Love To Hate You
Annie Silva

Annie Silva

CONTENTS

DEDICATION

To the beautiful souls who believe love is love, who fight society and their rules.

To the people who struggle with their mental illnesses.

And of course, to the readers who just love books with a long list of Trigger Warnings.

This one is for you!

PREFACE

I'D LIKE THE WONDERFUL readers who gave this book a chance to go into this with one thought in mind, NO ONE IS PERFECT. Definitely not my characters. I wanted a dash of reality in my story but also remember that this is strictly a work of fiction. Also, I am by no means a medical genius, a man nor have I ever done half the shit my characters do and so even though I did research, some things might not seem believable. If you can't handle topics like, suicide, depression, rape or relationships between two men then I implore you to kindly put this book down and go read some thing full of sunshine and rainbows. Though I wrote a happy ending it's going to take lots of patience and possibly tears to get there. I put all of my heart into this book. It has taken me a long time to put this baby together. I hope you love my characters as much as I do. The inspiration behind this book is really just a huge mix of books I've read, movies, and my own struggles with mental illnesses, love, trauma and figuring out my own sexual orientation. This is my first book. The first of many, I hope. There is a strong possibility that there will be errors I've missed because I have edited the fuck out this book MYSELF. Now that being said, go enjoy the story. I personally think it's a good one. Nah, it's a great one.

***

PLAYLIST!

As I wrote this book. I thought of songs that would go along with the way my characters were feeling or what they were thinking. It helped me channel the mood of some chapters.
Enjoy!
Broken heart collector- **Ekoh & Arankai**
Never enough- **Archers**

Bad Guy- **Falling in Reverse feat. Saraya**

I think I'm OKAY- **MGK, YUNGBLUD & Travis Barker**

Made for Love- **Archers**

My Serotonin- **Bishop Briggs**

Love Me Like You Do-**Ellie Goulding**

My Greatest Fear- **Benson Boone**

Strong for Somebody Else- **Citizen Soldier**

Different People- **JESSIA**

HEARTBEAT- **Isabel La Rosa**

F**k It All- **TX2**

Rescue Me- **Unions**

a Good Day To D13- **Arankai**

Dangerous- **Nick Jonas**

My My My!- **Troye Sivan**

Kiss the Boy- **Keiynan Lonsdale**

Beat It Upright- **Korn**

PROLOGUE

T HE CHEAP WHISKEY BURNED a familiar path down my throat. My reflection in the chipped glass showed a man I barely recognized. Dark curls plastered to my forehead, blue eyes shadowed with a weariness that twenty seven years had earned. Lily, my twin, sat across from me, a stark contrast in a pastel pink sweater and perfectly curled hair. She looked untouched, serene even, in this shitty apartment. A haven built on stolen breaths and cheap booze. Lily, had somehow found the strength to rebuild, while I drowned. My strong build, usually a tool for confidence and a weapon for flirting, felt like a cage.

We escaped our father together, ten years ago, but the escape only left half of the scars behind. Mine festered, deepened by every shot of cheap tequila, every stolen night. I relied heavily on my confident, flirty exterior. A carefully crafted mask to hide the monster my father created. A darkness lurked within me.

Lily reached across the table, her hand finding mine. Her touch, gentle and warm, sent a jolt through me, a stark reminder of the life we'd lost and the one we were fighting to build. The whiskey suddenly felt insufficient. She had a way of seeing through me, past the bravado and the alcohol induced haze, straight to the frightened boy trapped inside. She didn't judge the drunken nights or the careless flings. She understood the self destruction, the need to erase the past. Tonight, though, she saw something else. A vulnerability so profound, so raw, it startled even me. It was in the way she looked at me, with a mixture of empathy and unwavering love, that a flicker of hope ignited.

She spoke then, her voice soft but firm, "We escaped, Jasper. We're safe now. It's time to let him go."

The words hung in the air, heavy with meaning. Looking into her eyes, mirroring my own blue depths but filled with a strength I could only dream of, I knew she was right but I couldn't forget as easily as her. The whiskey bottle felt heavy in my hand. The past remained, a scar I'd carry forever.

"I can't let it go." I said, knowing my words would finally break her enough to leave me behind and continue prospering.

CHAPTER 1

JASPER'S POV

The music was booming and the crowd was buzzing with movement on the dance floor. Alcohol encouraging strangers to meet. The night was young and full of endless possibilities. Women throwing themselves at anyone who offers a good time. The club's lights were blinding and left you dizzy even without being inebriated. I downed way too many shots of tequila, my head was spinning like a carousel but I was having the time of my life not giving a shit about anything. My mask of confidence had been perfected. It was the perfect bait to catch the attention of an easy lay.

The bass vibrated through my chest, a rhythmic pulse mirroring the thump, thump, thump of my own heart. She stood next to me, a vision in sparkling silver, her blonde hair a striking contrast to the pale skin that flushed slightly as she spoke.

"Hey, Handsome. Want to dance with me?" Her voice, flirty and seductive in intention, yet almost shy in delivery. Perfect. Her lack of confidence was endearing, a refreshing change from the usual parade of perfectly polished, aggressively flirtatious women I encountered in places like this. Her eyes, a captivating hazel, held a hint of nervousness, a vulnerability that intrigued me far more than any practiced seduction. I was Jasper, twenty seven, with a reputation (deserved, I admit) for charm and a physique that didn't hurt. I wasn't looking for anything serious. She was not my type but who gave a shit. Certainly, not me.

"Yeah, I'll dance with you." I said with an inviting smile I knew no one could resist.

I downed two more shots and pushed through the throng of bodies with the blonde. With her hand in mine, I lost myself to the beat. Bumping and grinding, working up a sweat. Her shyness evaporates like smoke as she invites me to her place.

Stumbling through the door of her apartment, the kiss was urgent, the groping immediate. I didn't even know her name. I didn't care to ask. She wanted a good time, and I was there to oblige. Quickly, I unzipped my pants, bent her over her couch, and... well, did what I do best, fucked her. The screams, initially enthusiastic, were punctuated by a sudden, sickening thud—her vomiting on the carpet. She stumbled to the bathroom, leaving me standing there, the taste of cheap tequila souring in my mouth. I was too drunk for this shit. Annoyed, I slumped onto the couch, the room tilting precariously. Then, blackness.

***

"Hey! Hey, you! Get out of my house!" A nagging voice woke me up. The light was brutal, a blinding assault on my already throbbing head. It felt like someone had used my skull as a punching bag.

"Hello! Get out!" She nudged me again, this time with considerably more force.

"Alright, alright. I'm leaving. Just stop yelling already," I groaned, hauling myself up. My eyes finally adjusted enough to see I was... indecently exposed. Fantastic. Didn't even manage to zip up before passing out? Seriously, Jasper? This was peak embarrassing. I quickly fixed myself, putting my limp dick away. The whole situation felt surreal, like a bad dream I couldn't quite shake. Zipping my pants, I stumbled out of what I assumed was her apartment, the walk of shame beginning.

Dragging my feet through my apartment, my first thought is how desperately I need water and ibuprofen for this hangover but first, I jump into the shower to wash off that blonde off of my skin. As the hot water trickles down my body, I can't help but think that I'm such a shitty guy. The typical dude that never stays in a relationship and only picks out girls that just want sex. Why am I like that? I don't want to be like that. I guess I just haven't found the right one or maybe I'm not looking in the right places. No, truth is that I'm not looking at all. I'm not boyfriend material. My father raised me to be anything but

THAT. I could never forget the monster that I truly am. Not ever. My sister could never forget it either. That's why she left me behind and continued to blossom without me.

I finish up with my shower. Slicking my wet curly hair back. I wipe the foggy mirror with my hand and take a look at myself. I look like shit. I feel like shit. Like I've been hit by a bus. My blue eyes are slightly bloodshot and my skin is sickly pale. I look like a walking corpse.

At least, I don't work today. I wrap a towel around my waist and head over to the kitchen to make coffee. No sugar, no creamer and barely any coffee grounds. Damn, I need to go to the market. I quickly toss on some sweatpants and a fitted tee shirt. Grab my keys and head to the coffee shop around the corner.

"Welcome. What can I get for you today?" The cashier was a cute brunette with green eyes. I smirk at her, ready to charm my way into her pants. I notice her name tag—Cindy.

"Cindy. That's a cute name. I'd like a large coffee with cream and sugar, Cindy."

She blushes and tries to hide a smile.

"That'll be five dollars."

From my peripheral vision, I can see someone is watching me. My body is instantly on high alert. I turn to see who it is. A man with black hair falling over his eyes and tattoos crawling up his arms and neck, smoking a cigarette. His face seemed amused as he stared at me unabashedly. Ignoring the creep, I pay for my coffee. I noticed Cindy wrote her number on my cup. I wink at her like I have a million other girls and sit at a table to drink my coffee. I noticed that the stranger with the tattoos was still watching me. He jerked his head to the side so his hair was out of his brown eyes. It was weird and made me uncomfortable. So, I got up and left.

I needed to sleep off this hangover. I had daydreams of sleeping in my bed but I got a call.

"Marcus, what's up?" I answered my phone.

"Sorry, Jasper. I know it's your day off but boss is calling you in. Short on staff. So you have to train the new guy."

"Well, that's a fucking bummer. I'll be in shortly though."

***

I work as a bartender at The Velvet Rope, a strip club. The smell of alcohol right now is making me nauseous. The crazy lights and loud music are giving me a headache. I should have slept off my hangover but money was calling me. I never say no to making more money.

"Hey, Jasper. This is the new employee, Ezra." Marcus said.

I turned to face them and to my surprise, the guy from the coffee shop was standing before me. The freak that was staring at me. Yeah, him.

He swooshed his hair to the side and extended his tattooed hand.

"Nice to meet you, Ezra. Welcome to the team." I say, shaking his hand.

"Thanks. I think I'm gonna like it here." Ezra smirked, still holding on to my hand.

I yank my hand out of his grip and gave him a weird look.

"I'll leave you guys to do training. I have boxes to unpack out back." Marcus excused himself.

Great.. now I'm alone with this emo weirdo.

"Have you been a bartender before?"

"I know my stuff but I won't refuse training." He says, looking straight into my eyes. What is with this guy?

"Um, ok. Let's get started then. It's going to be really busy in here soon. The faster you learn, the better." I say as I look away.

As the night went by, Ezra was actually really good at bartending. He made the drinks quick and even showed off a little. Women and men were flirting with him, trying to get his number but he refused everyone. He wouldn't even peek at the pole dancers. It was like he was completely uninterested or like he was too good for anyone here. I couldn't help my curiosity.

"You got a girlfriend or something?" I blurted out. Ezra raised an eyebrow and laughs.

"No. I don't have a girlfriend."

What was so funny about that? I nodded my head and didn't say anything else. I could feel his eyes on me but I just ignored it. At least, I tried. Ezra made quick friends with most of our coworkers. Even the dancers. If it weren't for his creepy staring habit, he'd be a pretty cool guy. Since, he was staring at me, I took the opportunity to stare back. Challenging him to look away but he must have thought this was a game because he just grinned and let his eyes take all of me in. As though he was taking a mental picture.

What the fuck? I immediately stopped challenging him with my eyes and stepped away feeling naked, even though I was fully clothed. I think I will be avoiding Ezra from now on.

CHAPTER 2

EZRA'S POV

The strip club I'm working at "The Velvet Rope," where the clientele ranges from surprisingly diverse to ridiculously predictable, was throbbing with bass and bodies. A humid haze clinging to the air thick with the scent of cheap perfume and desperation. But my focus remained laser sharp on Jasper. A whirlwind of dark curls and confident smirks. His blue eyes, the color of a summer sky after a storm, caught mine for a fleeting second, and a jolt, something akin to static electricity, shot through me. Twenty eight, shaggy black hair falling into my brown eyes, and a demeanor that could best be described as "permanently unimpressed," I, Ezra, was utterly captivated by this...this confident mess. I poured tequila shots, handed out beers, deftly deflecting the clumsy advances of both men and women. Their attempts at flirtation felt as insubstantial as glitter falling from a dancer's costume. None of them registered, only Jasper's playful banter across the room did. I caught him watching me, a smirk playing on his lips, and a strange flutter took root in my chest. It was funny, really. Mr. "I'll charm the pants off anyone" was seemingly flustered by my presence. He was definitely flirting with everyone BUT me. He flexed his muscles and winked like a fuck boy.

A voice pulled my attention away from Jasper, "Nice tattoos. Did they hurt?"

A female, perched on a stool at the bar, was the source of the surprisingly inane question. Long, smooth legs and a beautiful smile were undeniable assets, but the cliché query grated on my damn nerves. I plastered on a friendly smile nonetheless.

"Yes, they hurt, but it was worth it. What can I get you?"

"Just a beer. Thanks," she replied, her smile widening as she subtly accentuated her cleavage. I couldn't help a grin at the transparent attempt to grab my attention.

Handing her the beer, I asked, "What's your name, sweetheart?"

"Becca. What's yours?"

"It's Ezra. What brings you to a place like this?" She leaned in, radiating flirtatious energy.

"A good time. Want to have a good time with me?"

This was getting predictable. I leaned in close, whispering in her ear, "You are really beautiful, but I'm gay."

The shock on Becca's face was almost comical. Her jaw dropped slightly, and a flicker of genuine surprise—not just feigned offense—crossed her features.

"You don't even look like you are," she stammered, a laugh following quickly. "I'm so sorry. I must be really drunk."

I couldn't help but wonder what exactly "gay" is supposed to look like, apparently something that doesn't involve meticulously crafted tattoos and a friendly demeanor. My gaze drifted back to Jasper, who was engrossed in a similar, albeit less subtly performed, display of mutual attraction with a woman whose huge breasts was the focal point of his intense stare. He was completely oblivious to the subtle art of seduction, or perhaps simply uninterested in anything beyond the purely physical. I rolled my eyes. It was time for a smoke break, a chance to clear my head and contemplate the baffling assumptions people seemed to make based on appearances. The irony wasn't lost on me.

"I'm heading out back, Jasper." I pat him on the back and he tenses up.

Outside, the cool night air was a welcome change from the smoky haze of the club. The cigarette tasted good, a small rebellion against the evening's absurdity. I hear the door opening behind me. I turn to face an agitated Jasper.

"What the fuck is wrong with you?" he asks, red in the face.

I take a long drag of my cigarette and puff out smoke.

"I'm not sure what you mean." I calmly reply.

He attempts to shove me but I don't budge. I guess that made him angrier because he pointed a finger in my face.

"Stay out of my way."

I take one last drag of my cigarette and blow smoke in his face. I flick the cigarette to the ground and stomp it out with my boot. I tilt my head to the side and look into Jasper's blue eyes.

"Why are you so offended?" I said, brushing one of his curls away from his forehead. The act made his eyes go wide and his eyebrows furrowed. The emotions on his face ranged from shock to confusion to finally settling on anger. Jasper swung a fist towards my face but I dodged it at the last second with incredible ease. He's surprisingly strong for a pretty boy, though.

"I'm not some homo fruity boy!" He spat. I don't even know what that means but I assume from the word 'Homo' that he means he's not gay like me. The irony isn't lost on me. He's the one practically vibrating with aggressive energy, while I'm as calm as a summer's day. I was still so calm. I actually smirked.

"I never said you were," I countered, my voice low and steady, "but you're the one in my face right now. So close we could practically be kissing." I say, eyeing his lips.

The words hang in the air, charged with something neither of us fully understands. At the realization of how close his face was to mine, he frantically took several steps back, his confidence momentarily shattered. A flicker of something else...vulnerability?... crossed his features before he could mask it.

"Nice form by the way. Your fist almost caught me. Sorry you missed," I say with a sly grin, enjoying the shift in our dynamic. The anger is gone, replaced by something akin to stunned curiosity. He clears his throat and avoids my eyes. I open the door and head back into work. I wonder what Jasper would have done if I kissed him like I wanted to. I would have gladly taken a punch to the face.

***

JASPER'S POV

I stood outside in the back of the strip club, the humid night air doing little to cool the fire of my anxiety. Ezra wasn't even bothered by my outburst, the sheer nonchalance of it all a stark contrast to the frantic turmoil inside me. I'd lost it back there, completely losing my temper with him during a particularly stressful shift. The memory of my hands flying, replayed in my mind like a broken record.

Fuck, I hope I don't get fired. This job, was more than just a paycheck. It was a routine, a structure that kept my days predictable, my mind occupied, and the ghosts of my past safely locked away. The fear of losing that stability was a cold knot in my stomach. The thought of facing my boss, a man who valued efficiency above all else, and the swift, ruthless replacement that would follow, sent a shiver down my spine. That's why I was here, tailing Ezra, despite my initial anger. I needed to make sure he wouldn't report me. Reaching out, I grabbed his arm. He turned, those startlingly brown eyes fixed on mine, his muscular arms folded across his broad chest. This guy could have easily retaliated, could have thrown me through a plate glass window. Why didn't he? We were almost mirror images, same height, same build. The unspoken question hung heavy between us.

"Hey!" I blurted out, the word sounding pathetically weak even to my own ears.

He didn't respond immediately, just studied me with an intensity that both unsettled and intrigued me.

"I prefer whatever hostility you hold against me to be left outside," he finally said, his voice low and steady, a stark contrast to the tempest raging within me.

"Actually," I stammered, "I wanted to apologize. I could have handled things differently. Way differently."

The words tumbled out, a rush of clumsy contrition. The image of my own violence, the raw, uncontrolled anger, still burned in my memory. He tilted his head slightly, a subtle movement that spoke volumes.

"There's nothing to apologize for," he said, his expression unreadable. "Misunderstandings happen."

Misunderstandings? The sheer understatement hung in the air, thick and heavy. I dared not question the casual dismissal, the lack of any visible lingering anger or resentment. It was unnerving, but it was also...a reprieve. I took the win, the unspoken acceptance of his silence, and turned to leave, determined to avoid any further confrontations. The incident, however, had irrevocably shifted something between us. It had broken through the careful wall I had built around myself, exposing a vulnerability I hadn't realized I possessed.

***

After work, I decided to follow him, a foolish impulse fueled by a potent cocktail of curiosity and something else I couldn't quite name. Then he hopped on his motorcycle, that low rumble a growl in the night, and caught me staring.

"Need a ride?" he smirked, that infuriatingly calm demeanor catching me completely off guard.

"Uhh.. No! I'm g-good." I stammered, my carefully constructed facade crumbling. He saw right through my clumsy attempt at stealth.

"It'll be easier to follow me, if you accept the ride. I got an extra helmet." Fuck. Busted. I pushed the embarrassment to the back of my mind and pretended like my confidence wasn't shaken.

"I've got a girl to meet. Cindy from the coffee shop." I lied, trying for casual. The lie felt flimsy, even to me, but his expression remained unchanged.

"Alright. Well, have fun with Cindy then." His motorcycle roared, speeding off, leaving me in a cloud of dust and the lingering scent of his cologne. I exhaled, feeling relieved his eyes were no longer observing my every move.

"Hey, Jasper! What are your plans for tonight?" Marcus calls out to me.

"Nothing, why?" I reply.

"Dude, come out with us! We're going to a pool party!!"

"Yeah, alright. I'll head out with you guys."

***

It was a short ride to the pool party. Not sure who's house this is but it was crowded with party people, a pulsating mass of bodies swaying to the relentless beat of the music. The air hung thick with the scent of chlorine, sweat, and cheap beer. I grabbed a plastic cup filled with something vaguely resembling punch and watched the chaotic dance floor from the relative safety of the periphery.

The music vibrated through the floor, a physical force that mirrored the nervous energy thrumming in my chest. There was a bit of commotion in the middle of the room, a swirling vortex of limbs and laughter. Curiosity piqued, I pushed my way through the dense crowd, navigating a sea of flashing teeth and sweaty bodies. It turned out to be nothing more than a playful tussle between a group of girls, their shrieks of laughter echoing through the house.

For a fleeting second, I thought I'd see Ezra there, a silly hope that quickly dissolved into the reality of the situation. I wasn't even sure why I expected him to be here. The thought of him, the unexpected flutter in my chest, felt out of place among the boisterous revelry. I excused myself from the throng, making my way towards the promise of quiet solitude by the pool in the back of the house. I didn't really plan on swimming.

Truthfully, I wasn't even sure why I was here. I didn't know anyone, and the prospect of forced conversations and awkward small talk didn't appeal to me. The idea of drinking myself silly or hooking up with a stranger held even less allure.

"You look lonely." I turn to my side to face some rocker chick with heavy black makeup around her eyes and a ton of piercings on her face. I realize I must have the typical frat boy look, though I'd like to think I'm a bit more than that. Confident, sure, maybe even a little flirty, but lonely? Absolutely not.

"I'm not lonely. I'm just alone. There's a difference." I try to fake a smile, mostly to see if she'd notice the dimples that usually work their charm. This girl, though... she's different.

"Whatever, dude. Want to get high?" She says, her voice surprisingly melodic despite the harsh exterior. I raise an eyebrow and think about it for a second. This is a party, after all. Anything goes, right?

"You don't even know me. Why would you want to party with me?" I asked, mostly out of curiosity. Her response, blunt and honest, surprised me.

"I don't want to be alone either." She grabs my hand, her touch surprisingly gentle, and guides me through the crowded house, up some stairs and into a bedroom.

The room is surprisingly tidy, a stark contrast to the chaos downstairs. She introduces herself as Raven. She's not really my type but she's right. I don't want to feel alone. I don't want to feel anything. She lights the blunt and passes it to me. I inhale but start to cough. Never been high before but there's a first time for everything. She laughs and pulls out a bottle of rum.

"Where did you get that?" I asked.

"What does it matter?! We're going to get fucked up." She smiles.

Before I knew it, I was ridiculously drunk and high as a kite. I couldn't comprehend anything. My limbs wouldn't function. Something was wrong.

"I don't feel so good." I try to say but the words don't come out. My body felt so heavy. My vision blurred. Everything fades to black.

***

EZRA'S POV

My phone is vibrating. I've got a few missed calls and messages. I'm at a red light on my motorcycle. So, I answer the phone.

"Ezra, I know we don't really know each other all that well but I need help finding Jasper. We're at a party but he's nowhere to be found. I'm freaking out, man." Marcus's words slurred, which immediately put me on high alert. I needed to remain calm though.

"Marcus, maybe he went home. You shouldn't worry."

"No, man! I'm telling you he's here somewhere. I need a sober friend right now. Help me find him." He pleads. Marcus is absolutely shit faced, and he needs my help. There's no way in hell he's going to drive himself or Jasper home. So, me being the good guy, I decide to help.

"Where are you? I'm coming to help you."

"I'm on Main st and Maple rd!" The light turns green. I'm not far from his location. Just a few minutes away. I pulled up at a sprawling frat house. This is definitely not my scene, but my new friends are in there, drunk and stupid. So I get off my bike and head inside, the bass throbbing in my chest. The air is thick with the smell of cheap beer and something vaguely floral, probably air freshener trying to mask the inevitable.

The chaos inside was overwhelming. People were dancing haphazardly, spilling drinks, and shouting over the music. I spotted Marcus almost immediately. He was slumped against a wall, looking utterly defeated.

"Ezra!! Over here!!" Marcus calls out to me. His voice was slurred, barely audible above the throbbing bass.

"Let's go, Marcus. You need water and a bed." He tried to stand, swaying precariously.

"No, we need to find Jasper. Can't leave him behind."

Jasper's disappearance, coupled with Marcus's inebriated state, was setting my teeth on edge.

"Stay right here and stop drinking. I'm going to find Jasper." I say, snatching his cup out of his hand and tossing it in the trash. The lukewarm beer splattered against the already sticky floor, a small act of rebellion against the overwhelming mess of the party. I scanned the crowd, searching for a glimpse of Jasper's familiar mop of dark brown hair.

I take a look around but I can't find Jasper. He's not in the kitchen, a whirlwind of activity with people making questionable food choices, not in the living room or dining area, both overflowing with people, definitely not outside by the pool where a few stragglers were attempting to cool off.

All that was left was upstairs where the rooms were. The air upstairs was thick with the lingering scent of cheap perfume and stale sweat. I opened a few doors, my heart sinking with each negative result. One was a bathroom, cluttered and smelling strongly of something I didn't want to identify. A few were closets, crammed with discarded clothes and forgotten belongings, still no Jasper.

Then, I opened a bedroom's door and the scene that greeted me stopped me dead in my tracks. There, sprawled across the bed, was an unconscious Jasper, a woman straddling him, riding his dick.

"What the fuck is wrong with you?! Get off of him!!" I shout at her, the words raw and furious. She panics, her eyes wide with fear, and stumbles off of him, her clothes askew.

"He wanted me to—" she begins, but I cut her off.

"Get out of here you fucking rapist!!" She runs, disappearing as quickly as she appeared.

My first thought was Jasper's safety. My anger was quickly replaced by a wave of concern. I checked for his breathing—slow, shallow breaths, but a steady beating heart. Relief washed over me, quickly followed by the need to get him out of there. He was out cold, his face pale. I gently shook him, but he remained unresponsive. Carefully, I helped him dress, pulling his pants back up his waist. The indignity of the situation fueled my resolve. I hoisted him over my shoulder and headed back downstairs, determined to find Marcus.

The party was a distant blur as I navigated the crowded house, the rhythmic thump of the music a dull drone in my ears. Reaching Marcus, I didn't bother explaining the details. The sight of Jasper, vulnerable and unconscious, had erased any remaining anger. Getting him the help he needed, ensuring his safety, became my absolute priority. The chaos of the party, the drunken revelers, faded into the background, replaced by the quiet urgency of the task at hand.

"Where are your keys, Marc?"

He digs in his pockets for the keys and hands them to me.

"What happened to him?" Marcus asks, gesturing towards Jasper draped over my shoulder.

"Alcohol happened. Let's get out of here." I said. I place Jasper in the back seat with his seat belt on. Marcus sits in the passenger seat. I drive. I'll have to come back for my bike. First, I drop off Marcus at his house. I didn't know where Jasper lives, so I drove to my place. The quiet of my apartment was a stark contrast to the boisterous party we'd just left. Carrying Jasper was surprisingly easy. I carefully lay him on my bed, his limbs falling limply around me. He looked so peaceful, completely oblivious to the chaos he'd created.

His dark curls falling in perfect spirals around his face. His lashes delicately fanned his cheeks, and his eyes slowly fluttered open.

"Hey, are you ok?" I ask, my voice barely above a whisper.

"Oh, it's you. Hey, you." He drunkenly smiles, a lopsided, charming grin. He seemed okay, just drunk. Maybe stoned? Definitely exhausted.

"Jasper, go to sleep. We'll talk in the morning." I say, starting to get up.

"Where are you going? Stay with me." he slurred, his voice thick with sleep. I hesitated, my initial plan to simply leave crumbling under his surprisingly insistent plea. I decided to stay, just in case he started to puke. Or at least, that's what I told myself.

"Alright. I'll stay, but you have to go to sleep." He mumbled something unintelligible, then focused on my arms.

"I like your... t-tattoos," he mumbled, his fingers tracing the intricate designs on my neck and arms.

"I have a thing for tattoos. M-makes you sexy," he confessed, his words slightly slurred, but strangely direct. I smirked, a genuine, unexpected smile. I didn't expect that to come out of a straight man's mouth. It was a little... exciting.

"Thank you, Jasper. I'll be sure to remind you when you're sober that you said so." I teased, my voice a low murmur. He blinked sleepily, his gaze drifting from my tattoos to my eyes.

"You make me nervous." he whispered, his voice barely audible.

"Why?" I asked, leaning closer, intrigued by his sudden vulnerability. A stark contrast to the mask of confidence he wore earlier.

"You make me feel... weird." he mumbled, before turning onto his side. His arm snaked around my waist, pulling me closer. I stiffened, unsure of what I should do. The unexpected warmth of his touch, the unexpected confession of attraction, and the intoxicating scent of his slightly musky cologne, all combined to create a surprising mix of apprehension and a strange, electric thrill.

His breathing slowed, becoming even and deep. He was asleep. The moonlight illumi-nated his face, casting soft shadows on his features. He looked peaceful, almost angelic. His head rested on my chest, his dark hair a soft, unruly cloud against my shirt. He was snoring softly, a low rumble that vibrated through me. Jasper Rowan, the impossibly straight, impossibly gorgeous, impossibly oblivious Jasper Rowan, was asleep on top of me. And I, the perpetually single, hopelessly romantic Ezra, was his unwilling, yet utterly enchanted, human pillow. I couldn't bring myself to move him. His weight was surpris-ingly comforting, a warm, solid presence against me. The thought of waking him and facing his probable mortification, however, sent a thrill of nervous anticipation through me. I wrapped my arms around him, the warmth of his body radiating against mine, and let the gentle rhythm of his breathing lull me into a surprisingly peaceful sleep. It felt...right, somehow. To have him here, close, safe. Even if it was only temporary, even if he'd likely forget the entire night. Even if he will definitely hate me in the morning.

CHAPTER 3

JASPER'S POV

I blink a few times, trying to figure out whether I'm alive or not. The raging migraine tells me that I'm not dead yet. I blink a few more times and the room comes into focus. I'm entangled with another body. My heart starts to pick up pace. How the fuck did I get here? Who is this person cuddling with me? I never fuck and cuddle. I sit up to look at their face. I blanched. How the fuck did I end up in Ezra's bed?! Am I naked?! I check under the covers. I'm fully clothed. I let out a breath of relief. I need answers. I shove him awake.

"Hey!! Wake up!! What the fuck did you do to me?!" Ezra doesn't open his eyes but he does speak.

"I saved your ass from a rapist." He mumbled.

"What are you talking about?"

"I found you unconscious being fucked by some crazy chick." He says, opening his brown eyes to look at me.

"Guys don't get raped. Why are we in bed together?" I said angrily. The words hung heavy in the air, the unspoken implications a stark contrast to the casualness of his response. His calm demeanor irritated me, the steady beat of his heart a mocking rhythm against the frantic pounding in my own chest.

"You're not any less of a man because you were violated. I won't tell anyone either." He says calmly. I hate how calm he is all the time.

The anger flared again, hotter this time, fueled by the vulnerability and the violation. His words, though intended to be reassuring, only served to highlight the horrifying reality of what had happened. The shame coiled in my stomach, a bitter poison. I wanted to lash out, to scream, to deny the truth of his statement, but the image of the woman, her face blurred and indistinct, remained sharp in my mind.

I clench my hands into fists. He gets out of the bed and continues talking.

"Nothing happened between us. I didn't know where you lived. So I brought you to my place and I would have slept on the couch but you asked me to stay. I didn't want you choking on your own vomit. So, I stayed. That's it. That's all that happened." He explains. "Then why were you all over me?!" I huff, my chest heaving.

"You were on top of me, Jasper. But I didn't mind." He smirks. I scoff at how ridiculous that all sounded. There's no way I asked him to stay or did anything as ridiculous as cuddling with a guy. I knew better though. I woke up with our limbs draped over each other and I was on top of him. My face reddens. What else did I do?

"Did I say or do anything else?"

"You were flirting with me and touching my arms. I told you to get your drunk ass to sleep but you just wouldn't leave me alone. Confessing your feelings for me." Ezra seemed too amused. He was teasing me. The shame burned hotter than the alcohol still lingering in my system. My denial crumbled, his words painted a picture far too familiar. The fragments of a blurry, alcohol soaked night began to coalesce into a coherent, humiliating memory.

"That's a lie. You're a liar. I don't have feelings for you. I just met you. I'm out of here." I said, clearly set on denying any of it to be true. He blocks the door, leaning against it with his eyebrows furrowed.

"I'm a lot of things, Jasper. But never call me a liar. I know you had a shitty night but that's not my fault. All I did was help you. You asked for answers and I gave them to you. I'm not the kind of guy that needs to take a drunk man home. Especially, not one stuck in the closet. Now you can leave."

I was stunned into silence. Stuck in the closet?! The absurdity of it hit me harder than the lingering effects of the cheap alcohol. I most certainly was NOT stuck in a closet. My memory of the night was hazy, a swirling mess of forced smiles, and the cloying scent of cheap perfume from the psycho girl who'd clearly taken advantage of my fucked up state. The shame burned hotter than any hangover.

I felt bad about accusing Ezra of lying, a pathetic attempt to deflect my own culpability and the crushing weight of my own poor choices. I wanted to apologize, to somehow bridge the chasm of misunderstanding that had opened up between us, but the tension thrumming in the air was a suffocating blanket.

He moved away from the door, his movements calm and controlled, a stark contrast to the turmoil churning within me. His obvious upset was masked by a quiet dignity, a self possession that was both captivating and infuriating. I couldn't help but watch him, his retreating figure somehow both heartbreaking and intensely alluring. His demeanor, so composed yet clearly wounded, stirred something deep inside me, a feeling I couldn't quite name, but desperately wanted to understand. The need to leave, to escape the suffocating weight of my own foolishness, became overwhelming. I couldn't believe how spectacularly my night had unraveled. That manipulative bitch... the memory seared itself onto my brain. The violation of trust left me feeling exposed and raw. I felt like a shattered vase, the pieces scattered and irreparable. I needed to escape this self inflicted mess, to find some semblance of order a midst the chaos. The haze of alcohol was slowly lifting, revealing the full extent of my disastrous choices. I needed to stop drinking so much, to regain control of my life before it completely spiraled out of control.

The immediate problem, however, was more pressing. I had no idea how to get out of this apartment. My surroundings were a blur, the unfamiliar layout twisting my sense of direction into knots. Panic threatened to overwhelm me.

"Ezra!" I shouted his name, the desperation evident in my voice. The embarrassment of my helplessness, of not even knowing my way out, amplified my already intense shame.

"What?" he replied, his voice tight but surprisingly even. He was standing behind me, silhouetted against the dim light filtering through the doorway. The air crackled with unspoken words, unresolved feelings. Taking a deep breath, I blurted out,

"I'm sorry I called you a liar. I'm... I'm not good with words, or... or cuddling. Not with girls, and definitely not with guys. I'm not even sure why my drunk ass would do that." The words tumbled out in a rush, a confession as much to him as to myself. The raw honesty, born of self loathing and a desperate need for forgiveness, hung heavily in the air. He simply looked at me, his expression unreadable.

"I think your drunk ass was finally honest with himself. Something your sober ass should try out." Then, slowly, a ghost of a smile touched his lips.

"I'll help you find the door." he said, his voice softer now, tinged with a hint of something akin to understanding. As he reached out a hand, I knew this day, despite its tumultuous start, wasn't over. It was only just beginning.

Before stepping out of the door, I grab my phone out of my pocket.

"Put your number in my phone." I said, my voice a little louder than I intended. He looked at me, a mixture of amusement and surprise dancing in his eyes.

"What?" he asks, confusion evident in his tone.

"Give me your number. I'm bound to be drunk again in the near future. I'm going to need a friend." I blurted out, a self deprecating laugh escaping my lips. The words hung in the air, a strange confession hanging between us. He smirks, a slow, deliberate curve of his lips that sends an unexpected flutter through my chest.

"I don't typically give my number out," he says, his voice low and husky, "but since you apologized, I'll make an exception."

He leans closer, his fingers deftly navigating my phone screen, creating a new contact. It kinda made me feel happy. I wasn't sure why, a strange warmth spreading through me despite the lingering headache and the gnawing uncertainty of the previous night. I ignored the feeling, grabbed my phone, and left, the air thick with unspoken things. I hadn't thought about how I was getting home or where the hell Ezra lived. My car was definitely not here, and my brain felt like a fucking scrambled egg. I can't think straight. Again, I'm a mess.

For whatever reason, I felt compelled to look up. From his upstairs window, I caught Ezra watching me. A cigarette smoldered between his lips, the faint orange glow illuminating his face. His expression was unreadable, a blend of concern and something else... amusement maybe? I quickly look away, my cheeks burning, and start walking to my right, pretending with all my might that I know where the fuck I'm going.

Hell yes, I was pretending. Anything is better than being caught standing outside like an idiot without a clue, my dignity hanging by a thread thinner than a spider's silk. The silence amplified my thoughts, making every thump of my heart echo in the stillness of the early morning. His number, a single, simple string of digits, felt like a lifeline in the midst of this self inflicted chaos.

I grab my phone out of my pocket and open the map app. I type in my address and it says home is a thirty minute walk from Ezra's apartment. You would think I would recognize my surroundings considering I've lived in this town all of my life, but no, I am dependent on the GPS. I'm such a mess. The streets blur through my tear filled vision, each one a harsh reminder of the darkness I carry inside.

My body feels heavy, each step a monumental effort. The silence of the early morning amplifies the turmoil within me, the rhythmic thump of my own heartbeat is the only sound that consistently breaks through the suffocating quiet. Shame coils around me, a venomous serpent tightening its grip with each passing block. I replay the night's events in my head, a nauseating loop of regret and confusion. Ezra's face, so kind and comforting, is a cruel mockery of the kindness I once believed in. The walk home feels like an eternity, each step dragging me further into the pit of despair I've fallen into. I just want to disappear, to erase myself from existence.

***

After exactly thirty minutes, I arrive home. First thing I want to do is shower and scrub my skin till it's raw. Erase all trace of that girl who took advantage of me. I strip my clothes and turn the water on. It's burning hot but I don't care. A sob escapes me. Fuck. I hate to cry. I haven't cried since high school, when my dad slapped my mom and she just took it. Those tears were fueled by anger. The tears I'm crying now are...sad, a raw, visceral grief that tears at my insides. The scalding water does little to soothe the burning shame that consumes me. I sit on the shower floor and just weep, the hot water a weak attempt to cleanse away the filth I feel clinging to me. I was raped.

What the fuck... that's so fucked up. I'm so fucked up. My alcohol consumption is a problem, I realize. How could I let this happen to me? The question gnaws at me, a relentless beast feeding on my self doubt and guilt. As I spiral in the shower, I can feel my exhaustion catching up to me. I decide to quiet my cries, finish scrubbing my skin, and head to bed. I need to forget. I need to escape. Since I'm not dead, sleep is the next best thing. Yeah, I need sleep.

CHAPTER 4

EZRA'S POV

It has been a week since I started working with Jasper at The Velvet Rope. He's been acting pretty normal. Watching him flirt with the customers is annoying but I can't deny he's actually good at it. His looks definitely help. God, he's so hot. It should be illegal to look that good. While my mind is occupied with all things Jasper, I drive my bike to the barber shop. I need a haircut. My eyes can't see a damn thing with the length of my hair in the way. I enter the small business and a bell rings.

"How can I help you?" One of the barbers said.

"Hi, I need a hair cut." I replied, stating the obvious.

The guy smiles and points to the chair at his station. I take a seat.

"Do you want it all chopped off or are you looking for a trim? I mean your bangs reach your nose."

"I want the back and sides shaved down and the top long."

He nodded and a few minutes later I was done. I ran my fingers through my straight, black hair and pushed the strands messily to the side. Just as I was paying the barber, my phone vibrated. It's a text from an unknown number.

> Unknown: Sober friend needed. Offer still good?

I immediately know that it's Jasper. I get excited and reply.

Ezra: Yeah. Where are you? I'll come get you.

Jasper: Meet me at the coffee shop.

There are a ridiculous amount of coffee shops in this town but I somehow know exactly which one he's talking about. The place I first set my eyes on him, while he flirted with the cashier.

I practically sprinted out of the barber shop, the cool air a welcome contrast to the sudden rush of adrenaline. My newly cut hair felt lighter, almost freeing, mirroring the lightness in my chest. Jasper needing a "sober friend"– it wasn't exactly a formal invitation, but it was close enough. The text felt like a secret code, a wink across a crowded room. He'd been acting normal. Possibly, even more overtly flirtatious with the customers at The Velvet Rope. I noticed, Jasper is observant. He'd catch my eye across the bar, a small, almost shy smile playing on his lips before he'd turn back to charm some unsuspecting woman.

It was driving me crazy, this subtle shift in his behavior, this tantalizing hint of something more. Maybe? The thought of seeing him, of finally being alone with him outside the chaotic atmosphere of the club, made my heart pound a frantic rhythm against my ribs. The coffee shop was just around the corner, and I found myself unconsciously accelerating, my bike weaving through the late afternoon traffic with an almost reckless abandon.

***

The coffee shop was bustling, the usual after work crowd huddled around steaming mugs and laptops. I spotted Jasper immediately, sitting in a corner booth, his head resting in his hand, his usually vibrant energy subdued. He looked...vulnerable. It was a side of him I had only seen once, a stark contrast to the confident, charming bartender I knew. He looked up as I approached, his eyes widening slightly, his cheeks turning pink. I smile.

"Hey." I greet him as I sit across from him.

"Um, Hi. I mean, Hey." He says nervously.

Is he being shy? I stifle a chuckle but I can't help the smile on my face.

"I didn't think you'd actually contact me. I thought you took my number just to be nice."

"Yeah. Well, I get drunk and do stupid shit all the time. Don't feel too special." He said. I laugh.

"Ok. I'll try real hard not to feel too special, Jas."

His face scrunched up.

"Jas? That's an awful nickname. Don't call me that."

"Oh, well in that case, you're stuck with it."

"Alright. Fine. Then I'll start calling you E. You've been reduced to a single letter."

Was that supposed to upset me? I kinda like this childish banter.

"My very own nickname? I'm starting to feel special, Jas. You should be careful." I chuckled. Jasper rolls his eyes and shakes his head.

"You're impossible. I'm done. I'm too drunk for this shit." He grumbles as he gets up from his seat. I follow behind him.

"Where are you going?" I asked.

"Home."

I quickly realize that Jasper lives across the street and around the corner from the coffee shop. Convenient. I watched him stumble a few times, his gait increasingly unsteady, and before I could stop myself, I was offering a hand. He accepted, his grip surprisingly firm despite his inebriation. I looped his arm around my shoulder to steady him as we navigated the steps leading up to his apartment building. His body tensed against mine, the proximity clearly making him uncomfortable, yet he didn't pull away. The keys slipped from his grasp, clattering on the floor. I retrieved them and, without a second thought, unlocked his door. The whole thing felt incredibly spontaneous, a series of impulsive actions driven by a sudden and unexpected surge of protectiveness.

"Alright. I'm fine. You can let me go now." he mumbled, a slight blush creeping up his neck. I respected his need for space and released him, stepping back to give him room. His apartment was surprisingly neat and tidy, a stark contrast to the slightly disheveled image he presented moments ago.

"Cool place." I commented, trying to keep my tone casual, despite the rapid thudding of my heart. He stumbled towards his couch, collapsing onto it with a soft thud.

"Cool haircut." he replied, his voice a little slurred but the words, somehow, felt pointed. A slow smile spread across my face.

"I'm feeling special again, Jas. You're doing it intentionally." I teased, enjoying the unexpected banter.

"In your dreams, Ezra." he retorted, his words laced with a hint of something I couldn't quite decipher.

"Dreams come true," I countered, unable to resist pushing the boundaries a little further. Jasper turned his head, his gaze locking onto mine. It was at that moment, seeing his intense blue eyes glare at me, that a flicker of something like vulnerability momentarily pierced his defensive facade.

"Stop looking at me like that." he said, his voice low and strained. I feigned innocence. "Look at you like what?"

His next words were blunt and hurtful, a stark contrast to the lighthearted exchange moments before.

"Like you're in love with me. I'm not into that gay shit." he spat out, the disgust evident on his face. The rejection stung, a sharp prick to my burgeoning feelings. I forced myself to remain calm, my composure a shield against his harsh words.

"I'm not looking at you in any particular way. Maybe you are a little too drunk, Jas," I smirked, trying to inject some lightness into the tense atmosphere.

"You're right. I need to sleep this off before work. Thanks for coming." he said, his voice weary.

With a final, lingering glance at his face, a mixture of disappointment and intrigue swirling within me, I turned to leave. As I walked towards my motorcycle, a strange mixture of emotions tumbled within me. Disappointment certainly, but also a stubborn, lingering hope that maybe, just maybe, things could be different next time. I wouldn't give up on Jasper that easily. He had beautiful blue eyes, and the thought of seeing him again tonight at work, fueled my anticipation.

***

JASPER'S POV

"Jasper!! You made it on time!!" Marcus said, his voice booming over the already lively chatter of the club.

"Ha ha. Fuck you, Marcus. I'm never late. You just arrive too early." I clapped him on the back, the familiar camaraderie easing the tension of my late night shift. Sliding behind the bar, I caught sight of Ezra, his new haircut catching the light. It was good, undeniably good. I tried to dismiss it as just a haircut, but the way the customers flocked to him, their flirty advances met with his effortless, charming rejections, only fueled a strange curiosity within me. The way he handled them, with a polite dismissiveness that somehow made him even MORE attractive, fascinated me.

It was a performance, a masterful display of self possession I envied. I fell into the rhythm of the night, mixing drinks with practiced ease, flashing my smile, flexing my biceps for the appreciative glances, the usual showmanship that kept my tip jar overflowing. The energy of the club was a familiar comfort, a vibrant hum that matched the beat in my chest.

"Hey, Ezra. Come check this shit out!" Marcus's voice cut through the music, his phone held aloft.

"What is it?" Ezra asked, his attention momentarily diverted from polishing a glass. "Look, look, look. Isn't she great?!" Marcus thrust the phone into Ezra's view, a picture of a stunning woman filling the screen. Ezra shrugged, his expression nonchalant.

"Eh, Not my type." Marcus's jaw dropped.

"The fuck you mean 'not my type'?! She's hot as fuck!" he exclaimed, incredulously. I couldn't help but eavesdrop, drawn in by their exchange.

"What's going on over here?" I asked, stepping into their conversation.

"Ezra, doesn't think this girl is hot! Unbelievable!" Marcus declared, his voice dripping with disbelief.

"I never said she wasn't hot. She's clearly not ugly. I just wouldn't be interested." Ezra clarified, a slow smile playing on his lips. I peered at the phone. The woman was a damn supermodel. What wasn't there to like?

"Wouldn't be interested? What kind of girl would interest you, E?" I pressed, curiosity outweighing my usual aloofness. Marcus's gaze switched to Ezra, mirroring my own expectant silence. Ezra's smirk widened, a glint of amusement in his eyes.

"There isn't a woman alive that could interest me." he said, his smile unwavering. The air shifted, the unspoken hanging heavy between us. He's gay. I knew it. I mean, the guy was so calm about cuddling in his bed. Of course, he's gay. Marcus' jaw drops, his usual boisterous energy momentarily silenced.

"You like men?! No fucking way. I don't believe you." he sputtered, his disbelief palpable. Ezra, ever calm, simply raised an eyebrow.

"Why not?" he asked, a hint of amusement in his tone. Marcus, flustered by his own surprise, stammered, "I mean, look at you! You look and act like a straight male!"

Ezra just laughs, a low rumble in his chest.

"Why? Because I'm not flamboyant and saying 'yass queen' every two seconds? I didn't expect you to believe in stereotypes, Marcus. I don't have to be feminine to like men." The casual dismissal of the expectation seemed to deflate Marcus somewhat.

"Oh. Well, I didn't mean anything by it. I support your community. No big deal." he mumbled, clapping Ezra on the back a little too hard. Ezra chuckles, seemingly unfazed. I, however, am still reeling. Is that why he kept staring at me so hard? The intensity of his gaze now took on a whole new meaning.

My mind raced, trying to reconcile the image of Ezra, the effortlessly charming, ruggedly handsome bartender, with the revelation of his sexuality. It shouldn't have surprised me, but it did. The realization felt like a seismic shift, rearranging my understanding of him, of us. Then, the unexpected happened.

"Ok. So, what kind of guys do you like?" I blurted out, the question escaping before I could stop it. The words hung in the air, thick with unspoken implications. Ezra smirks, a slow, deliberate curve of his lips that sent a shiver down my spine. His eyes, dark and intense, raked over me, lingering on my face, my hands, my body. The audacity of it, the blatant assessment, shocked me. He bites his lip, a small, almost imperceptible movement that somehow managed to be both innocent and incredibly seductive.

"Wouldn't you like to know." he purrs, the words a low, husky whisper. The action left my throat feeling dry. I was flustered. My heart started beating fast. What the fuck is wrong with me? Marcus, oblivious to the sudden shift in the atmosphere, simply laughs.

"Damn! You have to teach me to do that! Look at Jasper all red!" He exclaimed, pointing at me.

"Fuck you, Marcus." I muttered, flipping him off, my cheeks burning a fiery red. The casual dismissal of my obvious discomfort only fueled my inner turmoil. I retreated back to my station, plastering a friendly smile on my face as I resumed making drinks, my hands trembling slightly. But the image of Ezra's eyes, the feel of his gaze burning into me, lingered. His words, *"Wouldn't you like to know,"* echoed in my head, a tantalizing invitation.

I stole a glance at him, his usual calm demeanor replaced with a sly grin.

***

A few hours later my shift is over and I know I shouldn't be drinking again, but it beats going home right now. I want to have fun. Let loose. The dance club is a pulsating mass of bodies. The music is a relentless, throbbing beat that vibrates through my chest. The DJ is a maestro of manufactured euphoria, keeping the energy high, the crowd ecstatic. A brunette with eyes like melted chocolate hangs on my left arm, a blonde bombshell with a laugh that could shatter glass clings to my right.

They're both beautiful, both undeniably interested, and the thought of spending the night with them feels... exhilarating. The drinks flow freely, fueling the laughter, the dancing, the intoxicating feeling of invincibility. I lose myself in the music, the touch, the sheer, unadulterated pleasure of the moment. Nothing else matters. The world shrinks to this small space, this pulsing rhythm, these two women who seem to anticipate my every desire. Their hands are everywhere, their smiles knowing and playful. Regret? It's a distant concept, a shadow lurking at the edge of this dazzling present. The night is young, and I'm embracing every second.

"Come on, baby. I'm not wearing any underwear." the blonde shouts, her words barely audible over the music. I grin, a silent agreement. The brunette and blonde, a coordinated force of nature, steer me towards the exit, a blur of limbs and laughter. I'm ushered into a car. Black, expensive looking, but I don't register the make or model. Where we're going doesn't matter. The only thing that registers is the intoxicating blend of perfume, skin, and anticipation. The blonde's lips find my neck, leaving a trail of goosebumps. The brunette's hand is less subtle, her touch insistent, groping my crotch. Then, abruptly, the car stops.

A hotel, I realize, the imposing structure looming before us, its lights reflecting in the dark windows. We move like a single entity, a wave crashing towards the shore, into the elevator, the close quarters heightening the electric tension between us. Their hands are constantly on me, exploring, teasing, leaving me breathless.

Ding! The elevator doors open, and we stumble out, a little unsteady on our feet. I blink, momentarily disoriented, then I'm on a bed, sinking into its plush embrace like a cloud. The blonde is already pulling off my shirt, her touch surprisingly gentle, the hands numerous, exploring my chest, a symphony of sensations.

The brunette fumbles with my pants, a smile playing on her lips as she struggles with the buttons. I smirk, taking over the task myself, a sudden surge of self consciousness overcoming me for a brief moment. It's then, inexplicably, that Ezra's image floods my mind—the way he bit his lip when he smirked, the way his eyes held mine with a captivating intensity. My heart, momentarily stilled by the intoxicating experience, begins to pound again, a frantic rhythm against the slow, deliberate rhythm of the room. What the fuck am I thinking about him for?

The blonde's laughter pulls me back, and I realize that while my body is responding to these women, my mind was somewhere else. I had been so lost in thought that I hadn't even realized my pants being dragged down my legs and bunched up around my ankles. I smile and keep entertaining these girls. Again, Ezra comes to my mind. I'm not having fun anymore. I feel nauseous. I abruptly get up and pull my pants back up.

"Where are you going?" The brunette whines.

"Sorry. I have to go." I said.

"But we were having fun." The blonde said. I look at her breasts. Those are nice but no, thank you. I pick up my shirt off the floor. I take my phone out of my pocket and like the crazy person I am, I call Ezra. Because why not?

I stumble out the door and walk down the hallway, the cheap carpet a blurry landscape under my feet. My inebriated state is entirely to blame for the impulsive call to Ezra. "Hello?" A very sleepy, very deep voice answers, laced with a hint of amusement that I somehow missed in my drunken stupor.

"How mad would you be if I showed up at your apartment drunk right now?" The question hangs in the air, a ridiculous, desperate plea whispered into the phone. I hear rustling, the soft crinkle of sheets, and a brief silence thick with unspoken possibilities. "Jasper?" The question, though laced with concern, doesn't hold the sharp edge of anger I'd braced myself for.

"I'm coming over." I reply, the words slurring slightly, before abruptly ending the call. The walk, if it could be called that, is a hazy memory of stumbling through the night, the city lights blurring into an indistinguishable wash of color. I don't know how I made it, but suddenly, I'm fumbling with his doorknob, knocking with a clumsy thud.

He opens the door, his eyes, dark and shadowed in the dim hallway light, assess me with a mixture of exasperation and something else... something softer.

"I'm starting to think you're an alcoholic, Jas," he murmurs, his arms warm and surprisingly strong around my waist. He kicks the door shut, effectively shutting out the world. I smile, a goofy, uncontrolled grin that spreads across my face. I don't know why. I just do.

The warmth of his apartment envelops me as he guides me inside. The familiar scent of old books and something faintly woody fills my senses, grounding me just slightly. I notice, with a clarity that surprises me considering my state, that Ezra is shirtless. His skin isn't bare, though. Intricate tattoos, a swirling tapestry of ink, cover his body, a testament to a life lived with passion and perhaps a little recklessness, much like my own.

He lays me gently on his bed, the mattress surprisingly soft beneath me. The world tilts again, but this time, it's a pleasant kind of dizzy. He begins to take my shoes off, his touch surprisingly gentle, his fingers brushing against my skin sending shivers down my spine. He's handling me with the care one might take with a rare and fragile thing.

"Hi." I greeted him. Ezra stops what he's doing and looks up at me.

"Hi, Jasper. Go to sleep. We'll talk in the morning." He said and then continued to take my shoes off. Once he's done, he tries to leave but I quickly grab his hand to stop him.

"I hate being alone." I confess. Ezra nods in understanding. He climbs into the other side of the bed.

"I'm right here." He whispers. I'm comforted by his words and close my eyes. The feeling of safety wrapping me up in warmth like a heavy blanket. The demons can't get me tonight. Ezra is with me. I'm not alone.

CHAPTER 5

EZRA'S POV

Jasper's chest rose and fell with slow, even breaths. He looked peaceful, almost angelic, in the soft glow of the moonlight filtering through my curtains. His dark hair was tousled across the pillow, a stark contrast to the pale skin of his forehead. I couldn't believe he was here again, curled up in my bed, asleep after another drunken night. The last time this happened, he'd woken up in a panic, mortified and then began stammering apologies. The sheer audacity of him showing up again, trusting me enough to fall asleep like this, filled me with a strange mix of amusement and apprehension.

I had spent the better part of the night mesmerized, watching his face, tracing the line of his jaw with my eyes, resisting the urge to reach out and touch him. It felt wrong, invasive, even though the pull to do so was almost unbearable. The hope that this could be the start of something real, something beyond drunken accidents and awkward mornings, sparked a warmth in my chest, a feeling so potent it made me want to hold my breath. Finally, I decided to close my eyes, to try and get some rest myself, pushing aside the thrill and fear swirling in my stomach.

He stirred, a soft mumble escaping his lips. I opened my eyes, my heart leaping into my throat.

"Jasper, are you ok?" I whispered, my voice barely audible. He didn't respond, only shifting closer, his head finding a comfortable place nestled against my chest. My breath hitched. This felt so incredibly intimate, so incredibly wrong, yet so incredibly right. I held perfectly still, paralyzed by a mix of fear and fascination. He was so warm against me, his weight a comforting pressure.

The fear of his reaction in the morning threatened to suffocate me, but the feeling of his body pressed against mine was intoxicating. With the utmost care, I gently repositioned his head onto the pillow, releasing the breath I'd been unconsciously holding.

"You're going to drive me crazy." I muttered to his sleeping form, a smile playing on my lips despite the anxieties churning beneath the surface. I closed my eyes again, hoping for some respite, only to be jolted awake hours later by a persistent nudge.

"Ezra." he mumbled, his voice gaining strength. I groaned, feigning sleep, but he persisted.

"Ezra, wake up!" I opened my eyes to find him sitting beside me, his face etched with a serious expression.

"How does this keep on happening?!" he exclaimed, gesturing wildly between us. "Alcohol. That's how." I replied, a hint of amusement in my tone. He scoffed, rising to put his shoes back on.

"Nothing happened. You called me all drunk and came over. I put you to sleep. That's it. The end." I explained, my voice calm, trying to appear nonchalant despite the flutter in my stomach. He paused, turning back to face me, his earlier panic seemingly subsiding into a different kind of intensity.

"Nothing happened?" he questioned, his eyes searching mine. I smirked, leaning in slightly.

"Did you want something to happen?" He flushed.

"No!" he denied, but his voice lacked conviction, and in that moment, a midst the lingering scent of alcohol and the lingering warmth of his body against mine, I knew this wasn't the end. This was just the beginning I get up and stretch my tired body. I catch him looking at me. I like his eyes on me but I grab a shirt out of my drawer and put it on. I don't want to make him uncomfortable.

"Hungry? We can go grab a bite to eat." I said in attempt to keep him with me longer.

"I'm going to need something to absorb the alcohol I consumed."

That makes me smile. I get to spend a little more time with him. If he wasn't standing right in front of me, I might've done a little happy dance.

***

We head out and end up at a diner.

"Tell me about yourself." I said, shamelessly looking into his blue eyes. He squirms under my gaze, his nervousness palpable.

"Um, there's not much to tell." he mumbled. I raise an eyebrow, unconvinced.

"Bullshit. I don't believe that for a second." Jasper rolls his eyes, a playful exasperation in the movement.

"Fine. I'm 27. I'm a Leo. My favorite color is green. I have one sister. I don't talk to my parents. I never went to college. I have exactly zero tattoos and I live up to my reputation." he blurts out, all in one breath. I smile, now we're getting somewhere.

"I'm 28. I don't know my zodiac. My favorite color is black, but recently I've been obsessed with blue. I don't have any siblings. I have a degree in computer science, but that didn't interest me at all, so I tried culinary school instead. I have too many tattoos to count, and I don't think I have a reputation to uphold. Oh, and I'm gay."

Our pancakes arrive, fluffy stacks of sugary goodness, mirroring our shared, unexpected connection.

"How don't you know your zodiac? You can literally google it." he says, a hint of amusement in his voice. I laugh.

"That's all you grasped out of everything I told you?" I ask, amused. He pulls out his phone.

"When is your birthday?"

"January 1st." I reply. His head snaps up, his eyes widening in disbelief.

"You're a New Year's baby?!" he nearly shouts. I hate it when people call me that.

"Yes, but don't call me that. It's not a big deal."

"You're a Capricorn," he finally says, the revelation seemingly more significant to him than to me. I'm not sure what that means, honestly. I've never been one to obsess over my zodiac, but Jasper's interested in it, and I'm interested in Jasper. He leans forward, a playful glint in his eyes.

"So, Capricorn, tell me more. What's your favorite kind of pancake topping?" The question, seemingly lighthearted, feels intimate, a bridge built on shared syrup and surprisingly compatible astrological signs.

"Chocolate chips. When is your birthday, Jas?"

"August 8th." He said with a mouthful of pancakes. I make mental note of his birthday and dig into my food. The whole time we ate and talked. Made a few jokes and he laughed. I was shocked at first but then I decided that that was my favorite sound ever and I had to hear it again. It was a great fucking morning but then it came to an end and he had to go home.

***

JASPER'S POV

I'd like to think that I know myself inside and out, but the truth is, I'm a stranger to myself. The realization hit me hard, a cold wave of panic washing over me. It terrified me, this unknown residing within. My usual coping mechanism, drowning myself in alcohol and the fleeting oblivion of parties, felt inadequate, a flimsy shield against the overwhelming fear. But today was different. Today, I was facing my fear head on, trading the bottle for dumbbells, the throbbing bass of a nightclub for the rhythmic thud of my own heartbeat.

The gym's familiar scent of sweat and exertion was somehow comforting. It was a controlled chaos, a place where I could exert myself physically to try and tame the storm brewing inside. Each rep, each set, was a small victory, a tangible testament to my resolve. The burn in my muscles was preferable to the burn of self doubt, a preferable pain.

The heavier the weights, the better I felt, the more in control I seemed to be. I finished my weight routine, gulping down water like a parched traveler. The cool liquid helped to soothe my racing pulse, although the reasons for that pulse had shifted. I moved to the treadmills, the monotonous rhythm a counterpoint to the frantic rhythm of my thoughts. A gradual increase in speed from a walk to a light jog, then a full blown sprint, helped to clear my head, at least temporarily. That was until my phone buzzed, interrupting my carefully constructed sanctuary.

The call was from Ezra. His voice, warm and familiar, cut through my exertion, my carefully maintained composure crumbling. His casual question, an invitation for pizza and a casual evening, sent my carefully constructed world spinning.

"Hey, Jas. Are you ok? You sound out of breath." he'd said, his concern a balm to my anxieties. His concern for my breathing while I was clearly, and maybe foolishly, pushing myself so hard to the limit. It was his concern, his genuine concern, and not the alcohol I should have been reaching for, that unsettled me.

The sudden, unexpected call, the casual invitation...it all felt far too easy, too perfect. The near fall on the treadmill, a clumsy, adrenaline fueled stumble, served only to amplify my growing panic. My heart pounded not just from the exertion but from the realization of just how much his presence, his simple phone call, had the power to unsettle me. I was entirely unprepared for these feelings. I hate feelings.

I fumbled for an answer, my breathless reply a mixture of truth and avoidance.

"Um, sure. I'll bring over some beers." I managed, the words sounding hollow even to my own ears. So much for no alcohol today. There's no way I can be around the guy without being under the influence of alcohol. My nerves would never let me relax.

"Cool. I'll see you soon then."

"Um, y-yeah. B-Bye." I stutter, making him chuckle before hanging up. I curse myself for being stupid. I quickly head out to my car and drive home.

I strip out of my clothes and toss them into the laundry basket. I walk into the bathroom and turn on the shower. I look at myself in the mirror.

"Keep it together, Jasper. It's just pizza. What could go wrong?" I tell myself. I take a deep breath then walk into the shower. The hot water washes over me, a soothing balm against the unexpected turmoil churning inside. It's not the pizza... it's Ezra.

My best friend. The idea feels so foreign, so profoundly new. For years, my life was a carefully constructed social landscape, populated by acquaintances and fleeting friendships. Popularity had been my shield, a way to avoid the vulnerability of true connection.

Yet, Ezra…Ezra saw past the carefully crafted persona, past the polished surface. He saw me. The shower water cools as my thoughts spiral. This friendship, this unexpected intimacy, it's shaking the foundations of everything I thought I knew about myself. I quickly rinse off and turn off the water. I dry myself with my towel, the fluffy fabric doing little to absorb the nervous energy still thrumming beneath my skin. I spend way too long trying to decide what to wear, eventually settling on a simple black shirt and jeans. The beer in the back of my car feels heavy, a physical manifestation of the weight of my anxieties.

Driving to Ezra's apartment, the familiar streets feel strangely unfamiliar, each turn a hesitant step into uncharted territory. The beer feels like a crutch, a way to mask the nervousness bubbling up inside me. Now, here I am, standing awkwardly before his door, feeling foolish and exposed. His amused smirk only exacerbates the situation.

"Were you going to stand out here all day?" he asks, the question laced with playful mockery.

"Shut up." I walk passed him and make my way to his couch. I place the cases of beer on the table. Ezra closes the door and walks to his kitchen. He comes out with two plates of pizza. He hands one to me.

"You know, you should dry your hair before leaving your house." he randomly said. I furrow my brows. I had completely forgotten about my hair.

"People don't get sick from going outside with wet hair. That's a myth." I said, then took a bite of pizza. An explosion of flavor erupts in my mouth. Ezra sits next to me with a smile on his face. I never really noticed how nice his smile is. How soft and plump his lips are. Fuck. I take another bite of my pizza and try my damnedest to shut my thoughts down.

"That's not what my mom told me all of my life." he chuckled, a low rumble in his chest that sent a surprising shiver down my spine.

"I bet being an only child was lots of fun." I said sarcastically, attempting to deflect the unexpected flutter in my stomach. I open up the box of beers and drink one because I NEED it. The cold liquid helps to soothe the sudden nervousness that has taken root.

"It had its moments." he said between bites, his eyes twinkling.

"Where did you get this pizza? It's freaking awesome."

"I made it." I instantly stopped chewing and looked at him surprised. I know he told me he went to culinary school, but I didn't expect that he would cook for me. The revelation hung in the air, thick and delicious like the aroma of the pizza itself. My initial surprise morphed into something warmer, a slow burning appreciation for this unexpected gesture. He'd gone to all this trouble, prepared a meal just for me. It wasn't just pizza, it was a carefully crafted act of kindness, a silent offering of his time and skills.

"I thought you were going to *buy* some pizza."

"I was going to buy some pizza but then I decided to make it instead. Put my skills to work." He said. I decided that Ezra can cook for me forever. This is the best thing I've eaten like, ever. I won't tell him that though. No, I would die of embarrassment saying that out loud.

"You've got some serious skills. Why aren't you working at a restaurant or something?"

He puts his plate down on the table with a smile. Then leans back and faces me.

"I don't like being stuck on one thing. I want to learn to do a lot of things and keep growing."

"Why are you a bartender?" I asked, while grabbing another beer.

"It's not about the money for me. It's about the experience and the people I meet." He said, his eyes intensely looking into mine. I look away and drink my beer.

"I meet all kinds of people everyday. I end up with way too many phone numbers by the end of my shift. So, I know what you mean."

Ezra's whole demeanor changes after what I said but a second later he's smiling. Making me wonder if I imagined the whole thing.

"I get more numbers than you do. I just throw them away." He smirks. I roll my eyes and move on to my third beer.

At this point, I'm just chugging them down. Ezra stops me on my sixth beer. I ignore him, the cold glass a comforting weight in my hand, and continue to drink. The amber liquid slides down my throat, a temporary numbness spreading through my chest. Our conversation continues, a low hum against the background noise of my rapidly increasing inebriation.

He keeps a close eye on me, his expression a mixture of concern and something else... something softer, something akin to fondness? I can't quite decipher it through the haze of alcohol. On my tenth beer, I'm starting to feel relaxed, obviously very drunk, but I don't stop. No. I push on to my twelfth. Now I'm sloppy, babbling nonsense, making a complete and utter fool of myself. My words are slurred, my laughter too loud, my movements clumsy.

Absolutely embarrassing myself. Ezra, however, remains calm. He just observes me, this ridiculous, drunken mess sprawled on his couch, laughing at my lame jokes, the sound surprisingly gentle. The alcohol is washing over me, erasing the sharp edges of my anxiety, leaving only a dull ache behind. I lay my head on his lap, the denim surprisingly comforting.

I don't think he was expecting that because he tenses up for a few seconds, his body stiffening before slowly relaxing. He slowly lifts his hand, his fingers tentatively tracing the outline of my ear before gently weaving themselves into my hair. It feels so incredibly nice, a soothing balm against the turmoil within. The touch is light, yet incredibly grounding. My eyes grow heavy, the alcohol finally winning its battle against my weary mind. He's got that look on his face again, that same look that always makes my heart flutter, the one that suggests a depth of emotion I'm too afraid to acknowledge, a look that says he's... in love with me?

I shut my eyes, pretending that I don't notice, hoping to simply sink into the warmth of his presence.

"Why do you drink so much?" he whispers, his fingers now deep in my hair, the motion hypnotic.

"To forget." I whisper back, the words catching in my throat, the tears finally threatening to spill.

"Forget what?" he asks softly.

"Everything." I manage to croak out, the weight of unspoken words pressing down on me. He's silent after that, the silence heavy with unspoken understanding. So, I break it.

"You're my best friend, E." I murmur, the words feeling profoundly true despite the alcohol fog clouding my judgment. I don't know if he replied or anything after that.

The comforting weight of his hand in my hair, the gentle rhythm of his breathing beside me, the warmth of his body radiating out to me, all combine to create a haven of safety. In that moment, surrounded by his quiet strength and unwavering kindness, the fear recedes, leaving only a profound sense of peace. I feel safe again, completely and utterly safe, and I finally fall asleep, my head resting comfortably on his lap. The weight of "everything" is gone, for now, replaced by a gentle hope for the future.

CHAPTER 6

———◆○◆———

EZRA'S POV

I have a storm of emotions swirling within me right now. Sadness, anger, disappointment, intrigue, admiration—a chaotic cocktail stirred by the sight of Jasper, sprawled across my couch, a casualty of another night spent battling his demons. The empty bottles scattered around him are a testament to his struggle, a silent scream echoing the pain I sense beneath his usually boisterous exterior.

Someone who drinks themselves to death has clearly gone through something terrible, something that has chipped away at his soul, leaving him fractured and broken. I wish I could have saved him from whatever darkness claims him, pulled him back from the precipice. I'm angry at myself for letting him get this drunk again, for failing to intervene sooner. It's a familiar frustration, this helpless feeling of watching him self destruct.

I don't want to only be around him when he's too drunk to remember anything, to be a blurry, fleeting presence in his hazy memories. I'm bitterly disappointed that my feelings for him seem doomed to remain unspoken, relegated to the confines of a one sided affection. And yet, I'm fascinated by him.

Everything about Jasper, even his self destructive tendencies, intrigues me. I admire his strength, the resilience that keeps him going despite the relentless weight of his sorrow. The thought of leaving him there, alone and vulnerable, is unbearable. So, I gently replace my lap with a pillow, tucking a blanket around his shivering form.

I walk over to the window, the city lights blurring into a hazy watercolor painting outside. I pull out a cigarette from the carton on the windowsill, a small rebellion against the overwhelming tide of my emotions. The familiar ritual of lighting up, the sharp tang of tobacco, provides a momentary distraction. The smoke curls around my face, a fleeting companion in the quiet of the night.

Why have I gone and fallen for a straight man? The question hangs in the air, unanswered, as heavy as the smoke itself. I inhale deeply, letting the nicotine soothe my frayed nerves, a temporary balm for the ache in my chest.

Five minutes later, the cigarette is a dying ember, tossed out into the darkness. I turn off the lights, the sudden gloom mirroring the emptiness inside me. In my room, I shed my clothes, the simple act feeling strangely ritualistic. I crawl into bed, the cool sheets a welcome contrast to the turmoil in my mind.

I fall asleep eventually, exhausted from the emotional rollercoaster of the evening. I don't know how long I've slept, but then a weight crashes down on me. A heavy, warm weight. I open my eyes to find Jasper's head resting on my chest, his upper body draped across mine. The scent of his cologne, a mix of sandalwood and something faintly floral, fills my nostrils.

"Jasper?" I whisper. He hums, a low rumble vibrating through the mattress.

"What are you doing?" I ask, trying to keep my voice steady, but a tremor betrays my nerves.

"You smell good." he whispers back, his breath warm against my skin.

"You are going to hate me in the morning, Jas." I murmur, a warning and a confession all in one.

"Maybe." he replies, burying his face in the crook of my neck. I suppress a moan. The warmth of his body pressing against mine, the weight of his hand resting on my chest, sends a jolt of electricity through me. My heart is beating erratically, a frantic drum against my ribs.

"Jasper, you are really tempting me. I need you to move to the other side of the bed. Please." I beg, my voice barely a breath. But he doesn't move. Did he fall asleep? His nose and lips are pressed up against my skin, and I shiver, a mixture of apprehension and a thrilling, unfamiliar warmth. I slowly, carefully, lift him off me and onto the other side of the bed. I stare at him for a moment, the dim moonlight illuminating his sleeping face, soft and vulnerable. Wondering what the hell just happened?

Is Jasper attracted to me when he's drunk? That doesn't make any sense. If he is attracted to me when he is drunk, then, by some twisted logic, he must be attracted to me when he's sober. Holy shit. The thought is both exhilarating and terrifying.

The possibility hangs in the air, thick and heavy, a silent promise. There's still some doubt in my mind, a tiny voice whispering warnings of misinterpretations and drunken mistakes. But the weight of his presence, the lingering warmth on my skin, the memory of his nearness... it feels far too real to dismiss.

I close my eyes and try my hardest to fall asleep, the image of his sleeping face imprinted on my eyelids. After a while, I do, the uncertainty a strange, exciting companion in my dreams.

***

The jarring ring of a phone sliced through the blissful haze of sleep. Slowly, I peeled open my eyelids, the sight of him greeting me like a sunrise. Sleepy, his dark hair was a messy halo around his face, his eyelashes casting delicate shadows. We were a tangle of limbs, a comfortable, intertwined knot of human beings. His arms were a comforting weight around me, my own wrapped securely around his waist, our legs hopelessly entwined.

He stirred, a slight groan escaping his lips, and then his eyes fluttered open. Recognition dawned, a slow, dawning realization spreading across his features, followed by a sharp gasp. The ringing ceased, the silence amplifying the sudden awkwardness between us. I tried to disentangle myself, a clumsy, half hearted attempt to regain some personal space, but my arm was pinned beneath his weight, a testament to how deeply we'd slept.

"Sorry," I mumbled, my voice thick with sleep, "I tried putting as much distance between us as I could."

The extrication process was slow and fumbling, a dance of apologies and awkward shifts. Finally, we were free, the space between us suddenly vast and charged. I stood on my side of the bed, he on his, both of us breathing a little too heavily, the silence punctuated only by the gentle thump thump of our hearts. He didn't speak, just stared at me, his expression unreadable, his breath catching in his chest.

"Are you ok?" I asked, concern beginning to prickle at the edges of my own awkwardness. His gaze drifted from my face to my body, then snapped back up, a flicker of something...embarrassment? Mortification?... in his eyes. I looked down, and the reason for his sudden shift became horribly clear.

I was only in my underwear, and the undeniable evidence of my morning wood was hardly subtle. My hands flew to my crotch in a futile attempt to cover up. Scooping up a pair of sweatpants from the floor, I pulled them on, the sudden rush of blood to my cheeks mirroring the crimson tide I imagined painting Jasper's face.

He didn't wait for me to finish. He bolted, disappearing from the room with a speed that suggested a startled gazelle escaping a lion.

"Hold on! Don't go!" I shout and run after him.

"Hold on!" I grab his arm and stop him from leaving.

"Stop. Let me give you water and some painkillers. Maybe some breakfast."

"No. I have to go home." He said, while pulling his arm out of my grip.

"Ok, no breakfast. Just water and painkillers." I try to bargain. He sighs and nods.

I go to my kitchen and grab a water bottle.

I go to my bathroom and grab some painkillers from the cabinet. I bring it all back to Jasper. He opens the water bottle and puts two pills in his mouth then chugs the water. I just watched him. Searching his face for answers. When he's done, he turns around and leaves. Slamming the door shut on his way out. Fuck.

***

JASPER'S POV

I run out of Ezra's apartment like a bat out of hell. I go down the stairs two at a time and when that's not fast enough, I jump down like this shit is parkour. I climb into my car and grip the steering wheel tightly. I scream all of my frustrations out, a raw, guttural sound. I'm breathing heavily, chest heaving, a frantic bird trapped in a cage. All I'm thinking is, *WHAT THE FUCK... This isn't happening. This is...That was...I have no excuse. I liked it all.*

The images flash behind my eyelids. The sight of Ezra, practically naked, the sun light catching the damp sheen of his skin, the tantalizing outline of his hard cock pressed against the fabric of his underwear. Fuck! No! That's not possible. I'm a mess, a whirlwind of conflicting emotions and confusing desires. This can't be happening. I'm straight, aren't I? Or am I? The thought sends a fresh wave of panic crashing over me. I begin to hyperventilate, tears blurring my vision, hot and uncontrollable. I can't breathe. No air in my lungs. The world spins, threatening to pull me under. Suddenly, my car door is opened, a hand gently but firmly grasps my arm.

"Hey! Hey! It's ok. Look at me. Breathe." Ezra's voice cuts through the chaos, grounding me in the present. His hands cup my face, his fingers warm and reassuring, forcing me to look at him. His eyes, usually sparkling with mischief, are now filled with concern.

"Breathe, Jasper. I'm right here. Everything is ok. I'm right here. Nothing happened. You're ok." His voice, low and soothing, has an almost magical effect. Slowly, tentatively, my breathing returns to normal, the frantic rhythm easing into something steadier. He wipes away my tears with his thumbs, the gentle touch sending shivers down my spine.

I place my hands over his for a second, the warmth a comforting anchor in the storm raging within me. I close my eyes, swallowing the lump in my throat, trying to regain control. Then, with a sudden rush of shame and confusion, I remove his hands from my face. The reality of the situation hits me with full force. I can't deal with this now. Not like this.

"I have to go." I say, my voice barely a whisper. Ezra nods, understanding dawning in his eyes. He stands up, still shirtless, his body sculpted. I look away, unable to meet his gaze, the intensity of his presence almost unbearable. The vulnerability in his eyes, mirroring my own turmoil, makes my heart ache. I close my car door, the metal cold against my hand. I fasten my seat belt, the familiar click a small comfort in this overwhelming situation.

As I pull away, leaving Ezra standing there in the shadows, I feel a sense of relief, but also a profound unease. The questions remain, unanswered and swirling in my head like a restless storm. I need time, space, and a long, hard look in the mirror before I can even begin to understand what happened and what it means for me. The drive home is a blur, a silent journey of self discovery and uncertainty. I have to go home but I don't go home.

I go to the coffee shop around the corner from my apartment. I walk in and wait in line. When I finally reach the counter, I recognize the girl taking my order. Cindy.

"Welcome. What can I get you today?" She asked with a smile.

"Hey, Beautiful. I'd like a small coffee with cream and sugar." I smile. She blushes. I hand her the money for my coffee.

"You never called me." She said with a pout.

"Sorry. How about I take you out after your shift?" She twirls her brown hair around her finger.

"How many girls do you take out a day?" She asks. I chuckle.

"None." She looks surprised. She doesn't know that I don't date. I fuck around but I don't date. Maybe that's my problem. I need a girlfriend.

"Not a single one?" She asks, perplexed.

"Nope. How about we skip the small talk and I just call you my girlfriend?"

"Ok, pretty boy. You can call me your girlfriend. My shift ends at five. Don't be late." She said with a flirty glint in her eyes. That was easy. She hands me my coffee.

"I won't be late." I tell her. I walk away and exit the shop. I sit in my car and let everything that just happened sink in. I'm not a relationship kind of guy. I've never had a girlfriend. I've been with plenty of women. I just never took any of them seriously. They knew what they were getting with me. A good fuck and nothing more. That's not enough anymore, however. I need to try to commit to a girlfriend. Occupy myself with a relationship. Problem is I feel sick. I have no idea what the fuck I am doing and odds are I will fuck this up badly. I turn on my car and park it in my apartment complex parking lot. I forget all about the coffee I just bought.

I walk up the steps and enter the building. I climb the stairs to the third floor and find my apartment's door. I walk in my home, feeling lost. I shut the door and lean against it. I can't believe Ezra seen me cry. I hate to cry. Men shouldn't cry. My father would be disappointed with my tears. He would be disappointed with a gay son. I'm being a little bitch right now. The tears pour out of me so effortlessly. I don't even know why I am crying. I need to sleep this off. I walk to my bedroom and just let myself fall onto my bed. When I close my eyes, I just let myself drift away into a deep slumber.

***

I wake up hours later. It's three in the afternoon. Cindy gets off work at five. That gives me enough time to shower and get dressed. When I'm all done with that, I make myself a sandwich. Then I walk to the coffee shop, the familiar aroma of roasted beans and brewing coffee filling the air. I find a seat near the window, nervously checking my watch every few minutes. She notices me instantly, her presence a beacon in the otherwise bustling cafe.

She smiles wide, a radiant expression that lights up her entire face. Her green eyes sparkle, reflecting the warm afternoon light, and a blush creeps onto her cheeks as she approaches.

"Ready?" I ask, my voice a little shaky despite my attempts at nonchalance. She nods her pretty little head, her hand instinctively reaching for mine. The simple act sends a surprising jolt of nausea through me. We walk the short distance to my apartment, the silence comfortable yet charged with unspoken anticipation. I unlock the door, ushering her inside with a nervous laugh.

"Nice place." she says, her eyes taking in my modestly furnished apartment.

"Thank you. As my girlfriend, you can visit me anytime." I reply, the words tumbling out before I can fully process them.

"You're seriously my boyfriend now?" Her question hangs in the air, a mixture of surprise and delight. This is it. An opportunity to get out while I can, a tiny voice whispers in my ear, yet I find myself unable to back down.

"Of course, I am. I wouldn't joke about that. You're a pretty girl." I say, the words feeling slightly forced. Clearly, I am a masochist, I think to myself with a wry smile. She blushes really hard, the color blossoming on her cheeks like a summer rose, but the smile never leaves her face.

I guided her to sit down in my living room, the afternoon sun illuminating the dust motes dancing in the air. Suddenly, she blurts out, "Every time you come around to buy coffee, I always have this insane urge to kiss you."

Well, things are moving fast. I lean in, and kiss her. It wasn't terrible, but it wasn't great either. It lacked spark, passion, and hunger. A different set of lips danced in my mind's eye, and an image of Ezra's perfect full lips kissing me, instead of Cindy, came about without my permission. I shook the mental image away.

"Wow." she says once we pull apart, her eyes wide with wonder. She's practically glowing, radiating a happiness that feels both infectious and... slightly disconcerting.

"I'm going to need your number again, Cindy." I say, trying to shake off the lingering unease. I hand her my phone, and she saves her contact information. She saves her number under 'Baby Girl.' I text her so she has my number. She quickly saves it. I don't know under what name, but I don't care. It's not important to me.

We watch a movie, a lighthearted romantic comedy, her hand nestled comfortably in mine the entire time. Her presence is undeniably comforting, yet a quiet discord still plays within me. Afterwards, I drove her home. She lives in a charming yellow house in a quiet suburban neighborhood. I kiss her goodbye, a polite peck on the cheek, promising to see her tomorrow, the words tasting like ash in my mouth. On my drive home, I get a call from Ezra.

"Hello?" I answered, my voice trembling slightly despite my attempt at nonchalance. His voice, deep and warm, sent a familiar flutter through my chest.

"Hey, Jas." The simple greeting felt charged with unspoken emotions, a stark contrast to the casual "What's up?" I managed to muster in reply. His concern was palpable.

"I'm just calling to check up on you. You had a whole panic attack in your car. Left me worried about you." The words hung in the air, weighty and unexpected. His worry... it was unsettling, yet strangely comforting. The image of him witnessing my distress, his concern etched on his face, replayed in my mind.

I mumbled a weak apology, feeling the heat creep into my cheeks. The conversation stalled, a thick silence settling between us. Should I tell him about Cindy? The thought felt like a lead weight in my stomach. The truth felt like a betrayal, even though it was the honest truth. I couldn't bring myself to confess my complicated relationship. Instead, I deflected. His next words shifted the uncomfortable silence.

"We're hanging out tomorrow. I want to bake a cake and you're helping. So, I hope you have a sweet tooth." The invitation was surprising. Baking a cake? It felt like a deliberate attempt to steer the conversation away from the emotional minefield we'd just navigated.

The prospect of spending time with him, even in a seemingly mundane activity, was appealing despite the lingering guilt.

"I don't know how to bake a cake, E." I confessed, a hint of nervousness coloring my voice. His confident response, "Well, lucky for you, I do. Dinner at my place tomorrow and don't bother bringing alcohol," made me roll my eyes playfully. His insistence on no alcohol was both intriguing and slightly frustrating. I knew he was aware of my reliance on it to numb myself. Perhaps this was his way of helping me, a subtle intervention disguised as a baking session.

"Fine. I won't bring alcohol. I'll see you tomorrow." I grumbled, already anticipating the awkwardness of navigating a sober evening with him.

"See you tomorrow, Bye."

How am I going to survive dinner without alcohol? The thought echoed in my mind as I switched off the engine and stepped out of the car. The sober reality loomed large as I walked into my apartment. The day's events—the panic attack, Cindy, Ezra's call, the unexpected invitation—had left me feeling emotionally drained and confused. The weight of it all pressed down on me, a heavy cloak of conflicted emotions.

***

My phone buzzed, Cindy's name flashing across the screen. Breakfast? Sure, why not? I was trying to be the perfect boyfriend. Anything for Cindy. She was bubbly, feminine, all long brown hair and bright green eyes. I got dressed, a nervous energy buzzing beneath my skin. The drive to her house felt longer than it should have. When she stepped out, in a floral dress that clung to her curves, I felt a familiar pang of... something. It wasn't just lust, there was a disquiet nestled within the excitement.

"Hey, Babe." she chirped, kissing me.

"You look really pretty today." I managed, the words feeling slightly hollow even as they made her smile.

The diner was a blur of waffles and pancakes. The latter reminds me of Ezra, my best friend, and the unsettling question of my own sexuality that I am insistently trying to ignore. No, I'm straight, I told myself. Cindy talked incessantly, a relentless stream of words that I struggled to follow, yet somehow managed to respond to appropriately. The silence that followed when our food arrived felt thick and heavy, a stark contrast to her earlier exuberance.

After breakfast, she insisted on going shopping with me. The mall was a sensory overload. Cindy shopped and I bought, my credit card burning a hole in my pocket. Her happiness was infectious, but the relentless pace of our relationship felt suffocating. Too fast, I thought, but pushed the thought aside. Perhaps it was the sheer adrenaline, but the next thing I knew, we were parked in the mall parking lot and she was on top of me, riding my cock.

Afterwards, a strange calm settled over me. Maybe, just maybe, this was it. The answer to all my anxieties. That feeling didn't last. Lunch at my apartment, more pizza (Ezra again!), more fucking, and then she was gone. The empty apartment suddenly felt vast and lonely. I poured myself a drink, the alcohol burning a path through the growing unease.

The emptiness wasn't just about the loneliness, it was a profound sense of unease, a deep seated feeling of wrongness. The rapid progression, the almost desperate need for physical intimacy. It all felt like a frantic attempt to silence something within me. Cindy was beautiful, exciting, but the fleeting high didn't mask the underlying truth. The image of Ezra, his easy smile and genuine warmth, flickered in my mind.

The truth, harsh and unwelcome, finally surfaced. My frantic pursuit of Cindy was fueled by a fear of confronting my true feelings, a fear of what it meant to be truly happy, not just fleetingly satisfied. The cheap whiskey did little to numb that realization. The feeling of being dirty wasn't from the sex; it was from the lie I was living.

Now I'm drunk again, but I promised Ezra I'd bake a cake. So, I drive, not caring about the law. It's a blur, really, stumbling to his door. He opens it, a smile quickly replaced by a frown.

"You really are an alcoholic." he says, the disdain sharp.

"I didn't bring any alcohol." I slur, stepping inside, heading straight for the couch. Ezra shuts the door, his anger palpable. I've never seen him this mad, and it's unpleasant to experience. It's not the playful anger, this is raw, burning frustration.

"The point was I didn't want you drunk, Jasper! And you knew that!" he yells. The words sting, and I shrink, the confidence that usually shields my vulnerabilities crumbling.

"I'm sorry," I mumble, "Please, stop yelling."

His words hit harder than any punch ever could.

"I'm so fed up of seeing you drunk! You couldn't spend one day without fucking yourself up?! That's pathetic!" He's right, of course, devastatingly right. The shame burns hot, mixing with the alcohol.

"Okay. I'm sorry. Just get me some water."

"Get your own damn water, Jas." He leaves me alone, slamming the door to his bedroom. I flinch, the sound echoing the shattering of something precious.

I quickly come to terms that I hate it when Ezra's mad. It feels like a physical weight, crushing me. I get water, chugging it down. Then I head to his room, knocking insistently.

"Come on, E. Don't be mad at me. Open the door." I plead.

"If you don't open the door, I'm going to kick it down." It's a bluff, but it works. He opens the door, his eyes blazing, but I grab his wrist, pulling him slightly.

"I'm sorry. Don't be mad at me. I didn't mean to upset you."

"I don't accept your apology. Apologize to me when you're sober." he says, retreating into his bed. I follow him, collapsing onto the mattress.

"Are you really not going to forgive me?" I ask. He takes a deep breath.

"Jasper, I don't want you in my bed until you're sober. Because I hate it when you wake up and look at me like I've taken advantage of you." He's right again. It's a horrifying thought. He shoos me away, and I crawl back to the couch, the alcohol now a thick, suffocating blanket.

Seems like I'm always trying to sleep these days but I can't sleep. The frustration is a physical ache. It's all too much. The memories. Anything to forget. God, I have so much shit I want to forget. Like the crap parenting my father gave me or how my mother did fuck all to stop his abuse. I recall the day he placed a gun in my hand. No, don't remember that... just go to sleep, Jasper. Go to sleep but I can't sleep. These are the ghosts I drink to forget, the horrors that fuel my self destruction. Ezra is different, he sees through the bravado, the flirtatious charm, the carefully constructed facade I present to the world. He sees the scared, broken boy underneath just like my sister, Lily, did. But tonight, he can't reach him. Tonight, the alcohol wins, and I close my eyes, the weight of my past threatening to drown me once more. Sleep offers a temporary escape, but I know the morning will bring a new round of apologies and a painful reckoning with the man I am. The man my father created. No, the monster.

CHAPTER 7

EZRA'S POV

This morning I woke up to the smell of coffee. Jasper must be awake. My black hair was a mess, but the aroma was enough to pull me from the comfortable warmth of my bed. I get out of bed, my brown eyes already half focused on the day ahead. My usual morning routine in my bathroom— wash, brush, done —felt oddly peaceful this morning, a stark contrast to the usual chaotic energy that often followed Jasper's late night arrivals.

Leaving my room, I registered something else in the air, a subtle sweetness that battled with the coffee's robust scent. It was intriguing. As I entered the kitchen, the mystery was solved. Jasper, a whirlwind of dark curls and bright blue eyes, stood a midst a flour dusted battlefield, painstakingly frosting a cake that looked like it had survived a small explosion. It was terribly lopsided, the frosting a chaotic swirl, but it instantly melted away the remnants of any lingering irritation. I crossed my arms, a smirk playing on my lips.

"What are you doing?"

His eyes snapped up, his hands pausing mid swipe.

"Um, making an apology," he mumbled, a nervous energy radiating off him.

"It's not perfect, and I don't know if it tastes great, but I'm definitely sorry."

He looked so sincere, so vulnerable, that my carefully constructed walls began to crumble. I knew, deep down, that Jasper's struggles often led him to seek solace in the bottom of a bottle, and another late night escapade was a near certainty. But right now, seeing him like this, his usual confident swagger replaced with hesitant sincerity, made my anger melt away like butter.

"That's the sweetest apology I've ever gotten." I admitted, a genuine smile finally breaking through. He breathed a sigh of relief, that familiar flirtatious smirk returning, and my dumb heart did a ridiculous flip. I've got it bad. He has me wrapped around his finger, and he doesn't even know it.

"I made coffee. Want some?"

"I'll never say no to coffee." I replied, settling onto a stool. He moved with surprising grace, quickly preparing two mugs.

He handed me a mug, the warmth spreading through my hands. Then his phone vibrated on the counter. He picked it up, his brow furrowing as he read the message. The usual light in his eyes dimmed.

"I have to go, but I'll see you later. I'll call you." he said, slipping his phone into his pocket. A wave of disappointment washed over me. I had been relishing this quiet moment. But I knew better than to push.

"Okay. See you later." I replied, watching him leave, the aroma of his apology cake lingering in the air. He closed the door, leaving me with the lingering scent of coffee, the messy cake, and the undeniable truth. I was hopelessly, undeniably in love with him, flaws and all. I drink my coffee, the taste doing little to mask the bitter taste in my mouth.

My black hair falls into my eyes as I think about how to fill this gaping hole in my day. My phone, retrieved from my nightstand, vibrates with a message from Mariana. A trip to the diner to catch up sounds perfect. The quick confirmation sets my day in motion. Coffee downed, clothes on, keys, wallet, phone and I'm ready.

The rumble of my motorcycle engine is a welcome distraction as I head to our usual spot. The familiar diner smells of coffee and greasy spoons, but today, the aroma is overshadowed by a sudden, unwelcome sight.

Through the window, I see Jasper, his dark curly hair slightly windblown, getting out of his car, hand in hand with a woman. He leans in, kisses her. A million thoughts race through my mind, culminating in a silent, "WHAT THE FUCK?!" But then, a calmer voice reminds me, he's not mine. I shouldn't be mad. Yet, my appetite vanishes.

Making matters worse, they're heading straight for the booth next to mine. He scans the diner, then spots me. His eyes widen, and he visibly pales. The introduction is stilted, awkward.

"Hey, Jas. Fancy seeing you here. Who's this?" The girl, Cindy, steps forward, smoothly taking control.

"I'm Cindy. His girlfriend. Nice to meet you." Her handshake is firm, her smile practiced. I manage a weak smile in return, the polite facade barely clinging. Just then, Mariana bursts in. A huge bun that rivals a beehive and her signature bright red nails.

"Sorry I'm late!" she exclaims, sliding into the booth. "Que pasa?"

The situation's already tense, and with Jasper and Cindy awkwardly waving hello before retreating to their table, it only gets more strained.

"Was it just me, or were those two kinda weird?" Mariana asks, peering at the menu.

"I don't know about Cindy," I reply, "but Jasper was definitely being weird." She glances at me, a knowing look in her eyes.

"Well, weird or not, he was super hot." I roll my eyes.

"He is hot," I concede bitterly, "it's just too bad he has a girlfriend now."

"You sound jealous, Gringo." Mariana's chuckle stings. She doesn't know the half of it, I'm burning with a jealousy I hate. One minute he's in my bed, the next he's parading a girlfriend around town.

"I have no idea what you're talking about, Mari." I deflect, though my voice betrays my lie.

"Is it the pretty blue eyes or all the muscles?" she teases. I glare playfully, but the waitress arrives, interrupting our little game. I order coffee, Mariana, the entire menu. My thoughts are still on Jasper, but I force myself to engage. Needing a moment, I head to the restroom. As I wash my hands, Jasper follows.

"Ezra, I can explain." he begins. I continue washing, rinsing away the soap, the awkwardness, the anger, the hurt.

"You don't owe me an explanation." I reply, my voice firm despite the tremor in my hands.

"You're mad at me again, E. I can feel it." he sighs. I chuckle, drying my hands.

"I'm not mad, Jas. I'm surprised." I turn, standing toe to toe with him. My eyes travel his face, lingering on his lips. A subconscious lick of my own lips mirrors the undeniable pull, the magnetism that still crackles between us. Can he feel it too?

"Alright. I gotta go back now but I'm still going to see you later." He said, while looking away.

"Ok, Jas. I'll see you later." We walk out the bathroom. He heads for his table and I go back to mine. Where Mariana is happily eating everything she ordered. I sit down and prepare to spend the day with Mari.

***

JASPER'S POV

~A FEW MONTHS LATER~

I don't know how it happened, but Ezra became a big part of my life. Best friends. We do everything together. Any time I get drunk off my ass, he's a call away. Which is often. Every day I look forward to seeing him at work or the coffee shop. It makes my day to see his face. It makes me feel weird though. Unsure of myself.

So, I started dating Cindy. I don't typically date. In fact, I never do relationships. I needed to be sure of myself again though. She's my girlfriend now. We've been together for three months. A girlfriend doesn't change anything though. I still go out and get drunk. Only difference is now I don't go home with a stranger, I knock on Cindy's door.

She's been getting mad at me lately, however. So, I call up Ezra and he lets me stay on his couch. Though most of the time, I wake up in his bed. Which I happily ignore because all that ever happens is good friends falling asleep. Now I'm drunk again and knocking on Ezra's door at three in the morning.

"Jasper, I really thought you were joking when you asked for my number just in case you get drunk." he says, holding the door open for me. I stumble inside his apartment.

"That was months ago. Besides, Cindy won't be happy if I knock on her door this drunk." I slur.

"Jasper, go to sleep. I'm not in the mood to deal with your drunken-ness." He seemed annoyed. I don't like when Ezra's upset. He's a very calm person. So, if he gets mad then you just know you've fucked up and me being...well, ME...I fuck up everything.

"Aww.. don't get mad at me too, Ezra. I can't handle it when you're mad." I whine.

"I'm going to bed. Drink water before you die of dehydration on my couch." he moodily leaves me in the living room. I caught up and followed him into his bedroom. I've gotten comfortable around Ezra when I'm drunk. I know that I'm safe here. Plus, I like annoying him like the true best friend that I am.

"I don't like water. It tastes like...not good. Why are you mad at me?"

He stops in the middle of his room and turns to face me. His tattooed chest rising and falling slowly as he breathes, trying to find the patience to deal with me.

"I'm not mad at you, Jasper. I'm just tired of answering my door to find you drunk again. You never learn your lesson."

"Put a shirt on, you weirdo. Your nipples are staring at me." I say, walking past him and jumping onto his bed. The dim light catches the glint of his brown eyes, usually calm and steady, now filled with a frustrated tenderness. He sighs, a sound that somehow manages to be both exasperated and loving. Ezra rolls his eyes and gets into bed, his back ramrod straight against me. He's definitely mad, and honestly, who can blame him? I'd be tired of dealing with my shit too.

This is the only time I can truly feel okay, nestled in this comfortable numbness, because tomorrow, I won't remember any of this, or at least I can convincingly *pretend* I don't. His friendship is everything to me, far more important than I'd ever let slip. The alcohol is the only thing that shuts off the relentless noise in my head, the constant second guessing, the fear.

I don't overthink every little kindness from Ezra when I'm like this. I'm comfortable in the quiet of oblivion. If I quit drinking, reality's icy grip would squeeze the life out of me, forcing me to confront all the bullshit I've been burying. That's a Pandora's Box I'm not ready to open. The alcohol is a problem, I know Cindy hates it, Ezra's made that clear too. But I can't stop. I refuse to stop. My father—God, I hate fucking thinking about him—he'd be proud, see? Drinking like a "real man." The irony isn't lost on me, but the self loathing is a familiar comfort. I want to make Ezra happy again, to make things right. And then an idea sparks, dangerous and thrilling, one I hesitate to even acknowledge, let alone embrace... I like it.

CHAPTER 8

EZRA'S POV

Jasper always does this. He gets drunk and knocks at my door because he knows I won't say no. He gets into my bed and falls asleep holding me. It's never more than that. He tempts me though. His body so close, his warmth seeping into me, sets my skin on fire, but I never make a move. I don't want anything between us to be a drunken night. I'm jealous of Cindy. She gets to have him, really *have* him, in ways I can only dream of.

Tonight, though, I'm just annoyed. I turn my back to him, his beautiful blue eyes a torment I refuse to succumb to.

"Ezra.. Ezra..Ezzzrraaaa.." he slurs in a sing song voice.

"Go to sleep, Jasper!" I snap, stiffening at the touch of his hand trailing down my bare back. He's drunk, I tell myself, a mantra against the pull of his touch as his hand snakes towards my chest.

"Don't be mad at me." he whispers into my ear.

"I'm not mad at you. Go to sleep before you do something you'll regret." I say, my voice tight with barely contained frustration.

"You feel so warm." he whispers again, his hand inching lower, towards my abs.

"What are you doing?!" I snatch his hand away before it reaches my pants, whirling to face him. He doesn't reply, instead, he kisses me. I should have stopped him. I should have pushed him away. But three long months of longing, of watching him with Cindy, of silently aching for him... all that melted away under the pressure of his lips.

His tongue tasted of rum, a rough counterpoint to the sweetness of his kiss, and I didn't care. He shifted, his weight pressing down on me, the kiss deepening, heating. He's drunk, I remind myself again, a desperate attempt to cling to some semblance of control. Then, panic claws at me. I shove him away, the sudden action jarring us both.

"Jasper, I'm trying really hard not to take advantage of you right now. Please, go to sleep." I say, exasperated. I scramble out of bed, grabbing a shirt and pulling it on, needing the barrier between us, the space. I crash onto the couch, the distance a necessary buffer. But sleep won't come. My mind is a chaotic storm. He'll wake up tomorrow and never remember. Why did he kiss me? The chemistry, I always thought it was wishful thinking, a figment of my hopelessly devoted imagination. They say a drunk mind speaks with a sober heart...

I get up and light a cigarette, the nicotine a bitter comfort against the frustration. I lean against the window, the city lights blurring. I hate having blue balls. With Jasper, it's a never ending occurrence. Fuck. A drunk kiss. A stolen moment. A sliver of hope. The sobering truth, harsh as the cigarette smoke, hits me: maybe his drunken confession wasn't a mistake. Maybe it was the closest thing to a confession I'll ever get. Maybe, just maybe, he feels it too. The unspoken, the unsaid, the yearning that hangs heavy between us like the smoke curling into the night. The possibility, fragile as a whisper, makes the bitter taste of regret a little sweeter

***

JASPER'S POV

I woke up in an empty bed with the worst headache. I feel so fucking sick. Bits and pieces of last night flickered—stumbling through Ezra's apartment door, him kinda pissed...that's all. I must have fallen asleep speaking gibberish. My phone felt heavy in my hand, Cindy's name half typed in a text, but the rich aroma of coffee obliterated my intentions. The scent pulled me towards the kitchen.

Ezra, headphones on, was a symphony of motion. Shirtless, of course, those tattoos are a familiar, captivating sight. He was flipping pancakes with a rhythmic grace, his back muscles rippling beneath his skin, a silent invitation I couldn't ignore, even though I'd seen him shirtless a million times before.

It was always breathtaking. I stood there, mesmerized, until he turned, surprised to find me lurking. The headphones came off, tossed onto the counter.

"How long have you been standing there like a creep?" he asked, his voice a low rumble that sent a shiver down my spine.

Just woke up. The coffee lured me to your little pancake show." I joked, attempting a lightness I didn't quite feel.

"I figured you'd need some coffee to help with the hangover." he said, pouring me a steaming mug, his brown eyes—so calm, so steady—meeting mine. He handed me the coffee, the warmth spreading through my hands, mirroring the warmth that always radiated from him.

"Thanks. I'm gonna need it. Cindy wants to go to a party today. You should come." He placed a plate of pancakes before me, then sat, seeming lost in thought. The silence stretched, thick and heavy, until he finally broke it.

"What time?"

"5 PM. I can pick you up." I blurted, a smile blooming on my face despite my pounding head. The smile felt illicit, rebellious, given the chaotic mess of my feelings for him.

"Don't look so happy about it." he grumbled, that familiar smirk playing on his lips. "You better not drink yourself to death. I'm not babysitting you."

His glare was playfully menacing, only making my smile widen. I ate quickly, the pancakes were unsurprisingly good, and then I headed out. I had to get home, shower, and pull myself together. The party felt a million miles away, insignificant compared to the way he looked at me. A silent understanding that transcended words, the silent language of two people wrestling with themselves, each other, and the messy, beautiful chaos of love. He was cool, calm, Ezra, completely different from my usual confident, flirty self.

He saw through my bravado, my attempts to mask the uncertainty in my head.

***

5 PM couldn't get here faster. I beep the horn, signaling Cindy that I'm outside waiting for her. A few minutes later, she rushes out of her house in a glittery pink top, skinny jeans, and heels. Her brown hair was loose down her shoulders, her green eyes sparkling with happiness at the sight of me.

"Hey, Babe!" she greeted, pecking my lips.

"Hey, Cindy. You look great." I replied, smoothly driving towards Ezra's place.

"Why are we going this way? The party is in the opposite direction." she questioned, her voice laced with confusion. I mentally cursed myself. I'd forgotten to mention I'd invited Ezra. *Hope she doesn't mind.*

"Picking up Ezra. He's going to the party with us." I said, trying to keep my tone light. She didn't say anything after that, the silence stretching uncomfortably between us. I texted Ezra, letting him know I was outside his apartment.

Few moments later, he emerged from his building, a lit cigarette dangling from his full lips. He moved with a deliberate slowness, a cool swagger that made my pulse quicken. The breeze played with his straight black hair, slightly opening his leather jacket to reveal the tight fitting tee hugging his muscled chest.

As he approached my car, he tossed the cigarette to the ground and crushed it under his boot.

"What's up, guys? Let's party." he said, sliding into the backseat. I eyed him in the rear view mirror, my gaze lingering on the tattoos snaking across his neck. A detail that always captivated me. Suddenly, flashes of last night's blurry events flooded my mind. *Did I...kiss him?* My face burned crimson. He caught me staring, a smirk playing on his lips. My heart hammered against my ribs. Ok, don't panic. Why hadn't Ezra mentioned anything this morning? I glanced at Cindy. She seemed blissfully unaware.

The drive to the party was filled with awkward silences and forced conversation. My usual confident, flirty demeanor was shattered. The weight of my unspoken *feelings* for Ezra, coupled with the guilt of deceiving Cindy, felt suffocating.

Ezra's quiet intensity in the backseat only amplified my turmoil.

We thankfully arrived at the party in one piece. Cindy held my hand as we entered, Ezra trailing close behind. The music was a throbbing pulse, and Cindy, ever the dancer, instantly pulled me onto the floor. Ezra grabbed a beer, content to bob his head to the rhythm. I wanted to talk to him, keep him company, but Cindy's infectious energy was a captivating whirlwind.

A few songs blurred into one sweaty haze. I looked around for Ezra, but he wasn't where he'd been. My search, conducted while Cindy ground against me with enthusiastic abandon, found him a few feet away, locked in a passionate embrace with some girl. There wasn't an inch of space between them. He held her hips possessively, their bodies moving as one. His brown eyes met mine, a smirk playing on his lips as he pressed even closer, practically grinding his cock against her backside. Anger, hot and immediate, flooded my chest. Without thinking, I stalked over, grabbed his arm, and dragged him to the bathroom. I slammed the door shut.

"What the fuck are you doing?! Are you drunk or something?" I seethed, the words tumbling out in a rush.

"I've had a few, but I'm not drunk." he laughed, the sound grating on my nerves.

"You don't even like that girl! What the hell were you doing?!"

"If I didn't know better, I'd say you were jealous." he retorted, a cocky smirk curving his lips. I scoffed, crossing my arms, the heat rising in my face.

"I'm definitely not jealous!"

His response was sharp.

"You are so full of shit, Jasper. Why do you even care, huh? You have Cindy. She's literally out there waiting for you right now! You dragged me to the bathroom for what? To accuse me of having a good time?! Why can't you just admit that you got jealous, hm? Be honest. Oh wait, maybe it's because you're not drunk! Be a fucking man for once."

He started towards the door. His words, though harsh, cut through my carefully constructed facade. He was right, my ego was bruised, and his challenge was the catalyst I needed. Before he could leave, I caught his arm. He looked back, surprised. Without thinking, I pulled him close by the neck, my lips crashing against his. Ezra responded instantly, backing me against the wall, deepening the kiss.

I'd lost my goddamn mind, completely and utterly, but in that moment, I didn't care. His mouth tasted of beer and something else, something intoxicating. His hands tightened on my waist, pulling us together. The breathless feeling, the overwhelming need for more, was terrifying and exhilarating all at once. When he finally pulled away, the silence hung heavy.

"Honest enough for you?" I managed, my voice barely a whisper. His gaze lingered on my swollen lips, but then a shadow crossed his face.

"I like you, Jasper. More than just friends. I think you're really attractive. Kissing you...fuck... is amazing. But you have Cindy, and she's waiting for you. I can't be with a taken man. It's just not me." He took a deep breath, frustration etched on his features, and left me standing there, heart hammering, the taste of his kiss lingering, and the crushing weight of my unacknowledged truth pressing down.

CHAPTER 9

EZRA'S POV

It is taking absolutely everything in me not to turn back and make Jasper mine. I did the right thing though. My heart is beating wildly in my chest. The music, the people, the entire party was suddenly aggravating me. I just wanted to go home now. Unfortunately, Cindy caught sight of me and she was walking directly towards me.

"Hey, is everything ok? Where's Jasper? The way he left was so weird." She shouted over the music. I tried to think of something to say to her that would make her feel like nothing was wrong but all I could think about was the guilt I was feeling for kissing her boyfriend and enjoying it.

"Everything is fine. He's in the bathroom. He'll be out soon." I finally said with a fake smile. She nodded her head in understanding and went to talk to a group of friends.

A few minutes later, Jasper made his way to her. I awkwardly stood around, watching the party go on.

Feeling suffocated and uncomfortable, I decided to step outside. I light a cigarette and look at the moon. My mind races with a million thoughts. Why did I want to make Jasper jealous? What would I get out of forcing him to admit his feelings for me? He has a girlfriend. I should be a better friend to Jasper and Cindy. Maybe I should put some distance between us.

What am I even talking about? It was just a kiss. No big deal. It's not like Jasper confessed he's in love with me or some shit. I'm clearly freaking out over nothing. I laugh at myself. What is it about Jasper that makes me feel like an insecure teenager? He's all sharp angles and cocky smirks, a whirlwind of dark curls and sapphire blue eyes that seem to see right through me. He's everything I'm not. He's confident, outwardly assured, while I'm a quiet observer, my brown eyes usually hidden behind my black hair.

Maybe that's the attraction, the magnetic pull of opposites. Or maybe it's simpler than that: he makes me feel things, raw and intense, things I've never felt before. The stolen kiss tasted of rebellion and a desperate need for something more, something real beneath the surface of carefully constructed images. I take a drag of my cigarette and exhale smoke, the acrid taste mirroring the bitterness building in my mouth.

The moon hangs heavily in the inky sky, a silent witness to my turmoil. I stub out my cigarette, the glowing ember a tiny reflection of the burning questions within me. Maybe distance isn't the answer. Maybe honesty is.

Maybe, just maybe, Jasper feels the same way. But then, the thought of hurting Cindy, of shattering her carefully built world, brings me back to the cold, hard reality of the situation. I sigh. The night air is crisp and cool against my skin, a stark contrast to the burning heat in my chest.

Tonight, I choose to walk away. But tomorrow, I will talk to Jasper. Whether he admits it or not, I'll finally know where I stand. And I need to know. Because even though it terrified me, the thought of a future with Jasper, despite the complications, felt like hope. A fragile hope, but hope nonetheless. My phone vibrates in my pocket, breaking me out of my thoughts.

Jasper: Where are you?

Me: outside.

Jasper: why?

Me: smoking.

Jasper: come inside and have some drinks with me.

Me: I'm not really in the mood to drink.

Jasper: Don't be a party pooper. Come have drinks with me! :)

Me: lol no.

Jasper: Don't make me drag you in here kicking and screaming.

Me: nice try but I'm stronger than you. Lol

Jasper: I live in the gym. You are not stronger than me.

Me: Hey man enjoy your night. I'm going to head home in a cab.

Jasper: ....

***

The following morning I woke up to fifteen missed calls and four voicemails. I play the voicemails first.

"Ezra, it's Jasper. Pick up the phone! I need to talk to you!"

"Duuuddeee! I'm calling you. Why won't you answer?! I'm too damn drunk for this."

"Alright. I'm driving to your place and I'm knocking the door down. Since you don't know how to pick up the phone!"

"Hey, Ezra. It's Cindy. I'm calling from the hospital. Jasper got into a car accident. You're his best friend, he's going to need you. I'll keep you updated."

What in the actual fuck!? I quickly rush out of bed and throw on clothes. I run outside, start up my motorcycle and head to the closest hospital. I run to the front desk, asking the woman sitting there, for Jasper Rowan.

"Room 373. Take a left down that hall and take the elevator to the 5th floor." she directed, handing me a visitors pass. The directions were easy to follow. I knock on the door to room 373 and peek in. Cindy is asleep in her chair but Jasper is wide awake in the hospital bed, a constellation of wires and tubes attached to him. His face was bruised, his left arm in a cast. He definitely looked beat up, but even like that, he still looked beautiful. His blue eyes lit up when they caught sight of me.

"What happened to you?" I whisper yelled, trying not to wake his girlfriend.

"I'm fine. I'll be out in a few hours." he said, not bothering to whisper.

"Drinking and driving. Are you stupid?!" I shook my head.

"Don't be mad at me, Ezra. You know I hate it when you're mad at me." he groaned. I sat on the bed and just glared at him.

"You're lucky to be alive. I don't appreciate waking up to rush to the hospital in a panic. You need to stop drinking." I lectured him. Jasper smiles uncontrollably, making me frown. He's not taking this seriously.

"You were worried about me? You're so cute." he chuckled. I glanced at Cindy and then back at Jasper.

"Are you seriously flirting with me right now?" I whispered, incredulously. Before he could reply, there was a knock at the door and in came the doctor. The doctor's assessment was thankfully positive: no serious internal injuries, just a concussion and some bruises. He recommended rest, a detail that sparked a conversation between Cindy and the doctor while I turned my attention back to Jasper.

"What?" I said, catching him staring.

"Just thinking," he said in a low voice.

"About what?" Jasper gripped my shirt and pulled me forward, smashing his lips onto mine. I quickly pulled away, shocked.

"What are you doing?" I said, clearly surprised.

"Yeah, what are you doing?" Cindy spat angrily, having clearly woken up. Jasper blanched.

"Babe, I...What you saw...Um, I'm sorry," he stammered. The air thickened with awkwardness.

"I'm going to leave." I finally said.

"You don't have to leave." Jasper said quickly. Cindy scoffed and stormed out.

"What just happened?" I asked, still reeling.

"Doesn't matter. It has already happened." he replied.

"She didn't deserve that, Jasper." My voice was calm, even though my insides were a tangled mess of emotions. Jasper, all dark curly hair and stunning blue eyes, usually so confident and flirty, lay in the hospital bed, pale and subdued. His usual swagger was absent, replaced by a vulnerability that both scared and captivated me.

He'd kissed me, three times in fact, while his girlfriend, Cindy, was just a few feet away. He'd been in a car accident on his way to confess his feelings, or so he claimed. I was completely smitten, even if his methods were... unorthodox. The irony wasn't lost on me: I, the seemingly calm one, was utterly flustered by his chaotic confession and the mess he'd made.

His explanations were riddled with contradictions and evasions. One minute he was blaming his actions on some sort of hypnotic effect of my tattoos, cigarettes, and leather jacket (which was laughably untrue). The next, he was lamenting his relationship with Cindy, admitting it wasn't working out. His struggle with his sexuality was palpable, his discomfort a visible ache in the air.

It was a stark contrast to the Jasper I knew. The charming, almost reckless Jasper who once tried to punch me at work and freaked out when he woke up in my bed with a hangover. He didn't have answers for my questions, only a quiet desperation that mirrored my own yearning. His inability to articulate his feelings, coupled with his actions, spoke volumes. I knew he liked me, the kisses were not merely impulsive mistakes. But I ached for him to say it, to acknowledge the undeniable connection between us. In came a nurse with papers in her hands. She unhooked the monitors and took the IV out.

"You're all set to go." she said happily. My heart did a little flip. Jasper was finally being discharged. I took the papers and folded them up, my brown eyes never leaving his. He was pale, the usual confident smirk replaced by a vulnerability that tugged at my soul.

Even in his weakened state, his blue eyes held that captivating spark that had drawn me to him months ago, a spark I was now fully consumed by.

"You can crash at my place, if you don't have anyone else to watch over you. Where's your family? Do they even know?" I asked, my voice softer than I intended. Jasper rolled his eyes, a flicker of his usual self returning, and got up from the bed in the hospital gown. He was silent as he strategically angled himself so I couldn't see any nakedness and put his pants on.

The way he moved, cautious and self conscious, broke my heart. He untied the hospital gown, and I tried not to stare, but the sight of his bruised body, made it impossible to look away entirely.

"Can you stop staring at me?! I don't have family. Just a sister and she's busy planning a wedding. She doesn't need to worry about me." The raw emotion in his voice confirmed my suspicions. This wasn't just a physical ailment. There was a deeper struggle, a secret pain.

"Alright. Well, what's your next move?" I asked, trying to sound casual. The unspoken hung between us, heavy and charged. We walked out of the room and headed for the elevators.

"I need to deal with Cindy." he said, his voice low.

"Can you take me to her house?" A hint of pleading in his voice.

"Yeah, alright. I can do that." I replied, my mind already racing. Cindy. It felt like a turning point, an inevitable confrontation, a test of our fragile connection. The elevator doors slid open, revealing the bright, bustling hospital lobby. But for me, the only light visible was the one shining between Jasper and me, a light that, despite the shadows and uncertainties, felt brighter than ever. The journey wouldn't be easy, but as long as we had each other, even Cindy wouldn't be able to extinguish the flame that was starting to burn between us
.

CHAPTER 10

JASPER'S POV

"Thanks for the ride, Ezra. I'll call you if I need you." I watched him drive off on his motorcycle, his taillight a disappearing red spark against the suburban twilight. Cindy's yellow house loomed before me, a beacon of impending doom. I took a deep breath, smoothed down my curly hair, and marched up the steps.

My blue eyes, usually flashing with confident flirtation, felt heavy. I knew this wouldn't be easy. I, the guy who could charm the birds from the trees, was completely floundering. Cindy, with her long brown hair and perpetually bubbly personality, was everything I thought I wanted—until Ezra... and the kiss... and the party.

She opened the door, her green eyes blazing. The accusations flew, sharp and stinging. "You're gay and you used me!" The pain in her voice was a physical blow. I tried to reason, to explain, to drag this conversation inside before the entire neighborhood became privy to our spectacular implosion.

"I'm not gay," I insisted, "but... we're not working out. I'm breaking up with you." The words hung in the air, heavy and awkward. Her reaction, or lack thereof, was even more unnerving than her anger.

A simple, flat, "Okay." It felt wrong, too easy, like a script gone horribly awry. My carefully constructed confidence crumbled. This wasn't how it was supposed to go. My carefully cultivated image of effortless cool was shattering. The whole thing was irritatingly anti-climactic.

My discomfort morphed into full blown anxiety when she whispered, "How many times have you cheated on me?"

The question hung in the silence, a stark reminder of the party, of the drunken kisses, of the choices I made that led to this moment. Lying felt like a betrayal even worse than the truth. I confessed, the words tumbling out in a rush, each syllable a confession of my own inadequacy, my own inability to navigate feelings and desires I barely understood myself.

The aftermath was silence, heavy with the weight of unspoken words and broken trust. My charming, flirty self was gone, replaced by a raw, vulnerable version, left to face the consequences of his actions.

"How many times have you cheated on me?" She said so quietly that I almost couldn't hear it, but I did, and blanched immediately. Cindy, usually so bubbly and full of life, now looked utterly broken. Fuck!

Now I have to tell her about the party. Do I really? I could lie. The only other person who knows about the party is Ezra and I doubt he's eager to tell Cindy anything. I contemplated it, the weight of my actions pressing down on me, but inevitably told her the truth because I just don't have the energy to lie in this very moment.

"Three times. I kissed Ezra on three separate occasions." I kept a serious face, trying to hide my annoyance. The yellow house, her yellow house in the suburbs, felt suddenly suffocating.

"Why?" she questioned, tears welling in her eyes. FUCK. FUCK. FUCK. FUCK. FUCK.

I'm really not in the mood for this conversation anymore. Now she's crying?! Oh, for fuck's sake. The words tumbled out, raw and ugly.

"Because I felt like it, Cindy. I fuck around. I get drunk and I bang whoever I want. It's just who I am. Happy?!" The bravado was a flimsy mask, a desperate attempt to deflect the pain I felt rising within me, a pain that had nothing to do with Cindy's tears and everything to do with the confusing mess of my own desires and insecurities.

My sexuality, a battlefield I was constantly fighting within myself, was bleeding out into my relationships. I stormed out of there and slammed the door behind me. I don't need any of her shit right now. Talking about feelings or anything about Ezra. I need a drink. Yeah. That's all I need right now.

I took my phone out of my pocket to call a cab, but a drop of water fell on my screen. I look up to the sky, but it's not raining. I touch my face and there was wetness. Tears. I was crying. Wiping my face with my hand, I call a cab to take me home. I can't be out in public crying like a pussy.

The cab drops me off in front of my place, but the smell of freshly brewed coffee wins. I decide to walk to the corner cafe first.

"Welcome. What can I get for you today?" The cashier, a guy who looked like he'd rather be anywhere else, asks.

"Small coffee, cream and sugar." I reply, tossing him some cash. My blue eyes are scanning the room, catching a flash of black hair and a familiar tattoo peeking from under a worn leather jacket. Déjà vu. It's Ezra. He's sitting alone, a cigarette smoldering between his lips. He smirks, a silent invitation.

The confidence that usually radiates from me feels a little shaky. This whole "being out" thing, this figuring-out-my-sexuality thing, it's a lot harder than I thought. Yet, there's something about Ezra, that quiet intensity, that pulls me in despite my internal turmoil. I grab my coffee and head towards his table.

"You know, for such a softy you sure look like a bad boy. With your mysterious aura and shit," I tease, aiming for playful but landing somewhere closer to nervous. He smiles. A slow, breathtaking smile that makes my heart stutter. He stubs his cigarette out in his mostly empty coffee cup, a small act of defiance or maybe just habit.

"I don't know what you're talking about. I'm just a normal person having a bit of coffee before heading to work." he says, his voice a low rumble. That "innocent" act? Completely unconvincing. My casual flirting is a desperate attempt to mask my own confusion, my attraction to Ezra is undeniable.

Then, I blurt it out, "I broke up with Cindy." His face falls, serious and concerned, the expression twisting my own gut into knots.

"Sorry, Jasper. I have to go to work now." he says abruptly, rising from his seat.

"What? Right now? Coincidentally, after I said I broke up with my girlfriend?" I ask, a sting of hurt mixing with the caffeine buzzing in my system. He avoids my eyes.

"Jas, we'll talk later. I'll stop by your place after work." he says before hurrying out. I stand there, coffee lukewarm in my hand, feeling utterly deflated. Today is just not my day.

The walk home is silent, my usual arrogance replaced by a heavy uncertainty. I sip my coffee slowly, the bitter taste mirroring the strange mix of relief and disappointment swirling inside me. As I stepped into my apartment, a chaotic mess, I just kept thinking about everything that had happened. I hated how Ezra makes me feel. This unsettling, thrilling mix of anxiety and exhilaration. I'm not good at handling these sorts of feelings.

I usually run for the hills when things get serious with girls. Which was close to never because up until Cindy, all I was interested in was one night stands. Here I am, kissing instead of running. Not to mention, with a man. He is going to drive me crazy. Just absolutely mad. I could feel it. A guy making *me* chase him like a fool. Ugh.

What the fuck is wrong with me?! I don't do feelings. I don't do relationships. Yet, here I am, dying to be in a relationship with Ezra. Ugh, I did NOT just say that. Does this make me gay? Fuck, no. I rather not think about that.

Hours blurred into a restless haze. My phone vibrated on the nightstand, jarring me from a fitful doze.

Ezra: Are you awake?

My fingers, clumsy and slow, tapped out a response.

Jasper: Maybe.

Ezra: I'm at your door.

My heart hammered against my ribs, a frantic drumbeat against the sudden quiet of my apartment. I quickly got up, my reflection in the hallway mirror showing a man battling inner turmoil, his usually confident facade crumbling.

Throwing open the door, I found Ezra standing there, his black hair falling over his eyes, those usually hidden brown eyes now blazing with a quiet intensity that mirrored my own turbulent emotions.

"I knew you weren't sleeping." he said, a smirk playing on his lips, a smirk that I suddenly found incredibly sexy. Before I could even think, before the swirling chaos in my mind could fully process anything, I grabbed the back of his head and kissed him. A kiss born of confusion, desire, and a terrifying, exhilarating leap of faith.

The kiss was everything I hadn't expected, and everything I'd secretly craved. It was a collision of two worlds, two very different people, yet somehow perfectly compatible. His hands found their way to my waist, pulling me closer. In that moment, only one thought remained, I was gay for Ezra.

CHAPTER 11

EZRA'S POV

Jasper's lips moved hungrily against mine. I was surprised at first. It was so unexpected, a stark contrast to the carefully constructed walls we both maintained. But then, a familiar hunger bloomed in my chest, mirroring his. It was a wildfire, ignited by stolen glances and lingering touches. With my hands on his waist, I closed his apartment door with my foot, the sleek, dark wood cool against my skin.

All rational thoughts, the differences in our worlds, the whispers of doubt, evaporated. I wanted him. I'd wanted him since the first time our eyes met across the bustling coffee shop, his dark, curly hair a halo around his intense blue gaze. My own black hair fell into my brown eyes as I tilted my head, lost in the heat of the moment.

His mouth opened, and I snaked my tongue inside, the taste of him a delicious surprise. Jasper moaned, a low, guttural sound that sent a shiver down my spine. Oh god... what a sweet sound. I didn't even realize we'd made it into his bedroom until I was hovering over him on his bed, my hands on either side of his head.

The air thrummed with unspoken words, with the unspoken weight of his internal struggle. We were both breathing heavy, our bodies slick with sweat and desire. I gazed into his blue eyes, those captivating pools that held a depth I longed to explore. They were like oceans I wanted to drown in for all of eternity.

"What are we doing, Jas?" I managed to say, my voice husky. The question hung in the air, heavy with the unspoken implications.

He swallows before answering, his voice barely a whisper, "Not giving a fuck." He grasps my lips again, a possessive claim that felt both exhilarating and terrifying.

His hands sliding under my shirt. *Yes, touch me.* I mentally begged. I certainly don't give a fuck about anything but him right now. I take my shirt off and toss it on the floor.

He traces his fingers over the tattoos on my chest, a ghost of a smile playing on his lips. I kiss and suck on his neck, the taste of him intoxicating. He moans, a low rumble in his chest, music to my ears. I grind my hips against his, the heat between us palpable. My dick is so hard right now and by the feel of it, so is his. I don't want to move too fast though. So, I pull myself away, lying next to him, breathing heavy, the adrenaline still coursing through my veins.

"What?! Why'd you stop?" he asks, a hint of frustration lacing his voice. His curly hair tumbled around his face, his blue eyes wide with a mixture of confusion and desire.

"Trust me, I don't want to stop, but we should." I say, my voice husky.

"No, we shouldn't." he replies before kissing me again, his lips urgent, demanding. I pull away long enough to speak, "Jas, I really think we have to slow down."

But he doesn't listen. Instead, he rolls over on top of me, his weight a comforting pressure. He takes off his shirt, tossing it to the floor, and leans down to kiss my neck, his breath warm against my skin. His hands are all over my chest, slowly making their way to the button on my jeans.

The reality of the situation hits me then. This isn't just about lust. It's about something far deeper, something fragile and precious that needs nurturing, not rushing. His touch, his urgency, it was overwhelming.

"Jasper..." I moan out, the name a soft whisper against the plush comforter of his bed. The cool, calm exterior I usually maintain crumbles under the heat of his touch. His hand, strong and sure, grips my dick with confidence that both thrills and unnerves me. This isn't the "talk" we were supposed to have, not the serious conversation about his struggle with his sexuality, but some primal urge takes over.

I close my eyes, the steady rhythm of his stroke washing away my anxieties. This feels surreal, like a dream where all my deepest desires are finally being met. The urge to reciprocate is overwhelming. I slide my hands down his shorts, ignoring the sting of his recent injury, my fingers finding him instantly. The beads of precum on his shaft are a potent promise. I feel the pressure building in my own body, a dam about to burst. This feels embarrassingly good after the long drought.

"Jas, I'm so close." I groan, the sound thick with urgency.

"Look at me," he whispers, his voice a low rumble against my ear. "Cum."

I open my eyes, meeting his gaze. The lust burning in those blue eyes is intoxicating, a fiery contrast to his usually flirty demeanor. It's like looking into a burning supernova, and I'm utterly captivated. The pressure explodes, a wave of intense pleasure washing over me, coating my stomach and his hand.

"Ohh, fuck..." I moan breathlessly, my body arching. The satisfaction in his eyes deepens as the lust settles into something more profound. It's a silent understanding, a shared moment of intense vulnerability and raw connection. My hand is a blur as I pump his cock into my tight fist. Jasper's cum, warm and white, shoots out. Landing everywhere. He falls against me, our bodies entangled, breathing heavily, our hearts a frantic rhythm against each other. Sticky and messy, but oblivious to it.

"That was... fun." he says, a genuine smile breaking across his face, a smile that finally showcases his true beauty. It's a smile that melts away the calculated confidence, revealing a softer, more vulnerable Jasper.

"That was not the 'talk' I thought we'd have." I smirk, unable to resist a playful jab, even in the afterglow of our intimacy.

"We had a wordless conversation. What's better than that?" he replies, then throws off his shorts. The light catches the sculpted muscles of his body, the slight bruise on his cheek, the cast on his arm. My gaze is caught by the amazing details, his dark curly hair, full lips, broad shoulders, perfectly sculpted muscles, and a huge cock. He looks like a Greek god, even with his imperfections.

"Like what you see?" He laughs, that confident smirk back in place.

"The boner in my pants says yes." I reply, all thoughts of our earlier conversation, the one where he wrestled with his feelings, completely forgotten. He smiles devilishly and walks off to the bathroom. I hear the shower running. I quickly take off the rest of my clothes and walk in the bathroom behind him. He turns around, and his cheeks start to blush as his eyes take all of me in.

"Aww. You're blushing. Does that mean you think I'm good looking?" I teased, my cheeks hurting from smiling so much. He wraps his cast in plastic wrap to protect it from the water. He looked deep in thought.

"I've never been attracted to a man before but you—" he trailed off. The vulnerability in his voice, the hesitation, made me rethink my playfulness.

"I was just playing around with you, Jasper. It's ok." I said, taking his hand in mine and stepping into the shower, willing away the sudden rush of fear that he'd retract. His silence was heavy, but it wasn't a rejection. It was something else... something deeper.

"I'm not good with words, E." he finally mumbled, his gaze unwavering.

"You don't need to be good with words. Your sexy body speaks for you." I smirked, looking down at his growing erection.

"Who says that's because of you? It could be a random boner." he laughed, a nervous sound that somehow felt intimate.

I grabbed some soap and began washing up Jasper's body, starting at his chest and slowly making my way down. The water cascaded over us, washing away not only the soap but the tension that hung between us.

"You can pretend all you want, but I know the truth." I said before kissing his full lips, the taste of him both familiar and exhilarating. I love kissing him. Shit, I love him. I've been in love with him for months. He pulls away, his breath hitching, and grabs the soap, washing me with a smirk playing on his lips.

The playful banter was back, but underneath, something solid had shifted.

"Let's get the fuck out of here. I'm tired." he says, his voice raspy with something that sounded an awful lot like contentment.

I rinse off and turn off the water. My straight hair, plastered to my forehead, drips onto the bathroom floor. Jasper tosses me a fluffy towel, his dark curly hair a halo around his blue eyes. He's so effortlessly confident, a stark contrast to the nervous flutter in my chest.

Drying off, I stepped into his room. He's rummaging through a drawer overflowing with clothes, his brow furrowed in concentration.

"Hey, you mind if I smoke?" I ask, the question a little breathless. His face scrunches up in that way he has, a charming mixture of disapproval and concern.

"You really should stop smoking. Why do you smoke anyway?" he says, tossing me a pair of his sweatpants. They're soft, smelling faintly of his cologne. The weight of his disapproval settles on me, yet somehow, it feels... comforting. The thought of him caring enough to lecture me about my smoking habit, a habit that feels as ingrained as breathing, sends a jolt of something potent through me.

I slide the sweatpants on, the fabric cool against my skin.

"Um, I don't know," I mumble, searching for an answer that doesn't sound pathetically weak. "It's just a habit, I guess."

I walk over to the bed and sit beside him, the springs groaning slightly under my weight. He's still sorting through his clothes, his dark hair falling over his eyes.

"Well, you should quit." he states, his tone firm but not unkind.

"You want me to quit smoking?" I ask, a hesitant smile playing on my lips. The question hangs in the air, charged with unspoken things.

"That's what I said." he replies, his voice barely a whisper. I couldn't help but smile. He cares, I think, a wave of irrational happiness washing over me.

"Okay," I say, the word surprising even myself. "I'll quit."

His eyebrows shoot up.

"Just like that? You're just going to quit?" He sounds incredulous, bewildered.

"Yeah. Why?" I ask, genuinely puzzled. And then it all comes tumbling out.

"I pretty much forced you into bed with me before we could even talk like we planned to and now I'm asking you to stop smoking like some clingy girlfriend." he blurts out, annoyed with himself. I laugh, a genuine, unrestrained laugh.

"First of all, you didn't force me to do anything," I say, my voice still laced with laughter.

"I just wanted to slow things down, to make sure we didn't regret anything. Secondly, you're not some clingy girlfriend," I tease, my eyes meeting his. "Though," I add, leaning closer, "I'd probably like that."

The tension in the room dissipates, replaced by a comfortable silence. His blue eyes, usually filled with playful flirtation, soften, and a small smile tugs at his lips. My heart hammers against my ribs. Maybe, just maybe, this wasn't just a fling.

"But we do need to talk, Jas. You just got out of a relationship." I said, the mood turning serious. He groans out of frustration and gets up to walk away.

"What does that matter? She'll move on in a week. I don't care."

"Jasper, I care. I want to do things the right way." I said, following him around his apartment. His dark curly hair bounced with the movement, the blue of his eyes flashing with something unreadable as he turned to face me.

"What exactly is the right way? Did I fuck up already?!" He was clearly frustrated and angry. I'd wanted to avoid this, to control the situation, but it all started falling apart the moment I gave in to my desires. We should have talked before things got this far. The painful truth was, Jasper was stuck in the closet, and I'd complicated our friendship tenfold.

"Alright. Things are complicated. This is exactly why I wanted to slow down." I admitted, my voice betraying none of the turmoil in my chest.

"It's too late for that now. I can't believe I'm having this conversation with you right now." he spat back.

"And what conversation is that? The one where you admit you have a thing for guys? Because yes, we are, and yes, you do. Can't go running back into the closet now, Jasper." He scoffs and tries to walk away, but I grab his arm. I won't let him leave. Not until we're done talking. Not until he faces the facts.

"Go on. Admit it. Say it out loud." I insisted. He yanks his arm free, chest heaving, face red, eyes watery, hands balled into fists. I waited, but nothing came. The silence stretched, thick and heavy with unspoken words and unspoken feelings.

I started gathering my things from the floor, the hurt a dull ache in my chest. Nothing more could be done until he could admit his feelings. So, I needed to leave.

"Where are you going? Don't leave." he groaned, the confident facade crumbling completely. I stopped, turning to face him, trying to mask my pain. His words, raw and unfiltered, hit me like a punch.

"What do you want me to say?! I'm not good with words! I told you that! Isn't what we did enough?! You make my dick hard, what more is there to say?" His vulnerability was shocking, yet somehow, it felt... insufficient.

"No, it's not enough. Not for me. I don't use people like you do. I actually have feelings. Which you're so carelessly stepping all over, and I can't do whatever *this* is." I said, gesturing between us. The weight of his unspoken words, his fear, his inability to fully embrace himself, hung in the air between us, a chasm too wide to bridge.

"Ok, hold on! Don't...just don't leave. God, why is this so hard to say! I have..certain..feelings for you to." He takes a deep breath. "There. I said it."

The relief in his voice was palpable, a wave washing over the tension.

"That's more than I wanted you to admit. I mean I'm not mad at it but I definitely am surprised. I just expected you to say you were a little gay but this is a whole lot better than whatever I thought you'd say." I said, stepping closer, the months of carefully cultivated distance crumbling.

I kissed him softly, a tentative exploration that quickly deepened into something more urgent, more desperate. The taste of him sent a jolt through me.

"Awesome. Now let's go to bed. I'm tired." he mumbled, pulling me towards his bed. The touch of his hand in mine was electrifying.

This was different. This wasn't the drunken, sloppy affection of past nights. This was real. This was us. As soon as Jasper's head hit the pillow, he fell asleep, the exhaustion of his own internal battle finally claiming him. I gently moved a curly strand of his hair from his forehead, the gesture feeling oddly significant.

"Goodnight, Jasper. I love you." I whispered, the words echoing the truth of my heart.

CHAPTER 12

JASPER'S POV

Sunlight was peeking through the window and shining right in my face. I groan as my eyes try to blink away the sleepiness. When I finally managed to open my eyes fully, I was welcomed by the sight of Ezra sleeping on his stomach. The muscles on his back are on full display. The ink on his flesh, a swirling tapestry of colors, was undeniably enticing. I couldn't help but reach out and trace them with my fingertips. Waking up with morning wood didn't help.

My thoughts quickly turned sexual, a wildfire spreading through my usually controlled mind. Maybe I should go back to sleep. Anything is better than the torture I'm putting myself through right now, this internal battle raging between the Jasper I presented to the world and the insecure, unsure boy struggling to understand his own sexuality.

Suddenly, I was brought out of my reverie. Ezra shifted, his fingers twitching slightly before he opened his eyes. Slowly, his lips curved into a smile, a slow, knowing smile that sent a shiver down my spine.

"Why'd you stop touching me? It felt nice." his husky voice rumbled, a low vibration that resonated deep within me. It made my dick twitch, and I was hyper aware of it. He placed his head on my chest, his arm draping casually around my waist, the weight of him oddly comforting.

"Uh, I didn't want to wake you." I mumbled, my cheeks burning. My hand instinctively covered my face, trying to hide the blush creeping up my neck. I tried to will my erection to soften, a silent plea to the gods of awkwardness.

"Why is your heart beating so fast?" he murmured, lifting his head slightly, one brown eye peeking at me, waiting, patient.

"I'm not used to waking up to hot men in my bed." I admitted, the words tumbling out in a rush, a confession more to myself than to him. The embarrassment was overwhelming, a stark contrast to the playful banter we usually engaged in. He chuckled, a low, throaty sound, before burying his face back into my chest. The scent of his hair, something earthy and masculine, filled my senses.

"Want some coffee?" He mumbled, changing the subject for my sake. My heart hammered a frantic rhythm against my ribs, a counterpoint to the lazy Sunday morning light spilling across Ezra's tattooed arms.

"Only if it comes with pancakes." I retorted, my voice a little too breathy, a little too playful. Ezra didn't even fight me on it. He just mumbled an 'ok' and got up, his black hair falling over his forehead as he moved.

"Ezra, I was just kidding! You don't have to make pancakes. Come back here." The words tumbled out, laced with a desperate plea that I didn't dare analyze too closely. I quickly pulled off the blankets and chased after him, my bare feet slapping against the cool wood floors of my apartment. He was laughing, a low rumble in his chest that sent shivers down my spine.

If this were a game, and it felt awfully like one, I was determined to win. All I had to do was catch him. I chased him into the living room, a breathless pursuit fueled by a combination of playful competitiveness and something deeper, something that had been simmering beneath the surface ever since Ezra, with his calm demeanor and steady gaze, had walked into my life. He jumped over the couch, his body effortlessly clearing the obstacle, while I fumbled, my dark curls bouncing.

"You can't catch me." he said in a sing song voice, a smug smile playing on his lips.

"Oh, I'm going to catch you, and when I do, you're so dead!" The ridiculous chase continued, a dizzying game of leapfrog over the damned couch that seemed determined to thwart my victory. He was quick, a blur of dark hair and brown eyes, but I was relentless. I took a step to the right, he mirrored me to the left. Then, with a surge of adrenaline, I jumped over the couch again, but this time, I didn't just jump past him. I tackled him, sending us both sprawling to the floor in a tangle of limbs. I pinned his hands above his head, straddling him, my blue eyes locking with his.

"Oh, would you look at that... I seem to have caught a very naughty boy." I smiled, my blue eyes twinkling, as Ezra squirmed beneath me on my apartment floor.

"Indeed, you have. What are you going to do to me now?" he said, a seductive smirk playing on his lips. Oh, fuck. He was breathtaking.

"You're enjoying this too much." I murmured, leaning down to kiss him. The kiss was hungry, urgent, and instantly intensified the already crackling tension between us. His hands, usually so controlled, moved to my shirt, shedding it with a practiced ease that matched the way he always seemed to effortlessly disarm me. I kissed and sucked on his neck, a soft moan escaping his lips. The feel of his body beneath me was electric, and I found myself driven by an instinct I barely understood. I kissed, sucked, and licked my way down his chest, the anticipation building. I pulled his sweatpants down to his knees, his throbbing member springing into view. The sight of it... I'd never considered this before, not really. Not until Ezra.

I looked into his eyes, the question hanging heavy in the air. He shook his head, his brown eyes wide with a mixture of apprehension and desire.

"No, Jasper. Don't. Ja-Mm..." he struggled against my hands, his words cut short as I took him into my mouth. His fingers entangled in my hair, his lustful gaze never leaving mine. He tasted... incredible. It was completely unplanned, instinctive, a raw response to the overwhelming pull of the moment.

"If you don't... oh, god... slow down... Jasper! I'm going to..." I couldn't hear him clearly over the roaring in my ears, but I didn't slow down. I took him deeper, gagging slightly as his thickness filled my throat. It was exhilarating, terrifying, and completely intoxicating. His release was a wave that washed over me, and I swallowed, the taste lingering on my tongue.

"Fuuuck..." he moaned, his head thrown back, chest heaving for breath. I didn't stop. I kept sucking, savoring the moment, relishing the unexpected pleasure. This was so far outside of anything I'd ever imagined, a completely different level of intimacy.

"Jasper," he breathed, a whisper against the air.

I sat up, a triumphant grin splitting my face. I licked my lips, impressed with myself, and with the depth of my own feelings.

"Breakfast was great." I teased, the words tumbling out before I could stop myself. The unexpected confession hung between us, unspoken but undeniable. He chuckled, pulling up his pants.

"That was... unexpected, but you're still getting pancakes and coffee." He got up, and I followed him into the kitchen, the lingering taste of him, and the thrill of my own newfound boldness, a delicious secret between us.

"Unexpected? I mean that was my first time...well, you know... and that's all you have to say?" I said, trying to sound more nonchalant than I felt. He turns the stove on and places the pan down on the burner. A smug look plastered on his face.

"I don't know if I believe that was your first time. You definitely have skills that took me a few times to get right." He said. Suddenly, the image of Ezra blowing another guy pops in my head. I grimaced at the thought. The fleeting image felt like a betrayal, a crack in my carefully constructed facade.

"So, you've never been with a girl?" I asked, the question tumbling out before I could censor it. My blue eyes darted around the kitchen, seeking a distraction from the sudden vulnerability that threatened to overwhelm me. Ezra tosses butter in the pan and mixes the batter of pancake mix.

"I had a girlfriend in high school. Her name was Kimiko. She was fucking awesome until she wasn't. I lost my virginity to her. It was fucking awful." He said, as he flipped pancakes. The casual way he admitted this, the almost dismissive tone, surprised me.

"Then you like girls and guys." I said, trying to sound casual despite the butterflies fluttering in my stomach. He flops the pancakes onto a plate and starts up the coffee maker. I sit on a stool and rest my elbows on the kitchen island. My curiosity keeping me completely enthralled in the conversation. What if I don't like the answer? Oh, shit. Well, too late now. Ezra leans on the island and replies, his gaze intense.

"No. I had a thing for Kimiko. Before I realized I really didn't like her in a sexual way. So, when a guy came along, it felt right. So, I guess to answer your question I'm totally gay."

"I have fucked like a million girls." I said, the bravado a thin veneer over my inner turmoil. Ezra arched an eyebrow and pursed his lips. His silence was more revealing than any response could have been. In the distance, I could hear the sound of coffee pouring into the pot. Nothing could distract me from his face though. Not even the heavenly smell of fresh coffee. His reaction—that simmering jealousy—was unexpected, a raw emotion that felt intensely intimate. I kinda liked it a lot.

"Well, I'll happily be the first man in your life and just so you know, I don't do the casual sex thing. So, that little stunt you pulled makes you mine." He turns to pour coffee into two mugs, his movements fluid and effortless, the epitome of cool. The heat rising in my cheeks felt like a wildfire.

"Whoa. What happened to 'slow down'?" He just laughs, handing me a mug before settling down.

"Your face is priceless, Jas, but I'm serious. No more fucking anyone else. Not if you're fucking with me."

"And who says I want to fuck with you?" I retorted, trying to sound nonchalant, even as my heart hammered against my ribs. Ezra just smiles, casually cutting into his pancakes.

"Don't self sabotage. Pushing me away isn't going to change the facts." he says, mouth full. I couldn't eat. My stomach was a tangled mess of nerves. Did I somehow stumble out of one relationship and straight into another? I had said I had feelings for him, and it was true. It would be so much easier if I didn't. This was all moving too fast, too intensely.

"I'm not self sabotaging. I just didn't realize that sucking your dick meant I automatically got a boyfriend. Things are changing a little too fast."

He puts his fork down, his gaze intense.

"I don't just share my body with anyone, Jasper. I don't enjoy feeling like a cheap slut. I want to hold value in someone's hands." he said, his voice low and serious.

"You mean in my hands." I looked down at my hands, calloused and marked from countless sexual partners, none of which had ever meant anything. Ezra was different. He was my best friend.

Oh god. I blew my best friend and liked it. What the fuck is wrong with me?! The sheer terror of it all was overwhelming. I was in deep. Too deep. I don't know what the hell I am doing. I rest my hands on my lap.

"Preferably, in your hands." He said truthfully.

"You have shitty taste in men, Ezra. I don't do relationships. I suck at being a boyfriend. I tried it with Cindy and look what happened to her! I cheated on her with you. That's what I do. I fuck shit up." The words hung in the air, heavy and sharp, a stark contrast to the quiet hum of the refrigerator in my apartment. My confession landed like a grenade in the middle of our breakfast.

The clinking of my fork on the plate felt aggressive, almost violent, mirroring the turmoil inside me. My heart hammered a frantic rhythm against my ribs. I could practically hear it echoing in the silence. Should I apologize? The urge to retract everything, to disappear into the plush cushions of my own couch, was overwhelming. I'm such a prick. Ezra's cool facade cracked just a little, revealing the hurt beneath.

"Don't compare me to the females you fucked. I'm not some chick you picked up at a bar. What is so hard about being with me?" he said, his voice low and controlled. The anger simmered beneath the surface, a dangerous current. He rose, plate in hand, and tossed the remains of his breakfast into the trash, the gesture sharp and decisive. The way he moved, controlled yet radiating tension, was captivating even as my heart plummeted. He placed his plate in the sink, his back to me, a silent condemnation of my words. I'd done it. I'd completely blown it.

What had I expected? This was all so familiar. The pattern was ingrained: the charming flirt, the inevitable self destruction, the echoing ghost of my father's mistakes. I'm my father's son, indeed.

"There's nothing wrong with you. You're my best fucking friend, Ezra! This shit just got too fucking complicated really fucking fast! And yes, I said I have...well, you know...for you but it's all too fucking new!"

Ezra turned, his hands gripping the edge of the counter, the muscles in his arms flexing. His gaze, usually so calm and steady, was intense.

"Can you be honest with yourself for once?! You would get really fucking drunk and call me up. Get in my bed with those blue eyes of yours eating me up. Not to mention, the copious flirting and cuddling. We could have done far more, if I was the kind of guy to take advantage of the situation. This isn't that new. We've been playing this game for months." he said, his words a mirror reflecting my own carefully constructed avoidance. He was right, of course. He saw through my bullshit, my carefully crafted layers of denial and fear. The truth hung in the air, heavy and unavoidable. I couldn't deny it. I couldn't lie. All I could do was face the messy, terrifying truth of my feelings. I hate it when he's mad at me. I take a deep breath and let it out.

"I can't lie my way out of this one. So, you got me, E." I said.

"You're giving me whiplash, Jasper. You fight me one minute and then kiss me the next. I get that your sexuality is a bit to deal with emotionally but you can't just string me along. So, call me when you've made up your mind." He said, walking out the kitchen. I didn't do anything to stop him from leaving this time. I just sat in my kitchen trying to wrap my mind around what the fuck just happened. He didn't even say goodbye. I heard the door slam closed. Then silence.

CHAPTER 13

———◆◦◆———

EZRA'S POV

Leaving Jasper's apartment was rough. The air hung heavy with unspoken words, the silence echoing the chasm that had suddenly opened between us. I hate that we needed space, that time apart felt necessary to untangle the mess we'd made. I'd texted Mariana and Jeremiah, my two friends, needing the familiar comfort of their company. The Italian pizzeria buzzed around me, a chaotic symphony of chatter and sizzling pizza, but my mind was a million miles away, replaying our last conversation. The scent of oregano and garlic did little to soothe the ache in my chest. I sat, fiddling with the straw in my empty glass, lost in thought, until the familiar flash of red nails caught my eye.

"Hey! It's my favorite gringo!" Mariana's voice pulled me back to the present. Her brown eyes, bright and full of life, held a spark of mischief. Jeremiah, all swagger and cornrows, followed close behind, his chocolate skin gleaming under the pizzeria's warm lights. Their presence was a balm, easing the tension. Mariana, ever the blunt force of nature, immediately launched into questioning my state of affairs with Jasper.

She pressed me, her usual Latina sass a playful counterpoint to my hesitant explanations. I confessed to the kiss, the bittersweet taste of it still lingering on my tongue, the way his touch had sent shivers down my spine. The way I'd confessed my desire for something more, only to be met with his uncertainty, his hesitation. The realization that he wasn't ready for the same level of commitment, a cold splash of reality that left me reeling.

Jeremiah returned with the food, the aroma of melting cheese and simmering sauce a welcome distraction. Mariana leaned in conspiratorially, her voice low.

"You are so old fashioned. Nobody wants to wait until the third date to have sex anymore. We live in a world where Tinder exists. Just fuck the guy." Her bluntness was a stark contrast to the swirling emotions inside me. Jasper. My Jasper. The way he laughed, his perfect smile, the way his eyes crinkled at the corners... I wanted to spend a lifetime with him, not just a night. I would marry him tomorrow if I could. The thought of jumping into bed with him without the emotional connection, without the promise of something real, felt wrong, deeply wrong. I was calm on the outside but inside, I was hopelessly, hopelessly romantic. This Italian pizzeria, usually a haven of delicious chaos, felt suffocating today.

Jeremiah, our ever optimistic friend, oblivious to the turmoil raging inside me, interrupted with his pizza fueled chant: "Pizza! Pizza! Pizza!" He was a six foot tower of oblivious joy, a constant source of amusement and sometimes, surprisingly, good advice.

Mariana's laughter cut through the air, followed by her recounting of my predicament to him, my agonizing struggle with Jasper's fear of commitment. Jeremiah, mouth full of pepperoni, offered his pragmatic wisdom, "Listen, man. You a cool dude but don't you ever have fun? Like not everybody you like is gon' be relationship material. You can't cuff everyone. Some folks just a good time." His words stung, a tiny prick of doubt piercing my carefully constructed romantic ideal. Mariana squeezed my hand, her support a silent reassurance a midst the conflicting advice.

Mariana's words, while harsh, had a kernel of truth. Maybe I was being naive, clinging to a fairy tale in a world of swipes and hookups. Yet, something in my heart stubbornly refused to accept her logic.

"If someone doesn't want the incredible guy that you are then it's their loss." Mariana said, her small smile surprisingly comforting. Jeremiah nodded in fervent agreement, his face a masterpiece of cheesy pizza induced bliss. Across the table, Mariana was mid laugh, her brown eyes sparkling. Beside her sat Jeremiah, his easygoing demeanor a stark contrast to Mariana's fiery spirit. He was recounting a childhood anecdote involving his mother's surprisingly accurate aim with whatever kitchen utensil was closest at hand. I watched them, a quiet observer. Their banter felt familiar, comfortable, like a warm hug on a chilly evening.

"What about you guys? When are you two going to hook up?" I said, the question hanging in the air, light and teasing, yet carrying a deeper curiosity. They both looked at each other and laughed.

"Yo, I love this girl. She's a baddie but there ain't no way I'm going to be chased around with a sandal." Jeremiah joked. Mariana retorted, "Hey! It's 'la chancla' and you're right to fear its power. My ma still scares me and I'm a grown woman."

Their playful sparring continued, a dance of familiarity and affection that was both endearing and intriguing. Jeremiah's tales of his mother's disciplinary methods were met with Mariana's equally humorous stories of her own Latina upbringing. We traded stories drawing laughter and sharing understanding. My own contribution, a slightly embarrassed account of my mother's uncanny ability to dispense life advice with the sweetness of freshly baked cookies.

The easy flow of conversation felt right, a testament to the unlikely bond forged between these three vastly different personalities.

Then, Mariana announced, "Oh, guys! I totally forgot to tell you. We absolutely need to plan a road trip. Work has me stressed and I really need my boys. So, schedule some time off next month. Road trip!"

Jeremiah immediately asked, "Road trip to where?" I was about to suggest the coast, picturing Jasper beside me, when my phone buzzed, a sharp vibration cutting through the pleasant hum of conversation. I pulled it out and glanced at the screen.

"Jasper's calling." I said, my voice barely a whisper above the boisterous chatter of the Italian pizzeria. Mariana and Jeremiah exchanged worried glances. My brown eyes were now narrowed with concern. My tattoos peeked from under my leather jacket's sleeves—a silent testament to a life lived fully, a life that now revolved heavily around Jasper. We were an odd pair, him with his confident, almost cocky charm, me, the steady, tattooed anchor in his chaotic storm. We'd been dancing around each other for months, a delicate waltz of unspoken feelings, hidden glances and clumsy attempts at connection. The way he made me laugh, the way his blue eyes held a depth that mirrored the ink swirling on my skin—I was utterly, hopelessly in love with him. And right now, he was clearly in trouble.

"Hello?" I answered, bracing myself. His voice, when it came, was slurred and echoing, confirming my worst fears.

"E! Little problem. Like just a teensy weensy, tiny, soo tiny problem." he mumbled, the sound of a party thrumming in the background.

"Jasper, are you drunk?" I asked, the irritation battling the worry. He denied it, of course, but the 'Baby' he let slip out—a pet name he would never use unless he was thoroughly intoxicated—gave him away. He rambled on about me being on his mind, a sentiment that both thrilled and terrified me; thrilled because it suggested a reciprocation of my feelings, terrified because of the circumstances. He couldn't even tell me where the fuck he was, eventually settling on the vaguely ominous "Wilmington avenue, Baby! What a stupid name." The panic tightened its grip.

"Jasper, don't go anywhere. I'm coming to get you." I snapped, but the line went dead.

"Sorry, guys. I have to be a knight in shining armor." I muttered, a strained smile playing on my lips.

***

The pizzeria faded behind me as I raced out, the roar of my motorcycle a counterpoint to the frantic beating of my heart. Wilmington Avenue was a vast expanse; finding him drunk, disoriented, and possibly alone, felt like searching for a single needle in a haystack. My mind raced, picturing Jasper, his dark curly hair plastered to his forehead, his usually confident blue eyes clouded with alcohol. The thought of him alone, vulnerable, fueled my urgency. I found the house easily enough; balloons bobbed like frantic jellyfish in the humid air, and the music pulsed with a primal rhythm that vibrated through the earth. This wild pool party, a chaotic explosion of half naked bodies and throbbing bass, was the last place I expected to find him.

I parked my bike, the chrome gleaming under the afternoon sun, and pushed through the throng of half dressed bodies. The music swelled as I moved towards the back, the only fully clothed person in a sea of glistening skin and tangled limbs. I stood out like a sore thumb. It was a sensory overload. The smell of chlorine, sweat, and cheap beer. The pulse of the music; the flashing lights that strobes across sweaty bodies. My heart hammered against my ribs as I scanned the crowd, searching for a flash of dark curls, a glimpse of those captivating blue eyes. And then I saw him in the pool, two beers clutched in his hands, a lopsided grin plastered across his face.

"Jasper!" I shouted, but my voice was swallowed by the music. He was a vision of casual debauchery, completely at ease a midst the chaos. Relief washed over me, quickly followed by a wave of exasperation. I really didn't want to have to drag a grown man out of a pool.

Luckily, he spotted me. A wide, drunken grin spread across his face as he splashed around, somehow managing to walk on the pool floor and climb out. His muscular body, dripping wet, staggered towards me, a picture of confident chaos.

"You know, you're not supposed to wet your cast. Why are you drunk so early in the day?" I asked, my voice laced with a mixture of concern and frustration. He struggled to stand upright, losing his balance slightly.

"I'm not drunk. Relaaaaxxx. I'm chillin'." he slurred, draining the beer in his right hand before I snatched the other one away. Broken arm and he still manages to hold his beer just fine. I draped his arm around my shoulder, steadying him as we walked.

"Let's go. We're leaving. You need to sober up." He didn't protest. At the motorcycle, he clung to me with surprising strength, his damp body warm against mine. The ride home was silent, the roar of the engine a steady hum against the chaos of the party we'd left behind. Despite the circumstances, a strange sort of peace settled over me. He was here, he was safe, and somehow, a midst the chaos, we were together.

We arrive at my apartment, the scent of chlorine clinging to Jasper like a second skin. My apartment, with its minimalist decor and the faint smell of lavendar incense, feels starkly different from the chaotic energy he carries. My hair is messy from running after him, my brown eyes burning with a mixture of frustration and something else... something softer, something that scares me. Jasper is swimming in a blurry sea of intoxication.

"Jasper, you need to stop calling me drunk and what the hell were you thinking getting in a pool like this?! You could have drowned. You can't even stand up properly." I scolded him, the words sharper than I intended, but the worry was a raw, throbbing thing in my chest.

He slurs my name, "Ezra, Ezra, Ezra. You beautiful masterpiece," and collapses onto the couch, a boneless heap of limbs and damp clothes. The anger drains away, replaced by an aching weariness. He's safe. That's all that matters, right? He could have called anyone, anyone at all, after his drunken escapade at the pool party. He could have chosen to fuck with someone who wouldn't care. But he called ME. He stumbled his way to my number. And even though the whole thing is infuriating, even though the image of him nearly drowning still makes my heart pound, there's a strange, stubborn bloom of something akin to pride blossoming in my chest. A stupid, irrational pride. It's messy, this love, chaotic and infuriating. Maybe that's why it feels so real.

I watch him sleep, his breath uneven and shallow. The silence in my apartment is thick, broken only by the gentle hum of the refrigerator. The urge to light a cigarette, a habit I kicked only a day ago, claws at me. I resist. I need to be strong for him, even if he doesn't deserve it, even if he doesn't see it. This isn't easy. Jasper, with his dazzling confidence and breathtaking recklessness, is a whole universe away from my quiet, tattooed existence. But in this moment, as I watch him sleep, oblivious to the depth of my feelings, I know. I know, with a certainty that chills me to the bone, that this messy, complicated love is worth fighting for. Even if it kills me.

CHAPTER 14

JASPER'S POV

I woke up feeling confused. I look around in the dark. I'm at Ezra's apartment. God, this headache is killing me. My hair is plastered to my forehead, a testament to this afternoon's debauchery. I get up to find Ezra. I walk down the hall towards his room, open his bedroom door quietly and peek in. He's in bed asleep, his black hair a mess on the pillow. I crawl into bed with him, the familiar scent of his clean laundry and something else…a faint hint of lavender and something else indefinably him.

"You smell like chlorine." he said in a sleepy voice.

"I'm sorry. Did I wake you?" I said. He turns his lamp on and sits up, his brown eyes, usually so warm, assessing me.

"Doesn't matter. I was waiting for you to get up. You need to eat and wash up."

"You want to take care of me? Why? You should be angry that I called you drunk again. I don't even want to think about the stupid shit I said." I hide my shameful face in his pillow, the weight of my actions pressing down. Dreading the consequences of my actions as reality punches me in the gut. His bluntness is a comfort, a familiar counterpoint to my own turbulent emotions.

"You're still my best friend, Jas. Even if you don't want to be with me, I'm still going to be your best friend. So, get up and go shower. I'll make us something to eat." He gets up and walks out.

The hot water of the shower washes over me, a physical manifestation of the cleansing I desperately need. As the water runs down my back, I think about Ezra's quiet strength, his unwavering loyalty. No one has ever taken care of me like this. I've been on my own since seventeen, a lone wolf trained to kill, raised in a world devoid of love.

My father, a monster who used violence as currency, conditioned me to survive, not to feel. He would beat me but I preferred it to be me than my mother or twin sister, Lily. I escaped that life, but the scars remain. I was fine with that existence, the fleeting connections, the constant partying. Until Ezra, with his calm demeanor and tattooed body, walked into my carefully constructed world and shattered it.

God, I hate him sometimes. I was perfectly content in my self imposed isolation, until him. He messed everything up with his compassion, those gorgeous brown eyes, and that leather jacket. Man, those lips... being kissed by those lips leaves me seeing stars.

The chlorine smell hits me again, a reminder of the pool where I'd spent the evening before, drowning my sorrows (and maybe a little bit of my conflicted feelings) in alcohol.

"Hey, are you ok?" His voice interrupts my thoughts and my eyes snap up to look at his face. He looks concerned.

"Yeah, I'll be out in a few minutes." I said, the words a little breathless. The shower steam fogged the mirror, blurring my reflection. Ezra is still standing in the doorway though, his black hair falling over his forehead, those brown eyes, usually calm and steady, holding a hint of something I can't quite place.

"Did you need something else?" I asked, scrubbing quickly with the soap. He just smiles, a slow, warm curve of his lips that melts away some of the tension I'd been carrying since my last training session with my father at seventeen... the relentless drills, the cold, hard steel of the knife, a stark contrast to the warmth in Ezra's eyes.

"Just enjoying the view. Try not to wet your cast or you'll need to get it redone." He's so careful, so considerate. It's a stark contrast to the brutal efficiency my father drilled into me, a stark contrast to the violence I'm trained to inflict, the violence that sometimes feels like a part of me I can't shake.

I nod, finishing quickly. Stepping out, I grab the towel, the soft cotton a welcome comfort against my skin. It's one of a million small ways he cares for me, a million ways he soothes the savage within. But the towel only solves half the problem. My only other clothes are my swimming trunks, left in the hamper.

Guess I'm staying naked. I walk out, confident in my own skin, though the confidence feels a little...fragile. I've known Ezra long enough that my nakedness doesn't faze either of us. He's seen me at my most vulnerable, at my most broken. He's seen the scars, both physical and emotional, the lingering remnants of the life my father tried to force me to live.

"Can I borrow some clothes, E?" I call, but he's not in his bedroom. I find him in the living room, faintly illuminated by the glow of the TV. The faint sound I heard was a nature documentary playing softly.

"Hey, I was looking for you." He turns, looks up at me, and his smirk is instantaneous, shameless, as his eyes roam over me.

"You're not wearing any clothes." he states the obvious, his voice a low rumble.

"I asked if I could borrow something but you couldn't hear me." I shrug, sitting down next to him, the couch cushions soft against my bare skin.

"Put on clothes before I lose my self control." he says, eyes closed, a pained expression flitting across his face, the tattoos on his arms subtly shifting as he speaks. It's a different kind of control he's fighting, a control born not of violence, but of overwhelming affection. I take the opportunity, leaning in to kiss him, the taste of him both familiar and exciting.

"You're cute all hot and bothered." I murmur between kisses, my hand splaying across his chest, feeling his heart hammering against my palm, a frantic rhythm mirroring the frantic rhythm of my own life before I met him...before this quiet love found a way to bloom a midst the wreckage.

I liked the effect I had on him. It encouraged me to go farther. My hand slid from his chest, tracing the hard lines of his abs, my fingers playing with the waistband of his pajama pants. The soft cotton felt cool against my skin. He quickly clamped his hand around my wrist, stopping me. His touch, usually so gentle, held a surprising strength.

"No, Jasper. Please, go put on clothes. It's not in me to have meaningless sex. Even if it was, I don't want it to be meaningless with you." He said it slowly, releasing my wrist. The words hung in the air, heavy and unexpected. Stunned, I blinked a few times before finding my voice.

"So, you're like this with everyone? You never had sex outside of a relationship?" My tone, I realized, was sharp and accusatory. Ezra, calm as ever, didn't react to my tone.

"I've only ever had sex with people I'm in a relationship with. So, no, never. Please, go put on clothes now."

I found a faded band tee and some shorts in his dresser, the scent of his laundry detergent a sharp contrast to the lingering smell of beer on my breath. Pulling them on, I returned to the couch, the silence thick with unspoken things.

"What are you watching?" I asked, trying for casualness. My voice felt strained.

"I'm sorry." he said, his gaze fixed on the screen.

"Sorry for what?" I pressed, leaning forward.

"For complicating things. You—" He started, but I cut him off.

"Shut up, Ezra. The only one making moves was me. I'm the one that needs to apologize. I fucked up. Not you. I shouldn't have been calling you drunk or kissing you and I definitely shouldn't have blown you."

The words tumbled out, raw and honest. It was the truth, after all. My usual confidence, the carefully constructed wall my father had helped me build, crumbled. The confession, intended to ease the tension, backfired. His jaw tightened, fists clenching. That angry scowl, I hated it. That controlled rage felt so different from my own carefully cultivated chaos. His anger was a storm brewing, a tempest I couldn't quite understand. It was far removed from the controlled fury I was trained to wield. His was raw, vulnerable, a stark contrast to my own carefully honed facade.

"So, you regret everything that ever happened between us?! Like I'm just a series of mistakes in your life?! Even after you just kissed me five minutes ago?! Are you fucking serious right now?!" He raised his voice. My dark curls fell over my forehead, the blue of my eyes stinging with unshed tears. Ezra looked utterly devastated. My tongue felt thick, clumsy. I'd been trained to kill, to be precise, to be utterly in control, but words? Words failed me spectacularly.

"No, that's not what I meant. How am I fucking this up even more?! Ok, listen. I'm not good with words. I was trying to say that I'm at fault here. That's all." I said, trying to reach for his hand, but he pulled away. The hurt in his gaze was a physical blow, a violation of my carefully constructed walls.

"You implied that you have regrets. That you regret the connection we had." His voice softened, losing its sharp edge, replaced by a sadness that mirrored my own. My mind raced. He thought I regretted him? The thought was ludicrous.

"I regret a lot of things in my life, but you aren't one of them, E! Don't you see that I'm the one falling all over you! That you keep pulling me back in! I'm not the relationship kind of guy and it's terrifying that I want that with you! A man! I've been straight my whole damn life and then you walk into my life and changed everything! That's fucking scary!" The confession poured out, a torrent of emotion I'd kept bottled up for so long. Tears burned my eyes, but I blinked them back, taking a shuddering breath.

My heart hammered a frantic rhythm against my ribs. I leaned back against the plush couch in his apartment. Talking about feelings? Utterly foreign territory. But losing Ezra? Unthinkable. He was quiet, his expression unreadable for a long moment. Then, a slow smile spread across his face.

"Are you done fighting me? Will you finally just give in?" He said, the tension visibly leaving his body. A perverse sense of relief washed over me. His anger, at least, felt familiar compared to the vulnerability I'd just laid bare.

"We're inevitable. There's no use in fighting what we have anymore." I admitted, the words a surrender and a declaration of war all at once. Ezra tugged on my arm, pulling me against him. He pulled me down onto the soft cushions, his body fitting against mine with a comforting familiarity. I burrowed my face into the crook of his neck, breathing in the scent of him. The peace that settled over me was profound, a stark contrast to the turmoil of the last few minutes. In this moment, amidst the chaos of our conflicting emotions, I knew, with a certainty that transcended my training, my doubts, and my fear, that this was it. This was where I belonged. With him.

"I made us sandwiches. You should eat." He said. His voice, a low rumble that vibrated through the plush cushions of his living room couch. My dark, curly hair tumbled around my face as I leaned against him.

"I'm not hungry. I just want to stay right here." I replied, my voice barely a whisper. Ezra's arms, strong and comforting, tightened around me. His warmth enveloped me, a stark contrast to the icy chill that usually resided in my bones. Holding me tight, he pressed a kiss to my temple, the gesture so simple, yet completely disarming.

"I can't believe you're my boyfriend now." He said, a hint of disbelief in his voice. I hummed a reply, a low, throaty sound that expressed a contentment I hadn't known I could feel.

My sapphire eyes, usually sharp and calculating, were soft, focused solely on the comforting weight of Ezra's arms around me. Minutes bled into an eternity, the anxieties that usually gnawed at me, the ghosts of my father's brutal training, momentarily silenced. Shortly after, I felt a profound sense of peace. Ezra is all mine now. Surprisingly, that thought doesn't scare me like I thought it would.

The truth was, fear was a constant companion. My father had instilled in me a deep seated distrust of intimacy. He'd hammered into me the belief that vulnerability was weakness. Yet, here I was, nestled against Ezra, a man whose kindness felt like a dangerous indulgence, a luxury I didn't deserve.

Ezra, with his soft black hair, his calm brown eyes that seemed to see right through me, yet held no judgment, was an anomaly. He didn't flinch from the darkness I carried, the shadows clinging to the edges of my soul. He saw past the carefully constructed facade of confidence and flirtatiousness, the masks I'd worn since childhood, and loved the flawed, damaged man beneath. The sandwich sat untouched on the coffee table, a small, forgotten detail in a moment of immense significance. The quiet hum of the town outside seemed to fade as the weight of my past lessened, replaced by the warmth of Ezra's care.

CHAPTER 15

EZRA'S POV

~Six weeks later~

"Come on, Jas! We're going to be late for your doctor's appointment and if you miss this one, who knows how much longer you'll be stuck in that cast!" I said, putting my dirty plate and mug in the kitchen sink. Jasper was running back and forth, a picture of charming chaos as he tried to get dressed.

He's been staying with me most days the past month and a half. The other days, I'd stay at his apartment. A clear difference to my small, cozy space. His place was all sleek lines and modern minimalism whereas mine is a comforting jumble of books and mismatched furniture.

Things have been... good. Since that night at the pool party, when his drunken vulnerability cracked open the carefully constructed walls he'd built around his heart, things have been...electric. He still parties, still get those late night, slightly slurred phone calls, but now there's a sweetness mixed in with the alcohol fueled bravado.

He's handsy but in a way that feels cherished, not aggressive. I like the touch, the closeness, the way he makes my quiet world feel brighter.

I'm head over heels. My black hair feels perpetually pulled back in an attempt to keep up with his energy.

"Alright! I'm finally ready to go. I can't live with this thing on my arm any longer. Let's go!" He said, jogging to the door, a flash of that familiar playful smirk on his face.

"Finally! I was ready half an hour ago." I muttered, a smile tugging at the corners of my lips despite my teasing words.

The drive to the clinic was filled with his usual playful banter and my quieter observations, a comfortable rhythm we'd fallen into. The differences in our personalities seemed to fuel our connection instead of hindering it. His confidence tempered my quiet nature. My calm demeanor soothed his occasional anxieties. I found myself falling deeper into this unexpected love, a love built on stolen kisses and late night talks, on differences that complemented each other rather than clashed.

***

Sitting in the waiting room of the clinic, I realize that I don't go to the doctors, like at all. And here I am, with Jasper. It's not like going to the supermarket together. This is way more personal, a glimpse into his life he's choosing to share with me. It's just a simple cast removal, no big deal, really. But internally? My chest is doing the Macarena.

I'm crazy about Jasper, completely and utterly smitten. Anything he wants to share with me, even something as mundane as a doctor's appointment, is a monumental event in my carefully curated world.

"I'm really fucking bored." he whined, his curly hair falling over his forehead. His ocean eyes, usually sparkling with mischief, held a hint of genuine restlessness.

"You thought a trip to the clinic was going to be fun?" I teased as I leaned closer, a smile playing on my lips.

"Ha ha, very funny," he glares playfully, but the boredom is evident. Just then, a nurse called his name.

We followed her to a room, the sterile scent of antiseptic filling my nose. She pulled out a cast saw—a whirring, buzzing machine that looked surprisingly menacing. Jasper sat down, a mixture of apprehension and excitement on his face, eagerly anticipating the freedom of his arm.

He was instructed to stay very still as the lady powered on the saw. I watched, fascinated by the process, my calm exterior masking the nervousness bubbling beneath. After a few minutes, the satisfying *snip* of the saw announced the end. The cast was off.

The smile that spread across Jasper's face was worth more than all the diamonds in the world. He examined his arm, flexing his bicep, a confident glint in his eyes.

"Wow. Do you work out?" the nurse asked, her voice far too bright and her eyes lingering a little too long on his arm. My blood ran cold.

"Yes, I do. Hard work pays off." Jasper replied, his tone casual.

"Bet your girlfriend enjoys your hard work." she added, her words laced with an inappropriate flirtatiousness. Suddenly, a wave of irritation washed over me, a prickly heat spreading across my skin.

Jasper made eye contact with me, his gaze apologetic, before looking down at the floor. "No, I actually don't have a girlfriend." he said quietly, his voice laced with an awkwardness that only he could pull off. My annoyance didn't exactly melt away. It simmered, transforming into something sharper.

"Are we done here? I'd like to go home." I said, my irritability obvious, my voice firm but not unkind.

The nurse wrote something on a piece of paper and handed it to Jasper. Her phone number. The audacity.

"You are free to go. Have a great day." she said. Jasper nodded politely and stood up to leave. I walk out of the room, making my way towards the parking lot, a knot forming in my stomach. I could hear Jasper's footsteps close behind. I got into the passenger seat, buckling up. He sat in the driver's seat, but didn't start the car.

"Are you seriously jealous of the nurse?" he asked, his tone laced with amusement.

"You told her you didn't have a girlfriend. When you could have simply said you were with someone and then you took her phone number. That's not nothing." I retorted, my voice tight.

"It's not like I was interested. I was being polite." he replied.

"And you could have politely told her to fuck off. I can't even be mad at her. She thinks you're straight." I snapped, feeling the unfairness of it all.

"Low blow, Ezra." he said, finally starting the car. I felt like an asshole. I definitely didn't want to upset him, but the truth stung. Being back in the closet, for the sake of our relationship, felt suffocating. The irony wasn't lost on me. I know for damn sure that females are going to flirt and throw themselves at him all the time. That wouldn't really matter to me normally. I mean, we work at a strip club.

What bothers me is not being able to say he's mine or that I'm his. It's a small thing, really, a detail lost in the grand scheme of our complicated relationship, but it stings. Jasper has this infuriating habit of being both completely captivating and maddeningly secretive.

"I'm sorry. I was just being stupid." I said.

He glances at me before parking the car in front of my place. The silence stretches, thick and uncomfortable, a familiar tension hanging between us. I wait, the unspoken words echoing in the cramped space.

Finally, he speaks, his voice low and laced with something that sounds like vulnerability.

"What you said wasn't fair. It's my secret to tell. It took me forever just to admit it to you and you already knew." His confession hangs in the air, heavy with unspoken implications. I know he's referring to our differences—my quiet, introspective life juxtaposed with his vibrant, public persona.

He's from a world of chaos and secrets, I'm content with my books and quiet evenings. The secret, I suspect, is about his family, a world that wouldn't understand my quiet existence, or perhaps even me.

"I know. I said I was sorry." I said. "Anyway, I'll see you at work tonight."

A quick, almost desperate kiss, and I'm out of the car, the air suddenly cold.

I unlock my apartment door, the familiar weight of my keys, a small comfort in the face of the larger uncertainties. The thought of facing the boisterous crowd at the bar where I work tonight fills me with dread.

I'm not in the mood to be charming, to craft cocktails for people celebrating lives I barely understand. All I want is to be able to shout from the rooftops, to finally claim him as mine, to let the world know that despite our differences, our quiet moments of shared intimacy are more valuable than any public declaration. But Jasper's secret, like a fragile bird, remains safely tucked away, a constant, low hum of frustration and unspoken love under the surface of our otherwise perfect romance.

***

JASPER'S POV

I'm stoked to be back at work, doing what I do best. Now that my arm is cast free, I can finally get back to a normal routine and do things for myself without struggling and without Ezra freaking the fuck out. I love how caring he is but fuck, I'm excited to care for myself.

"Hey! Welcome back to work! We missed you around here!" Marcus said, as I stepped in through the club's doors.

"It's good to be back, Marcus." I shouted over the music. The bar was full of people ready to purchase alcoholic drinks. Behind the counter was my favorite person, Ezra. He smiled at me when his eyes landed on mine but it was short lived as he attended to some people.

My curly hair bounced as I moved, my eyes scanning the crowd.

Two Malibu strawberry cocktails were next, for a pretty brunette.

"No problem. Coming right up." I flashed her a toothy smile and winked, showing off a bit as I made her drink. The tips flowed in, along with the harmless flirting. One redhead with impossibly blue eyes kept returning.

"Aren't you drunk by now, Miss?" I joked with her, expertly mixing another round.

"No way. I'm having a damn good time. I'll have some more beers." she giggled.

"Alright, but after this I'm cutting you off. You've definitely had too much to drink." I grabbed her beers, my confidence radiating.

"Aw, you're no fun. I kinda thought you'd be the kind of sexy guy into a good time." she flirted, her words playful yet suggestive.

"Me? Sexy?" I flexed my biceps, a playful wink escaping.

"Woo! Why aren't you up on that stage stripping?!" she called out.

"I don't have a stripper name." I replied, leaning over the counter.

"Jasper, get back to work." Ezra demanded, his face dead serious. His protectiveness, though sometimes overwhelming, was a testament to his love.

"Sorry, I have to attend to some other customers now." I smiled at the redhead. She pulled out a napkin and pen, writing something before handing it to me with a wink. I looked down at the napkin: 'Call me. XOXO, Riley.' I stuffed it in my pocket and continued to work.

"I'm taking a smoke break." Ezra announced, his voice barely a whisper above the throbbing bass of the club. I frowned. My Ezra hadn't touched a cigarette in weeks. He'd promised, sworn on his life, no more smoking. I followed him to the back, the scent of cheap beer and desperation clinging to the air.

"What the fuck are you doing?! Did you forget your promise to me?" I yelled, my blue eyes flashing. He wasn't amused. That much was clear in the stillness of his expression.

"Do you see a cigarette in my hands?" he asked, his voice unnervingly calm. I looked, my anger momentarily deflating. Empty hands.

"Um, no."

"Then obviously I'm not smoking and I haven't broken any promises." he said, a hint of irritation in his voice.

"You... did I hear you wrong? I thought you said you were taking a smoke break?" I reached for his hand, but he subtly pulled away.

"I knew you'd follow me back here if I said I was smoking," he continued, his voice low.

"I wanted to get your attention, Jasper. We need to talk about your...nonstop flirting with every damn girl that comes through the door." The anger evaporated, replaced by a warmth spreading through me. He was jealous. My cocky, confident, flirty self, the one that thrived in the chaotic energy of "The Velvet Rope," was melting under Ezra's concern. It was... adorable.

"They don't mean anything, E. You're being silly." I smirked, my usual bravado returning, but with a softer edge.

"Yeah? What about that redhead? Are you interested in her?" he pressed, his gaze intense. I stepped forward, closing the distance between us. Cupping his face in my hands, I kissed him, the taste of his lips a familiar comfort.

"No," I breathed, pulling back slightly. "I'm interested in you."

The words hung in the air, heavy with unspoken promises and the understanding that spanned the gulf between our vastly different worlds. His smile, when he finally broke it, was worth more than all the tips I'd ever earned. Dropping my hands, the relief washing over me was palpable. I took a step back, winking.

"You're such a fuck boy, Jasper. Stop winking and flexing your damn muscles." Ezra's voice, usually so soothing, held a sharp edge. I grinned, flexing again, the muscles in my arms burning with the exertion and the attention.

"What? I'm not a fuck boy. I mean I *was*, but not anymore. And you like these muscles. You're just mad because I'm sexier than you." I joked, my blue eyes sparkling. He laughed, but it wasn't a genuine sound, more like a tight, strained exhale.

"Ok, Baby. Let's see how you like a dose of your own medicine." The playful tone in his voice was gone, replaced by something colder, and a sudden chill went down my spine. That's when I knew I was in for it.

He walked back into the club, his usually calm gait purposeful. I followed, a knot of unease tightening in my chest. A gorgeous blonde approached the bar, ordering whiskey. I watched, helpless, as Ezra effortlessly charmed her, his brown eyes twinkling with a playful light I'd only ever seen directed at me.

He mixed her drink with a practiced grace, and she left, her number clutched in his hand. My jaw tightened. Even though I knew Ezra was gay, and that this was his way of showing me how my behavior affected him, the jealousy burned. He didn't stop there. Oh, no...he flirted with every customer, winking and charming his way through orders. The climax came when a group of guys, openly asked him to fuck. He laughed, a genuine sound this time, before casually replying, "Sorry, boys. I have a boyfriend," glancing at me with a knowing smile. The guys backed off.

That glance, that subtle acknowledgment of our unspoken understanding, broke through the wall of playful antagonism. His little act had worked. It made me see myself through his eyes. I didn't like it.

***

The workday was finished, and we both walked out to the parking lot. I was pissed off. I couldn't even think straight from how angry I was. My dark curls bounced with the force of my frustrated strides. Ezra called out to me. I ignored him, my blue eyes blazing, heading straight for my car. Of course, he followed. He always did.

"I get it, Ezra. You're sexy. Everyone thinks you're the finest piece of ass." I spat, the words sharper than I intended. The irony wasn't lost on me; I, Jasper, the confident, flirty king of the Velvet Rope strip club, was reduced to this childish outburst. It felt humiliating, but the sting of his blatant flirting right in front of me, still burned.

"You sound jealous, Baby." he chuckled, that infuriatingly calm tone doing little to soothe my frayed nerves.

"Not funny, E." I snapped, my temper threatening to boil over. He was right, though. I wasn't exactly a saint when it came to flirting with customers. It was part of the job. But his casual charm was different, a whole other level of playful seduction that felt like a betrayal.

"I won't flirt with the customers anymore." I said. My "fuck boy" act wasn't cute...it was hurtful. The playful competition had a point: he wanted me to understand the impact of my actions. Seeing him effortlessly deflect the advances, wearing his affection for me like a shield, was a humbling and touching experience.

I suddenly felt a surge of feelings for him, stronger than the initial pang of jealousy.

"Just never put me through that torturous crap again, E. Meet up at my place." The words "meet up at my place" held a desperate plea, a need for his touch, his comfort, to mend the crack in our carefully constructed world.

I got in my car, the air conditioning was a welcome relief against the simmering anger still coursing through me. I watched him take off on his motorcycle, the rumble of the engine a low growl in the parking lot's silence. He was my rock, my Ezra, the one who'd shown me a tenderness I didn't think I deserved. He'd fallen for the confident Jasper, but tonight, he saw the vulnerable, jealous child underneath. And that child, for the moment at least, just wanted to be held.

Before I could take off, the redhead tapped on my window. I rolled it all the way down. "Hey, you mind giving me a ride home? I'm totally drunk. You were right." she giggled. I couldn't just leave her there, drunk. What if something happened? I couldn't just leave her. The guilt would've eaten me alive. So, I did the gentlemanly thing.

She stumbled into my car, a cloud of cheap perfume and desperation. I helped her buckle up.

"What's your address?"

"Oh, I live at 72 Summer Rd." Another giggle. I drove quickly, the silence punctuated only by her uneven breathing.

"Alright. Take care." I said, hoping she got the hint.

"Can you help me get to the door?" I sighed, but I couldn't leave her stranded on her doorstep.

I opened the door to her house and helped her stumble inside. Before I knew it, she was all over me, kissing me, fumbling with my belt. Caught completely off guard, I fell backwards, her weight crushing me.

"Whoa...I...can't!!" I managed between kisses, pushing her away roughly. She landed with a thud.

"I can't!! I can't!! I'm with someone!! And they're actually really fucking important to me!!" The words tumbled out in a frantic rush. I scrambled to my feet and bolted, my heart hammering against my ribs. The walk back to my car felt like a marathon.

My phone vibrated. It's Ezra. Fuck. The contrast between this disastrous encounter and the gentle warmth of my boyfriend felt insurmountable. This whole situation, the drunk girl, my near betrayal, the overwhelming feeling of guilt felt like a weight. It felt wrong on so many levels. It felt wrong on every level.

Sitting in my car, Ezra's name flashing on my screen, I knew I had to tell him everything. The truth, messy and uncomfortable as it was. He deserved that much, at least. My dark curly hair fell into my eyes as I wrestled with the steering wheel, the leather cool against my sweaty palms.

"Hello?" I answered, trying to keep my voice calm, a stark contrast to the turmoil inside. My eyes darted around my car, a sleek machine that usually felt like a symbol of my confident, flirty exterior, now just a cage of anxiety.

Ezra was the only thing that mattered. He was my grounding force, my safe harbor in a life that often felt like a storm.

"I've been at your place for awhile now. Where are you?" his voice, usually so soothing, carried a hint of worry.

"E, the craziest thing just happened. Please, don't be mad." I held my breath, trying to find the courage to explain the shit show that had just unfolded.

"What happened? Are you ok?" His concern was palpable.

"The redhead from the club needed a ride. So, I thought I'd be nice and give her a lift home but once I got here, she threw herself at me." Listening to myself say it out loud, it sounded incriminating. And I definitely should have figured out her intentions sooner. My gut twisted. It was dead silent on his end. So quiet that I had to check if he'd hung up.

"Ezra?"

"I'm still listening." he finally said, his voice laced with disappointment. The silence stretched, thick and heavy, each second amplifying the weight of my stupid mistake. "Nothing happened, E. I threw the bitch off of me and stormed out of there. I swear it. I'm on my way home. Please, don't leave." I pleaded, the words tumbling out in a desperate rush. The casual confidence I usually projected was gone, replaced by a raw vulnerability that terrified and exposed me.

"I won't leave." he assured me, but the sadness in his voice was a knife twisting in my gut. The disappointment was evident. This will surely be the end of us, I thought, the reality sinking in with bone jarring finality. I fucked up. I really fucked up.

Chapter 16

---◆---

EZRA'S POV

I'm not sure what to think right now. I knew that girl wanted to fuck Jasper.

Would he cheat on me? Am I enough for him? Can I even believe anything he says to me? I really wish I could smoke right now but I still value the promises I made to him.

"Ezra? Babe, are you here?" He sounds like he's shitting bricks.

"In the kitchen." He quickly rushes over to me and gives me a tight hug. I slowly wrap my arms around him.

"I thought you left." He seemed genuinely afraid of losing me. Like what I thought about the situation actually mattered to him.

"I thought about it but I wanted to hear you out like the adult that I am." I said, letting him go. What I saw next broke something inside of me.

"I already explained it to you, E. I was just trying to take a drunk girl home safe and she attacked me." His words hung in the air, thin and unconvincing.

"Is that why you have lipstick all over your mouth and your pants are unbuttoned?" His hands shot up to his face and wiped his mouth. His fingers were stained red. His eyes went wide with the realization, a flicker of something... fear? Guilt?...darting across his usually confident blue gaze.

The carefully constructed facade of the charming, flirty Jasper, the man I loved, cracked, revealing something darker, something I couldn't quite comprehend. His hair was disheveled, adding to the sense of disarray. My calm, collected demeanor, usually so effective at diffusing tense situations, crumbled. The carefully constructed peace of my world shattered around me. My eyes felt hot and stinging.

"I'm sorry, Ezra!" He panicked, the words rushed and unconvincing. I quickly got up to leave. The apartment, once a haven of our shared laughter and whispered secrets, felt suffocating.

"Ezra, wait! Don't leave, please! Wait! It's not what you think, I swear! She attacked me!" I stopped in my tracks at the sound of his desperation. Jasper, my Jasper... reduced to this pleading mess. He couldn't have cheated on me, right? His story sounded like bullshit though.

"Did you fuck her, Jasper?" The words were sharp, clipped, leaving no room for misinterpretation. He grabs my hand, his touch surprisingly gentle, pulling me around.

"No! I didn't fuck her, E. She asked for help to get inside. Then she threw herself at me. Yes, she kissed me, but I pushed her off. Then you called, and I told you everything."

The relief in his voice was palpable, but the lingering scent of another woman's perfume still clung to him. He cups my face in his hands, his touch warm against my skin. His forehead rests against mine, and in that moment, I see the genuine panic, the vulnerability behind the usual bravado. There was a long silence, filled only with the frantic beat of my heart.

"Ok. I believe you." I finally said. He tries to kiss me, but I stop him.

"Wipe that shit off your face first." The words were harsh, but necessary. His immediate reaction, his unhesitating dash to the bathroom, spoke volumes.

He returned, scrubbed clean, and this time, his kiss was soft, hesitant, apologetic. As he held me, the pasta water boiled over on the stove, a mundane interruption to the intense emotions swirling around us. The scent of garlic and simmering tomato sauce hung heavy in the air, a comforting aroma. Jasper leaned against the kitchen counter, watching me with that familiar intensity.

He was beautiful, a captivating contrast to my own quiet calm. He was confidence and flirtation personified. I, a quiet comfort in his chaotic orbit. The pasta was almost ready, a simple dish mirroring the simplicity I craved in our relationship. A stark contrast to the complexity of his unspoken secret. He wrapped his arms from behind me and slowly kissed my neck.

"I've been meaning to ask you something," he murmured against my skin. "Want to be my plus one to my sister's wedding?"

"Are you asking me to meet your family?" I said, turning to face him, wrapping my arms around his neck. A smirk played on my lips, a mixture of excitement and apprehension.

"Yes. Is that okay? It's just my sister. She's all the family I have." he replied, his voice laced with a vulnerability I rarely saw.

"I'd love to be your plus one, Jas, but I don't think that's the best time to come out of the closet. Stealing the bride's thunder is frowned upon." I joked, though the underlying truth hung heavy. He buried his face in the crook of my neck, a soft hum escaping his lips. The silence that followed was thick with unspoken words.

"You will tell someone eventually, right? I don't want to be hidden forever." I whispered, my brown eyes meeting his blue ones. I needed him to understand. I craved a relationship that wasn't lived in shadows. I ached for the freedom of holding his hand without fear, for a world where our relationship wasn't a secret.

"I will. One day. Just not yet, E. I need time." he confessed, his voice low. The words hung in the air, heavy with his unspoken reasons. I understood the need for time, but my heart ached with the weight of his secret.

"Alright. Well, I want to take you out on a date." I blurted, the words tumbling out in a rush. His immediate reaction—the surprised lift of his head, the straightening of his posture—was exactly the response I'd hoped for, and yet, it also held a hint of something else, something playful and teasing. The relief that washed over me was almost intoxicating.

"A date?" he echoed, a grin slowly spreading across his face.

"Don't act so surprised. Of course, I want to take you out on a date. Might even buy you flowers too." I said, a genuine smile finally breaking through my own nerves. The playful banter that followed was typical Jasper, a mix of flirty charm and unexpected vulnerability.

"That's the girliest shit I've ever heard you say." he laughed, but the affection in his voice was undeniable.

"Alright, but no roses. I'm not a chick." he added, his smile widening. The image of him, my confident, sometimes brash boyfriend, willingly accepting flowers, sent a wave of warmth through me. My elation spilled over. I kissed him, a soft progression from forehead to lips, a tender gesture that he, predictably, turned into something far more intense. His strong arms scooped me up, surprising me with their strength and the unexpected tenderness.

"Where are you taking me? The food is going to burn!" I chuckled, breathless.

"Who cares?! I'm only hungry for you." he laughed, his eyes sparkling with an intensity that mirrored my own. The rest of the night blurred into a haze of laughter, whispered secrets, and the intoxicating intimacy of two souls finally finding their rhythm. The planned dinner was forgotten, replaced by a much more satisfying feast of shared touches, quiet moments of understanding, and the unspoken promises that hung heavy in the air between us. Eventually, exhaustion claimed us both. We fell asleep intertwined, the scent of him filling my senses, a tangible reminder that despite our differences, our relationship was real, raw, and undeniably ours.

***

I woke up, the next morning, naked in Jasper's bed. Sunlight streamed through the large windows of his bedroom, illuminating dust motes dancing in the air. The scent of his cologne still clung to the crisp white sheets. I could hear the shower running. My heart thumped a little faster. The memory of last night's passionate frotting still vivid in my mind. Getting up, I padded over to the bathroom, intending to join him.

Instead, I caught him masturbating, mid stroke, his head thrown back, strong hand rhythmically stroking his length, droplets of water tracing paths down his skin. He was completely unaware of my presence.

A small, almost imperceptible smile played on my lips. His stifled moans, as if he didn't want to wake me, were oddly endearing.

"Please, tell me you're thinking of me in there," I said, my voice low and husky, the words meant to tease, but with an undercurrent of genuine longing. The sound of my voice jolted him.

"Jesus fucking Christ, Ezra!" He whirled around, eyes wide with surprise and a touch of mortification. His reaction was both hilarious and endearing.

"Well, don't stop," I teased, leaning against the door frame, arms folded across my chest. "I was enjoying the show."

He sputtered, "Privacy, E!"

"You left the door wide open," I countered, my amusement bubbling over. "You practically invited me in here."

His annoyance was palpable, his tone heavy with it, but it only made me laugh more. His cock, however, remained stubbornly defiant, a testament to the lingering heat between us
.

"Ugghhh, did you need something or what?" he grumbled, but even his grumbling was sexy.

"You'd think you've had enough after last night," I purred, stepping closer, "but since you want more... I'm ready to please. So should I bend over in there, or should I wait for you in bed?"

Jasper's mouth fell open in shock, his blue eyes glazing over with lust. He ran a hand through his dark, curly hair, the gesture both disheveled and captivating. This would be a first for us... a full, uninhibited surrender. This was a huge step. Something felt undeniably right about this moment, about the raw, unfiltered intimacy.

"Well, what are you waiting for?! Get your ass in here." he grinned, his schoolboy grin radiating pure, unadulterated joy. I knew he couldn't say no to me. The steam from the shower, a modern glass enclosure, clouded the glass as I slid the door open. My black hair plastered to my forehead, my brown eyes fixed on him, a confident smirk playing on my lips. He was a vision.

Wasting no time, his lips found mine, a hungry kiss that mirrored the urgent need thrumming in my own body. His hand, firm and possessive, found its way to my dick, the touch igniting a fire within me. I can never get enough of him, the way his skin felt against mine, a shiver of pure pleasure followed by a rush of heat. I closed my hand around his dick, the rhythm of my touch mimicking the pounding of my heart. He moaned, a low, guttural sound that sent shivers down my spine, his lips finding my lower lip in a tender bite. The sounds of his pleasure, a siren's call that drew me deeper.

"Stick it in, baby." I breathed, turning, bracing myself for the exquisite pain I craved. His confident smirk softened with concern.

"Won't I hurt you, E? I read somewhere about prepping you first."

He wasn't wrong, of course. But in that moment, surrounded by the steam and the intoxicating scent of Jasper's soap, logic was a distant whisper. I shook my head, my need overriding any reservations. He spread my ass cheeks, the head of his cock coating my hole with precum, the anticipation building into a searing tension. He pressed slowly, inch by agonizing inch, until he stretched me to my limit.

"Fuck, Babe. You're so fucking tight. I'm trying my best not to hurt you." he murmured against my ear, his voice thick with exertion.

"Rip me a new one. I don't give a damn. Just fuck me, Jas." The words hung in the air, a raw confession of my desire. He didn't need more convincing.

His hips moved hard and fast, a relentless rhythm that matched the frantic beat of my own heart. His nails dug into my hips, leaving crescent shaped marks that would bloom into bruises, a testament to the passion we shared.

"You feel so good. So fucking good, E." he groaned, his voice a primal sound lost in the steam filled air.

"Harder. Fuck me harder." I urged, the words raw and desperate. The sensation was euphoric, a symphony of pleasure amplified by the intensity of my love for him.

His confident smirk was usually flirty, but right now, it felt possessive, and utterly intoxicating. Everything felt just right as he talked dirty in my ear.

"You love my cock in your pretty little ass, huh?!" The words, rough and demanding, sent a shiver down my spine, a delicious contrast to the warmth spreading through me.

"Yes!" I moaned, the sound swallowed by the roar of the water, yet somehow amplified in the intimate space between us. He moved deeper, the friction against my prostate a potent wave of pleasure that stole my breath.

His hands, calloused yet gentle, gripped my hips, urging me closer. The porcelain of the shower walls was cool against my chest, a grounding sensation a midst the overwhelming heat of the moment. He was so sure of himself, so comfortable in his own skin, and it was infectious.

"Tell me you love me." he demanded. Without thinking, without hesitation, the words spilled from my lips.

"I love you, Jasper. I really fucking love you." It felt liberating, powerful. The confession, whispered against the rush of water, felt as natural as breathing. The high of being fucked so good completely consumed me, eclipsing any reservations.

"I'm so fucking close, E. Say it again." he growled, his rhythm quickening. His breath hitched, and I knew this was it.

"I love you, Baby. Cum for me." With a few more powerful thrusts and guttural grunts, he came inside me, then released a tidal wave that washed over me. Fuck, I came hard too, the pleasure exploding, leaving me clinging to the cold tile wall, the warm water a comforting embrace against the tremors shaking my body.

The steam clouded the glass, obscuring our figures, leaving behind only the lingering scent of sex, sweat, and the undeniable truth: I loved him. I loved him fiercely, desperately, wholly. Weak at the knees, Jasper pulls out and sits down under the running water. I straddle him on the shower floor and kiss him with everything I've got. He pulls away and we stand up. Washing up quickly, turning off the water, he has this odd look on his face.

"Did you mean it?" he questions me, his voice soft, a complete difference to the intensity of moments before.

"Every damn word. I've known for awhile." I said honestly, my own voice still a little husky from the afterglow.

"How long?" he presses, his blue eyes searching mine, a flicker of disbelief in their depths.

"Since the moment I saw you at the coffee shop." I reply, the memory vivid – his dark curly hair catching the light, the confident smirk playing on his lips. I couldn't understand why he was getting upset. I've never lied to him, but somehow it was hard for him to believe that I could love him at first sight. He frowned, stepping out of the shower, the water sheeting off his skin, and I followed close behind, the steam clinging to us like a second skin.

"Bullshit. You didn't even know me then." he says, his tone sharper now. His disbelief stung, a bizarre twist to the intimacy we'd just shared.

"I didn't have to know you. I just knew. It just clicked." I explained, trying to convey the inexplicable certainty that had settled over me that day. The way he'd moved, the subtle curve of his smile, the intensity in his gaze. It all spoke to something deeper, something undeniable.

"Ezra, if you said it in the heat of the moment, it's fine. Just don't fucking lie to me." His words, though laced with something vulnerable, rubbed me the wrong way. My calm exterior, usually so steadfast, threatened to crack. I was trying really hard not to snap, to keep the love and the lingering heat of our passion from turning to ashes.

"I consider myself a really calm guy, but you are really pushing my buttons right now, Jas," I said, my voice low but firm. "I would never lie to you about something so damn important. I love you, and now that I've finally said it, I'm not going to stop saying it because I mean every damn word. The day you walked in at that coffee shop, I couldn't get my eyes off you. I was 100% sure that I never wanted to lay eyes on anyone else ever again. I was in love with you since then. It was a happy coincidence that I showed up to my new job that same day and you were there. I took it as a sign. Now here we are fucking each other senseless. Driving each other crazy."

Jasper just stood there, stunned. My annoyance, however, remained. I stepped out of the bathroom, ignoring the lingering steam and dampness, and threw on some clothes, needing space, needing him to process, needing the quiet aftermath of a declaration that felt both explosive and eternally true.

His curly hair was plastered to his forehead, droplets of water clinging to the tips. Blue eyes, usually sparkling with mischief, were clouded with something I couldn't quite decipher. My own black hair was probably a mess too, after the steamy aftermath in his shower. Jasper's modern apartment, minimalist and sleek, felt strangely intimate in this moment, the aftermath of passion replaced by a confusing tension.

"I'm sorry. I ruined the moment. I'm a prick." he mumbled, the words hitting me harder than any argument ever could. He closed the distance between us, the scent of his shower gel still clinging to him.

"You're everything to me, Baby. So get it through your thick skull." I said, my voice steadier than I felt. His reaction, however, was immediate and familiar. That flinch, that retreat.

"You're starting to scare me, E. Quit talking about feelings already. I heard you." he said, already pulling on a pair of jeans and a tee shirt. The casual dismissal stung, a practiced defense mechanism I'd come to recognize. I watched him from the bed, his movements jerky, his face flushing a rosy pink. The confidence he so easily projected crumbled away, leaving a vulnerable core exposed.

Why was he so afraid? Who hurt him? It wasn't about me. I knew that. It was about him. About some deep seated fear that kept him from fully embracing the intensity of our connection. One moment he craved to be loved, the next he pushed it away, a dance of push and pull that was both exhilarating and exhausting.

"Jasper," I whispered, his name a soft anchor in the turbulent sea of his emotions. He stopped, turning to face me. Our eyes locked, a silent conversation passing between us before I finally spoke. "You're safe with me. Whatever it is that scares you about what you're feeling, we can work it out together. I swear it." The words felt heavy with a promise I intended to keep. His gaze dropped to the floor, his hands flying up to cover his face, but I saw the tears before they fell. I got up and hugged him tightly, his body trembling against mine.

"I hate you." he mumbled into my chest, his voice muffled and choked with emotion. I smiled, a bittersweet ache in my heart.

"Yeah, I know." I chuckled, knowing he meant the complete opposite.

CHAPTER 17

—◆◇◆—

JASPER'S POV

I'm not sure what possessed me during sex with Ezra, but it was the best sex I've ever had. The raw, animalistic power of it, the way his touch ignited something deep within me. It was terrifying and exhilarating all at once. Hearing him say he loves me, a phrase I'd scoffed at for years, surged a powerful sensation through me. A tidal wave of something I hadn't even known existed.

He's my favorite drug, and the high he gives me is phenomenal. He makes me feel things I've never felt before. Like I was living my life in black and white before him, but now everything is vibrant with colors I didn't even know existed. He's changed me, irrevocably. Suddenly, I can't picture my life without him in it. The thought alone is agonizing. I hate him for it. I hate him for changing my life so much. I hate him for picking me out of the millions of people in this world. ME, Jasper, the boy trained to kill since childhood by a man who saw nothing but a weapon in his son.

Now I don't know what to do with myself, how to reconcile this overwhelming emotion with the icy shell I'd built around my heart for so long. I need some distance, a way to numb myself, to fortify the cracks forming in my carefully constructed defenses.

"I hate you." I mumbled, the words a pathetic whisper against the roaring tide of my feelings. Tears fell, hot and unwanted, tracing paths down my cheeks. He held me close, his black hair falling over his forehead, his calm brown eyes filled with an empathy that both comforted and unnerved me. His touch, so gentle, felt like a betrayal of everything I'd been taught. Everything my father had drilled into me. Strength, control, detachment.

"I know." he chuckled, the sound laced with a sadness that mirrored my own.

I pulled away, wiping my face roughly, hating the weakness my tears exposed. I hate to cry. Especially in front of other people. It shows vulnerability, and vulnerability is weakness. I look into Ezra's beautiful brown eyes, eyes that held a depth of love I'd never believed existed, a love that threatened to shatter the carefully crafted walls I'd spent a lifetime building. He makes me weak. He makes me soft, gentle. He melts the ice around my heart, revealing a vulnerability that both terrifies and intoxicates me.

"I can't believe you're in love with me." I whispered, more to myself than him, the confession hanging heavy in the air between us.

"Why is that so hard to believe?" he frowned, his concern palpable. I looked down at my bare feet, the polished floor cold beneath them.

"I've never been worthy of love," I confessed, my voice barely audible. "I use people and then discard them. That's who I am, E."

The truth, stark and unforgiving, hung between us, a chasm I wasn't sure we could bridge. I stepped away, putting a painful amount of distance between us. I could see the hurt in his facial expressions.

"For someone so beautiful. You have a shitty self esteem. You fake confidence so well but now that I really see you, you're really fucking broken but that's ok because I'm going to love you anyway. I'll love you until you love yourself and even after that I'll still love you, Jas."

He left me in my room after that. His words, sinking into my mind slowly. Even though I don't believe in a god, I found myself praying that I don't fuck up whatever I have with him. The way I ultimately fuck everything up in my life.

The thought of my past, of the brutal training my father put me through, of the cold, calculated kills I was trained to execute as a child, threatened to overwhelm me. But Ezra's words, his unwavering acceptance, were a lifeline. I put my shoes on and made my way down the hall towards the kitchen, drawn by the sweet smell of his coffee. A mundane comfort in this chaotic reality of mine.

"Would you like some?" he smiled, a knowing look in his eyes, a look that said he understood more than he let on.

"Duh. You make the best coffee. I'll never say no." I replied, the carefully constructed wall of my confidence crumbling just a little. We sat down at the table with our mugs.

"My sister's soon to be husband is having a bachelor party tonight. I've been invited but I don't want to go without you. Want to join us?" I say, trying to make casual conversation. He sips his coffee and then speaks.

"Like alcohol and strippers?" He smirks.

"Is it even a bachelor party without alcohol and strippers?" I reply, a playful challenge in my tone. He raises an eyebrow and puts his coffee down on the table.

"You know I'm gay as fuck, right? Looking at girls give lap dances isn't exactly my idea of fun." He said, his voice calm but firm. A small pang of guilt hit me. I knew he wasn't keen on such things, but the thought of facing that party alone was unbearable.

"Aw. Come on, E. I want you to go with me." I whined, already knowing how persuasive I could be. My dark, curly hair fell over my eyes as I leaned forward, the blue in my eyes intense. Ezra finishes his coffee and brings his mug to the sink.

"Alright, but I'm gonna need a wicked amount of alcohol in me." He joked around with me, his usual calm demeanor giving way to a playful smirk. Relief washed over me. He was coming. He was my sanctuary, a stark contrast to the violent world I'd been forced into. Getting up, I walk towards him, pecking him on the lips, a quick, stolen kiss that said more than words ever could. The taste of his coffee and the soft feel of his lips against mine were my grounding force, the only thing that anchored me to a reality that was free of the ghosts of my childhood.

"Maybe before we leave, I can strip for you." I wrap my arms around his waist, peppering his neck with kisses, relishing the warmth of his tattooed skin against mine. The scent of my shampoo and something uniquely Ezra, filled my senses, a welcome distraction from the thoughts that threatened to engulf me.

"You are insatiable." He laughs, his voice a low rumble in his chest. The sound, the feel of him, it's everything I needed and craved.

"I just can't get enough of you, E."

***

Few hours and one hot sex session later, it was finally time to head out to Jonah's bachelor party. I wore a short sleeved, black button down shirt with black jeans. My dark hair, usually tamed, was allowed its natural curly freedom. I felt good, a confident swagger filling me as I checked my reflection. The blue of my eyes seemed sharper, brighter, reflecting the happiness humming beneath my skin. Happiness, tinged with a familiar undercurrent of unease.

Ezra, waiting patiently, was a stark contrast. He, in his gray shirt, black jeans, signature leather jacket, and combat boots, looked effortlessly cool. His black hair fell messily, framing brown eyes that held a quiet intensity. He was calm, my anchor in a world that often felt like a tempest. He didn't know about the tempest in my past. About my father's brutal training, the years spent honing skills I'd rather forget, the cold efficiency that still flickered beneath the surface. He just loved me, simply and completely, and that was the most terrifying and most wonderful thing in the world. Ezra's groan broke through my thoughts.

"Jasper, it's not a beauty pageant. Hurry up." I bit my lip, resisting the urge to smirk at his frustration.

"It takes time to look this good, Babe." I retorted, giving him some playful finger guns. He raised an eyebrow, a hint of a smile playing on his lips.

"Alright, Princess. Let's go. I'm ready to get drunk."

"Rude! I'm a king!" I scoffed jokingly, grabbing my keys and wallet. Jonah, marrying my sister Lily, was a good guy, but his bachelor party... well, it promised to be a wild night. The thought sent a ripple of anxiety through me, a reminder of the careful facade I maintained.

***

Moments later, we arrived at the venue. A dimly lit club throbbing with bass. My polished exterior cracked slightly as I watched Ezra navigate the boisterous crowd. He moved with that same quiet confidence, his arm occasionally brushing mine, a silent promise of comfort and protection. Music was blaring, girls were already draped around the groom's shoulders and the smell of alcohol filled the air.

"Hey! You made it!" Jonah shouted happily.

"Couldn't miss your last week as an unmarried man, bro!" I shouted over the music while giving him a bro handshake and hug. Jonah was oblivious to the coiled tension in my own life, the carefully constructed facade I presented to the world. Ezra stood beside me, his usual calm demeanor slightly ruffled by the chaotic energy of the bachelor party. I introduced him to Jonah and his friends, acutely aware of the secrets I carried, secrets that could shatter the fragile happiness we'd built.

Ace, Jonah's best man, complimented Ezra's jacket, breaking the ice slightly. Bryan, Jonah's brother, then handed us tequila shots. Ezra, usually measured in his drinking, surprised me by downing five in a row. The cheers that followed felt jarring, a stark contrast to the quiet intimacy we shared.

His normally calm exterior was dissolving, and the carefree smile was a little too bright, too wide. I tried to slow him down, worried about his tolerance, worried about the secrets I held close. The worry was a constant shadow, a reminder of the life I tried to leave behind. He assured me he was fine, that easy confidence masking something else, something that mirrored my own suppressed anxieties. I could only clink my glass to his, raise it in a toast to my sister's impending nuptials, and pray that this night wouldn't shatter the delicate balance we'd created.

The rest of the night blurred in a haze of tequila and forced laughter. I watched Ezra, his eyes sparkling with a mixture of exhilaration and something else... vulnerability, perhaps?...And my heart aches. The carefully crafted wall around my emotions threatened to crumble.

"It's time for some VIP action! Show me the ladies!" Jonah drunkenly slurred, his words echoing in the dimly lit club. Out they poured, a gaggle of women in tawdry bridal gowns, their movements calculated, their smiles practiced. My stomach churned. My gaze drifted to Ezra, his usual calm demeanor subtly strained. He sipped his tequila, the amber liquid catching the light in his dark eyes. He was so different from me. Quiet where I was vivacious, grounded where I was... well, a trained killer. My father's "gift," a legacy I'd painstakingly buried beneath layers of charming confidence and flirtatious smiles. Ezra knew nothing of that past, of the hands that had taught me to disarm, to kill, to disappear. He loved Lily's brother, the one who thought I was just a charming, successful man. The thought of revealing my true self to him, of seeing the confusion in those kind eyes, was almost unbearable. I smiled weakly at my own reflection in the swirling smoke.

"You better be faithful to my sister, Jonah." I warned, the words laced with more sincerity than sarcasm. Ace, ever the voice of reason (or at least, his attempt at it), chimed in,

"Let the man live tonight. He's going to be chained to one woman for the rest of his life in less than a week!"

"When did you become a fag, Jasper?" Bryan's crude joke about my sexuality stung, but my real concern was for Ezra. He excused himself to the bathroom after that, his departure a silent protest. Bryan's eyes followed mine, his voice booming,

"Holy shit! You are a gay bastard!" The revelation hung in the air, thick and suffocating.

"What are you talking about? This guy has had more pussy than all of us combined." Jonah said, but momentarily sobered, frowned, Ace's earlier observation—my lack of interest in the women—now making sense.

"You know, now that I think about it. You've been joined at the hip with that friend of yours." Jonah said.

The tension was palpable, the room's noise fading into a dull roar. My carefully constructed facade crumbled, and the weight of my secrets, threatened to suffocate me. My dark curly hair felt suddenly heavy, a physical manifestation of the anxiety tightening my chest.

"What? I'm not gay. Ezra is just a friend. You guys are just being drunk assholes." I said, forcing a smile that felt brittle and unconvincing, even to me. The truth that Ezra, with his calm demeanor and deep brown eyes, was more than just a friend was a secret I guarded fiercely, a secret born from a childhood so brutal it had shaped my adult life into a carefully constructed performance of confidence and flirtatiousness. Bryan was pushing.

"Let's take these pretty girls to a hotel. Let the real party begin." He was testing me, trying to crack the carefully crafted shell I'd built around my heart.

He wanted me to say the words, to confess, but the fear was a physical presence, holding me captive. The fear wasn't just of rejection, but of the unraveling of everything I'd worked so hard to build. The fear was rooted in the memories I kept locked away, memories that threatened to shatter the illusion of the carefree, flirty Jasper everyone saw.

So, instead of confronting the truth, I played along. I encouraged the idea of the hotel, nodding enthusiastically, pushing down the rising tide of panic. The charade was exhausting. Ezra returned from the bathroom, his black hair damp from the water, his usual calm replaced by a slight furrow in his brow. The moment the guys filled him in on the "plan," his eyes met mine. That look, filled with unspoken concern and a hint of suspicion, spoke volumes. The way he looked at me, so perceptive and loving, instantly shattered my carefully constructed lies in his eyes. The air shifted, and I saw the suspicion bloom on the faces of the other guys, sensing the unspoken question hanging heavy in the air.

I watched Ezra, his calm exterior masking a storm I knew he was too kind to unleash on me. We were at a crossroads. The revelation of my secret life that existed outside of the persona I presented to the world, hung between us, thicker than the smoke from the cheap cigars.

***

The air hung thick with the smell of cheap perfume and desperation. My hair felt sticky with the humidity, a stark contrast to the icy dread that was settling in my gut. Jonah was sprawled on the hotel bed, two naked women draped across him like expensive scarves. Ace and Bryan were equally engrossed, their laughter echoing off the cheap motel walls. I, usually the life of the party, the flirty one with the confidence to charm the birds from the trees, felt a cold knot of discomfort tighten in my chest.

Ezra stood stiffly in the corner, a single beer clutched in his hand, his usual calm demeanor replaced with a barely contained fury. His black hair seemed darker, his brown eyes shadowed. The way he watched me, the way his jaw clenched...it felt like a silent accusation. I desperately wanted to go to him, to reassure him, but the weight of the situation, the absurdity of it all, kept me rooted to the spot.

Jonah, oblivious to the tension, gestured towards the woman who'd just left his lap.

"Show this pretty lady a good time, Jasper." he slurred, his words thick with alcohol. The woman, all painted smiles and predatory grace, approached me. I mumbled something about it being Jonah's night, trying to subtly push her away. Ace and Bryan chimed in, their words meant to be jovial but sounding like taunts.

"Come on. What's the harm, Jasper? You're not dating anyone. She's a hot girl. Don't make her feel bad." Ace said. Their casual disregard for my discomfort, their blatant dismissal of my feelings, felt like a punch to the gut.

Bryan's insistence that I was "a fag" (a label he threw around like confetti) was the final straw. The pressure mounted, the air thinning, the cheap champagne fizz turning sour on my tongue. I felt trapped, like a fly caught in a sticky web of expectations, unable to escape the suffocating atmosphere.

"The Jasper I know would have had her on her knees already." Jonah pressed on.

Ezra's quiet exit was the only break in the stifling atmosphere. He didn't storm out. He simply turned and walked away, leaving behind a silence more deafening than the previous cacophony. Ezra left me alone. My throat felt dry, my hands clammy, and the knot in my stomach tightened with each passing second. I should tell them to fuck off. I want to scream, to make them leave me alone.

I don't need to prove anything. So why can't I just say the words? It's Jonah's bachelor party. A disastrous decision to even attend, especially considering it's in a sleazy hotel room. Ezra wouldn't understand my desperate need to prove something, to prove anything that could somehow fill this hollow emptiness that's been gnawing at my soul since he left me alone with these...men. I was trapped, utterly, sickeningly alone in this suffocating room. The brunette knelt, her bare breasts bouncing slightly as she settled between my legs.

"Honey, you don't have to do anything," I managed, my voice barely a whisper. "I really don't feel comfortable...making you blow me in front of these assholes."

I hoped she'd get the hint. Her smile was predatory, her long, fake eyelashes fluttering.

"I *want* to blow you in front of these assholes." she purred. The words hit me like a physical blow.

"Please, get up. I don't want this." I pleaded, but the words were lost in the rising tide of panic. The guys cheered, urging her on. My drunken stupor prevented coherent thought. The panic was a suffocating blanket. Before I could react, she was on me, her mouth on my dick. I squeezed my eyes shut, fighting back tears. My body was betraying me. Fuck! The sensation was too good, a jarring contrast to the horror churning in my gut.

My heart hammered against my ribs, a frantic drumbeat against the silence of my own screams. I covered my face, wanting to disappear, to escape this body that seemed to have a will of its own. I didn't want this. I didn't want to enjoy this.

The tears flowed freely now, mingling with the sweat on my skin. The shame was a physical weight, crushing me under its immense pressure. And then a single, terrifying thought pierced the haze of panic and pleasure.

This wasn't just about the men in the room. This was about the unspoken, the hidden desperation, this was about proving my worth in a way Ezra would never understand. The truth felt colder than the room. I wasn't proving anything to anyone. I was destroying myself. Jonah's raucous laughter echoed in my ears, a cruel mockery of the horror unfolding.

"I told you he's not a faggot! That right there is a king!" he'd sneered, the words a sickening soundtrack to the violation. The stripper, her painted smile a grotesque mask, continued sucking and licking, but the nausea was overwhelming, a physical manifestation of the filth clinging to me. I couldn't cum, the act a twisted parody of pleasure.

My body felt broken, my spirit crushed. I opened my eyes, the stinging tears blurring the sight of Ezra's brown eyes, wide with a silent scream. His hands were fists, knuckles white. The dam finally broke. Tears streamed down my face, a torrent of shame and despair. Seeing his pain, something inside me snapped. I shoved the girl away and scrambled after him, zipping my pants as I ran.

"E, wait!" I shouted, my voice cracking with desperation. But the hallway stretched endlessly before me, swallowing Ezra whole. My legs felt weak, my breath ragged. The sickness, a churning vortex of regret and self loathing, threatened to consume me. I stumbled toward the exit, my heart a frantic drum against my ribs. I saw him just as he hopped into a cab, his face a mask of hurt I didn't deserve.

"Don't leave!" I screamed, but the words were lost in the rush of traffic. He was gone. Bile rose in my throat, burning its way out onto the cold pavement.

Fuck. I'd fucked up monumentally. My phone! Where was it? I fumbled it out, the screen reflecting my distraught face. I called Ezra, the automated voicemail message a cruel punch to the gut. Bryan appeared, his smug face a grotesque caricature of indifference.

"What happened? Trouble in paradise?" he taunted, his voice dripping with malicious glee.

"Fuck off, Bryan!" I snarled, the words a desperate attempt to stem the rising tide of panic. He retreated, leaving me alone with the suffocating weight of my actions. The air felt thin, my chest tight. Spots danced in my vision, blurring the edges of the world. Why couldn't I breathe? I blinked, and darkness swallowed me whole.

***

I woke up in the hotel room, on the most uncomfortable chair. Jonah was sprawled across the bed, a smug smirk playing on his lips even in sleep. Bryan snored softly on the floor, a discarded stripper's feather boa draped across his chest. Ace? I didn't even register his absence. My curly hair was a mess, my blue eyes stinging. The taste of cheap alcohol and something far worse lingered in my mouth.

The memory of the night, a blur of forced laughter and sickening violation, clawed at the edges of my consciousness. I grabbed my phone, my fingers trembling as I dialed Ezra's number. It went straight to voicemail again. Twenty calls later, sober me was screaming at drunk me. I needed to see Ezra, my anchor in this storm. I had to get to his house.

A few minutes later, I was pounding on Ezra's apartment door.

"Ezra! Open the door, E! Please!" My voice cracked with desperation. No answer. Each unanswered call was a hammer blow to my already shattered composure. I stood there for what felt like an eternity, hoping, praying for a glimpse of his calm brown eyes, the familiar comfort of his presence.

Five fucking hours bled into a torment of unanswered pleas. The gnawing emptiness in my gut told me something was wrong, something beyond a simple disagreement. I went home, defeated, my hope replaced by a cold dread. The next few days were a relentless cycle of unanswered calls and unanswered doors. The reality settled in with the crushing weight of a tombstone. Ezra wasn't coming back.

It wasn't just the rejection. It was the violation, the betrayal by people I thought I knew, the sickening knowledge that Jonah, who was marrying my sister Lily, was responsible.

The nightmares began, vivid and terrifying replays of the night at the bachelor party, the cheap hotel room filled with the reek of cheap liquor and the chilling silence of complicity.

Ezra's absence intensified the horror, leaving me adrift in a sea of grief and betrayal. The confident, flirty Jasper, the one who'd always known how to charm his way through any situation, was gone, replaced by a broken shell. I understood now. Everything was truly, irrevocably fucked up. My best friend, my Ezra, was gone, and the pieces of my life lay scattered and broken at my feet.

By the time the work day came up, I convinced myself that nothing mattered anymore. I'd walk into my job and be who I always am. Jasper, the flirt. The fuck boy that everyone knew me to be. It was a shield, a flimsy one, but it was all I had left after... after that night.

The dark curls of my hair felt heavy, a curtain hiding the blue eyes that usually sparkled with confidence. Tonight, though, they felt dull, reflecting the grey emptiness inside. The Velvet Rope felt like a cage, but it was also a stage. I could play my part, the charming Jasper, and maybe, just maybe, forget for a few hours.

As I entered, I spotted Ezra taking care of a customer. He smiled, that gentle, caring smile that melted away the ice around my heart... usually. When he saw me, that smile vanished, replaced by something... guarded. I rolled my eyes, the practiced gesture of a man burying his pain under a layer of bravado, and stepped behind the bar, the familiar coolness of the polished wood a small comfort.

"What can I get you?" I asked the customer, but my voice felt flat, devoid of its usual playful lilt. I didn't hear his answer. My gaze was locked on Ezra. The way he moved, the careful grace in his movements. The way his black hair fell over his eyes, the way he bit his lip when concentrating, every small detail a sharp, painful reminder of him, of us.

Of everything we'd lost that night at Jonah's bachelor party. The memory was a bitter poison, constantly churning in my gut. I should've protected myself, should've been stronger, but I was... I was broken. And he saw it, etched on my face. I knew he saw it. The customer's voice, sharp and impatient, pulled me back from the brink.

"Hello?!" he snapped.

"I'm sorry," I mumbled, my usual charm a pathetic imitation. "What can I get you to drink?"

"One beer." he grunted. I poured the beer, my hands steady, the practiced motions a practiced performance. I forced a smile, a carefully constructed mask, offering the drink with the practiced ease of a seasoned bartender.

"Here you go. Sorry for the wait." The lie tasted bitter on my tongue, as bitter as the truth. I was drowning, and even in the glittering artificiality of The Velvet Rope, Ezra couldn't pull me out. Not anymore.

***

The night was long and exhausting. The whole time was spent avoiding him. It was ridiculous, really. All the weaving through the sweaty bodies, the forced smiles at leering customers. All to avoid Ezra. But the truth was, I craved his touch more than oxygen but tonight, I couldn't bear to face him, to see the sorrow reflected in his usually calm brown eyes. I took a break and headed to the back of the club like I always do. Stepping outside, the cool air felt nice on my skin.

The door opened and Ezra stepped out. He muttered something under his breath. Probably a few cuss words, his way of processing things.

"I can leave. I already got some fresh air." I said, already moving towards the door. But he was blocking the way, his silhouette stark against the neon glow of the city. The casual dismissal felt false even to me. Beneath the bravado, my heart hammered against my ribs.

"That's all you have to say to me?" he finally asked, his voice low and strained.

"Yeah, that's all I have to say. So, can you move out of the way." I replied, my voice harder than I intended. He narrowed his eyes, disbelief etched onto his face.

"Fine, but we're over. I'm breaking up with you, Jasper."

Nothing prepared me for the hurt that followed, the sharp, agonizing sting. It felt like a punch to the gut, a physical manifestation of the emotional turmoil I'd been suppressing. It fucking hurt.

"Why are you so upset about this?! We were just fucking! You and I, were just fucking around. That's all." I snapped, wanting to hurt him. Wrong choice of words, but it's me, and of course, I fuck up everything. The look in Ezra's eyes, usually so warm, was now a chilling, intense storm. I took a few steps back, my blue eyes darting away from the pain etched into his face.

"I'm going to warn you once, Jasper. Once. Never accuse me of using you like some fuck buddy," Ezra's voice was low, controlled, yet laced with a raw hurt that cut deeper than any insult. "You and I both know that we made love. You might be too chicken shit to admit it, but we were in a fucking relationship. I invested 100% of my fucking heart." His words hit me like a punch to the gut, the truth of them undeniable. The shame was a suffocating weight. I'd tried to bury it. Ezra... he saw past my carefully constructed lies.

"You want to tell yourself lies to make yourself feel better for being so shitty to me, fine, but when you see me you'll be reminded of the cold truth. You were gay for me and you loved every minute of it."

"I might have had a speech like you a few days ago, had you picked up the phone or opened your damn door but clearly, I didn't matter all that much to you. So, save your bullshit speeches for someone else, E."

His deliberate steps towards me were measured, each one a hammer blow against the fragile wall I'd built. His hands, usually so gentle, were clenched into fists.

"What could you possibly have to say? I was there. I saw it with my own eyes. It was hard to miss a chick blowing you in the middle of the room." His words were a cold, hard reality. I couldn't deny it. The tears threatened to spill over, but I blinked them back. I couldn't unravel here.

"Then you must have seen that I certainly didn't want it to happen," I choked out, my voice barely a whisper. "I was crying like a bitch, frozen to my seat. I panicked. I was pushed into a corner and I didn't know what to do." The truth hung between us, heavy and suffocating. The confident Jasper, the flirty bartender, was gone, replaced by a broken man, finally facing the wreckage of his denial.

The conversation about Jonah's bachelor party, about what happened to me that night—the sexual assault—hung between us, thick and suffocating. This conversation was too much for me to deal with right now. I stepped to the side to leave but Ezra blocks me. Now I'm getting angry.

"This conversation isn't over. You don't get to leave just because it's difficult." he said, his voice low and dangerously steady.

"What do you want from me, Ezra?! I fucked up. You hate my guts. You broke up with me. There's nothing more that I can do. I'm sorry, ok? Just let me go. I can't do this at work." I pushed him out the way, the force of my anger surprising even myself. He stumbles back but still doesn't let me open the door.

"Yes, you fucked up big time and maybe I should hate you. I sure as fuck want to hate you but I don't. I'm still madly in love with you. I just don't know how we can fix this. The damage is done. You broke my heart, Jasper." His words, blunt and raw, hit me like a physical blow. The carefully constructed walls I'd built around my guilt crumbled. The tears fell freely down my face now, hot and relentless. He may not hate me, but I surely do

.

I hurt the only person that meant a damn thing to me. The weight of my actions, my failure to protect myself, my failure to tell him sooner, crushed me. I gently place my hand on his face and looked deeply into his brown eyes, those usually calm pools now reflecting my own turmoil.

"I'm really fucking sorry. I should have been a man and sent them all to hell. If I could go back in time, I would have done everything differently. You are the last person I ever wanted to hurt. I don't deserve you. You're too good for me. I'm really sorry." My voice cracked, but the words, each one heavy with remorse, were true.

I kiss his forehead, a small gesture against the vastness of my regret. I wiped away the wetness on my face with my hands. The alcohol haze of the bar, the usual buzz of the club, fades into the background as all my attention focuses on Ezra's pain, my pain. His pain reflects my own, an unbearable mirror of my failings. The future, once bright with our shared laughter and shared dreams, now seemed a distant and uncertain place.

"Take care of yourself, E." I whisper, my voice barely audible above the pulse of the music. Turning, I walked away, leaving behind not just the bar, but a piece of my heart, a piece I fear I may never fully recover.

"Why does that sound like goodbye forever?" He whispered. I didn't have an answer for him. Ezra's voice, usually so calm, was tight with unshed tears. His black hair fell over his forehead, framing those warm brown eyes that always saw right through me. All that remained was the hollow shell left behind in Jonah's bachelor party, a night I'd rather erase from existence. Instead, I opened the door to the back of the club and walked straight to management. My boss looked at me with a questioning expression.

"I quit." I said. Just as swiftly as I walked in, I walked out. I grabbed my belongings and hopped in my car.

I drove aimlessly for hours, a blur of highway lights and the echoing silence in my car. The escape felt good, the initial rush of adrenaline masking the deep ache in my soul. I finally stopped at a gas station, the harsh fluorescent lights illuminating the stark reality of my situation. I'd driven out of the state with nothing but the clothes on my back.

The beer seemed like a quick fix, a numb escape from the searing pain that gnawed at me. I bought a few cases, the cashier's questioning gaze barely registering. Back in my car, the cold aluminum of the cans felt like a temporary shield against the overwhelming despair. An hour later, the empty cans littered the car floor, testament to the flood of tears that had accompanied the beer. My self loathing was a suffocating blanket. I didn't deserve to live, a mantra that echoed in my mind, leading me to the bridge.

The cool night air whipped against my face as I climbed the ledge. My phone rang uselessly in my car. I didn't even bother to check it. Headlights flashed, cars slowed, people watched. A silent audience to my final act. I counted to three, closed my eyes, and let go. In that terrifying plunge, before the impact, a single, sharp regret pierced through the darkness... I never told Ezra I loved him. His quiet kindness, his unwavering support. He deserved more. Then there was nothing. Only the painfully cold embrace of the dark abyss, swallowing me whole, a final, bitter irony in my desperate escape.

CHAPTER 18

———◆◇◆———

EZRA'S POV

Jasper kissed my forehead and I savored every second of it. His touch, usually a spark of playful electricity, felt different this time; warm, grounding, and profoundly sad. But the warmth vanished the instant his lips left my skin, replaced by an ice cold emptiness that spread through me, leaving me feeling like a hollowed out husk.

"Take care of yourself, E." he whispered. The confidence that usually radiated from him was gone, replaced by a weary quietude. I frowned, my fingers itching to reach for him, to hold onto him, but I didn't. There was a finality in his words, a weight that settled heavily in my chest.

"Why does that sound like goodbye forever?" I asked, my voice barely a whisper. He remained silent, his gaze distant, before turning and walking away. I knew he needed space, so I didn't chase after him, the unspoken words hanging heavy between us in the dimly lit corridor of The Velvet Rope.

Back in the club, the usual cacophony of music and laughter felt muted, replaced by a dull thrum of anxiety.

"Dude! What happened?! Jasper just quit his job." Marcus blurted out, as soon as he found me.

"What? What are you talking about?" I asked, my hands shaking slightly. Jasper wasn't behind the bar, his usual playful banter absent. The chilling truth slammed into me. His goodbye wasn't just a temporary separation, it was a farewell.

"Where is he, Marcus?!" I demanded, my voice tight with panic. He shrugged, his usual jovial demeanor gone, replaced with concern.

"He grabbed his stuff and stormed out of here like a bat out of hell. You need to tend to the customers he left behind." The usual calm that defined me shattered.

I mechanically started making drinks, my movements automatic. The smiles I plastered on felt grotesque and hollow, mirroring the emptiness inside me. I knew Jasper. I knew his silences and his disappearances stemmed from the pain he kept hidden, the aftermath of being twice violated. He wasn't just leaving The Velvet Rope, he was leaving me, leaving this life to confront his demons. The few hours before the next shift felt like an eternity. I didn't care about the customers, about the money, about anything except reaching him. Something was wrong, I could feel it in the pit of my stomach.

A cold dread, a knot tightening with each passing minute. Don't do anything stupid, I told myself, but my hands were slick with a nervous sweat. I kept glancing at the clock, the numbers blurring in my anxiety. Jasper should have been home by now.

Finally, after what felt like an eternity, it was time to clock out. I rushed to my motorcycle, the engine roaring a welcome release of tension, and sped off towards his apartment. I ran up the stairs, my heart hammering against my ribs, a frantic rhythm mirroring the fear building inside me. I banged on his door, shouting his name, the sound echoing in the quiet hallway. His neighbor, a tiny woman with a cloud of white hair, emerged, her face etched with concern.

"Excuse me, sir," she said, her voice trembling slightly, "The gentleman that lives here hasn't come home. Please, stop shouting."

"How do you know he isn't home?" I demanded, the bluntness in my voice surprising even myself.

"Well," she explained, "He always leaves my mail on my doorstep after work, but today, I didn't get any." The simple statement hit me like a physical blow. The sickening feeling in my stomach intensified, a cold dread settling deep in my bones.

"Sorry to have disturbed you, ma'am." I mumbled, my voice thick with despair.

"I'll just leave. Thanks."

Where could he be? Why isn't he home? The thought of him, alone and vulnerable, sent a fresh wave of panic through me. I had no choice but to go home, my phone dead, leaving me stranded in a sea of unanswered questions. I undressed numbly and fell into bed, waiting for my phone to power on, the weight of my worry too heavy to fight. I fell asleep, the unanswered questions hanging in the air like a shroud.

***

I opened my eyes and cursed at myself. How could I have fallen asleep? My apartment, a small but cozy space, was dimly lit by the predawn light filtering through the blinds. My brown eyes, now wide with a growing sense of dread. I immediately grabbed my phone. I called Jasper, but he wouldn't answer. I must have called about ten times, each unanswered ring a hammer blow to my gut. The tenth unanswered call felt like a confirmation of my deepest fears. I attempted to call one more time and finally, it went through.

"Jasper, where are you? I've been—" I was interrupted by a female voice.

"Hello, I'm Deputy Bradshaw. Your friend is currently being rushed over to the hospital. Is there any way you can come down to answer some questions?" she said, her voice tight with urgency. My heart lurched.

"Which hospital? Is he ok? I can be there right away."

"I don't know his condition, sir. He is going to Mary Saints Hospital. We have his belongings and need someone to sign for them. Can I have your name?"

"Mary Saints Hospital? My name is Ezra Valenti. Where is that located?" I questioned, a cold knot tightening in my stomach.

"Western County, sir." she replied.

"There isn't a Western County in my location."

A beat of silence, then, "Sir, we're in Delaware."

Delaware? The sheer impossibility of it sent a shiver down my spine.

"It's going to take me hours to get there." I managed to say, my voice trembling.

"Please, get here quickly. My name is Deputy Fran Bradshaw. I'll be waiting for you at the hospital. I have to go now."

What the fuck is going on?! The words hung in the air, unanswered. A wave of nausea washed over me. It was a gut feeling, a certainty that had been gnawing at me all evening, a feeling I'd tried to ignore, a feeling that had led to my restless sleep. I knew something was wrong. I knew it. The thought of him possibly in a Delaware hospital...It was unbearable. I quickly grabbed my keys and hopped on my motorcycle, the engine roaring to life, a desperate cry against the suffocating silence of fear. I shouldn't have fallen asleep. I knew something would happen. The road blurred into a frantic race against time, a race against an unknown, terrifying future.

The drive was long and agonizing, but I finally made it to Mary Saints Hospital in Delaware. My brown eyes darted around frantically as I made my way to the front desk.

"I'm here to see a patient, Jasper Rowan." I said, my voice betraying none of the fear churning in my stomach. The receptionist, thankfully, didn't seem to notice my inner turmoil. She scribbled a room number and a crude map onto a scrap of paper, and sent me on my way.

I ran, a maniac possessed, weaving through the crowd, past murmuring patients and harried nurses, until I found his room. A man, a doctor, judging by his crisp white coat, stopped me just as I reached the door.

"Are you here for Jasper Rowan?" he asked, his tone strangely gentle.

"Yes," I managed, "Is he okay? What happened?"

The words that followed ripped the world from beneath my feet.

"I'm sorry to inform you of this," he began, his voice flat and devoid of emotion. "Jasper jumped off a bridge. He was intoxicated and drowned. EMTs were able to resuscitate him, but he went into cardiac arrest. He's currently stable, but hasn't woken up. He runs the risk of organ failure due to the lack of oxygen to the brain. Right now, it's unclear if he'll ever wake up. I'm so sorry."

The carefully constructed wall of calm I'd maintained crumbled. I started crying, hyper-ventilating, the earth shattering beneath me. This can't be happening. This curly haired, blue eyed man, the confident, flirty Jasper, my ex boyfriend, my Jasper... suicide? The image of his laughing face, of his touch, of the way his blue eyes sparkled...it felt like a cruel joke, a cruel and impossible twist of fate.

"Sir, are you alright?! Please, sit and have some water." The doctor's words were a blur. I couldn't focus, couldn't breathe. I needed to see him. I needed to be with Jasper. Ignoring the concerned medical staff, I pushed past them and into his room. A police officer sat in a chair, her expression grim.

"Deputy Bradshaw?" I guessed, my voice a rough whisper.

"Yes sir, you must be Ezra." Her sad smile didn't reach her eyes. I nodded, my gaze fixed on Jasper. He lay still, a tangle of wires and monitors attached to his chest. I sniffled, then sobbed, the sound raw and uncontrolled.

"I know this is a hard time, but I need you to answer some questions." Deputy Bradshaw said gently, her voice barely a murmur above the rhythmic beeping of the machines.

"Why is he handcuffed to the bed?" I croaked, the question catching in my throat.

"That's just a safety precaution. He can't hurt himself this way. He's on suicide watch." she explained. The words hit me like a physical blow. Suicide. Jasper had tried to end his life. She asked about depression. I shook my head, truthfully. He'd never hinted at anything like that to me. Then came the question that ripped open the wound.

"Any clue as to why he would do this?" The tears flowed freely now, blurring my vision.

"I... I broke up with him," I managed, the confession a bitter taste in my mouth. "He's been struggling with... his sexuality. Some people... they made him do things... and he didn't handle it well." The words felt inadequate, a feeble attempt to explain the complex turmoil I knew he'd been facing. Her pen scratched across the notebook.

"What sort of things?" she pressed, her tone professional but empathetic.

"Sexual things." I whispered, shame burning in my chest.

"He was sexually abused?" The question hung in the air.

"He said he didn't want it to happen. And... some months ago... he was raped. By a woman." The admission shattered me, the weight of my guilt crushing me. I should have been there for him. Instead, I left him alone, vulnerable, to face the darkness. The beeping of the machines felt like a morbid metronome counting down the seconds of my life, where every breath is a regret, each beat a painful reminder of my failure.

His blue eyes, usually sparkling with mischief, were closed, heavy lids concealing the soul that held mine captive.

"Does he have any family that we can get into contact with?" the officer had asked.

"He only has a sister but she's getting married. I don't have any contact information for her." I'd mumbled, my voice a hollow echo in the sterile room. The calm exterior I usually maintained cracked, revealing the raw, desperate fear clawing at my insides. My pounding head felt heavy, a physical manifestation of the grief threatening to consume me. This wasn't the way it was supposed to end. Not with him lying here, cold and unresponsive, after his... attempt.

"His car was towed." The officer's words still hung in the air. The triviality of it stung, a jarring reminder of the mundane world continuing while mine crumbled. I tucked the towing information into my pocket, the flimsy card feeling like a weight, a symbol of the practicalities that now seemed insurmountable. His hand in mine, felt lifeless, chilling me to the bone.

"Please, Baby. Open your pretty blue eyes. I can't live without you. I love you more than you could possibly imagine. Please, come back to me. I'm sorry. Ok? Do you hear me? I'm so fucking sorry. Don't leave me. Please..." My voice cracked, a desperate plea lost in the sterile silence. I leaned down, pressing a kiss to his forehead, tasting the faint antiseptic scent that mingled with his familiar cologne, a ghost of the man I loved. The tears finally came, hot and silent, as I held his hand, a desperate anchor in a sea of uncertainty.

Later, as I sat in the hospital parking lot, staring at the empty space where his car should have been, a strange calm settled over me. The calm wasn't acceptance, not yet. It was the chilling realization that even if he woke up, things would never be the same. His attempt, the secrecy surrounding his sister, the sudden absence of any real communication. It all painted a picture of a man I barely knew, a man who had built a wall around his heart, one I hadn't been able to breach. The towing card felt insignificant now, overshadowed by the much larger task before me. Understanding and possibly, ultimately, letting go of Jasper.

***

Days bled into nights at Mary Saints Hospital. I spent them by Jasper's side, only leaving when visiting hours ended. The doctors were baffled. His vitals were normal, the tests came back clean. He just... wouldn't wake up. They mumbled about possible head trauma, but it didn't fit the circumstances. The attempted suicide. It was a surreal experience explaining everything to his sister, Lily, over the phone. She'd postponed her wedding, she said, for "personal reasons". Now, here she was.

Lily arrived, a whirlwind of long, dark curly hair and those same stunning blue eyes that mirrored Jasper's. The resemblance was uncanny. She was everything Jasper was, but somehow... softer.

"Hey, I'm Lily. Jasper's sister. We talked on the phone." she said, her voice trembling slightly. I just sat there, awkwardly, my usual bluntness replaced by a profound awkwardness. This wasn't how I envisioned meeting Jasper's family. The silence stretched, thick and heavy, until Lily's direct question broke through the tension.

"You're in love with him. Aren't you?" The words hung in the air, stark and clear.

"Yes," I replied, my voice low, "I am very much in love with your brother." She nodded, a faraway look in her eyes as she gazed at Jasper's still form.

"Is he in love with you?" she whispered, a blush creeping onto her cheeks. The question hit me hard. In all the months we'd been together, Jasper, with his confident smirk and flirty banter, had never uttered those three little words. He never even said he liked me, for that matter. His affections were communicated through subtle cues. A crinkle of his nose, the curve of his lip, a blush, the intensity in his eyes. Those were the signs, only visible to those who knew how to read him.

"I don't know," I finally answered, my throat tight. "You should ask him when he wakes up."

It wasn't my place to speak for him, to define his feelings or lack thereof. The truth was, I didn't know if he loved me or if he ever would. Whether or not he loved me, was almost inconsequential at that moment. He was alive. And, I would wait for him. I would sit here, amongst the beeping machines, and I would wait for him, to wake up and tell me what he felt.

"My twin is so closed up. Jassy would never admit to having feelings. Plus, he's totally not gay. Sorry to tell you that." She'd smiled sadly, a heartbreaking gesture that only intensified my grief. If only she knew. If only she knew how fiercely, how desperately, I loved him. The revelation of a twin was a shock, a detail that shifted my understanding of Jasper in a way I hadn't anticipated.

Lily's stories, though meant to be lighthearted anecdotes of their childhood, painted a richer, more complex picture of Jasper than I had ever known. She spoke of his protective nature, his pranks, his unwavering loyalty. The way he'd covered for her teenage escapades resonated with the way he'd always covered for me, always shielding me from his own vulnerabilities.

The stories filled in the gaps, highlighting a side of him I'd only glimpsed. A softer, more vulnerable Jasper hidden beneath a layer of confident bravado. Hearing them made me happy, a bittersweet happiness that was quickly overtaken by the crushing weight of his absence. He'd attempted suicide. That much, I knew. The gravity of it pressed down on me as Lily left, leaving me alone with the man who still held my heart captive.

I held his hand, the coolness of his skin a chilling reminder of his fragility. The simple act, a gesture of love and heartbreak combined, was all I could manage. As I rubbed gentle circles with my thumb, a tear escaped, then another, and another until the dam broke. I closed my eyes, the sobs racking my body.

"Ezra?" Jasper's hoarse voice spoke. My eyes snapped open and settled on his. His dark curly hair, usually perfectly sculpted, was a mess against the crisp white pillow. Those stunning blue eyes, the ones that once held a playful glint, were now clouded with pain, yet sparkling with a familiar spark of defiance.

"Oh my god! Jasper you're awake!" I peppered kisses on his beautiful face. Relief, a tidal wave of it, swelled in my chest, pushing aside the lingering fear that had choked me for what felt like an eternity.

"You scared the fucking hell out of me! How could you do something so reckless?! Don't you know I can't live without you?!" I said in between kisses, my voice thick with emotion. My calm exterior, the one I usually presented to the world, shattered into a million pieces.

The bluntness that usually defined my demeanor was replaced by raw, unfiltered love, a love I thought I could bury deep after our tumultuous breakup.

"Everything hurts." He croaked, his voice a fragile whisper. The sight of him, pale and weak, triggered a surge of guilt. Had my anger, our final argument, driven him to this? The thought sliced through me, sharper than any blade. I quickly ran out, my heart hammering against my ribs, and found the medical staff. I felt a strange sense of detachment as I directed them back to his room, my black hair falling across my face as I watched them examine him. It was as if I was watching a movie, a tragic drama unfolding before my eyes, yet I was a mere spectator.

"You've made a miraculous recovery, Mr. Rowan. You must have one hell of a guardian angel." The doctor said, his words a strange mix of clinical observation and almost mystical wonder. He smiled, tucking his stethoscope around his neck, a small, knowing smile.

"Why am I handcuffed to this bed?" he rasped, his voice weak, the words a painful reminder of his suicide attempt. The doctor's explanation —"to protect you from yourself"—hung in the air like a suffocating shroud. My heart ached. Part of me wanted to scream at him, to shake some sense into him, to demand an explanation for the terror he'd put me through. But another, larger part of me just wanted to hold him, to erase this nightmare.

He was angry, his attempts at yelling reduced to frustrated whispers.

"The only way you can go home is if someone takes responsibility for you and signs you out." The doctor's words landed like a heavy weight. Jasper's plea, "E, please. It'll never happen again," cracked my carefully constructed composure. His desperation was palpable, raw. He'd never begged me for anything. Never. The weight of his words pressed down on me.

"I don't know, Babe. What you did is serious. You could have died. Correction, you did die and they brought you back." I replied, my voice strained. The reality of it hit me again. The sheer terror of the call, the frantic race to the hospital, the gut wrenching wait, and then the doctor's words, "drowned, clinically dead, but we managed to revive him."

The image of his lifeless body flashed before my eyes, a stark, horrifying reminder. His repeated assurances, "I swear. It won't ever happen again. Please, take me home," were a desperate cry for forgiveness, a plea I was hesitant to grant. Could I trust him? Was this a reckless act of love or a terrible mistake? His usual playful glint in his blue eyes, was gone, replaced by a desperate vulnerability that both terrified and captivated me. The doctor placed the release forms in front of me.

The pen felt heavy, mirroring the weight of my decision. My brown eyes, usually calm and collected, darted between the papers and Jasper's pleading gaze. Could I really forgive him? Could I risk it all again? A single tear escaped, tracing a path down my cheek. It was a risk, a gamble on a love that felt both fragile and fiercely strong. The pen hovered over the signature line. Sighing, I took a deep breath and signed.

"If you ever do this shit again, I'll never forgive you." I said, my voice firm, a final warning hanging in the air.

"Lily is going to kill me when she finds out." I whispered mostly to myself.

"My sister? Why would...wait, you met her? How long have I been asleep?" Jasper's brow knits together as he tries to put the pieces together in his head. I hand over the papers back to the nurse.

"You weren't asleep. You were in a coma. You've been out for many days, Babe. Your sister postponed her wedding and we spent time getting to know each other while sitting in this room. I should actually call her and let her know you're awake." I explained calmly. I kissed his forehead and stepped out of the room to make the call.

CHAPTER 19

JASPER'S POV

After Ezra called Lily, it didn't take her long to come and see me.

"Jassy!" She exclaimed with excitement.

"Lily, you know I hate it when you call me that." I said, but she just laughed it off.

Ezra stood around, smiling at our interactions, the familiar sibling banter a comforting balm.

"Alright, Babe. I'm going to get some coffee. I'll be right back." he said.

My sister looked at me wide eyed. Ezra hadn't even realized what he called me, but I did. That "babe" hung in the air, thick and sweet like the aroma of freshly brewed coffee. I knew Lily would have questions, but I wasn't afraid to answer them. Not anymore.

The coma had been a strange, silent world, unlike the chaotic life I'd led before, a life of calculated movements, deadly precision, and a father who'd taught me to kill before I could even tie my shoes. Mary Saints Hospital felt strangely peaceful compared to that.

"Go ahead. Ask your questions. I know you're just dying to know." I told her.

"He's in love with you, you know." she said, her voice barely a whisper.

All I could do was smile.

"He better love me or I'd make a pretty annoying stalker." I laughed at my own joke, the dark humor a familiar comfort. Lily just continued to stare at me incredulously, speechless. Her reaction annoyed me. Why was it such a big deal? Was it the contrast, the unexpected tenderness blossoming a midst the wreckage of my past?

"Lillian, he makes me happy. So, shove your judgments up your ass, k?"

She smiled at my remark and started to squeal like a high school teenager, the sound echoing in the sterile hospital room. Her relief was palpable, a mirror to my own quiet joy.

"Oh my god, Jassy! Tell me everything!" Lily giggled, her voice echoing slightly in the room.

"No, no, no, no! We're not having a girl talk. I'm not a chick. I'm not going to start wearing dresses or anything like that. I just so happen to love a guy. That's it." I said, trying to sound nonchalant, but my heart hammered against my ribs.

"Oh my god! You love him?!" she shouted, her usual composure shattered. I winced.

"Keep your voice down. He doesn't know it yet. I'm not even sure if we're in a relationship." I groaned, running a hand through my dark curls. She quickly covered her mouth with her hands, her eyes wide. I noticed she wasn't wearing a wedding ring. A wave of relief washed over me. Lily deserved better than Jonah, that stiff, self absorbed, piece of sh it.

"Why didn't you get married?" I blurted out, the question escaping before I could censor it. The sudden shift in topic hung heavy in the air. Lily's hands fell to her lap, her vibrant energy dimming. Her normally bright blue eyes clouded over with a sadness that mirrored the sterile white walls surrounding us.

"I postponed the wedding. I wanted a few extra days to think. Plus, I wanted my brother to be there." Her voice was barely a whisper. The guilt slammed into me, a physical blow. I hadn't even considered how this would affect her, hadn't thought about the ripple effect of my near suicide, the impact on our relationship. I hadn't thought at all, lost in my own turmoil. My own selfish escape.

"I'm sorry, Lily." The words felt inadequate, pathetic. The guilt was a lead weight in my chest.

"It's ok because now that you're free to go, we'll have time to spend together. My wedding doesn't even matter." She offered a weak smile, but her eyes still held a fragile sadness. I reached out, taking her hand. The coolness of her skin sent a shiver down my spine, a stark reminder of the fragility of life, the precariousness of happiness.

Just then Ezra walked back in the room with an officer. I raised an eyebrow and shot him a what-the-hell-is-going-on look.

"Time to remove the handcuffs." The officer said, answering my silent question.

As soon as my hands were free, I rubbed my wrists. My first thought was to use them to pull Ezra's face closer to me and kiss his full lips. I didn't do that, however. I wasn't sure if he wanted to kiss me. Not after all of this. My hospitalization didn't change anything. I still fucked up and he's still heartbroken about it. He's only here because I fucked up again.

"Are you ok?" Ezra's voice interrupted my thoughts.

"Yeah, get me the hell out of here." I said as I began to rip off the wires attached to my body. My sister and the officer left the room so that I could dress myself. The Hospital felt like a suffocating tomb. I'm surprised that they released me so soon after my... incident. But hey, I'll count my blessings and just be glad to get out of this hell hole.

Ezra was waiting by the door, his usual calm demeanor somehow amplified by the sterile environment.

"Need help?" Ezra asked, his voice a low rumble. I didn't need any help, not really, but I nodded anyway. The gesture was as much for him as it was for me. He untied the back of the scratchy hospital gown. I could feel his eyes on my back, a familiar warmth despite the circumstances. A thrill, dangerous and exhilarating, ran through me. I wanted his touch, desperately, a silent plea echoing in the sterile air. But he didn't reach out. He knew better than to violate the fragile space between us. I turned around, letting the gown fall to the floor. He gulped, his brown eyes wide.

"Nothing you haven't seen before, E." I smirked, testing the waters. The playful tone was a mask, hiding the raw vulnerability still clinging to me.

"Jasper." he warned, his voice tight with barely contained emotion.

"My name sounds so good on your lips." I purred, pushing further. His blush was a delicious reward. Ezra turned away, covering his face with his hands, his shoulders shaking slightly.

"Put your clothes on, Jasper. Before I lose my self control." The words were a confession, a raw display of the love that existed beneath the surface of our turbulent relationship. A laugh escaped me, unrestrained. He was so cute, all hot and bothered and I loved it, that power, that lingering pull I still held over him.

As I dressed, the room faded into the background. All that remained was him, me, and the chaotic, beautiful mess of our complicated story. I patted him on the shoulder.

"You can look now. I'm dressed." I said, fighting back a grin as I subtly adjusted my cock, hiding the evidence of my unexpectedly strong reaction to seeing Ezra again.

"You did that on purpose. I was trying to be a gentleman." he mumbled, his cheeks a beautiful, flustered pink.

"You are a gentleman, you big softy. I just couldn't resist teasing you. I mean, look at those rosy cheeks on a guy who looks like he could front a hardcore metal band!" I laughed, pinching his cheek. He swatted my hand away, a playful annoyance in his eyes.

"I was the lead singer in a hardcore metal band. In high school. Back when my hair was long." he admitted, the gruffness melted away slightly. I could already picture the teenage rebellion, that was Ezra in his teens. Screaming out angry lyrics.

"Tell me you have videos of this!!" I exclaimed, as we walked out of the sterile hospital environment and towards his motorcycle, a beautiful black machine that mirrored his own quiet intensity. Ezra chuckled, a low rumble in his chest, clearly amused by my enthusiasm. He hopped on, my arm instinctively around him as I settled behind him.

The roar of the engine was exhilarating, the wind whipping through my hair as we sped off. The closeness of our bodies sent a familiar shiver down my spine. Arriving at a small, secluded hotel, he parked the bike and took my hand, the gesture surprising yet utterly comforting.

We walked inside, hand in hand, the simple act sending a jolt of unexpected electricity through me. He glanced at me a few times, a slow, sexy smirk playing on his lips that had the power to melt any resistance I might have mustered. It was a look that spoke of shared history, of unspoken understanding, of a future I desperately hoped we would build. He unlocks door 32B and leads me inside to his room.

"I figured you'd want to shower and change. I have clothes you can wear." he said. He was right. Ezra handed me a bag full of clothes. Everything inside was new, still tagged. The gesture felt both incredibly tender and jarringly strange, considering the circumstances. Before I could process it all, the words tumbled out, "Will you join me?"

My voice was shaky, a pathetic whisper against the backdrop of our complicated reality. His gaze locked onto mine, a flicker of something unreadable crossing his features.

"If I join you, it'll be strictly to bathe you. Which I know isn't what you truly want. We can't stress your heart. So, no. I won't be joining you. I want to join you but I don't trust myself not to have sex with you."

"You want to have sex with me?" The question felt absurd, yet utterly fitting given the raw, emotional landscape of this hotel room. His answer was blunt, devoid of the playful flirting I usually expected from him.

"Is that a trick question?" He countered. I paced, the cheap hotel carpet rough under my bare feet.

"I'm just going to get straight to the point. You broke up with me but you're calling me 'Babe' and doing things for me. Now you're implying you would have sex with me and I just need to know what it all means." His hands settled firmly on my shoulders, grounding me in the present.

"Yes, I did break up with you but that doesn't mean everything just goes away. I'm still attracted to you. I still love you but I can't just jump right back into the way things were between us. You tried to kill yourself. I'm angry about that. You gave me some bullshit goodbye and then you jumped off a bridge." The words hung heavy in the air, the unspoken accusations more potent than any shouted argument. The elephant, massive and ugly, was squarely in the room. My attempt at suicide, my failed escape, stared me in the face.

He released his grip, the sudden absence of his touch leaving a hollow ache. He sat on the bed, the weight of his unshed tears palpable. The anger in his eyes softened, morphing into something akin to hurt, a vulnerability I'd almost forgotten he possessed. I opened my mouth to speak, to explain, to apologize, but the words wouldn't come. So, I offered a pathetic excuse.

"I was drunk, E."

"Bullshit. It was more than that. Was it me? What pushed you to do such a thing?"

I couldn't look at his face. It filled me with guilt.

I never thought I'd have to explain a suicide attempt because I didn't think I would survive. Now I'm staring the consequences of my actions dead in the face and I didn't like it. I sat in the chair by the window, my reflection a stranger, my hands trembling.

"I just thought that I didn't deserve to live. All I do is hurt people and it fucking sucks. So, I thought if I end my life then everything would just stop. I just hated that I hurt you and I just couldn't live with myself anymore." I said as tears slowly fell. Ezra got up and knelt before me. With gentle hands, he wiped away my tears.

"You're the most infuriating person I've ever met. It's like you don't hear me at all. You are human, Jasper. You're allowed to fuck up sometimes. Yes, I'll be upset occasionally but none of that will change my love for you. I shouldn't have broken up with you. That was my mistake. I didn't even mean it. Almost losing you reminded me of just how short life really is and I don't want to live it without you." He said softly.

Stunned by his words, I remained speechless for a brief moment. I parted my lips to speak but closed it when nothing would come out. My voice was stuck in my throat. My heart beating wildly in my chest. Finally, the words rolled off my tongue.

"I love you." I said. Then it was Ezra's turn to be speechless. "My last thought before I hit the water was you. How much I am in love with you. It sounds stupid saying it out loud."

Ezra shook his head.

"It's not stupid. It's not stupid at all." He said with a smile so wide. He leaned forward and kissed my lips softly. It was a simple kiss, a peck of the lips that lingered but filled me with a soothing warmth that I could only describe as love. His kiss filled me with a love so big that my heart felt it would burst with happiness. It was a foreign feeling but I welcomed it nonetheless.

I could feel the colors slowly seeping back into my life. The tears that fell from my eyes now, weren't of sadness or anger any longer. Ezra was perfect. Perfect for me. I didn't care who knew it now. Fuck, let the whole world know.

His precious brown eyes looked deeply into my blue ones. Silently, he pulled me to my feet and lead me to the bathroom. He turned the shower on first then proceeded to undress me until I stood naked in front of him. My skin screamed for his touch. I couldn't hide my arousal.

"I'll be right outside the door, if you need me." he said, his voice a low rumble that sent shivers down my spine.

"You're not going to stay?" I frowned, the question laced with a childish petulance I couldn't quite control.

"I want to stay. God, do I want to stay, but it's a bad idea. Your health comes first." He stepped out and closed the bathroom door. I just stood there for a few minutes, staring at the door and hoping that he came back in, but he didn't. Honestly, I shouldn't have expected anything less from Ezra. His morality and kind heart were golden. He never did anything wrong. He kept his promises, stayed faithful and loyal.

Unlike me, who got drunk, broke hearts and never gave a shit about anyone. All of that was changing though. This wasn't just another fleeting encounter. This was Ezra, the man who saw past my messy, self destructive tendencies, the man who loved me despite my flaws.

I stepped into the shower and let the water fall down my body. I thought about pleasuring myself but instead, I shifted the temperature of the water to as cold as it could get. Scrubbing myself down with soap, I mentally groaned. Stupid recovery. Stupid heart. Stupid boner. Everything was stupid.

I rinsed off the cold soapy water and looked for a towel but there wasn't any. I heavily sighed, rolling my eyes at the same time. Walking out dripping wet, the chill of the hotel room air hit me like a slap, raising goosebumps across my damp skin.

"Ezra, where are the towels?" I called out, my voice echoing slightly in the quiet room. He was asleep, curled up on the far side of the bed, his black hair a dark halo against the crisp white sheets.

The sight of him, so peaceful, struck me hard. I hadn't thought about the sleepless nights he must have endured while I was in the hospital, the nights spent worrying about me, about whether I'd make it. This whole situation—me, a recovering suicide attempt survivor, sharing a hotel room with my ex, who had somehow forgiven me and became my boyfriend again—felt surreal. Guilt gnawed at me, a familiar companion. My big secret weighed heavily on my mind. Would Ezra leave me again, if I told him?

I grabbed a fluffy blanket from the foot of the bed and carefully tucked it around Ezra. He stirred slightly, murmuring something unintelligible, then settled back into sleep. The sight of him, vulnerable and peaceful, tugged at something deep inside me. It wasn't just guilt. It was a profound sense of gratitude. A gratitude that transcended the messy complexities of our relationship.

Looking around the room, my eyes landed on a stack of neatly folded towels on a small table. Relief washed over me. A small victory in a week filled with monumental ones. I grabbed a towel, its softness a welcome contrast to the rough edges of my recent past. As I dried myself, the scent of lavender from the soap lingered, a subtle reminder of the calm I was striving for. When I was finally dry, I pulled on the clothes Ezra had laid out for me.

"Ah, shit. I fell asleep." Ezra said, his voice heavy with exhaustion. I walk over to his bed side and sit on the edge.

"You looked so peaceful. I didn't want to wake you."

His brown eyes looked at me adoringly but I could also see the sadness that stole the light in them. The dark circles from lack of sleep, evidence of the hell I put him through. Guilt was crawling up my spine like the fingers of decay and strangling my heart. I really fucked up. I'm still fucking up. My secret was at the tip of my tongue.

'I was trained to kill, E. My father raised a monster.'

"You should have woken me up, Jas. We have things to do." He said, sitting up on the mattress. I looked away from his face, I couldn't bare to see what I had done to him. I couldn't tell him now.

"What is there to do? Besides, get my car back." I said. He reached over and gently turned my face to his but I closed my eyes.

"Are you ok?" His voice was etched with worry. "Why won't you look at me?"

I hated that I began to cry silent tears. When did I become so emotional? He wouldn't let me go. That strong hand on my jaw felt both comforting and suffocating, a physical manifestation of the complicated mess we were.

"How can you stand the sight of me?! All I do is hurt you." I choked out, the words raw and laced with self loathing. He wiped away my tears, his touch gentle yet firm, and kissed me. The kiss started softly, a balm to my raw nerves, but quickly intensified. It was a desperate craving, a collision of longing and pain. The need to feel something, anything, other than the hollow ache inside that consumes me.

My hands explored his chest, the heat flaring between my legs. I kissed and sucked his neck, leaving a mark, a testament to our volatile connection.

"Jasper, we need to stop," he said, his voice strained. But I couldn't. Or maybe I could but I didn't want to. I touched him, feeling the hardness beneath his clothes, a raw energy mirroring my own.

"You want me. So, have me." I whispered, the words a challenge to him, a challenge to myself.

"Fuck, Jasper. I said stop." he finally managed, his voice thick with a mix of desire and frustration. The abrupt halt was as jarring as the previous intensity. The sudden silence in the room was deafening. I pulled away, the heat between my legs fading as quickly as it had ignited. The distance I created wasn't just physical. It was an emotional chasm. I stood, the cheap carpeting cold beneath my feet. The raw need was gone, replaced by a chilling emptiness.

"Ok, I'll stop." I whispered, my hands in the air in a placating gesture. Ezra was staring at me, concern etched on his face.

"Your health is important to me. We won't be able to do anything for a few weeks."

"A few weeks?! Ezra, you're kidding. Right? You can't be serious." I said, the panic rising in my throat. He got up, his black hair falling slightly over his forehead, and walked over to the mirror hanging on the wall, his reflection a stark contrast to the chaos in my head.

"I'm entirely serious, Babe." He said, gently touching the mark I'd left on his neck, a testament to the passion that burned between us, a passion that threatened to consume me. All I could think about was giving him more, pressing my lips against that smooth skin again and again. How was I supposed to resist the sexual urge I have for him, when he looks like he's been sculpted by the sex gods themselves? He's my everything.

"Bring a man back from the dead and give him hell on earth, instead." I groaned, the words tumbling out before I could stop them. The irony wasn't lost on me. Here I was, a self destructive force of nature, now clutching at the edges of a relationship that felt like the only thing keeping me tethered to reality. Ezra sighed, his patience wearing thin.

"You can't take matters into your own hands either." He said, his voice low and firm. The unfairness of it all struck me.

"Oh but you can?! That's not fair." I retaliated, my frustration boiling over. He's dictating the rules of our rekindled relationship, the rules of my recovery.

"Yeah. Well, I didn't jump off a bridge. Did I?" His words, though blunt, stung with a truth I couldn't deny.

"Low blow, Ezra." I muttered, but even as I said it, I knew he was right. He grabbed my hand, his touch surprisingly gentle, and pulled me towards the exit. Leaving the hotel room felt like leaving a pressure cooker, the air outside suddenly crisp and clean.

"Let's go. We have to get your car and make the long ass drive back home." He said, walking down the hall of the hotel with my hand in his. I wondered if he would make a habit out of holding my hand in public. I admit, it felt natural but it didn't stop my heart from beating erratically.

\

CHAPTER 20

EZRA'S POV

Every day has twenty four hours, but today felt like such a long day. The minutes went by so slowly. It felt like forever before I finally made it home to my small, cluttered apartment. Jasper immediately stripped down to his underwear and belly flopped onto my bed. He could be over the top sometimes, but this wasn't one of those times. The exhaustion was real, palpable. My bed looked like heaven to him, and honestly, to me too. But I couldn't indulge fully. My mind, a battlefield of worry, refused to let go.

Sleeping seems impossible these days. A gnawing paranoia that Jasper would die, a constant, chilling presence in my thoughts. Or the nightmares, vivid, horrifying visions of finding him lifeless. I should see someone, a therapist, actually. We both should. Jasper and I, navigating this dark, gloomy shit together, needing guidance. Maybe holding his hand would ease the terror, the constant fear of losing him. I just want to hold him and never let go.

I watched him as he drifted off, his ocean eyes disappearing under heavy eyelids. My anger still flickered. A raw, burning ember. I wanted to be understanding, truly, but the memory of his selfish act, jumping off that goddamn bridge, threatened to consume me. What if he'd succeeded? The thought clawed at my throat, a silent scream raged within me. How could he do that to me? To us?

Then, I looked at his face, peaceful in sleep, and the anger melted away, replaced by a wave of profound relief, a gratitude so immense it almost ached. He survived. He's here. I get a second chance, a chance to heal, to understand. To correct my mistakes. A small smile touched my lips as I watched the slow rise and fall of his chest, his features relaxed, worry banished from his face for a few precious hours. I would just lie here, keep my eyes on him, guard him with my very being. Until sleep finally claimed me. My eyelids fluttered closed, a heavy blanket of exhaustion pulling me under.

***

I'm running. The panic is rooted deep within my chest, a familiar ache mirroring the one that settled there after Jasper's... incident. The near drowning. He'd been so sure then, so final in his despair. Now, here he is again, on the edge of a skyscraper, the wind a howling beast mirroring the storm raging inside me. My black hair whips around my face, blurring my vision as I desperately try to reach him. My brown eyes are wide with terror. His dark, curly hair is tossed by the wind, his blue eyes wide with a fear I know too well.

A shadow, inky black and vast, clings to his shoulders, its claws digging into his flesh, whispering promises of oblivion.

"Jasper!" I scream, the sound swallowed by the wind, my voice cracking with unshed tears. Then the shadow turns. Its face is a grotesque parody of humanity. Hollow eyes, a jagged smile revealing far too many teeth, and a patchwork of red scars marring its skin. A monstrous, nightmarish appearance. It's the face of my own deepest fears, amplified, made tangible. The monster's hideous grin is almost a mocking imitation of Jasper's playful smirk, the one that always melted my resolve.

I can almost feel the warmth of Jasper's hand reaching for mine, almost touch his skin before it's gone. He falls. The shadow dissolves. Only the wind whistles a mournful song. A cold whisper snakes into my ear, its voice a chilling rasp, "You can't save him." I whirl around to face the disembodied voice, only to meet the same horrifying face, its jaws agape, a suffocating darkness yawning before me. It's monstrous head looms closer, filling my vision, erasing the city, the sky, everything except its grotesque grin. It consumes me.

***

My eyes snap open. My breathing is labored. I shoot up right in my bed. It was just a dream. Fuck. I fell asleep. When will these fucking nightmares end?! The familiar icy grip of panic constricts my chest. It's always the same...the churning water, Jasper's face, pale and lifeless, slipping beneath the surface. I try to calm myself. Focus on my breathing, instead. I check my phone for the time. It's four in the morning.

"Are you ok?" Jasper croaks out, heavy with sleep. His voice, a low rumble that usually sends shivers of a different kind down my spine, only adds to the unsettling quiet of the predawn hours.

"I'm ok. Go back to sleep." I manage, my voice raspy. He turns over and softly snores. Doubtful that I'll be able to sleep, a familiar wave of exhaustion washes over me, but not the kind that lets you rest. I get out of bed and stand to my full height, my black hair falling over my eyes. The familiar routine begins. Jasper is going to want pancakes later. So, I'll just make them now. Cooking is a good distraction.

The rhythmic chopping, the careful measuring, the sizzle of butter in the pan. It's a ritual born from necessity, a way to channel the restless energy that threatens to consume me. Mise en place. This is what my life has come to. Making breakfast food at the crack of dawn because I can't smoke the anxiety away. Man, a cigarette would be heaven right now. Just one sweet inhale of nicotine as the paper turns to ash. The craving hits hard, a physical ache in my chest. I mix the ingredients into a batter and turn the stove on. This is the longest I've gone without smoking since I was fifteen. I don't even remember why I started smoking in the first place.

I'm kind of proud of myself for keeping my promise to Jasper. I'd do just about anything for him. Which is why these night terrors are freaking me the fuck out. The nightmares aren't just about the near drowning. They're about the fear of losing him again, a fear so profound it threatens to drown *me*. The pancakes are almost done, golden brown and fluffy. Just as I flip the pancake, I hear footsteps behind me.

"What the hell are you doing?" Jasper says while rubbing his eyes.

"Um, pancakes." I point to the stove with the spatula in my hand.

"Yeah, I see that but why?"

"Honestly, I couldn't sleep." I replied as I place the pancake on a plate.

"Stop. No more pancakes. Bed. Now. Come on." He said while removing the spatula from my hand and turning the stove off.

"Jasper!"

"No, don't 'Jasper' me. Let's go. Only crazy people cook at the ass crack of dawn." He grabbed my hand and dragged me to my room.

"I can't sleep, Jas. There's no point." I groaned. He wouldn't listen. I got dragged all the way to bed and he laid his head on my chest. A full proof plan to keep me in place. I couldn't resist digging my fingers through his curly hair and slowly a smile crept onto my face. His stubbornness to continue to fight me never fails.

"See? You're already relaxed." He said with a smile. Truthfully, I was relaxed but I wasn't sleepy. More than anything I just wanted to kiss his plump lips and make him orgasm. That would be a much better distraction. Far better than cooking or smoking. My body easily exposed what my mind was thinking and though I'm not ashamed of it, I didn't really want to explain how my mind went from sleep to sex in a matter of seconds.

"Jas, can I get some space?" I try to say nonchalantly but it really came out more strained.

"What? You never want space." He said as he lifted his head to look me in the eyes. Those blue eyes, usually sparkling with mischief, held a genuine question.

"Move, Jasper. Please." He rolls over on his side and looks at me perplexed. I quickly get up and run to the bathroom. The cool tile against my bare feet was a small comfort.

"Ezra, are you trying to hide a boner?" I could practically hear the smile in his voice. Jasper, always perceptive, always teasing. I mentally curse how well he knows me.

"What makes you say that?" I said through the closed door. He knocks and jiggles the doorknob. The sound of his laughter echoed through the bathroom, a sound that usually filled me with joy, but now felt like a mocking soundtrack to my mortification.

"Come on, E. Open up." This is becoming more and more embarrassing as the seconds tick by. A grown man hiding in the bathroom due to an inappropriate boner. Not the distraction I would have hoped for.

"Jasper, privacy." I managed to say, as I tried to force my cock down.

"Open the door. So, I can fix your problem. I don't understand why you're hiding it." The amusement was clear in his tone. He was enjoying this a little too much. Needless to say, I reluctantly opened the door. He had a sexy smirk and a mischievous glint in his blue eyes. He stepped forward and fervently kissed my mouth. An action I wholeheartedly allow myself to get lost in. Tongues clashing and teeth biting. He's more than just a distraction. He's my favorite drug. For a moment I reciprocate the passion but my mind let one negative thought through and ruined the high. I pulled away from Jasper and fought the urge to cry. *You can't save him.*

"What just happened?" Jasper furrowed his brows and had concern etched in his facial expression. I step to the side and exit the bathroom without a word.

"Ezra, I'm talking to you. What's wrong?"

What could I say? Lying was never easy for me but the truth felt stupid to me. I should be able to be unaffected by nightmares and stupid thoughts. I'm not typically the kind of guy who needs to puff out his chest and act tough to feel like a man but right now I feel like I need a bit of that because I'm being a damn pussy over some silly dream.

"Sorry, Jas. How about we just go back to sleep, yeah? Sex can wait. We can't stress your heart anyway." I managed to say.

"You're starting to freak me out, E. What aren't you telling me? Whatever it is, you can tell me." I can feel his warmth as he stands close behind me. I close my eyes and think of a way to put my feelings into words.

"I don't know how to say it without being an asshole but your suicide attempt has fucked me up in ways that I'm not handling very well."

I turn around to face him. Guilt is all over his face and I immediately feel like an asshole. Fuck. I try to cup his face in my hands but he dodges me.

"I'm not going to do it again. I promised you." He said. I take a deep breath because I know the next few words out of my mouth is going to start an argument. The words tumbled out in a rush, raw and unfiltered.

"It doesn't matter. I'm still paranoid. I still have nightmares about it every fucking night and I'm still pissed that you would do it in the first place. Everything isn't all better just because you said sorry and made a few promises. Watching your body lay lifeless in a hospital strapped to all kinds of monitors and wondering if you'd ever wake up has fucked me up! The damage is done, Jasper!"

I didn't mean to raise my voice but my emotions are running high. I haven't slept properly in days and I've been stuck in this depressing fog. Shit was starting to get to me. Jasper frowns and takes two steps back.

"That's not fair. I was in a dark place. My thoughts made sense to me at the time. I had been drinking. And I didn't just apologize for the sake of being forgiven. I meant every word. If I could change it all, I would." He said. The tension between us was unbearable. The dark cloud hanging above us grew darker and heavier. I could feel the wedge tearing us apart. I sit down on my bed and rest my elbows on my knees, my head hanging low.

"Jasper, I'm not attacking you. I'm just going through a really tough time. I need space to avoid saying or doing something that I'll regret." I lift my head to look him in the eyes. You can see the soul through the eyes. I just want to get a glimpse of his perfect blue eyes and find understanding. He just stands still. Like he's processing everything that just happened. It's a little nerve wracking.

"Do you want me to go now?" He said.

"No. Don't be silly. We're going back to bed." I said, holding my hand out for him. He looks at my hand for a second and then back at my face. I was going to give up but then he grabbed it. I pull his body between my legs and rest my forehead on his toned stomach. Jasper uses his free hand to lift my chin.

"It took me a long time to admit my feelings for you and now that I have, it feels like you're walking away. I won't go to bed with you, if that's the case. This feeling is exactly why I stay away from relationships." He said. I could feel the walls he began to put back up around his heart with every word he spoke. The wedge was growing bigger. Fuck.

"We're not breaking up. I just got you back. Space does not mean break up. So, come to bed with me." I said. Jasper pushes me back onto the bed and lies on top of me, his face hovering over mine.

"Good."

I place a chaste kiss on his lips and we both lay properly on the bed. My head on my pillow and my blanket covering my lower half. I'm actually exhausted. Which sucks because I have to go back to work today.

CHAPTER 21

JASPER'S POV

It's been three weeks of no sex. Nothing. Zilch. Nada. My libido's screaming bloody murder, a symphony of blue balls only I can hear. The doctor, that sanctimonious prune, refuses to give me the all clear, even though I feel perfectly fine! Perfectly fine, except for the simmering rage that's threatening to boil over and scorch the already charred remains of my patience. I'm losing it. Seriously losing it. I quit my job. A monumental act of idiocy. And now I'm staring down the barrel of my savings account. My apartment now feels like a suffocating mausoleum.

Ezra's been a saint, practically my nurse, but his recent need for "space" has morphed into an icy chasm. He's started seeing a shrink and tried to convince me to join him. Me? Spill my guts to some stranger? HELL. NO. He says it's for his night terrors, but I'm not buying it. If therapy was really helping, wouldn't he be less...distant? This whole situation is driving me batty.

The real kicker? Liam. Ezra's "friend" from group therapy. They're practically conjoined at the hip, their daily coffee dates a constant, irritating reminder of my own desolate existence. Every time Ezra's on his phone, it's Liam this, Liam that. Pictures of them laughing together, Liam's arm casually draped across Ezra's shoulder.

It's a blatant display of affection, and the jealousy is a bitter, unwelcome guest. I should be happy for him, I tell myself, but the truth is, my insecurities are twisting this into a grotesque parody of support. I watch him slip away, becoming more distant each day, and I feel a cold dread settling in my chest. It's not just the lack of sex. It's the growing sense of being replaced, of being superfluous in the life of the man who once swore he loved me.

The man I still love with every fiber of my being, even as he drifts farther and farther away

.

I grab my phone from the nightstand to check the time. It's two in the morning. Ezra is working a shift at the club while I lay here in bed, struggling to sleep. I really need to start applying for a job of some kind. Get back into a routine of some sort.

"Fuck this." I whisper to myself. I get up from my bed and turn the lamp on. I can't just sit in the dark, staring at my ceiling. I'm going out. I don't fucking know where but I'm going. I walk over to my dresser and open a drawer full of folded clothes. I pull out a red tee shirt and some gray sweatpants. After I dress myself, I grab my car keys and head out.

I don't have a destination in mind. I'm just driving aimlessly, the highway blurring under the glow of streetlights. It's 3 AM, the world outside muted and sleepy, a drastic difference to the restless energy buzzing inside me. The urge to keep moving clashes with a gnawing emptiness, a void only a sugar rush and maybe... some human connection can fill.

That's how I end up at a 24 hour convenience store, the fluorescent lights harshly illuminating the aisles. I grab a ridiculous amount of junk food... chips, candy bars, soda. A monument to impulsive desires, and drop it unceremoniously on the counter.

"Wow. All of this just for you?" The cashier, a girl with shoulder length brown hair and big, expressive brown eyes, asks with an oddly cheerful nosiness. She's undeniably cute, radiating this bright, almost aggressive optimism.

"Do you question all your customers?" I retort, a smirk playing on my lips. She just smiles, a mischievous glint in her eyes, and starts scanning the items.

"Just the really hot ones." she flirts shamelessly.

I can't help but smile. It's been a while since anyone has flirted with me with such unapologetic boldness. It's disarming, refreshing even. I take a moment to really look at her. She's petite, maybe five foot three, all bright energy contained in a surprisingly small package. There's a genuine sweetness to her, unlike the jaded cynicism I've grown accustomed to.

"Yes, this is all for myself." I answer her earlier question, my voice softer now, a little warmer.

"You're cute when you smile." She giggled. There was something joyful in her eyes. As if nothing could ever go wrong in her world. So strange.

"Thank you but I'm in a relationship." I awkwardly answered. She laughed some more as she finished up scanning the items on the counter and bagged them.

"You're just so adorable! It's ok, though. I respect that you have respect for your relationship. Which only makes me like you more. So, I'll tell you what..this is my number and I hope you use it because I make an amazing friend. Also, your snacks are free." She scribbled her phone number on my hand and never stopped smiling as she handed me the bag of junk food.

"I really can't walk out of here without paying for this stuff." I smiled nervously. This girl was crazy. Wouldn't she be fired?

"Dude, I own this little shop. I'm just covering one of my employees' shift because they had an emergency." She said.

"That's all great and all but I still wouldn't feel right not paying you."

She squinted her eyes and leaned against the counter. I suddenly felt uncomfortable under her gaze. I shifted awkwardly on my feet. Then she smiled.

"Ok. Then you owe me coffee in exchange for those snacks."

I debated for awhile but ultimately decided that she seemed harmless. A little strange for sure but definitely harmless. Ezra would like her.

"What's your name?" I asked her.

"Emmie. You?"

I wondered if that was short for something but decided not to ask.

"Jasper." I replied. Just then my phone began to ring in my pocket. "Um, I have to take this but I'll definitely call you for that coffee, Emmie."

I walked out the store and answered Ezra's call.

"Hello?" I said, settling into my car, the leather cool against my skin.

"Where the heck are you?" Ezra's voice was laced with irritation.

"How do you know I'm not home?" I challenged playfully, already picturing his dark hair, his intense deep brown eyes, probably slightly narrowed in that adorable way he had.

"Jas, I'm in your apartment. Where are you?"

"I'm sitting in my car, E." I sighed.

I heard muffled sounds from his end, like he was pacing. Then silence.

"So, you came by to visit me?" I purred into the phone, already planning my grand entrance.

"I'm just gonna go home, Jas." His voice was flat, the calm betraying nothing of what I knew was going on inside him. Panic flared in my chest.

"No! I'm on my way! Don't leave!" I blurted out quickly. I toss my phone and it lands with a thud on the passenger seat. The engine roared to life, and I sped towards home, my heart pounding a frantic rhythm against my ribs. I parked haphazardly, the crooked angle a testament to my haste, and burst through the apartment door.

"Baby, I'm home!" I shouted, the bag of snacks I'd bought almost forgotten in my hand.

"E! Baby! Where are you?!"

My bedroom was empty, the air thick with the faint scent of his cologne. For a split second, despair threatened to engulf me. Then, the telltale sound of running water. The shower. A smile spread across my face, chasing away the fleeting anxiety.

Knowing Ezra was naked in there, his gorgeous body slick with water, sent a thrill of anticipation through me. I pushed open the door, the steam hitting me like a warm wave, and the sight stole my breath. I couldn't even help myself. My cock hardened instantly, a painful, delicious throb against my jeans. Something about how the water trickles down his muscular, tattooed body. How it drips from his overgrown hair. I dropped the snacks with a clatter, the sound swallowed by the roar of the shower. My own clothes felt suddenly like a suffocating prison. I shrugged them off, the fabric pooling at my feet, and stepped into the steaming enclosure. My arms instantly circling around his narrow waist. My cock pressed against the crack of his perfect ass, a silent question hanging in the steam filled air. Ezra didn't flinch, didn't turn, didn't even seem surprised by my sudden invasion of his personal space.

"Hey, I thought you left." I said softly, my voice echoing slightly in the tiled expanse of my ensuite bathroom. Ezra pushed his wet, black hair back. He turned, his deep brown eyes, tired and shadowed.

"Hey," he replied, his voice a low rumble. "You're finally home."

I leaned in, kissing his lips. A kiss that tasted of rain and something else, something indefinable that sparked a flicker of unease. I missed him, desperately, but the chasm between us felt wider than the ocean.

"Ezra, what's going on between us?" I asked, the question hanging heavy in the air, thick with unspoken accusations.

He furrowed his brows, his calm facade cracking.

"What do you mean?" His voice edged with agitation. I didn't want to fight, I truly didn't. But the words tumbled out, a torrent I couldn't stem.

"What do I mean? I mean you've been spending more time with fucking Liam. Instead of me. I barely see you. We don't talk anymore, Ezra. I miss you. I'm going fucking insane and you don't seem to give a fuck. That's what I mean." The words hung in the air, sharp and cruel, echoing the cold tile of the shower walls I leaned against. He looked as though I'd slapped him, the color draining from his face. His usual placid demeanor was shattered, replaced by a raw vulnerability that almost broke my heart. But then, the anger flared ag ain.

"Jasper, I'm going to say this one more time. Liam is just a friend!" His voice was tight with frustrated exasperation. He turned the shower off, the sudden silence amplifying the tension. As he stepped out, the water clinging to his skin like a second layer, I followed. He continued, "I've never given you any reason to distrust me. I'm allowed to have friends."

He stared at me, his brown eyes pleading, but there was a hard edge of defiance there, too.

"I never said you couldn't have friends!" I exploded, the words tumbling out in a rush. "But Liam is not trying to be your friend! He's worming his fucking way into your pants and you're stupidly falling for it! Anyone with fucking eyes can see that guy's intentions!" Steam still hung in the air, a hazy curtain around the fight that had erupted between Ezra and me, a fight that somehow found us naked and arguing instead of fucking each other until exhaustion took over. My blue eyes were blazing. Why couldn't he see what was so blindingly obvious? I swear I was about to punch that smug fucker Liam in the face.

"Jasper, I'm exhausted. Can we not argue every goddamn moment we have together?" Ezra said, his voice flat, almost resigned. He skipped the whole drying off and getting dressed bit, instead flopping onto my bed, his black hair plastered to his forehead, the intricate designs of his tattoos visible under his damp skin. I watched him, a familiar ache tightening in my chest. The opportunity to study him, from head to toe, as I always loved to do, was there, but it brought a wave of sadness. I never got to touch him anymore. He'd pulled away, this calm, blunt man I loved, and I didn't understand where it all went wrong.

"I don't want to fight either," I said, my voice softening. "You've just changed, and I don't know where my boyfriend is because he certainly isn't whoever is here." His deep brown eyes, usually so full of warmth, met mine. He sat up quickly, approaching me.

"You don't mean that. I'm still your boyfriend. I'm still the same guy who fell in love with you. I'm sorry I've been a little distant. I'm just afraid of losing you." he confessed, his hands finding mine. Afraid of losing me? By distancing himself? The logic was baffling.

"The only way you're losing me is if you keep this shit up," I said, the anger fading into a raw need. "I can't deal with all this space, Ezra. I want my boyfriend back. Also, please fuck me. I'm dying to be touched!"

A genuine smile, the one that used to melt me, finally broke through his guarded expression. His hands moved to my ass, his fingers digging in, pulling me against him. The familiar scent of his skin, washed over me as his body pressed against mine. Damn. I loved this man.

"I want to make love to you but—" he began, that hesitant start always a prelude to something I dreaded.

"No 'but'. I don't want any excuses. I just want you." I said, my voice firmer than I felt. His hand reached for me, and I knew what was coming.

"BUT we don't have clearance from your doctor." He finished, and a groan escaped my lips. This was the ongoing saga of my life. A carefully constructed health plan that clashed violently with my desire for intimacy.

"BUT we don't have clearance from your doctor." He finished and I groaned. I stepped away from his hold and searched my dresser for clothes. I settled on some shorts and a tee shirt. Ezra got the hint and put some sweatpants on but stayed shirtless, leaving his inked upper body exposed.

"Alright, I'm going to sleep." I said, pulling the sheets up to my neck, a small act of defiance against the frustration simmering beneath the surface. He climbed into bed, spooning me from behind. His arm, warm and solid, settled around my waist. Everything felt peaceful after that. My eyes closed and I forgot all about the junk food or even the argument. All that mattered was him and I. I drifted to sleep, lulled by his gentle breathing against my neck.

CHAPTER 22

———◆○◆———

EZRA'S POV

I was immediately greeted with the gorgeous sight of my sleeping boyfriend's face. He went to sleep all grumpy, a simmering pot of jealousy left bubbling on the stove of our relationship, but right now he looks peaceful. The morning sun, a benevolent painter, streaks gold through the blinds onto the pale sheets. I want to get up and make coffee, the rich aroma a much needed comfort, but staring at Jasper for a moment longer, while he's unaware to protest my admiration, seems like a better use of my time. His words are still ringing in my ears.

"Why are you always so distant? Why are you always spending time with Liam?" Why is he acting all jealous all the time? He knows I love him. Isn't that enough? And what the hell does he mean by *"You've changed"*? I haven't changed. I still feel like the same Ezra I've always been. My phone vibrates on the nightstand, a jarring interruption to my quiet contemplation. I turn around and pick it up. Liam sent me a text message.

> Liam: coffee?

> Me: sure, dude. Just woke up.

> Liam: cool. See you soon.

I put my phone down and look at Jasper again. It's just coffee. Not a big deal. I get out of bed and borrow some of Jasper's clothes. A pair of dark blue jeans and a white shirt.   I head out the door and walk to the cafe around the block. I smile to myself, remembering how I met Jasper for the first time here, the chipped paint on the windowsill a silent witness to our awkward, fumbling beginnings.

My black hair falls forward, obscuring my deep brown eyes as I search for Liam. He's easy to spot. A splash of vibrant blue in a sea of beige. His long blue hair, intricately braided, makes him look like a modern day Viking, a stark contrast to the muted tones of the cafe.

"Hey, man. How's it going?" I say, my voice a little gruffer than intended. He looks up, his hazel eyes crinkling at the corners as he grins.

"Hey, Ezra. Took you long enough. I took the liberty of ordering your coffee ahead," he says, sliding a steaming mug towards me. The familiar scent of dark roast fills my senses.

I take a seat opposite him, the warmth of the coffee spreading through me. His hazel eyes watch me with a quiet happiness that feels strangely comforting.

"Am I the best or am I the best?!" he jokes, his playful tone cutting through the lingering melancholy. We met at group therapy, an unlikely meeting place for a friendship. Liam, with his boundless energy and unwavering optimism, was a beacon in the darkness of my anxiety and grief.

He'd listened patiently to my endless venting about Jasper, about the incident, the heart-break, the sheer terror of navigating life afterward. He'd never judged, always offering a comforting presence that I desperately needed.

"So, what are your plans for today? I got invited to a party and I definitely don't want to go alone." he says, his usual cheerfulness slightly dimmed. The idea of a party fills me with dread. The thought of forced interactions and shallow conversations sends a shiver down my spine.

"No way. I'm not going to a party. Getting drunk and being surrounded by a bunch of horn dogs sounds boring." I say, my bluntness escaping again. Liam's face falls slightly. He pleads, "Aww, come on, Ezra. I'll be there, and we don't even have to get drunk. We can just have a few drinks and play games or even dance. You've gotta come."

His words, laced with genuine desire for my company, tug at something inside me. It's my turn to be a good friend, to step out of my comfort zone for him, the same way he'd been there for me. So, I reluctantly agree. Maybe, just maybe, this stupid party will be unexpectedly okay.

"Alright. Alright. I'll go but you so owe me." I said.

Liam smiled, his hazel eyes crinkling at the corners, but the warmth instantly vanished. His gaze drifted past me, settling on something behind my back.

"Um, isn't that your boyfriend with... that chick?" His voice was low, hesitant. My heart felt heavy in my rib cage as I turned. There he was, Jasper. My Jasper. And with him, a woman who looked like she'd stepped out of a magazine. She was striking, all curves and confident smiles. The deep brown of my eyes narrowed as a wave of anger, sharper than anything I'd anticipated, washed over me. I didn't even think. I just stood, pushing my chair back with a harsh scrape, and marched towards them. Liam watched, his expression unreadable.

"Jasper." I said, my voice tight with a mixture of hurt and disbelief. He looked up, startled.

"E, baby. I thought you left." he said, his voice a little too casual, a little too smooth. The casualness made me angrier. I pointed at the woman, her brown eyes widening in alarm.

"Who's this?" I demanded.

"This is Emmie," he replied, his calm almost infuriating. "A new friend."

A new friend. He'd never introduced "new friends" to me like that before. The girl, Emmie, looked genuinely scared. The whole situation felt cheap and wrong, like a poorly written soap opera. This wasn't like Jasper or was it? This wasn't the caring, supportive man I'd fallen for. Jealousy, raw and ugly, clenched at my chest. It wasn't just the attractiveness of this "friend"... it was an inadequacy that I couldn't quite explain settling in my b ones.

"Hi, I'm Emilia. Emmie is my nickname. You must be the boyfriend." She said with a friendly smile. I gathered that Jasper must have told her about me because there's no way she could have guessed that.

"Yeah, I'm Ezra. The boyfriend. Nice to meet you, Emilia." I faked the biggest smile I could offer, still feeling uncomfortable with her. Her presence felt...invasive. This wasn't about jealousy. It was about the subtle shift in the familiar dynamic Jasper and I shared.

Just then Liam walks over. I had completely forgotten he was here.

"Dude, your coffee is getting cold." He said. I quickly glance over at Jasper and he is absolutely livid. His jaw ticks and his hands fist on the table. My eyes darted between the three of them. I needed to diffuse the situation before shit went down.

"Forget the coffee." I told Liam. The sudden shift in my voice surprised even me. It held an edge of command I rarely used.

"Jas, I know what you're thinking. Please, relax. Enjoy your time with Miss Emilia. I'll talk to you later, ok?" I leaned over and kissed him on the cheek. Mostly because he turned his face so I couldn't kiss his lips. Telltale signs that he's pissed off. I'm assuming he's trying to keep his cool for the sake of his new friend. Whatever the reason, I was happy a fight didn't break out.

"Let's go, Ezra. Shit is getting weird now." Liam said. I walked out of the coffee shop with Liam, his long blue hair catching the morning sun. He was a stark contrast to Jasper, my boyfriend who is all brooding intensity and dark curls.

Liam, he had a way of seeing past my usual bluntness, a kindness that felt both comforting and unsettling given the simmering tension with Jasper. I knew Jasper wouldn't approve of this coffee date. He'd already made that abundantly clear with a pointed glare from across the room. The uneasy feeling in my stomach was a familiar companion these days. A constant hum of anticipation for the next fight. I really hated arguing, but it seemed inevitable given the current trajectory of my relationships.

"What time is the party?" I asked, pushing down the anxiety that threatened to spill over. The party, a sprawling, all day affair thrown by some ridiculously wealthy kids Liam knew, was supposed to be a distraction, a break from the emotional turmoil. Liam's easy laugh, however, couldn't quite mask the underlying tension.

"It's an all day thing. Too early to drink, though, so how about we leave at five?" he conceded, mirroring my own thoughts.

"5 pm. Got it." I hopped onto my motorcycle, the rumble of the engine a welcome distraction. But even the familiar comfort of my bike couldn't fully silence the concern gnawing at me.

"Hey, Liam…You're doing okay, right?" I asked, staring at him. His quiet was a heavy silence. My worry was justified, he looked vulnerable, pale and tired.

"I don't want to ruin your fun, but I'm concerned you're coping negatively." I confessed. His smile felt a little forced, but he insisted he was fine, attributing his attendance to the sheer fun of it, and my presence as a comforting anchor. I believed him. He'd always been honest.

"Alright. Cool. Then I'll see you at 5pm. Now I have to get home. See you later." I said, pulling on my helmet. The roar of the engine as I pulled away felt like a release, a temporary escape from the complexities of my life. Jasper's disapproval, Liam's quiet struggles, my own problems. It all hung heavy in the air, waiting for me to return. But for now, the wind in my hair and the open road offered a brief respite.

"Later, dude." Liam called back, his voice a fading echo as I accelerated away.

***

The day went by agonizingly slow and I still haven't heard from Jasper since the coffee shop. I couldn't worry about it though. It was finally time to get ready and meet up with Liam. I'm honestly not in a partying mood but I'm hoping with an optimistic attitude, I can get through it. I start to undress, making my way to the shower. The water is running but before I could step in, I heard a knock at my front door.

I mutter under my breath a few profanities but I wrap my towel around my waist and head over to answer the door. The banging on the door was persistent. Someone better be dying. I was surprised to see Jasper.

"Why are you in a towel?" He asked, while shamelessly ogling my body. I ignored his question.

"Why are you banging on my door like a crazy person? Get inside." He quickly steps into my apartment but doesn't answer my question.

"Do you make a habit of answering your door naked?" He said with frustration. Alright, here we go, I thought. The arguments are beginning. I sighed and began to walk back towards my bedroom. He followed me.

"Jasper, you caught me before I jumped into the shower. You were banging on the damn door like it was urgent. Obviously, I don't make a habit of being naked in front of others."

He followed behind me and replied, "Why the fuck were you with Liam today? You didn't even say goodbye. You just left me in bed and decided to meet up with fucking Liam."

I knew it was coming. Even still I couldn't help the anger that boiled in me. I try to remain as cool as I can despite my frustration at having to have the same conversation about Liam again.

"Jasper, we are just friends. Why is that so difficult for you to understand? Liam is no threat to our relationship. You are the only guy.. No, the only PERSON that I am crazy about. I don't know how much clearer I can be." I said, facing him and looking into his eyes. It did nothing to remedy his frustration. He looked conflicted or maybe like he was trying to find the words to make me understand his point of view. I don't know.

He grabbed my face with both of his hands gently and as calmly as he could said, "Baby, I am not worried about you cheating on me. I'm telling you that Liam is not your friend. He has ulterior motives. Why are you so blind that you can't see that?"

I tried not to laugh because he just seemed so serious. He let go of my face.

"Ulterior motives? Seriously? What could Liam possibly want from me, other than being my friend?" I fold my arms across my chest and arch an eyebrow.

"You know he just wants to have sex with you!"

"Fuck it. I'm just going to get dressed and shower later. I'm wasting my time." I turn around and walk off into the bathroom to shut off the water.

"Where are you going?! We're in the middle of a conversation!" I hear Jasper shout from where I left him. I walk back to my room and remove the towel from my waist. He just watches me dig in my drawers silently. I look over my shoulder and see him adjusting his pants. I smirk, looking away.

"I'm going to a party. I was invited last minute." I said, deliberately leaving out that Liam was the one who invited me. I just don't see the point in upsetting him.

"You rarely ever go to parties. So, who is dragging you to one?"

I zip up my black jeans and button them while trying to think of a way to tell him it's Liam but I couldn't think of anything. So, I just blurted it out.

"Liam."

Jasper's face contorted with anger and he walked away towards the door to leave but not before punching a hole in my wall the size of a crater on the moon.

"Jasper! What the fuck?!" I followed him out.

"Don't talk to me right now, Ezra!"

"Hey! You can't just punch a hole in my goddamn wall and just storm out! Look at me!" I tried to grab his shoulder to turn him around but he shoved me off.

"Don't! Just fucking don't, E!" He shouted and then slammed the door shut.

What the fuck just happened? I glide a hand down my face to calm the frustration I feel. Should I follow him or follow through with my plans with Liam? I walk back to my room and grab my phone from the nightstand. I call Jasper. No answer. I try again and again but it always goes to voicemail. I check the time. Ten minutes before it's five. I finish getting dressed. Liam sends me a text, saying he's here.

Well, shit couldn't possibly get worst. So, I grabbed my keys, my wallet and put my leather jacket on. Out of the building I went.

I found Liam waiting for me, leaning his back against his car door. His blue hair in a bun on the top of his head and tattoo sleeves on display. He never just wears a tee shirt. So, I was surprised to see he had ink. Liam smiles when he sees me, a genuine warmth in his hazel eyes that momentarily overshadows my lingering worry about Jasper.

"I didn't know you had tattoos!" I smile back, trying to shake off the lingering anxiety. He looks down at his arms like he forgot the tattoos were there.

"You didn't ask." He replied, getting into his car. I sat in the passenger seat and put my seat belt on.

"I love getting tattoos. What else don't I know?" He started up the car, and I watched as he pulled out into traffic.

"There's nothing else that's interesting about me. I'm boring." He said, a hint of shyness in his voice. I felt like he was just being modest and humble. Which didn't surprise me because he's always shy about talking about himself. The truth was, I found him far from boring.

"Shut up. You're not boring. "

As we drove, the initial frustration over Jasper faded. The rest of the ride we were both in a comfortable silence. I looked out the window and watched the town blur by until we were in a rich neighborhood with lots of green lawns and trees. I instantly felt out of place and under dressed. Especially when we drove up towards a huge mansion that screamed luxurious wealth.

"How do you know these people? This is nothing like my crappy apartment downtown. I'm going to stick out like a sore thumb." I said. Liam just laughs at my nervousness and exits out of his car. So, I follow suit and get out as well.

"Relax. Friends of my family. No one is kicking us out." he says with a smirk on his face. What the fuck? Friends of his family? Is Liam wealthy? I'd known Liam, with his long blue hair and hazel eyes, for weeks. He was friendly, always cracking jokes, and always seemed genuinely interested in my life. But he'd never mentioned anything about being rich. He'd even joked about his "boring" life.

"I thought you said you were boring. This is far from boring!" I said as I followed him into the damn place. The moment the doors opened the music came blaring out. Inside was like a club only for the elite.

"Shut up. Being rich is boring. Perfection is boring. Let's just focus on this party, yeah?"

Immediately, drinks were placed into our hands and sweaty bodies pushed up against us as we tried to navigate the throng of drunk people. Not the kind of party I was expecting in a huge mansion. This is wild. The music pounded in my chest, a chaotic rhythm mirroring the nervous flutter in my stomach. Liam, surprisingly, seemed completely at ease, navigating the crowd with a practiced ease that only someone used to this level of opulence could possess. He was talking to people, laughing, effortlessly charming. I clung to his side, my black hair plastered to my forehead from the humidity. My brown eyes darted around, taking in the extravagant surroundings. Crystal chandeliers, priceless artwork, people dressed in designer clothes.

"That girl keeps looking at you. Go dance with her." Liam shouted into my ear over the music. I turned to look, and just as he said, she was staring shamelessly. Silver hair, striking eyes. She was pretty, I'll give her that.

"I'm not dancing with her. I'm good right here with whatever is in this cup." I shouted back, swirling the amber liquid.

"Why don't you dance with her?" I added, gesturing vaguely towards the persistent admirer. He leans in, his hazel eyes crinkling at the corners.

"No way. I can't dance."

"Lies! Show me your moves." I teased, smiling.

"I'm not drunk enough for that. Let's drink." he countered. So, that's what we did. We drank at Liam's friend's mansion party. A sprawling, opulent space that felt worlds away from my life. We drank copious amounts, joking like a pair of drunken idiots. But the girl, and the idea of dancing, stuck in my mind.

Eventually, fueled by liquid courage (and maybe a little stubbornness), I grabbed Liam's hand.

"You are definitely drunk enough now." I laughed, dragging him onto the dance floor. We stumbled between bodies, a chaotic ballet of limbs. He started bouncing around like a caffeinated octopus with jazz hands. Completely out of rhythm, a hilarious mismatch to the smooth R&B playing.

"No, no, no. You have to move your hips to this song like this." I instructed, demonstrating, a hot image of Jasper dancing flashing through my mind. Liam looked at me wide eyed.

"My hips must be broken because I can't do that!" He exclaimed. I grabbed his hips and guided them.

"See, now you're getting the hang of it! Now go show that girl those moves." I said, grinning. Instead of heading towards the girl, he looked at me, a different sort of intensity in his hazel eyes.

"How about you dance with me instead?" he asked, his voice surprisingly steady considering the amount of alcohol we'd consumed. The question hung in the air, the music a muffled backdrop. The girl faded from my awareness. I didn't see a problem with it. We were friends. Nothing more.

"Alright." I said, and grabbed his hand, spinning him into the throng. We were close, our bodies almost melting into each other in the crush of bodies. His hair, neatly tied back in a bun, had come loose, falling to his broad shoulders. It looked soft. I liked his hair. He finally started to move, a hesitant shuffle at first, then a confident sway.

He smiled, his hazel eyes crinkling at the corners, and put his hands on my shoulders. The pressure of his touch was surprisingly grounding a midst the chaotic energy of the party. This was a Liam I hadn't seen before, relaxed and playful. I was kinda happy in that moment that Liam invited me out. All my stress melted away like snow in the summer sun. My body felt light as a feather, and I let it move, fluid and instinctive, like a snake hypnotized by the music. My hands were on his waist, and we moved together, a strangely harmonious dance in the middle of the ocean of people.

A girl tugged me around and started dancing with me. I looked over my shoulder to Liam. He seemed fine. Still dancing. So, I focused on the girl as she pressed up against me. Suddenly, strong hands gripped my hips from behind and I felt Liam pressed against me, grinding into my backside, his breath warm against my neck.

"I thought you were dancing with me." he murmured, his voice low and husky, surprising me. He was different, almost a stranger. He spun me around, away from the girl, his hazel eyes locking onto mine with an intensity that sent a jolt of something unfamiliar through me .

"Whoa." I breathed, genuinely stunned. He smiled, a devilish glint in those eyes, and maybe it was the alcohol, but it was undeniably hot. I played along, mirroring his smirk, removing his hands from my hips and placing them on my shoulders. My hands found their place on his hips, pulling him close as we moved together.

"I'm the leader. You follow my lead." I declared, a playful challenge in my voice. His response was immediate and unexpected. He removed my hands, taking control of my hips, pressing his body even closer, the intimacy electrifying.

"I don't think so, Ezra." he murmured, his smirk widening. His face was so close I could see his hazel eyes dilated. Was he high? Or was this... something else entirely? The dominant, almost possessive way he held me. Was he really trying to dominate me?

"You're definitely drunk, Liam. Let's get some water, yeah?"

"No, I don't want water. I want to dance." He said.

"Dude, your eyes," I try to explain, gesturing to his slightly glazed gaze, "they're... a little off."

"I don't want to talk about my eyes. I feel good. I just want to dance." He said. I guess dancing a bit longer wouldn't hurt. We weren't drinking anymore. We could sweat it out. He hasn't let go of my body. I put my arms around his neck and let him move me in sync with his body.

"I thought you couldn't dance? You're moving perfectly fine now." I said in his ear, surprised by the unexpected grace of his movements.

"I'm not sure what I'm doing but it feels nice." He replied.

I'm so damn drunk but I feel good too. I understand what he's saying. I feel so light. I don't have a care in the world. Nothing matters in this moment. The friction between our bodies feels good. Too good. I'm getting horny. Too much fucking alcohol. My skin feels hot. Where's Jasper? I want Jasper. I close my eyes and I can see his gorgeous face. His curly hair, his blue eyes, his plump lips, everything. I need my Jasper.

I open my eyes and Liam is smiling at me. He's handsome. He's definitely attractive but he's not Jasper. The realization hits me like a cold wave. This isn't right. The warmth, the closeness, it felt intoxicating, but it was fueled by alcohol and a moment of vulnerability. It wasn't Jasper. It wasn't love. It was a hazy, drunken mistake waiting to happen.

"Take me home." I said abruptly, the words cutting through the music and my fogged mind. He frowns.

"Why? We're having fun." He said, his voice laced with a hint of something...more than just drunken camaraderie. I pull away and push through the crowd of people. The bass throbbed in my chest, a physical manifestation of the chaotic energy swirling around Liam's friend's mansion. It smelled faintly of expensive perfume and something vaguely floral, overlaid by the stronger scent of spilled beer.

I should call Jasper. My phone, clammy in my hand, unlocked easily. I dialed his number. It's ringing and ringing. Just when I thought he wouldn't answer, he picks up.

"Hello?"

"Baby, can you hear me?"

"I can hear you, Ezra."

"Are you busy?"

"No, Ezra but clearly you are. I can hear the party in the background."

"Come get me, Baby. I'm going to share my location with you." The words felt childish, even to my ears, but the need for Jasper was a sharp, urgent ache.

"Why can't Liam take you home?" Jasper's voice was laced with a dryness that hinted at amusement and something else... annoyance?

"Jas, I'm drunk. I want to go home with you."

"Fine. I'm coming to get you." Then the phone hung up. I find the exit and stumble out into the cool night air.

Waiting on the steps, the cool night air did little to sober me. The mansion loomed behind me, a monument to wealth and noise, a stark contrast to the quiet comfort I craved. I don't know how long I actually sat outside because I'm too damn drunk, but the world swam in and out of focus, the sounds of the party fading into a dull roar.

Eventually, the familiar rumble of Jasper's car cut through the night. He rolled down the window and I saw him, his dark curly hair slightly ruffled, his blue eyes holding a mixture of concern and that familiar, infuriating smirk. He got out of his car and, with a practiced ease, helped me up, his hand warm and firm against my back. The contact sent a strange jolt of clarity through my drunken haze. He looks irritated, but I'm smiling so wide my cheeks hurt. The sight of him was a familiar comfort a midst the chaos.

"Why are you smiling like that?" He says.

"I'm happy to see you. Kiss me." I said, still smiling like an idiot. The bass thumping from the party vibrated through the ground, a counterpoint to the frantic beat of my own heart. Jasper just arches an eyebrow. He's used to my bluntness, my obliviousness to the lingering glances Liam keeps throwing my way. He knows I only have eyes for him.

"Come on, E. Get in the car."

"No. Not until you kiss me." I pouted, leaning against his car, the cool metal a pleasant contrast to the humid night air. He finally rolls his eyes and gives in, the kiss as familiar and comforting as my own heartbeat. I smirk as he closes the distance, grabbing the back of his neck, deepening the kiss, exploring his mouth with a hunger that matched the raw need building within me.

The air crackled with unspoken desire. As we pulled apart, breathless, I spun us around, pressing him against the car. This wasn't just lust. It was a deep, primal connection, a silent language spoken through touches and stolen breaths. This urgent need to be close, to lose myself in him, felt different tonight, almost frantic.

Maybe it was the party, the overwhelming sensory input. Perhaps it was Liam's presence, a silent observer to our passionate display. The kiss moved from his lips to his jawline, then lower, eliciting a moan that was the most beautiful music I'd ever heard. I kissed him again, harder, deeper, until I couldn't take it anymore.

"Backseat. Now." I demanded, the words tumbling out of me in a rush.

"What?" he breathed, his voice husky with desire.

"Get in the backseat and take your dick out. I can't wait anymore." He didn't waste any time arguing. The urgency in my voice, the intensity of my gaze, it must have shown him exactly how much I wanted him. As he reached for the door handle, I caught a glimpse of Liam, still standing by the mansion entrance, his expression unreadable in the shadows. But in that moment, it didn't matter. All that mattered was the promise of Jasper's touch, the raw, unfiltered passion that was about to explode between us in the backseat of his ca r.

Jasper opened the back door to his car and I climbed in behind him. It was a bit cramped but I would make do. He laid down across the seat and pulled his pants and underwear down to his ankles. His manhood sprang free and at the sight of it, I knew exactly what I wanted to do. I opened my mouth and swirled my tongue around the head of his cock, until the tip of my tongue found the slit and licked up the precum.

I groaned, his taste driving me wild with need. I sucked on him, worshiping him in the only way I knew how. He threw his head back, his hands grabbing fistfuls of my hair. That only encouraged me. I bobbed my head up and down his length, listening to the sexy noises coming from his mouth, but I didn't want him to cum yet. So, I abruptly stopped.

"Why the fuck did you stop?!" he whined. I chuckled, the sound muffled against his skin.

"Be patient, Baby boy. Help me take my pants off. I'm too drunk to get the damn button." He sat up, his blue eyes, usually alight with mischief, now clouded with desire. He unbuttoned my jeans, then unzipped them, dragging them down to my ankles. Lust was clear in his eyes as he eyed my dick. The look made my cock twitch, beads of precum dribbling down my shaft. The intensity was electrifying, a raw, untamed energy that mirrored the passion simmering beneath the surface of our very different personalities. It was this contrast, this push and pull, that drew us together. I toed my shoes off, then took my jeans completely off and sat on his lap.

"Ready?" I asked. He nodded, his breath hitching. I grabbed his shaft, spit on it, and guided the tip to my hole. Slowly, he entered me, inch by delightful inch, filling me up to the hilt. Spreading my hole wide with his girth. He gripped my hips tightly and moaned.

"Oh, fuck!" he grunted. I liked that. I liked how good I made him feel. I began to move, bouncing on his cock as he thrust upwards. The windows began to fog up, the car rocked, but we didn't give a damn. He felt so good inside me, the tip of his cock rubbing against that magical little spot every single time.

"Look at me." I demanded. His eyes snapped up to mine. God, I loved his blue eyes. Blue is absolutely my new favorite color. I smiled as I continued to bounce. Riding his cock until it felt impossibly bigger inside me.

"Fuck, tell me you love me." he said, his voice ragged.

"I love you, Jasper." I whispered, the words as raw and honest as the cum I was about to release.

"Fuck, yes. Don't stop." he panted, thrusting deeper and harder. I quickly lifted his shirt, exposing his abs, just as I found my orgasm, releasing a hot load all over his skin. He looked so fucking pretty, sticky with my cum on his abs. That was all it took for Jasper to climax, his body shuddering against mine, his brows furrowed and his mouth fell open but his ocean eyes looked deeply into mine. I could see the love he holds for me in them and fuck, does that drive me crazy. We were both out of breath, our chests heaving.

"Sorry, I made a mess. I didn't think that one through. How are we going to clean up?" I said.

"Shut up. It was fucking great. I don't care about the mess." He smiled. I climbed off his lap, moaning as his cock pulled out of me. I plopped next to him and pulled my jeans back on. Jasper just pulled his shirt back down, leaving my mess underneath.

"What was the point of avoiding making a mess on your shirt, if you're going to rub it in like that?" I teased.

"Nothing a shower or laundry machine can't fix, Babe. It's not a big deal." He said.

The air in Jasper's car was thick with the scent of sex and something vaguely floral. Probably the air freshener he'd stubbornly refused to replace despite its age. My hair was a mess, plastered to my forehead with sweat. I opened the car door and made my way to the passenger seat, feeling the familiar thrum of contentment mixed with a touch of exhaustion. Jasper, ever the showman, hopped over the center console, from the backseat into the driver seat.

"You couldn't use the door like a normal person?" I laugh, my drunk mind finding everything hilarious for no reason at all. The truth was, I was still buzzing from the raw intensity of our encounter. The way Jasper's hands had moved over my body, the way his eyes had darkened with desire. It was a whirlwind, our relationship, fueled by passion and a stubborn refusal to let the differences in our backgrounds define us. Jasper smiles at me while starting up the car.

"Let's get you home." He said. The words were simple, yet they carried a weight of unspoken promises, of shared futures navigated carefully, one bumpy road at a time. As we pulled away from the mansion, leaving behind the remnants of our passion, I glanced at Jasper. Liam's lingering gaze from earlier today flashed through my mind, but I quickly shoved it away, choosing to focus on the warmth radiating from Jasper's hand resting on my thigh.

***

It took approximately twenty five minutes to get to my apartment, but we finally made it. I stumbled the whole way up to my front door and struggled with my damn keys, Jasper and I dying of laughter at how shitfaced I really am.

"I'm so going to regret drinking this much in the morning." I said through a fit of laughter, the words slurring slightly. The heat from the car sex still lingered on my skin, a pleasant warmth against the sudden chill of the night air. I began to leave a trail of clothes on the floor as I made my way to my bedroom, each discarded item a testament to our passionate ride.

"Don't worry, E. I'll take care of you, Baby." Jasper said, his curly hair bouncing as he followed close behind me, ready to catch me if I fell. My bed never looked so inviting as it did right now, a haven from the dizzying world spinning around me.

I didn't even realize when Jasper got under the covers with me, his confident smirk replaced by a gentle tenderness. His blue eyes, usually sparkling with playful mischief, held a soft concern. His touch was light, reassuring. The lingering scent of him was comforting. I heard the shower running at some point, a distant sound that faded in and out of my awareness. The warmth of his body pressed against mine, a silent promise of care amidst the chaos of my drunken state. The world outside my bedroom faded, replaced by the rhythmic lull of his breathing. I was knocked out as soon as my head touched the pillow. That night, nightmares didn't plague me. I fell into a dreamless sleep, a deep, restorative slumber that washed away the alcohol and the worries of the day.

CHAPTER 23

---◆〇◆---

JASPER'S POV

I don't know what time it is, but the sunlight blinding me tells me it's probably time to get up. I would have buried my face under a pillow and said "Fuck it," if it weren't for Ezra moaning and groaning like he couldn't be anymore miserable.

"Fuck..." he grunted.

"Can I kill Liam now, for letting you get this drunk?" I mumbled, my voice still hoarse from sleep. Ezra immediately turned his face to glare at me, his black hair a messy halo around his head.

"Don't start with me, Jasper. I don't feel like arguing with you right now." he said, his voice deep and husky. Fucking sexy. Wonder what he remembers about last night. So, I voiced my thoughts, "What do you remember?"

I watched as he furrowed his brows like he was trying to concentrate and backtrack his steps. His brown eyes, usually so warm and inviting, were bloodshot and irritated, darting everywhere but at me. When they finally landed on me, a flicker of something crossed his features. Confusion?

"I was drinking and cracking jokes, then I was... um, dancing... with... Liam. Then I don't remember shit else. How did I get here?"

I would be lying if I said that tidbit of information didn't piss me off. Of course, that motherfucker Liam took advantage of the alcohol Ezra was consuming. The way Liam's eyes linger, the sly smile... Ezra, with his caring nature, was completely oblivious. I felt a surge of protective anger. It wasn't just jealousy... it was a deep seated frustration at the unfairness of the world. Ezra and I, had found love, a love strong enough to withstand the friction caused by our differences, but not strong enough to overcome the opportunistic actions of some people.

"Of course, you don't remember me saving your ass or fucking me in the backseat of my car. Just the parts with fucking Liam. Ugh."

I must have said something wrong because he instantly jolted straight up into a sitting position and looked...shocked? Maybe.

"What?! We fucked?!" He said, exasperated.

"Well, don't look so disappointed. It's not like it's been forever since we've fucked or anything." I said sarcastically. Ezra immediately pinched the bridge of his nose and shut his eyes like he was praying for patience to deal with me.

"You know it's not like that, Jasper! You don't have clearance from your doctor! I could have killed you!"

I rolled my eyes at that one. He's being so dramatic. I'm perfectly fine. I got up from his bed in my boxer briefs to go to the bathroom connected to his room.

"Do I look dead to you? Besides, you did all the work. All I did was cum. I would have died happy." I shouted from the bathroom. Ezra walked in a few seconds later as I pulled my dick out to pee. The look on his face told me he was annoyed as fuck with me but you know what? I'm still really annoyed with him to. He's lucky he's hungover or I would have demanded he explained to me what the fuck was he thinking getting that damn drunk with Liam. Of all people. He began to brush his teeth.

"Jasper, you knew better. I was drunk. Obviously, I wasn't thinking straight."

"E, Baby, you were throwing yourself at me. Pinned me against the car and started to grind your dick against mine. 'No' was not exactly in my vocabulary at the time." I smirked at the memory. I flushed the toilet and put my dick away. Ezra just rolled his eyes and continued to brush.

"Well, I hope it was worth it because it's not happening again until you get the ok from your doctor." He mumbled. I didn't like that. I moved him over and grabbed my toothbrush with a frown on my face.

"I survived a fall off a bridge. I doubt the big guy upstairs would waste a miracle just to kill me with sex." I said bluntly. I don't even know if I believe in a God but if there was a God, it would be stupid to save me just to kill me a few weeks later. I mean how many people really die from sex? It's just so unheard of. Only creepy old men die from sex. However, Ezra was just not convinced of my invincibility and he was less than pleased to be reminded about the bridge incident. We finished brushing our teeth and leave the bathroom.

"Jas, you may not care but I do. Now I need some damn coffee in my system and some painkillers or I won't be such a friendly guy to be around." He grumbled on his way to the kitchen. I decided to get dressed but quickly remembered the mess Ezra made on me last night and so I'm going to need to borrow his clothes today. We're the same height and the same build. Well, I definitely lift more than he does but my point is, we fit in each other's clothes. So, I grab a tee shirt with some band he listens to on the front of it and toss on my jeans. I glide a hand through my curly hair and try to tame it. I walk into the kitchen and there's Ezra in nothing but his boxers hugging his ass just right. I can't even help feasting my eyes on all of him. I lick my lips, thinking about all the dirty things I'd want to do to him.

"Are you just gonna stand there staring at me?" He said. I could hear the smile in his voice. I don't know how he knew I was staring at his backside but it made me grin.

I walk up to him and grab onto his waist. Peppering kisses along his neck.

"Can you blame me? You know what the sight of you does to me." I reply. He turns around and faces me. I kiss his perfect lips and I let my tongue invade his mouth. He tastes like coffee but I don't mind. He pulls away, knowing how our kisses tend to escalate quickly.

"You look good in my clothes but you better return my shirt. Where are you going anyway?" He said.

"It's not my style, anyway. You'll get your clothes back and if not, you know where I live. And I'm going to hang out with Emmie." I said, as I let go of his waist to go put my sneakers on. He follows me to the front door, where I left my shoes.

"You mean the really attractive female that you introduced to me the other day? THAT Emmie?" He questioned, looking annoyed.

"Um, Yes. Is that a problem?" I arched an eyebrow.

"Nope. Have fun hanging out with your supermodel friend."

Is that jealousy? I couldn't help but smirk. A dose of his own medicine. Must taste bitter as fuck. He stomped off to his room.

"Whoa. Wait, a minute. No goodbye kisses?" I teased. He turns enough to glare at me and continues to storm off. I chuckle and head out to my car. I start up the ignition and change the gear into drive. An hour later, I pulled into the parking lot of Daisy Farms, the crisp air already hinting at the coming chill. Emilia really wanted to hang out picking out pumpkins.

I park my car and head on over to the entrance. And there she is, Emmie, perched on a stack of hay, a vision in blue jeans and a red plaid flannel shirt, unbuttoned just enough to reveal a glimpse of her white fitted tee. Brunette waves framed her smiling face, brown eyes sparkling with that infectious optimism. She looks beautiful.

"Hey!" She squeals and gives me a hug. I squeeze tight around her small, curvy frame.

"I made it." I said, while letting her go.

"Cool shirt. I didn't know you listen to heavy metal." She said. I had to look down at the shirt I was wearing.

"Oh, I don't. I borrowed it from my boyfriend." I smiled. She looped her arm through mine and began walking into the farm.

"Well, you should tell him he has great taste in music." She said.

"I didn't peg you as the type to listen to aggressive music." I replied, while taking in all of the pumpkins on the ground. I want to pick one that is perfectly round.

"What do I look like I listen to?" She asked amused by the topic of conversation.

I looked at her and pretended to think really hard.

"Hmm.. I would say pop songs or indies."

Suddenly, she was distracted. Pulling me towards some farm animals.

"Oh, look some cows!"

"Wow. Cows." I wasn't really impressed by some cows but she seemed really happy. So, I looked at some damn cows and then some pigs but eventually we went back for some pumpkins.

"Thanks for coming here with me. I know it's lame but it's kinda fun, right?" She said, with a stunning smile. The kind of smile that is contagious and makes you smile.

"I'm having loads of fun. Look at this pumpkin! It's huge." Of course, I tried to lift it. It must have weighed like fifty pounds. Totally easy to lift. I could bench press her, if I really wanted to.

"Let's take a picture!" She quickly takes her phone out of her pocket and took a few selfies with me and the damn pumpkin. I, somehow, ended up taking home the damn beast of a pumpkin and Emilia followed me there. We decided to cook dinner together.

"Ok, so what are we making?" I said, holding the refrigerator door open. She quickly took a peek in. She then opened the freezer door open but didn't find anything. She raided my pantry.

"This is such a dude home. Let's order pizza." She said. I laughed because usually Ezra's the one cooking. His apartment is the one that is stocked full of food.

"Alright. How about we watch a movie?"

She agreed and that's how we ended up on my couch, stuffing our faces full of pepperoni pizza and laughing at the chick flick she picked. Overall, it was a good day. I just couldn't help but wonder what Ezra has been up to today. So, I texted him.

> Me: Hey Baby

Ezra replied pretty quickly.

> Ezra: Took you long enough.

That made me smile. I didn't think he was waiting on a text message from me.

> Me: missed me?

> Ezra: Not even a little bit.

Me: Don't be like that. I missed you. Are you feeling better?

Ezra: Yeah. I just spent the day at home. Now I'm heading into work.

He seemed busy. So, I stopped texting him. The movie credits started rolling on the screen. I tossed the remote to Emmie. She smiled, that bright, genuine smile that could melt glaciers, and picked another movie. This one was a horror/thriller.

"Aren't you going to be too afraid to watch this?" I teased.

She threw a pillow at my head. The impact was surprisingly soft, but the playful aggression was undeniable. I grabbed a pillow and whacked her back, a laugh escaping my lips. My blue eyes met hers, and I knew this was going somewhere fun.

"Oh, it is so on! Pillow fight!" She squealed, her laughter echoing through my apartment. She stood up, her brunette hair bouncing, and started stalking towards me.

"No, no, no! This isn't some girly slumber party. We are two grown ass adults. Emmie, put the pillow down! Emmie! Shit!" She wasn't listening. She whacked me with a pillow, a gleeful cackle escaping her. Her direct, friendly nature shone through even in the chaos of our pillow fight. I whacked her back, and started jogging around the couch, trying to avoid her attacks. The apartment, usually meticulously organized, was now a battlefield of scattered pillows and laughter. She jumped on the couch, launching herself forward, swinging with the ferocity of a tiny, brown eyed warrior. I dodged that blow but managed to get her back. Her laughter was infectious.

"You hit like a girl!" She teased, her brown eyes sparkling with mischief.

"Rude! Take it back!" I said, my confidence a little bruised but my playful spirit un-yielding. I tossed her over my shoulder, a surge of adrenaline coursing through me. Her laughter, light and airy, filled the space.

"Put me down, Jasper! I won't hit you anymore! I promise!" But I didn't believe her.

"Nope. Take it back." She giggled.

"Ok. Ok. I take it back. You don't hit like a girl."

Finally, I tossed her onto the couch, the fight, and the laughter, subsiding into comfortable silence, punctuated only by the low hum of the horror movie playing on the screen, now utterly forgotten. My phone was buzzing. So, I answered the call.

"Hello?"

"You stopped texting me. Who's that laughing in the background?" Ezra's voice made me stop in my tracks. He seemed annoyed. I didn't feel the need to hide anything from my boyfriend, so I replied honestly, "I felt like you were busy, E. And that's Emilia. We're watching a movie." His scoff was audible even through the phone.

"She's still with you?" he asked, the edge in his voice sharper now.

"Um, Yes." I managed, a knot tightening in my stomach. Then, the line went dead. I stared at my phone, confused. The sudden silence felt heavier than any argument. Emilia, oblivious, was mid sentence about the hilarious scene from the movie, her laughter echoing in my apartment. This wasn't how I'd envisioned the evening unfolding. Ezra's possessiveness was a known fact, but this felt different... more intense, almost... threatening. Fuck, I hate it when he's mad at me.

"Hey, Emmie. Something came up. I gotta get going, but we should hang out again sometime soon. Today was fun." I said, the words feeling forced even to my own ears. The forced cheerfulness felt like a thin mask over a growing unease. Emilia, ever optimistic, didn't seem to notice.

"Alright. I'll call you." she replied, already pulling on her boots. I watched her go, a wave of guilt washing over me. I liked Emilia. She was genuinely fun but my boyfriend came before everyone. Even, her. I put my shoes on, grabbed my keys, phone, and wallet, and headed out of my apartment.

CHAPTER 24

―――◆◇◆―――

EZRA'S POV

The girls were topless and spinning on poles. The music was blaring, a throbbing bass that vibrated through the floor and up into my feet. The crowd, a sea of sweaty bodies and eager eyes, were all enjoying the entertainment. My job? Keep the drinks flowing, keep that crowd happy.

"Long Island Iced Tea, please." The female ordered. I wiped my hands on a towel, tossed it over my shoulder, and plastered on my most welcoming smile. I prepared the drink, the familiar motions soothing in the chaos, and handed it over. Then, a familiar voice cut through the noise.

"Ezra." I looked up and there he was, Liam, strolling towards me, a smirk playing on his lips. What the fuck was Liam doing here? He gave me a bro hug over the counter, his blue hair brushing my cheek.

"Liam. What are you doing here?" I asked, genuinely surprised.

"I'm here with some buddies," he replied, "Didn't know you worked at... this place."

I didn't think Liam, with his seemingly upstanding image, would ever step foot in The Velvet Rope. He was full of surprises, apparently.

"Having fun?" I asked, mostly out of curiosity. He grinned mischievously, his hazel eyes twinkling in the dim light.

"Do you have fun working here?"

His question hung in the air, a challenge, maybe even a bit of a judgment. I considered my answer carefully. Honesty was always my best policy, even with Liam.

"Look at this place," I said, gesturing around at the swirling bodies and flashing lights. "It's full of people with cash who want to drink. That's money in my pockets. Of course, it's fun making easy money."

It wasn't entirely untrue. I was damn good at my job, a fact that had initially drawn me to The Velvet Rope. Being single and impulsive, the easy cash and the thrill of the night life had been a siren song. But the truth was more nuanced. It had started because of Jasper. His killer blue eyes, full lips, and broad shoulders had kept me coming back for more. Now, Jasper was my boyfriend, and I stayed because the work was satisfying, not just financially but because there was a certain thrill in mastering the chaos of a busy bar, the artistry of a perfectly crafted cocktail.

Liam just laughed, the sound surprisingly melodic against the club's soundtrack. He looked good tonight. His blue hair was loose around his shoulders, falling in soft waves, and his short sleeved button down shirt showcased a collection of well done ink.

Suddenly, I hear someone else calling my name. I look around and spot my boyfriend walking towards me. Shit. He has the worst timing.

"Ezra! I came to-" he cut himself off, when he saw Liam, leaning against the bar, nursing a drink.

"Hey." Liam awkwardly greets Jasper. Of course, Jasper just scowls and ignores him.

"What are you doing here, Jas?" I said, wiping down the counter, the sticky residue of spilled tequila clinging to the surface, a familiar testament to another night at The Velvet Rope.

"I decided to come see you. Surprise! Can you make me a drink?" He said, trying to plaster a smile on his face. I glance at Liam and then back at Jasper.

"Consider me surprised, Babe. What do you want to drink?"

"Surprise me." He smiles, a thin, tight line that doesn't quite reach his eyes. I know he's upset, trying hard to be civil, but the jealousy is practically radiating off him in waves.

"I'll see you around, Liam. You should head back to your friends." I said, my voice sharper than I intended. He nodded and left, disappearing into the hazy, smoky atmosphere of the club.

"Why is it that Liam seems to always be around?" Jasper groans, his voice low and dangerous. I make him a strong drink, something potent enough to hopefully numb the edge of whatever was bothering him, and hand it over.

"We are not starting this argument again. Not at my job, Jas." He knocked back that drink in seconds. Maybe he should just go home. I can't have him distracting me at work. He seemed to read my mind.

"I'm not arguing with you. It was just an observation. I came here because you hung up on me and I didn't feel right just leaving things like that." He said, his tone softening. I hadn't meant to hang up, but Emilia is the epitome of everything Jasper seemed to find attractive before me. She's fucking gorgeous and that makes me feel... insignificant. A pang of jealousy, sharp and unexpected, stabbed through me. How long before he wants to be with a woman like Emilia again? I'm actually jealous of a woman. Ugh. What the fuck?

"I'm sorry, Jas. It won't happen again. I don't even know why I reacted that way but listen, go home. I'll head over to your place after my shift." I said, trying to sound reassuring, even to myself. He nodded, gave me a quick kiss, a little less passionate than usual, and left the club, leaving me to grapple with my own unexpected insecurities.

∗∗∗

A few hours later, I finally clocked out. I grab my belongings and head out to my motorcycle, my black hair catching the last of the setting sun. Sitting on the curb was a man with a familiar shock of blue hair, Liam.

"Liam?" I say, my voice calm despite the immediate concern that floods me. He turns slowly, hazel eyes widening in recognition. His face lights up, a fragile, drunken happiness.

"What are you doing out here? Where are your friends?"

He slurs, "Those assholes left without me. They said I was too gay or whatever."

Anger, hot and sharp, pricks at me. No one deserves that kind of treatment, especially not Liam, who possesses a heart of gold. Homophobia is a festering wound on society, and seeing it impact someone I care for fuels a protective instinct I can barely contain.

"Come on, Liam. Get up. I'm taking you home." I grab his arm, the feel of his tattooed skin surprisingly comforting under my touch. I help him to his feet, guiding him towards my bike.

"Whoa. I can't ride on THAT." he stammers, eyes wide, pointing dramatically at my sleek machine.

"Relax. As long as you hold on to me, you'll be fine." I smile, handing him a helmet.

I settle onto my bike, the familiar weight of the machine grounding me. Hesitantly, Liam climbs on behind, his arms wrapping tightly around my torso. His fear is palpable, making me chuckle softly.

"Ok! Holy shit! I'm really doing this!" he panics, or maybe that's excitement?

"You're doing great." I reassure him, starting the ignition. The engine roaring to life. At first, he's rigid with fear, his grip tight. But as we hit the highway, a transformation occurs. The wind whips through his hair, the speed exhilarating. His fear slowly melts away, replaced by a thrill, his arms loosening around my waist. I'm a little nervous about his grip, knowing he's drunk, but the ride is smooth. A smile touches my lips. His first motorcycle ride, and he's sharing it with me.

A few short minutes later, we arrive at Liam's house. A ridiculously luxurious place, all gleaming marble and hushed opulence, a stark contrast to my own modest apartment. Liam is definitely loaded. I helped him stumble inside, his long blue hair a messy halo around his flushed face, tattooed arms draped loosely around my shoulders. His hazel eyes, usually sparkling with mischief, were now glazed over with drink.

"Where's your room? Shhh... be quiet. You're going to wake up your mom." I hissed, as I navigated the dimly lit hallway. His vague directions led to a series of wrong turns. A bathroom, a closet, and then, incredibly, his sister's room. The awkwardness was palpable, thick enough to cut with a knife. Finally, we reached his room. I attempted to lay him on the bed, but he erupted into childish giggles, refusing to cooperate.

"Liam, I have to go. Jasper's waiting," I said, my patience wearing thin. "So go to bed, you drunk idiot."

He lurched towards me, seeking assistance, but his equilibrium failed him spectacularly. Down we went, a chaotic tangle of limbs hitting the floor with a thud. I groaned, the impact jarring my ribs. Liam landed on top of me, his weight surprisingly heavy, a peal of laughter echoing in the quiet room.

"Alright, get off me, dude. You crushed all my organs." I muttered, my voice tight with a mix of pain and exasperation.

"I'm sorry, I'm sorry, I won't ever drink again." he mumbled through giggles.

"Yeah, I'm sure you will." I replied sarcastically. The laughter subsided, replaced by a heavy silence. Lying there, with his body pressing down on mine, I felt a strange blend of annoyance and... something else. The air grew thick with an unspoken tension.

"What?" I finally asked, breaking the uncomfortable quiet. He didn't answer with words. Instead, he leaned down and kissed me. A soft, unexpected kiss that tasted faintly of whiskey and something else entirely. Something vulnerable and raw. Then, as quickly as it began, it ended. He stood up, leaving me sprawled on the floor, utterly baffled. The kiss hung in the air between us, heavier than the scent of expensive cologne that clung to his clothes. He climbed into bed. My brain finally started working again and I quickly got up. Leaving his house without another word. I tell myself that Liam was just drunk and didn't mean to kiss me.

***

I drive to Jasper's apartment like my life depends on it. The urgency isn't about some impending doom, but the overwhelming need to be near him, to erase the lingering taste of Liam's kiss from my lips. The memory, unwelcome and sharp, still stung. Rushing inside, I barely register the familiar hallway before I'm at Jasper's door. It's unlocked, as always. I push it open and head straight for his bedroom, shedding my clothes as I go.

The only thought in my mind is collapsing into his arms. I climb into bed, the cool sheets a welcome contrast against my skin. He's there, my Jasper. Curly hair plastered to his forehead, eyes closed, full lips parted slightly in sleep. He's breathtaking. So perfectly, utterly mine. That thought, that certainty, soothes the residual unease Liam had stirred. I lean down, pressing a soft kiss to his lips, the warmth of his skin erasing the coldness of the previous encounter. I close my eyes, the feeling of his nearness finally anchoring me. I must have fallen asleep because the next thing I know, sunlight streams into the room.

Jasper isn't beside me. Panic, a fleeting shadow, crosses my mind before I remember he's a creature of habit, a morning person unlike myself. I find him in the living room, sprawled on the couch, a bowl of cereal in hand, lost in some mindless TV show. Relief floods me, quickly replaced by a mischievous grin. I plop down next to him, cuddling close, enjoying the warmth of his body against mine.

"Good morning." I murmur, my voice still thick with sleep.

"You slept in. It's noon." he replies, the crunch of cereal oddly comforting.

"Got any plans today?" I ask, the idea already forming in my mind.

"Nope. You?" His answer, delivered with a hint of his usual playful confidence, fuels my resolve.

"I'm taking you out on a date today." I announce, kissing his cheek before standing. The spoon halts mid air. He stares at me, his blue eyes wide with surprise.

"What?" he asks, his voice a mixture of confusion and disbelief.

"You heard me. We're finally going on a date. It's about time. So stop looking at me like that." I smirk, turning to leave. His reaction is immediate, a blend of incredulity and mock outrage.

"Ezra, I'm not a chick! I don't need to go on dates to know you're mine! Ezra! Ezra!" He shouts after me, his voice echoing through the apartment. I don't respond, simply smiling to myself, completely enjoying his hilarious, endearing outburst. The lingering shadow of Liam's kiss is finally, completely gone. The date, a playful rebellion against the lingering discomfort and a reaffirmation of our bond, is precisely what we need. I get dressed to head out and plan a great date for us. Jasper walks in the room.

"Ezra, I'm not playing around. Stop it."

"I'm not playing around either. We made a deal. I won't buy you roses or treat you like a princess and you join me on a date." I say, my smile growing wider. He groans and flops on his bed. I chuckle.

"I'll pick you up at 4pm. Be ready." I said, as I walked out. My mind bursting with ideas for a great date.

CHAPTER 25

---◆◇◆---

JASPER'S POV

I've never been on a date before. It wasn't exactly a necessity when I could charm anyone to get my dick wet. Cindy never complained about not going on a date. So, I never had to go on a date. Ezra planning a romantic outing makes me want to throw up. I'm nervous that it'll be too lovey dovey and full of mushy feelings. Please, no candles and rose petals. God, please. I'll literally walk out the door. I look in the mirror and observe my reflection. Dark, curly hair in perfect spirals, blue eyes sharp, a smirk playing on my lips. I hope I'm dressed for the occasion because I've opted for a casual look.

A simple shirt and jeans. There's a knock at my door. I look at my phone. It's four on the dot. Ezra is punctual today. I walk over and open the front door. There stands my boyfriend in his leather jacket and black everything with his hands behind his back. His black hair falls over his eyes as usual. He's got a smile on his face.

"What's behind your back?" I questioned. He reveals a single rose in his hand.

"I couldn't resist. Don't be mad." he said.

I grab the rose and try not to beat him with it.

"You romantic sappy motherfucker." I grin. He laughs.

"Grab your jacket and let's go." he said. I jog to my bedroom, place the flower down on my nightstand grab my denim jacket and head out.

***

Ezra starts up his bike, the engine roaring a low growl that vibrates through my body as I cling to him from behind. Not my first time on this particular death defying thrill ride, but the thrill hasn't dulled. It's not fear exactly, more a healthy dose of adrenaline mixed with... well, let's be honest, a healthy dose of appreciating my boyfriend's strong back against me. And, yes, I enjoy feeling him up. It's not exactly a secret. Not anymore.

The wind whips through my curly hair, the scent of pine and damp earth filling my nostrils as we finally arrive at our destination. A clearing deep within the woods.

"You're not going to murder me, right? Because this seems a lot like a place you'd murder someone." I joke, already grinning at his knowing smirk. He's got those intense brown eyes, always watching, always assessing.

"Ha, ha. Very funny. I'm not going to murder you," he says, his voice a low rumble, "Yet."

The playful threat sends a shiver down my spine, a familiar tingle that comes with being with Ezra. He's blunt, sometimes even brutally honest, but beneath that tough exterior lies a caring heart. I love that about him.

"Seriously though, what are we doing out here?" I ask, hopping off the bike. He takes my hand, his grip surprisingly gentle. He leads me to a picnic blanket spread out in the middle of nowhere, a wicker basket resting beside it.

"I know you hate romantic shit," he says, a hint of a smile playing on his lips. "So, I didn't plan a fancy dinner or set up a room full of candles. I did something better. Something you'll like." My curiosity is piqued.

"Romantic picnic in the middle of nowhere?" I ask, my eyes widening as he pulls out two paintball guns from the basket. A slow grin spreads across my face.

"No. Well, there are sandwiches, but that's for later. You know, after we get hungry from shooting each other with paintball guns." he says casually. My father's training floods back. The precise aim, the controlled breathing, the satisfaction of a perfectly placed shot.

"You want me to chase you around and shoot you with paint?" I laughed, the sound echoing strangely in the stillness of the woods. He has no clue what he signed up for, considering that I never speak about the gun training my father put me through. The familiar weight of the paintball gun in my hand felt almost... comforting. My fingers, despite the years, still felt that familiar itch to pull the trigger. A phantom sensation honed by years of a grim childhood.

Ezra, my sweet, oblivious Ezra, with his dark hair and kind brown eyes, smiles back, completely unaware of the predator lurking beneath my confident exterior.

"Ready?" he asks, his own paintball gun held loosely at his side.

"Start running, Baby." I reply, my voice a low purr. He takes off, a flash of black hair disappearing behind a cluster of ancient oaks. Finding him is almost too easy. His heavy breathing, the snapping of twigs under his feet...it's a symphony of noise only I can appreciate. I let him get a good head start before I start the chase, the thrill of the hunt coursing through my veins. A quick aim, a sharp *thwack*, and the satisfying groan of my boyfriend clutching his side fills the air. The initial sting doesn't seem to slow him down. He spins, paintball gun raised, but his shot flies wide.

I smirk, the distance between us widening. Panic flickers in his eyes as he breaks into a run, his movements clumsy compared to my practiced agility. The years of training, though brutal, have left me with a hunter's instinct, a preternatural ability to anticipate movement, to anticipate him. Another shot, this time aimed for his thigh, a precise hit that stops him in his tracks.

"Damn, you got me!" he admits, his voice laced with a mixture of pain and grudging admiration. He drops his gun and raises his hands, surrender etched on his features, yet a smile plays on his lips. I approach, feigning another shot, trying to muster my most menacing glare, the years of training whispering tactics in my ear. It's a game, but a game with real stakes, even if the stakes are only temporary welts.

"Fuck, you're good at this." he pants, his breath coming in ragged gasps.

"Give up, Baby?" I ask, pointing the gun dangerously low. I can see the empty threat turning him on as his pants tent.

"Whoa. Let's play nice, Babe. You got me." he says, his eyes sparkling with amusement and something akin to awe. I lower the gun, laughter bubbling up from my chest, a sound that feels both liberating and dangerous. I drop the gun completely and grab the back of his neck, kissing him hard. All playfulness gone, replaced by a primal need. I push him against a tree, my fingers tracing the line of his jaw, and begin to kiss his neck, leaving behind my mark, a promise of more. He moans, a low, guttural sound that makes me grin. His brown eyes are heavy with lust when I pull away, the air thick with unspoken desires. I grind my cock against his through our pants, the friction a welcome addition to the already heightened tension.

My hand glides under his shirt, the skin beneath smooth and warm. I pinch his nipple, the gasp that escapes him is music to my ears. I'm so fucking turned on, so very horny. I would have had my way with him right there, bent him over and fucked his ass but I know he wouldn't let me. He cares too much about what my doctor has to say. Which makes no sense to me because I can run, climb and exert energy just fine. My father's training was brutal, but it forged me into something resilient.

"So, sandwiches?" I ask, a hint of a smirk still lingering on my lips.

"Yeah, sandwiches." he manages, a breathless chuckle escaping him. We pick up our paintball guns, the playful intensity of the game still lingering in the air, and head back to the blanket. Great date, indeed.

***

EZRA'S POV

It's been a week since the date with Jasper. It's also been a week since Liam, drunkenly, kissed me. My hair felt tangled, mirroring the mess in my head. Brown eyes stared at the worn wooden floorboards of my apartment, Liam's impulsive act a heavy weight on my chest. I can't let more time go by without talking to him. It's not right. He needs to know that it can never happen again. The guilt gnawed at me, especially considering Jasper's joyous news. My boyfriend, usually brimming with confident flirtation, was radiating a different kind of energy.

"Guess what?!" Jasper said, bursting through the door. Something big had clearly happened.

"I got a new job! Emmie helped me get a job as a bartender for weddings. Also, we can finally have sex because I finally have the ok." I get up and hug him, a genuine wave of relief washing over me. I don't love the close friendship he has with Emilia, but I can appreciate a good friend helping him out. He's finally getting back to normal.

"Congratulations. That's great news, Jas." I said, pulling back and attempting a smile. It must have fallen flat because he frowned instantly.

"What's wrong? You don't seem excited." It wasn't that I wasn't happy for him. It's just that the Liam situation loomed large, a dark cloud threatening to spoil everything. Telling Jasper would be a disaster. He'd overreact, and there's nothing to really freak out about.

"I'm excited. I am. I just have some things to deal with and it's stressing me out." A half truth, but not a complete lie.

"Oh. Well, maybe I can take your mind off it." he purred, his voice a low rumble. I want to have sex with Jasper but not while I'm feeling guilty about Liam. So, I think of something he'll say 'no' to.

"Alright but I top this time." The shock on Jasper's face was almost comical. He'd never seen me attempt to take control like that. I'm usually the submissive one in our relationship. This was a desperate attempt to put a stop to things before they started.

"But you never top, E."

"Exactly. I always bottom but this time I want to top you. What do you say?"

He sits on my bed. I follow and sit next to him. I hold his hand and intertwine our fingers. He's quiet like he's actually thinking about it.

"I can't believe I'm about to say this but sure, we can try it out. Just not right now. I forgot that I have to go meet up with Emmie." he'd stammered, the words hanging in the air like smoke. Emmie? Seriously? The relief that washed over me was almost as potent as the guilt. A simple excuse, so perfectly timed. I played along, a carefully constructed facade of nonchalance, hiding my surprise and relief at his almost too convenient excuse.

"Ok. That's fine. I have to head out soon anyway. So, meet up back at your place later?" He smiles and gives me a quick kiss on the lips.

"Ok, I'll see you later." He said and then he left.

As soon as the door shut behind him, I texted Liam to meet me at the coffee shop to talk. He agreed.

**

I spotted Liam sitting at a table in the back. His blue hair like a beacon, made him hard to miss. He waves me over, hazel eyes twinkling with a familiar warmth.

"Hey, I haven't heard from you in a week. What gives?" he said, his voice a low rumble. Does he not remember? The question hangs heavy, unspoken. I sit across from him, my black hair falling forward as I try to meet his gaze.

"Sorry, Liam. I've been busy with Jasper." I reply, the words feeling flimsy even to my own ears. He looks at me, a subtle shift in his expression, like he's sniffing out a lie.

"Or maybe you were mad at me for something." His voice is softer now, tinged with a vulnerability I hadn't expected.

"I wasn't mad at you. Why would I be mad at you?" The question feels defensive, even to me. He looks down at the table, drumming his fingers a restless rhythm against the wood. The silence stretches, thick and uncomfortable.

"Maybe because I kissed you." The words hang in the air, a fragile confession. He looks up at me, his hazel eyes searching, pleading for understanding. A wave of heat rises in my cheeks.

"I wasn't mad that you kissed me, Liam. I was confused and completely caught off guard. Please, tell me you were just drunk." The words spill out, a desperate plea for a simple explanation. A way to erase the unsettling memory, to neatly file it away under 'unfortunate drunken incident.' He doesn't answer, a silence more damning than any confession. Instead, he gets up, muttering something about getting us coffee. The flimsy excuse only serves to solidify my growing dread. It wasn't a drunken mistake. The thought hits me with the force of a physical blow, leaving me reeling. My heart pounds a frantic rhythm against my ribs, a frantic drumbeat of anxiety. What do I do now?

When he sits back down, the steam from two cups of coffee curls into the air, momentarily obscuring his face. He hands me a cup, the warmth surprisingly comforting. I take a tentative sip, the rich, dark liquid a small solace in the brewing storm within me. The caffeine's doing its job. Sharpening my senses, making the blurry edges of the situation a little clearer.

"You're right. I was absolutely drunk and I wasn't thinking. It won't happen again." He said. He sips his coffee.

"If we're going to be friends, it can never happen again."

Liam smiles and looks to the side then back at me.

"Are we good now? Can we just hang out?"

I chuckle feeling relieved.

"Yeah, we're good. How has your week been?" I said.

"I had to visit my therapist and work has been kicking my ass but overall, not bad. My mom told me to thank you for getting me home safe. She was pissed off with me even though I'm 23 and pay all the bills." He traces the edge of his cup with his finger. I found myself listening more intently than I'd anticipated, noticing details I hadn't before. His hazel eyes, flecked with unexpected green, were captivating. The way the sunlight caught his long, wavy blue hair, the subtle flash of a new tattoo on his neck... it was as if I was seeing him for the first time.

"I keep forgetting how young you are. I'm five years older than you." He smiled, a genuine, unguarded smile, as if my comment were a funny inside joke.

"You act like you're 80. You aren't that much older than me."

"You have pretty eyes." I blurted out, my own words surprising me. They hung in the air, clumsy and awkward. His face turns red and he stays quiet.

"What? It's true. I just noticed. My eyes are a shitty brown. You're lucky." I added. Just then my phone started vibrating in my pocket. I pull it out and see that Jasper is calling me.

"Hello?"

"Hey, Baby. I just wanted to know what time I should meet up with you later."

"Why? Miss me already?" I smirk, even though he can't see it through the phone. Jasper chuckles.

"No. Not even a little bit." He said. In the background, I could hear Emilia saying something but I couldn't hear what.

"You sound busy, Babe."

"I kinda am. Emmie can't drive to save her life. So, I'm busy trying not to die—That was a stop sign you just ignored! Oh my god. Pull over, I'm driving.—Hello? Babe?"

"Yeah, I'm here. Just text me when you're free and we'll meet up then, Jas."

I look up towards Liam. He looks bored and impatient. I feel kinda bad.

"Ok. I'll talk to you later, E." The phone call ends. I put my phone back into my pocket. I sip on my coffee. Yuck, it's cold.

"So, what are your plans for today?" Liam asks. My eyes look up into his hazel ones.

"I'm supposed to meet up with Jasper later. Whenever he's done hanging out with his friend, Emilia. Otherwise, I'm totally free."

He raises an eyebrow at the sound of that, the slight quirk of his lip hinting at something unspoken.

"She's way too attractive to just be his friend. How do you trust him with her?"

The casualness of his question irks me, a familiar sting of insecurity twisting in my gut. It's not the first time I've fielded these kinds of comments about Jasper and Emilia, and frankly, I'm tired of them.

"Are you implying my boyfriend can't keep his dick in his pants?" My voice is sharper than intended, the words tumbling out before I can censor them. Liam's face falls, the friendly demeanor dissolving into stunned silence. I see the immediate regret flicker across his features.

"Um, no. I was just saying...she's just...um, nothing. Forget it."

I stood up, the chair scraping against the tiled floor, the sound echoing my irritation.

"Alright. Well, I'm heading out. See you later, Liam." My voice is flat, devoid of warmth. He scrambles to his feet, his blue hair swaying. His eyes are begging me to stay, pleading for another chance. The desperation in his eyes almost makes me reconsider, but the sharp sting of his words remains. The unspoken jealousy is too much.

"Don't be like that. I'm sorry. Don't leave." But I don't care anymore. I walk away, leaving Liam to deal with the consequences of his thoughtless words.

CHAPTER 26

JASPER'S POV

"You're never driving my car again. Where did you get your license?" I said, as I kept my eyes on the road and drove towards the tattoo parlor. Emmie, a whirlwind of brunette wavy hair and infectious optimism, giggled from the passenger seat.

"Oh, stop it. I wasn't that bad. You're being dramatic." I glanced at her, incredulously.

"Not bad?! You ran two red lights, drove through a stop sign, and nearly didn't brake in time to avoid that kid crossing the road!" Her response?

"Nobody died, and your car's in one piece." It's like nothing could dampen her mood. She finds the silver lining in everything, a quality I both admire and find slightly terrifying. Her relentless cheerfulness is contagious though, and I found myself smiling. She's absolutely ridiculous, crazy, and always up for an adventure

"You are unbelievable." I said, the words tumbling out despite my simmering anxiety. Emmie smiles, her brown eyes crinkling at the corners.

"Shut up. You love me. I'm your bestie and besties bail each other out of jail." she retorted, her voice brimming with that familiar, infectious optimism. I pull into the parking lot, the stark white building of "Ink & Iron" looming before us. My reflection in the rear view mirror shows a dark haired, blue eyed mess. Even Ezra wouldn't recognize the nervous twitch in my jaw.

"I'd definitely bail you from jail, Emmie. Let's get this show on the road." I murmur, already regretting this impulsive decision. Stepping out of the car, Emmie loops her arm through mine, her warmth a strangely comforting presence against the sudden chill in my veins.

The air inside Ink & Iron hums with the buzz of needles and the low thrum of conversation. The scent of antiseptic mixes with something faintly sweet, a strange perfume unique to tattoo parlors. My heart hammers against my ribs, a frantic drumbeat against the rhythmic whirring of a tattoo gun in the distance. A gun I am not acquainted with. Go figure. I would rather take a bullet than get a tattoo that I have to commit to forever.

"You look like you're going to throw up. It's just a tattoo. Come on." Emmie says, her voice a reassuring counterpoint to the rising panic within me.

"This shit is forever," I protest, my voice a strained whisper. "I don't want to look stupid with an ugly tattoo stuck on my body for the rest of my life. I can't believe you talked me into this." The thought of a permanent mark, a visible commitment etched onto my skin, fills me with a sudden, overwhelming dread. Emmie's giggle breaks through my anxiety.

"Then get something that you know you'll love forever." she says, her usual bright demeanor somehow amplified by the intensity of the moment.

"What are you getting?"

She blushes and moves her hair behind her ear as if she were suddenly shy.

"I'm getting the letter J right below my ear. J for Joy because I'm so joyful."

Simple and cute. Just like her. We make our way to the front counter, where a heavily tattooed petite woman with neon yellow hair sat. She asked us if we had an appointment to which we replied no but she was nice enough to fit us in anyway. Emmie went first and was done pretty quickly since it was a tiny letter J.

I decided I wanted my first tattoo on my ribs, right below my pec. I felt the familiar confidence bloom as I took off my shirt, revealing my toned chest. I lay back on the chair, the sterile scent of the tattoo shop a strange contrast to the nervous flutter in my stomach. Emmie blushed crimson. The female tattoo artist shamelessly checked me out. Honestly? I didn't mind the attention. It was the playful smirk tugging at my lips that gave me away. Watching Emmie's reaction was far more entertaining. I winked at her, and her blush deepened.

Soon, the rhythmic buzz of the tattoo machine filled the air, the needles pricking my skin with a surprisingly manageable pain. The anticipation had been far worse. Not that I was afraid of the pain to begin with, I've been through worst. Emmie, ever the optimist, snapped a picture of me tilted to the side, arms behind my head, sporting a devilish smirk. It was a damn good shot. She'd captured the moment perfectly.

The buzzing stopped, and a strange mixture of relief and exhilaration washed over me. The artist meticulously cleaned the area, her movements precise and efficient. My new ink felt both alien and utterly right. I pulled my shirt back on, the fabric a comforting weight against my skin. Paying at the front desk felt almost anticlimactic. The thrill of it all was still buzzing beneath my skin, a physical echo of the needle's dance. The anticipation of Ezra seeing it, though... that was a different kind of electricity.

***

I text Ezra that I'm finally free. The anticipation prickles, a familiar excitement that always accompanies our reunions. It takes him a bit, but the familiar knock on my apartment door (A rhythmic tap, tap, tap that I recognize instantly) sends a jolt of pure happiness through me. I fling the door open, the scent of his cologne already filling my senses. He's all sharp angles and dark intensity, his black hair slightly tousled, those intense brown eyes softening as they meet mine. I grab the back of his neck, pulling him into a kiss that's both urgent and tender. Only when we run out of air do I finally pull back, my heart hammering a wild rhythm against my ribs.

"I missed you." I breathe, my voice husky. He smirks, that charming, slightly crooked smile that always melts away my defenses.

"I noticed." I grab his hand, pulling him towards my bedroom, the thrill of anticipation building with each step. I want to show him what I've done, more than just show him, I want him to feel it.

"I got something to show you." I say, a playful edge to my voice as I seat him on my bed. I stand between his legs, the familiar comfort of his presence settling over me like a warm blanket. Slowly, deliberately, I begin to take off my shirt, enjoying the way his eyes follow every movement.

"I like where this is going." he murmurs, his tongue tracing a path across my abs. I toss my shirt to the floor, a silent offering. He looks up, his eyes widening, the playful teasing replaced by something deeper, something akin to awe. He stops licking me. His expression is unreadable.

"Do you like it?" I ask, my voice a little breathless. He's staring at my chest, his gaze fixed on the beautiful calligraphy that spells out his name. The ink is still a little raw, but already vibrant against my skin.

"You tattooed my name on your body?!" His voice is a low, husky whisper, tinged with disbelief. I smile, a wide, radiant smile that reflects the content in my heart.

"Emmie wanted to get tattoos today, and I wanted something I'd love forever. The only thing I could think of was you." I explain. His hands find their way to my waist, his thumbs stroking my skin gently. He leans down, kissing the delicate curve of my hip, then looks up again, his eyes filled with a tenderness I've only seen in rare moments.

"I love it," he says, his voice thick with emotion. "Best gift I've ever gotten."

I push him down on my bed and climb on top of him. He smirks, that knowing glint in his intense brown eyes. I kiss his lips, a fierce, demanding kiss that melts into a softer exploration of his skin. My fingers trace the lines of his tattoos, the rough texture a stark contrast to the smoothness of his skin. I leave a trail of kisses down his neck, pressing hard enough to leave faint marks, barely visible amongst the ink. His scent, a mix of his own musky fragrance and the leather of his jacket, fills my senses. I shrug off the jacket, then his shirt, tossing them carelessly to the floor.

"Are you sure you want to top me? You know you love it when I'm in charge." I murmur, my fingers playfully toying with the button of his jeans.

"I do love it. I just asked to top to see what you'd say." He admits.

The audacity of it, to challenge my dominance, to test the boundaries of our relationship. It's intoxicating. I raise an eyebrow, a silent question hanging in the air.

"Did you expect me to say no?"

"Honestly, yes. I didn't think you'd trust me."

My fingers work swiftly, unbuttoning his jeans, the zipper a satisfying whisper against the denim. I pull them down, along with his underwear, revealing his hard, throbbing cock. The air crackles with anticipation. His vulnerability is a delicious weakness. The trust he craves, the trust he's dared to ask for, is freely given.

"I trust you, E. Fuck me." I demand, the words raw and urgent.

He grins, that cocky Ezra grin that always throws me off balance, and flips me onto my back. I didn't expect that. The sudden shift in power, the way his dark eyes, intense and brown, held mine. He kicks off his shoes and then his black jeans, the tattoos snaking across his legs a breathtaking sight, makes my mouth water.

He hovers, leaving a trail of kisses across my chest, each one a tiny spark igniting a fire. I grab a fistful of his black hair, lust pooling in my eyes as I watch him. He removes my pants and boxers with practiced ease, his touch both gentle and urgent. God, he makes me feel so good, so utterly seen. He takes my dick into his warm, wet mouth, and the moan that escapes me is involuntary, pure, unadulterated pleasure.

While his head bobs rhythmically, expertly working his magic, he slips two fingers into my mouth. I suck them, coating them in my saliva, a strange, delicious exchange. He pulls them out, and then, with a sudden shift, pushes a finger into my hole. I hiss, a sharp intake of breath, but the exquisite torture of his mouth wrapped around me drowns out the sting. He slowly moves his finger in and out, a teasing rhythm that builds the tension.

Then, a shift, a magical touch, a point of pressure that makes me moan again, a sound deeper and more desperate this time. My grip on his hair tightens, my knuckles white. He adds a second finger, curling them against my prostate, a wave of pure, overwhelming sensation washing over me.

"Fuck!" I cry out, the word a raw expression of the pleasure that tears through me. Ezra deep throats my cock, simultaneously thrusting his fingers inside, a brutal, beautiful symphony of sensation. He swallows, a guttural sound, while I'm deep in his throat, and the combined sensations send me soaring. He pulls his fingers out, stops sucking me, leaving me breathless and wanting more. A cocky smirk plays on his lips as he spreads my legs with his knees. He grabs hold of his dick, spits on it, the act both shocking and arousing. I feel the tip of his head pressed against my hole, the anticipation a taut, almost painful thing. I'm so fucking nervous, my heart hammering against my ribs.

"Relax," he murmurs, his voice a low rumble. "I'm going to go slow. Tell me if you want me to stop." I nod, barely able to speak. He slowly enters me, inch by agonizing inch, until he's completely inside. He doesn't move, giving me time to adjust to his size. It hurts, a raw, burning ache, but I've gotten this far. I'm not stopping now.

"Are you ok? Can I move?" He looks at me with concern. I nod again. Too damn speechless to talk.

"Are you sure?" He asks, again.

"Oh, for fuck's sake! Move, Ezra." My hair was plastered to my sweaty forehead, my blue eyes probably wide and unfocused. Ezra had always been soft, tender, caring. But this...this was different.

"Fine, but I won't be gentle, Baby. I'm going to fuck you into this mattress. So, hold on tight." He doesn't hesitate. He thrusts into me confidently. The pain is mixed in with pleasure and I can't tell if I love it or hate it. It's a raw, primal sensation that overrides everything else. The familiar comfort of my bedroom, usually a haven of playful flirtation and easy charm, feels suddenly charged with a potent energy. The sharp sting of his invasion becomes a dull ache, quickly superseded by something more.

Ezra doesn't hold back. He fucks me hard and fast, leaving me a moaning mess, as he consistently hits my prostate. He wraps his right hand around my throat, the unexpected pressure a jolt. That's new. He smirks, a darkness flickering in those intense brown eyes. Not evil, no, but predatory. And I'm his prey. I've never seen this side of Ezra before... this raw, untamed possessiveness. It's surprising, exhilarating, terrifying.

"Mine!" he growls, possessively, kissing my lips with a hunger I've never felt before. His grip around my neck never falters, it tightens, the pressure somehow only heightening my arousal. His thrusts, unrelenting and powerful. My moans are muffled against his lips, tears trickling down my face. The usual playful banter and flirty confidence that defines our relationship is absent, replaced by an overwhelming sense of surrender. I am his, I undoubtedly concede, and he is mine. I don't want anyone else. He stops kissing me and stares into my eyes, pounding into me relentlessly. He removes his hand from my throat and strokes my weeping dick instead.

"You're so fucking pretty when you cry. Look at you taking my dick like a good boy. Your ass was made for me. Now cum for me." His words, dripping with dominance, are the final trigger. The orgasm rips through my body with such ferocity, my release sticky between his fingers, coating my abs and my face. Ezra smiles, satisfied. A few more thrusts, and he comes inside me, filling me to the brim. I watch his muscles flex under his tattooed skin. Damn. He's so sexy as his face contorts with pleasure. We're both breathing heavily. He pulls out, drops next to me. A huge grin on his beautiful face.

"Where the fuck did that come from?" I ask, while looking at the side of his face. My dark curls are plastered to my forehead, a testament to the heat of our encounter.

"What?" he murmurs, voice deep.

"You were choking me. What the fuck?" Ezra turns, his intense brown eyes boring into mine.

"You just looked so good under me, my little cum slut." He said it with a smirk, a playful glint in his eyes. I roll my eyes, despite the heat rising in my cheeks. The audacity.

"Well, I'll be doing the fucking from now on." I declare, surprising even myself with the firmness in my voice. Ezra just smiles, a slow, predatory smile that both thrills and unsettles me, and leans in to kiss my lips.

"Whatever you want, Baby." He smirks. I get up, the soreness in my ass a stark reminder of his intensity. His cum drips down my thighs, a sticky trail of our passion. I can hear him chuckling.

"Shut up!" I shout, needing to reclaim some control.

I turn my shower on and adjust the temperature of the water. While waiting for the water to heat up, Ezra's hands glide around my waist and up my abs, not minding the sticky mess on me. His lips kiss my neck.

"I love you." He whispers. I remove his hands and pull away, stepping under the spray, his warmth following me.

"Say it back." he demands, his tone shifting, the playful edge replaced by something more demanding, more urgent. The water cascades over me, a cleansing ritual against the lingering feeling of being dominated, even though I'd craved it, even though I'd initiated a large portion of it.

"You know that I do." I say, the hot water soothing my sore muscles. But even the cascading water can't quite wash away the lingering feeling of... powerlessness. I'm used to being in control.

"I know you love me but I want to hear you say it, Jas." His hands find my body again. I turn to face him.

"Why?" I ask, my voice tight. I know I'm being difficult. It's easy to say "I love you," but the words feel weighted, burdened by the power play in the bedroom. The feeling of being his "bitch", though fleeting, still clung to me. This isn't just about the words. It's about the control, the subtle shift in the balance between us. Ezra's eyes darken with frustration.

"Because I just do. Say it." He said. I hate it when he's mad at me. This is Ezra. My boyfriend. I shouldn't feel this way. Pushing down my pride, I cup his face in my hands, the hot water washing over us both.

"I love you, Ezra. You are my first and only love." I murmur, the words finally freeing themselves. I turn, the soap suds a temporary shield against the lingering vulnerability.

"I'm your first love?" He asked, excitedly. His intense brown eyes, usually so guarded, held a vulnerable hope that made my heart clench. I rinse off the soap, the water cascading over my dark curls, and study him for a moment before answering.

"Yes. I didn't give a fuck about any of the girls I fucked." I admitted, the words raw and honest.

"Not even Cindy?" His questions just keep on coming. He looked at me expectantly and I sighed, running a hand through the lather on his heavily tattooed back.

"The only reason I even dated that girl was to get rid of my feelings for you because I was in denial that I felt anything for a man." I confessed. He stepped closer, the water swirling around us. Cindy. The name tasted like ash in my mouth. I hated thinking about her, about the wasted time, the hurt I'd caused myself and Ezra. I'd been such a fool.

"I can't believe THE Jasper Rowan, King of all fuck boys, has fallen in love and is in a serious relationship with ME. I feel special." he smiles, a genuine, unguarded smile that makes my heart ache with a love so profound it feels almost painful. I glare, but the grin threatening to split my face is impossible to suppress. He rinses off, the water turning to a gentle trickle as he switches it off. We step out, grab our towels.

"You are...special." I say, after a while. Ezra stops toweling his hair, his eyes wide with disbelief. I stop too, a grin stretching my face. I break the eye contact first, retreating to put on my boxers. Ezra follows, eventually, and I toss him some underwear. He catches them and puts them on.

"I'm hungry." I grumble, as I walk out of my bedroom.

"I'm cooking." Ezra announces, following me out.

Yes! I love it when he cooks but my kitchen is never stocked. So, the mystery of what culinary masterpiece he'll conjure from the sparse ingredients is always exciting. We reach the kitchen. I perch on the stool, elbows propped on the island, a silent observer to his graceful movements. His messy black hair falls over his brow as he searches the cabinets. I find myself captivated, not just by his culinary prowess, but by the sheer beauty of it all. The defined muscles flexing beneath his inked skin, the glint of his several earrings catching the light. Ezra has reduced me to a lovesick fool. I can't believe he's actually mine. Ezra catches me staring at him.

"If you keep looking at me like that, I'll bend you over right here, right now." He said, smirking at me.

"Yeah, yeah. Whatever." I roll my eyes playfully, as a blush colors my cheeks. I walked away in an attempt to hide it. He chuckles. The rest of the night was spent together. Ezra would get on my nerves and I'd annoy him back. Which isn't easy to do considering he's so damn calm all the damn time. He'd sigh dramatically, his brown eyes betraying a hint of amusement, before pulling me closer, the scent of his cologne wrapping around me like a comforting blanket.

We moved from the couch to my bed, a seamless transition fueled by laughter and whispered jokes. There was a playful fight over the blankets, a battle of wills ending with us entangled in a ridiculous, human pretzel of limbs. The absurdity of it all, the sheer joy of being wrapped in his arms, brought a smile to my face. It wasn't just physical closeness. It was the comfort of knowing, truly knowing, that we had found something real. My last thought, before sleep took me, was...I'm really happy. He makes me really happy. I smiled in the dark and held on a little tighter to Ezra's body, his warmth seeping into my bones. The thought of someone trying to sabotage this, to pull this carefully constructed happiness from under me, sent a shiver down my spine. Silently, I wished that nothing fucks this up.

CHAPTER 27

―◆◇◆―

EZRA'S POV

Every day I wake up and it gets a little easier to breathe. The nightmares don't keep me up anymore. Therapy still really helps but I don't feel scared anymore. I still worry about Jasper and sometimes I wonder if his smile is real or just a mask covering up his pain but most days, I just don't stress about things that I can't control. I have to trust him and hope that he'll keep his promises.

Overall, I just spend my days loving him because that's all I can do. I keep myself busy with work and friends. Like right now I'm with Mariana. Her curly brown hair is flowing in the wind and her hands with the red fingernails are wildly gesturing while she speaks. Even in the chaos of Mariana's tirade, a quiet contentment settles over me. It's a far cry from the anxiety that used to choke me.

"Gringo, I told that fool he'd catch these hands and I wouldn't think twice about it. I'm a crazy. You know I am. I would snatch his soul out of his body. Ugh! He makes me so angry!" She said, walking through the park. My intense brown eyes meet hers, a silent understanding passing between us.

"Why are you so violent? Relax. I bet he won't even bother you again." I replied, my hands shoved deep in my leather jacket's pockets.

"How do you stay so calm? It's creepy." She retorts. I chuckle, the sound a low rumble in my chest.

"My mom raised me to be pretty calm. It takes a lot to bother me."

She looks at me and smiles, then looks straight ahead.

"How's your boy toy?" She asks, while wiggling her eyebrows.

"He's not my boy toy. He's my boyfriend. I fought for that title. Use it." I said through a grin. The way her expression softens, a hint of respect in her eyes, speaks volumes.

"Fine. How's your *boyfriend*?" She said. My phone vibrates, distracting me from Mariana's question. I pull it out and see a message from Liam.

> Liam: hey are you busy??

I think about replying. Should I even reply? The last time we saw each other, things were awkward. Especially after I warned him about ever kissing me again. That could never happen again. Jasper means too much to me. But I do miss Liam, my confidant.

I typed out my response and hit send.

> Me: Hey. I'm with a friend. Why?

> Liam: I wanted to hang out.

> Me: Coffee?

> Liam: Coffee sounds great.

Mariana's voice, sharp as a tack, yanked me back to the present.

"Hello?! Earth to Ezra!" She punched my arm playfully, making me look up at her and put my phone away.

"Jasper's great. I'm going to marry him one day." I said with absolute confidence. Her squeal was genuinely enthusiastic.

"I can't believe I haven't met him yet!" She punches my arm, again.

"You'd scare him away. I can't trust you not to threaten him." I joked, mostly.

"I can be nice! I will just politely suggest that he doesn't break your heart or else." She grins.

"C'mon. Let's go get coffee. Liam is coming." Her eyebrows shot up.

"Who's Liam?" She asks. I ignore her question, the unspoken complexities between Liam and me swirling in my mind. We walked towards the coffee shop, the rhythmic tap, tap, tap of my boots on the pavement a counterpoint to the turmoil within.

Who is Liam to me? I keep telling myself we're just friends, but is that really true? The easy way Liam slipped back into my life, the unspoken understanding between us... it felt like more than friendship, a lingering echo of something deeper, something I'd tried so hard to bury beneath my commitment to Jasper.

A few minutes later, we're at the entrance. I open the door and look around but don't see Liam anywhere. I sit at a table, the worn wood cool beneath my tattooed hands. Mariana sits across from me, her expression unreadable. A minute later, Liam arrives, a flash of vibrant blue hair against the muted coffee shop tones. He's even more striking in person. The hazel in his eyes catches the light, a playful glint contrasting with his slightly shy demeanor.

I wave him over and he waves back, a hesitant smile touching his lips. Introducing them feels oddly formal, like I'm orchestrating a scene I'm not entirely sure I understand. Mariana's compliment about his hair is genuine, I can tell. Liam blushes, a charming reaction that makes the urge to pinch his cheeks almost overwhelming. But I'm Jasper's boyfriend, and loyalty is tattooed onto my soul as deeply as the ink on my skin. Liam's escape to the counter for coffee provides a brief reprieve.

Mariana's blunt declaration, "I don't like him," hangs in the air. My frown deepens. It's jarring, especially considering how little interaction they've had.

"You just met him." I retort, but I already know the underlying current.

"How does Jasper feel about Liam?" She asks and I sigh.

Her question about Jasper cuts deeper. His jealousy is a known factor, a simmering tension I've carefully managed.

"Jasper doesn't like him either," I admit, my voice low, "but he's just jealous. Liam and I are just friends." I add quickly, glancing towards the counter to ensure Liam's still occupied.

Mariana's words, "Ezra, this is going to end badly," chill me.

I want to argue, to explain the depth of my feelings for Jasper, the impossibility of this situation escalating into anything more, but Liam returns, breaking the heavy silence.

"Do you like Ezra?" Mariana asks Liam, no fucks given. I just look at her like she's crazy. Liam, with his long, wavy blue hair and hazel eyes, smiles that charming smile of his.

"Of course, I like Ezra. He's a cool dude." he replies, but I can see the discomfort etched around his friendly demeanor. His eyes, usually sparkling with mirth, are slightly downcast. Mariana, oblivious to Liam's subtle distress, sips her coffee, her dark eyes unwavering.

"No, I don't mean as a friend. To me it's very obvious that you like him more than just a friend. I don't like it." Liam glances at me, almost pleading, a silent SOS in his hazel eyes. But the smile remains plastered on his face, a fragile mask. He's so good at hiding things. Almost as good as I am at hiding my own complex feelings about this situation.

"I'm sorry you feel that way. I think maybe I'll leave now," Liam says, rising. He turns to me, his expression softening slightly.

"Uh, Ezra, I'll see you later. Enjoy your coffee." The way he says it, though... that slight hesitation, that careful phrasing, makes me want to scream. My boyfriend, Jasper, wouldn't be so subtle. He'd barge in and tell Mariana exactly what he thought. I watch Liam go, a wave of frustration washing over me.

"Liam, you don't have to go. She's just being an annoying overprotective friend." I call after him, but he's already out the door.

"Shit." I muttered, staring at my cup of coffee. Mariana, her own intensity dialed up a notch, levels me with a look.

"You better not break Jasper's heart. I will kick your ass if you do. Anyway, I'm going to leave now." She rises, the scrape of her chair against the tiled floor loud in the suddenly quiet coffee shop. The air is thick with unspoken tension, the lingering scent of burnt coffee beans oddly fitting the bitter aftertaste of the conversation.

"Your total lack of faith in me really hurts. I love Jasper. Liam knows that." I said with a shake of my head. This whole situation is exhausting. Liam is a great guy. He's kind, funny, and undeniably charming. But he's just not Jasper. He's never going to be Jasper.

The intensity of my feelings for Jasper, the many moments of laughter and tears shared, the unspoken understanding that passes between us— none of that can be replicated. It's a bond forged in the fires of shared experiences, a history richer than any fleeting attraction. I watch Mariana leave, her shadow falling across the cafe floor, and I sigh. I know myself.

I'm not the kind of man who cheats. I've never cheated on anyone and I won't start now. I pull my phone out and text Liam an apology. He didn't reply back.

I get up and leave the coffee shop. I head home. Only to find Liam parked in front. He's leaning against his car, tattooed arms crossed. I approach him.

"Liam?" I manage, my voice raspy. His silence is a heavy blanket, suffocating the air between us.

"Look, I'm sorry about Mariana—" I begin but he cuts me off.

"It's true." he says, his voice low and gravelly.

"What's true?" I ask, leaning against his car, the cool metal a contrast to the heat rising in my chest. He stands before me, his tattooed arms a stark contrast to his soft features.

"I like you more than just a friend, Ezra." The words hit me like a punch to the gut. He just...ruined everything.

"Take it back!" I shout, the desperation clawing at my throat.

"I can't." he replies, his gaze unwavering. My frustration boils over.

"Take it back!" I shove him, a pathetic attempt to regain control. He grips my shoulders, his touch surprisingly gentle, and pushes me back against his car.

"I can't! I can't take it back!" He's persistent, unyielding.

"Take it back or we can't be friends." I plead, my voice trembling.

"I won't take it back. I like you, Ezra." he says, his voice firm, unwavering.

"I'm in love with Jasper! He's my whole world. I won't choose you over him, Liam. Take it back. So, we can be friends." I gasp, my breath coming in ragged gasps. His calmness unnerves me.

"Forget Jasper for just a second and tell me you don't feel anything for me." he presses, his hazel eyes boring into mine. He steps closer, our faces inches apart. His hands remain on my shoulders, a warm, yet suffocating pressure.

"I can't forget Jasper. He's too important." I whisper, looking away, unable to meet his intense gaze. He grips my chin, forcing me to look at him. The desperation in his eyes mirrors my own.

"We can't be friends anymore." I manage, my voice a solemn declaration.

"That's fine. I don't want to be your friend. I want more than that. Admit that you like me too. Just once." he persists, that hopeful gleam in his eyes. I take a deep breath, the air heavy with unspoken feelings.

"I like you," I confess, the words tasting bitter on my tongue, "but that means nothing because I love Jasper. I find you attractive and I think you're awesome, but Jasper is breathtaking. So, anything I feel towards you means nothing in comparison. Maybe if I met you first things would be different, but even if I met Jasper second, I'd still end up with him." The admission hangs between us, heavy and final. He smiles, a knowing smile, his grip on my chin still firm, but gentle.

"I don't care that I'm in second place and Jasper is in first. The fact is I'm in the running. You steal glances at me and think my eyes are pretty. You like me back."

"Liam—" I try to protest, but I don't get the chance because he kisses me and stupidly, I responded. I kissed him back. His tongue slipped into my mouth and danced around with mine. My hands find their way into Liam's blue hair and he moans against my mouth. He grinds his hips into mine and I can feel his hardness against my thigh. My tongue is down his throat. What am I doing? This is wrong. I shouldn't be kissing him. But before I can push him away, before I can even process the betrayal, a shadow falls over us.

"Get the fuck away from him!!"

Oh no...Jasper.

CHAPTER 28

JASPER'S POV

I decided to surprise Ezra with a visit. I really missed him. I reach his street with a smile on my face but that smile fades instantly. My heart, trained to withstand so much, felt like it was being ripped apart. I parked the car haphazardly, the screech of tires a fitting soundtrack to the chaos blooming in my chest. My only thought is to remove that fucker's lips off of my boyfriend.

"Get the fuck away from him!!"I screamed, the words raw and laced with years of suppressed rage. I yanked Liam away from Ezra, the force of my pull sending him stumbling. But he wouldn't get away that easily. My left hand clamped around his collar, my right a blur as I punched him hard in the face. He went down, but my rage was a wildfire. I didn't stop. I straddled him, raining down blows. Blood blossomed across his face, his lip split, his eye swelling shut. My father's brutal training, a childhood nightmare I'd buried, resurfaced with terrifying ease.

"Jasper, stop! You're killing him!" Ezra's desperate shout finally broke through my haze. He pulled me off Liam, his voice cracking with fear. My focus shifted to Ezra, the man I loved, the man who had betrayed me. His brown eyes, usually so full of warmth, were clouded with worry. He didn't know the true extent of my capabilities, the deadly potential my father had instilled in me. Looking at him, the betrayal hammered home, a physical pain throbbing in my chest.

"How could you, huh?!" I shrieked, shoving him back. He stumbled but stayed on his feet, his hands outstretched pleadingly.

"Jasper, let me explain." He begs, his hands still trying to reach for me.

"I saw you, Ezra! I saw you eating his goddamn face! Just friends?! You fucking liar!!" My eyes watered. I won't cry though. He won't get to see me cry. I won't give him the satisfaction.

"Baby, please! I love you!" He had the audacity to say. His stupid beautiful face stained with tears.

"We're over, Ezra! We're done!" I shouted in his face.

"No! Wait, You don't mean that! Take it back! Don't go! Let's talk! Baby, let's talk! Please!" He begged. I stormed off to my car. I start it up and hit the gas, the tires screeching. This can't be happening. I must be dreaming, right? But I knew it was all too real. The irony was brutal. My heart shattered like cheap glass by the man who had shown me a different kind of strength, a different kind of love, a love that my carefully constructed walls couldn't protect me from.

I shouldn't have let my guard down. My carefully honed instincts should have screamed at me to stay away, to see the warning signs that I, in my blind adoration, had missed. My father would have sneered. He'd have told me to move on, to eliminate the problem. But this wasn't a target, this was Ezra. My fucking Ezra...Fuck.

I subconsciously drove all the way to Emilia's house, my hands clenched tight around the steering wheel. The image of Ezra kissing Liam burned behind my eyelids. I didn't even register getting out of my car, just the need to breathe on my mind.

I banged on her door, a primal scream trapped in my throat. My lungs felt like they were on fire. Each breath a ragged gasp. *Please, open the door. Please.*

A few seconds later, she opens the door. The relief that flooded me as she opened the door was almost as overwhelming as the pain. I fell to my knees, hugging her torso, sobbing hysterically. She's stunned at first but then hugs me back.

"Jasper, what happened? Oh my god. Honey, what's wrong?" She said. I couldn't speak. The words were choked by the raw agony in my chest. She helped me to my feet, her touch gentle but strong, guiding me to her couch.

Sitting beside me, her small hands wiped away my tears. I just cried as I clung to her body.

"What happened?" She asked softly.

"Ezra...Ezra, he...he cheated on me." I said and whole set of fresh tears poured out of me again.

"I'm so sorry, honey." She said with a frown etching itself onto her beautiful face. I laid my head on her lap.

"I broke up with him." I whispered, the words a fragile weight I could barely bear.

"It's ok. I'm here. I'll hold you. I'm right here. I won't let go." She whispered back, her fingers caressing my hair. With Emilia, I felt safe, accepted, unjudged. A man allowed to break down without shame. I fell asleep in her arms, exhausted from the emotional turmoil.

Waking up with a splitting headache, I found myself still nestled on Emilia's lap. She was asleep, her face serene and peaceful. Sitting up, I checked my phone—thirty missed calls. All from Ezra. I didn't bother calling back. Emilia stirred, a yawn escaping her lips.

"I'm sorry I fell asleep on you." I mumbled, embarrassed. She smiled, waving it off.

"I said I wouldn't let go." she said, that sunshine smile illuminating her face.

"Thank you." I whispered, sheepishly.

"Now," she said, her eyes twinkling, "start from the beginning and tell me what happened."

***

EZRA'S POV

I have grown to really hate hospitals, but here I am, sitting in a sterile room with Liam. His nose has stopped bleeding, but he looks utterly wrecked. Jasper really did a number on his face. I can't believe he broke up with me. Well, actually I can believe it. He caught me in the worst possible situation, and he had every right to be angry. What was I thinking?! I wasn't thinking...and it cost me everything. My heart feels like a black hole has been punched into it. I just hope Liam doesn't press charges against him for assault and battery.

That would really be the icing on this already disastrous cake. I've called Jasper so many times. He won't answer his phone.

"Are you going to talk to me?" Liam asks, his voice raspy.

"No." I reply, my voice tight.

"My face hurts, but it was worth it." he says, a strange glint in his hazel eyes. I scowl.

"None of this was worth it." I seethe, the words bitter on my tongue.

"You're just angry because you admitted you have feelings for two people." Liam states, his tone almost accusatory.

"No. I'm angry because you messed with my relationship even though I told you I don't want you." I snap, my brown eyes blazing. He chuckles, a sound that grates on my nerves. What the fuck is so funny?

"The way you kissed me back begs to differ. You wanted me then. How far would we have gone, if we weren't interrupted?" he presses, his blue hair falling across his bruised cheek.

"I was going to push you away. I just didn't get the chance. Jasper ripped us apart before I could." I retort, bitterness lacing my voice. He laughs again, a full bodied sound that feels like a slap in the face.

"Bullshit. You had your tongue in my mouth. Why are you trying so hard to deny it? I get that you're angry because he broke up with you. That was never my intention, and I'm sorry about that, but denying what we both know is true just makes you look stupid, and you are not stupid. So, why deny it?"

His words hit me like a punch to the gut. My heart pounds in my chest, a frantic drumbeat against the silence of the hospital room. I can't look at him. The truth is a bitter pill, and I'm choking on it. I broke Jasper's heart. That's my fault. I wasn't thinking when I kissed Liam back. The weight of my actions crushes me, heavier than any guilt or anger. This wasn't about Liam or Jasper, it was about me, and the terrible choices I made.

"I wanted you for like a split second. Kissing you was great but not for the price it cost me. I will never want you the way that I want Jasper. I would fuck you. I wouldn't marry you. But I'm not the kind of man to have meaningless sex. You and I will never happen, Liam." I said. The words heavy on my tongue.

"It wouldn't be meaningless. You care about me and I care about you. I mean you're sitting in a hospital with me." He smirks. Before I could reply or comment on how delusional Liam is, a nurse walks into the room followed by the doctor.

"Hello, I'm Dr.Kim and this is Nurse Abigail. What brings you in today?" The man in scrubs said. I thought doctors were supposed to be smarter than this.

"His face, obviously." I said, exasperated. Liam chuckles, a low rumble in his chest.

"I tripped into a fist. I'm very clumsy." He said.

Dr. Kim, seemingly unconcerned, felt around Liam's nose. Liam winced, a brief grimace that vanished as quickly as it appeared.

"It's not broken. So, that's good news. Did you lose consciousness?"

"No."

"Alright. Well, I can give you something for the pain and an ice pack for the swelling. Then you should be good to go."

That's it? No X-rays or tests? Really? I'm flabbergasted. I could have done that at home. Such a waste of time. Dr. Kim's nonchalant dismissal felt almost insulting.

"Thank you, doctor." Liam said.

"Be more careful about tripping into fists. It could be fatal next time. Have a good day, Gentlemen." Dr.Kim leaves the room and the nurse hands Liam ibuprofen with a cup of water. He swallowed the pill, the whole interaction absurdly casual given the circumstances.

"I'll be right back with the ice pack and discharge papers." The nurse politely said and then exited the room. I looked at Liam. He met my gaze with a knowing smile, his hazel eyes sparkling with a mischief that only intensified my confusion and anger. The kiss, the fight, losing Jasper, the incompetence of the medical staff...it all seemed to mock the very fabric of my reality. The crushing weight of it all threatened to suffocate me. He knew exactly what I was thinking. He'd seen it, the rollercoaster of emotions painted across my face, from furious to heartbroken to hopelessly lost.

"Let's get out of here and go back to your place." He said, while getting up from gurney.

"My place?" I questioned.

"I can't go home looking like this and we still need to talk."

"Alright. Let's go." I sigh. Forgetting all about the ice pack and discharge papers.

We leave the room and walk down the hall to the elevators.

I push the button and we silently wait for the elevator doors to open. I pull my phone out from my pocket and desperately try to call Jasper again. It rings and rings then goes to voicemail. I don't know what I would even say but I know I'd beg for forgiveness. I want him back. I miss him. I don't feel whole without him. Ding!! The elevator doors open and we step in. I push the button. The doors close. I glance at Liam and he looks...uncomfortable?

"This might be a stupid question but are you ok?" I ask.

"I don't do well in elevators. I have a fear of getting stuck." he confessed, his voice barely a whisper, eyes squeezed shut.

"Shit. Why didn't you say anything? We could have taken the stairs."

"I'm a grown man. I can handle taking the fucking elevator." He snapped.

"Right. That's why you're having a panic attack. Hold my hand and breathe." He places his shaky hands in mine and tries to breathe evenly.

"Ok. I'm freaking out, Ezra. I'm freaking the fuck out." He squeezes my hand tight.

"Hey! Look at me. Focus on me, ok?"

He nods his head and looks into my eyes. I take in his beat up face. A black eye, busted lip and slight bruising around his nose but he's still attractive. I hate myself for thinking that. Ding!! The elevator doors open. I break eye contact first and pull Liam out of the elevator with me. His hand is warm in mine but it's not Jasper's hand. That simple realization hit me hard. The sadness settles back in, heavy and suffocating, the taste of unshed tears bitter on my tongue. I let go of his hand as we reached his car. I open the driver's side door. Liam sits in the passenger seat. I start up the car and drive home. I'm so ready for today to be over.

***

I park the car and head out to the apartment building. Avoiding the elevators and going straight for the stairs. Liam follows me, his hair swaying with each step. We get to my apartment door and I unlock it, stepping inside. The air hangs still, the scent of burnt coffee lingering from this morning.

"Do you want some water or anything?" I break the silence, my voice a little too loud in the quiet apartment.

"No. I just want to talk." He said, taking a seat on my couch.

"Ok. Go ahead." I sit next to him.

"First of all, can we agree to be honest with each other?" Liam asks, his hazel eyes intense.

"Sure. I'll be honest." I said. I mean what could go wrong? I already lost Jasper. He won't even pick up my calls.

"Do you have feelings for me?" He asks. Shit.

"I love Jasper."

"Ezra.."

"I care about you. I valued your friendship." I sigh, feeling frustrated. His smile is infuriating. I glare at him.

"Was your plan to break us up? Did you want Jasper to break up with me?" I asked.

"No! I would never do that to you. I would have happily shared you with him. Not that I think you're a two timer or something like that. I just mean... I'm gonna shut up now." he mumbles, fidgeting with his fingers, a blush creeping onto his cheeks.

"Yeah, that wouldn't have happened. I belong to Jasper. I wouldn't have given myself away to anyone else." I stated. He arched an eyebrow.

"Ezra, you did give yourself away. The moment you kissed me back, you gave yourself to me."

"That was a mistake." I shot back, my voice sharp. He nods his head slowly.

"Fuck you, Ezra." He gets up and runs his hands through his long hair. I was taken aback.

"Excuse me?" I scoff. He turns around and cages me in with his arms.

"I said FUCK YOU. You are so full of shit. You forget that I know you. I know when you lie. News flash, you're a shitty liar, Ezra."

"It was a mistake! I lost Jasper because of you!"

"I don't give a fuck about Jasper. He's rude, conceited, selfish and throws temper tantrums like a child. Frankly, I don't know what the fuck you see in him. He looks like a basic bitch and he should be jealous of me. You know why? Because he doesn't have all of you. A piece of you belongs to me. You can hate it all you want. That's the truth. You're attracted to me, you have feelings for me, you enjoyed that kiss and now you're angry because I'm right. I was just the only one with the balls to act on it. Now what do you have to say, huh? Going to deny it?" He ranted, his face an inch away from mine. I sc owl.

"Fuck you! Don't you ever disrespect Jasper! The only one green with envy is you because you can't have me!" I shouted.

"Oh, is that right?" he challenged, his lips curving into a smirk.

"Yes!! Ye-" he shut me up with his lips on mine. The kiss was rough and fueled by anger. I shoved him off of me.

"Stop kissing me!"

"Stop kissing me back!"

"I don't want you! I'm in love with Jasper! I'M IN LOVE WITH JASPER! I want Jasper's lips! I want Jasper's arms! I want Jasper's dick! I want Jasper! He is the only one I will ever want! My heart belongs to Jasper!" I screamed, as tears fell from my eyes.

"If that were true, you wouldn't kiss me back, Ezra. The lies you tell taste bittersweet and if I didn't know you so well, I would have believed them. But I'm done arguing now. I don't like seeing you cry." He said, calmly.

I get up from the couch and storm off to my bedroom. I slam the door shut. I pull out my phone and call Jasper again. He doesn't answer. I call twenty more times. No answer. Fuck. I messed up. I ruined everything. I broke his heart and now he doesn't want me. I should have listened. I should have stopped being friends with Liam the moment it became a problem in Jasper's eyes. If I could just go back in time and change everything. The tears run down my face. I lost Jasper...my heart and soul... I lost everything.

The silence in the apartment is deafening, broken only by my ragged breathing and the occasional sob. His absence is a physical weight, a crushing emptiness that mirrors the hollow ache in my chest. The vibrant colors of our life together seem to have drained away, leaving behind only the stark, brutal reality of my mistakes. The phone lies limp in my hand, a silent testament to my unanswered calls, my desperate attempts to reach a man who had already walked away, leaving me alone in the wreckage of my own making.

CHAPTER 29

―◆◇◆―

JASPER'S POV

I'm in Emilia's bed. She's sleeping soundly on my chest, her breath soft against my skin. Her presence is a comforting weight. The faint green glow of Emilia's alarm clock illuminates the numbers: 3:00 AM. Shit. Sleep is a distant dream. My mind keeps thinking about Ezra. He has called me about a million times but I just can't seem to answer any of his calls. His voice would break me. I miss him and I still love him. That's the worst part. The pain of being betrayed by the only one you love is excruciating.

The urge to end it all, to finally silence the screaming in my head, is a heavy weight, pressing down. But I made him a promise. A promise to keep living, even though he shattered every promise he ever made to me. I have Emilia. She doesn't know about my suicide attempt but her quiet watchfulness is a comfort. She said I shouldn't be alone, and she's right.

I don't want to be alone, not tonight. I don't want to replay the agonizing tape of everything I changed about myself for him—the compromises, the sacrifices, the foolish trust. I don't want to think about how a man managed to fuck with my head, my heart and my dick. I gave him everything. Tears blur my vision, and I blink them back, the pain too raw, too real. Slowly, carefully, I slip out of bed, not wanting to disturb Emmie's peaceful sleep. I grab my phone and head to the kitchen, my heart a frantic drum against my ribs. I call Ezra. After the third ring, he picks up.

"Hello?" Ezra's sleepy voice answers. The lump in my throat won't let me speak.

"Jasper, say something."

"Why?" I whispered. He doesn't need to ask. He knows what I'm referring to.

"Baby, I'm sorry. It just happened. I should have stopped it but I didn't. I'm sorry. I never wanted to hurt you." He said, his voice laced with genuine remorse. The tears I'd been holding back finally spill over.

"Did you even really love me?" I whispered. I don't know why I'm whispering. I just can't seem to find the energy to yell at him.

"Of course, I love you. I'll never stop loving you, Jas. I never lied to you about that." He replies, his voice urgent.

"Do you love him?" I ask, the question a knife twisting in my gut. I need him to deny it. I need him to say no.

"I'm in love with you." He said.

"That's not what I asked." I raised my voice slightly. He sighs.

"I care about him. He was my friend. I love things about him but I'm not in love with him. I'm in love with you." His words break me. They shatter what little hope remained

"So, you love him." I cry. Goddamn it, this hurts.

"Yes, but I love you more." he counters, his voice pleading.

"That's not good enough. I only love you. I deserve someone who can reciprocate that, Ezra." I sniffle.

"Don't cry, Jasper. I love you, ok? Only you. I just want you. I swear."

"I have to go, E."

"No, don't hang up, Baby. Hold on. I want to fix this. I can fix this. I can—"

I hang up. I shouldn't have called him. I didn't need to know that he loves him. I shouldn't have called. Fuck.

"Jasper?" Emmie's gentle voice calls to me. I look up at her and run into her arms. I fall to my knees and she falls down with me. She holds me as I cry like a baby. This hurts more than any training my father put me through. That broken little boy, way deep inside of me, resurfaces and cries with the weight of the world weighing down on his shoulders.

"He said he loves him." I croak out.

"Shh. It's ok. I'm here." She soothes me. We get up from the floor and she guides me to her room. We lie down and she holds me. I fell asleep in her arms.

***

One week turns into three weeks. Time just kept moving forward. I haven't talked to Ezra for three weeks. I haven't seen him either. I've gone to work and then come home to Emilia. She's been my rock. I haven't cried anymore. I'm just numb now. I deserved what I got. I cheated on Cindy and this is karma coming to get me. I deserved it.

"Did you grab the eggs and milk?" Emmie asks, walking down the aisle of the supermarket.

"Nope. That's next on the list." I smile. I push the cart and walk to the next aisle.

"That should have been first on the list, Jasper."

"What does it matter if it's first or last? It's all going in the cart eventually."

I grab a few boxes of cereal and toss them in the cart. Emilia replied but I didn't hear any of it because I ran into the last person I'd ever want to see. His signature blue hair was loose around his shoulders and the urge to cut it all off his head was strong. Liam smiled when he saw me and actually dared to approach me. This motherfucker really wants to fuck with me today? I'm so ready to bash his face in again but instead, I pull a page from Ezra's book and remain calm.

"Are you two finally together? You make a great couple, honestly." He said. Emilia holds my hand to comfort me. I smirk and tilt my head to the side.

"As a matter of fact, we are together. I'm perfectly happy now." I lied through my teeth. Emilia caught on and kept the act up.

"Hey, Babe. We really gotta get going." She said. Her smile was bright and seductive. I lean down and kiss her head. Liam stands there, wide eyed.

"I'll be sure to tell Ezra how happy you are." Liam said.

"I don't give a fuck what you tell him. Anyway, you heard my girlfriend. I gotta go." I said and pushed passed him. I roll the cart towards the milk section. Emilia sighs.

"Sorry you had to deal with that. He was the last person I thought we'd run into here." She said. I grab a gallon of milk and put it in the cart. I smile at her.

"Did you see his face when I kissed you on the head? Fucking priceless." I chuckled. I moved on towards the eggs. She follows me.

"We definitely sold it. He must have been so disappointed to see you smiling instead of crying."

We grabbed everything we needed and headed to pay for everything. While in line, I see Liam telling Ezra something. My heart nearly leaps out of my fucking chest at the sight of him. I quickly hug Emilia from behind and bury my face in her neck.

"He's here, Emmie." I whisper to her. She looks to the side and spots them. Whatever Liam told Ezra must have upset him because he looks right at us with a frown on his face. He walks right towards us. I hold on to Emilia's body a little tighter.

"Jasper." He said. I haven't heard his voice in so long. It still sends a shiver down my spine, even now knowing it was filled with lies. I lift my head from Emilia's neck and rest my chin on her shoulder. I look into his brown eyes. They're still so beautiful.

"Ezra." I smile. He sees how close Emilia and I are, and the pain in his eyes is almost palpable. I swallow the lump in my throat and keep smiling.

"It's true? You moved on?" He asks.

"Baby, tell him if it's true." I tell Emmie. She turns to face me and kisses my lips. I grab her ass and stick my tongue in her mouth. She bites my lip and then smiles.

"Seems pretty true to me, Baby." She said. I look up at Ezra's face. His eyes well up.

"Oh, I'm happy for you." He says, wiping the tear that escaped his eye.

"Thanks. Never been happier." I lied. He waved goodbye and ran out the supermarket.

"You didn't have to be a dick." Liam said, then ran after Ezra. I let go of Emilia, the adrenaline draining away.

"Oh my god. Oh my god. Oh my god. I can't breathe. I can't believe I did that. I could practically see his heart bleeding out of his chest." I said, my hand gripping my shirt over my heart tightly.

"Hey, you did nothing wrong. He deserved it for breaking your heart." She said, her hands on my shoulders, grounding me.

"Yeah, you're right. Thanks for playing along so well." I said, sheepishly. She smiles.

"I didn't bite your lip too hard, did I??"

"No. You're great kisser, Emmie." I chuckled, a little halfheartedly. We finally paid for all of our groceries and put everything in the trunk of my car. Ezra's heartbroken face replaying in my mind on an endless loop.

CHAPTER 30

EZRA'S POV

I couldn't believe my fucking ears. Emilia and Jasper? Together? No fucking way. I looked around the fluorescent lit supermarket, the air thick with the smell of bleach and ripening bananas, until I spotted them. I frowned deeply, my brown eyes stinging, when I saw them standing in line, her back pressed firmly against his front, his arms wrapped possessively around her. I couldn't even resist the urge to stomp my way over to them, my heart a frantic drum solo in my chest, my stomach doing flips worthy of a Cirque du Soleil audition.

"Jasper." I called out, my voice a shaky whisper that surprised even me. His stupid, beautiful face, the face I'd memorized in the dead of night, looked up, and he smiled. That smile. A smile that used to be just for me.

"Ezra." he said, my name a casual throwaway on his tongue, so cold, so devoid of the warmth I craved. I missed him so much it ached. I just needed to know for sure. I needed to know if I'd really lost him.

"Is it true? You moved on?" The sadness in my voice was a knife twisting in my gut, but I didn't care.

"Baby, tell him if it's true." he told her, the flirtatious smile never leaving his face. Emilia turned, her lips devouring his, a blatant show of affection that felt like a physical blow. The world tilted, the bright supermarket lights blurring, a punch to the gut that stole the air from my lungs. I watched, numb, as Jasper got lost in the kiss, his hand splayed possessively across her ass. I blinked back tears, each one a tiny explosion of pain.

"Seems pretty true to me, baby." she said, her voice smug. Jasper looked at me, his lips swollen from the kiss, a blatant disregard for my feelings. I wiped a tear away, feeling utterly exposed.

"Oh, I'm happy for you." I managed to choke out, the words tasting like ash. I tried my best to mean it, but the truth was a raw, searing wound. I wanted Jasper, and only Jasper, for myself. I waved goodbye, the gesture feeling hollow and pathetic, and fled.

I jumped into my car, the cold leather a stark contrast to the burning heat of my tears. I gripped the steering wheel, knuckles white, and sobbed uncontrollably. Fuck. Liam hopped into the passenger seat.

"You didn't deserve that. He's a fucking prick." He said.

"I love him so much. It fucking hurts, Liam." I choked out, the words caught in my throat.

"You still love him after that fucking show he just put on? Are you fucking kidding me?" he replied, his voice sharp with disbelief.

"I don't care. I want him back." I wipe my face with my hands. I start the car.

"He doesn't want you back but that's fine because I want you." he stated, his words a cruel twist of the knife.

"I don't want you, Liam. You and I will never happen. I don't know how many times I have to tell you the same thing. I don't want you." I drive out of the parking lot and onto the main road.

"You're a damn liar. You want us both because you have feelings for the both of us. You just can't admit it to yourself." He said, while looking out the window. I'm tired of repeating myself. I just want Jasper. Nobody else. If anyone is in denial, it's Liam.

"You're delusional. I won't kiss you ever again. I'm going to get Jasper back."

"Yeah, we'll see about that. He looked really happy making out with that supermodel. He's definitely not missing you while he's deep inside her." He said, bitterly. I swerved, pulling over, anger finally eclipsing my grief.

"Fuck you, Liam!" I shout and then exit the car. I stormed off.

"You can't walk all the way home, idiot. Get back in the car and stop acting like a child."

I ignore him and flip him off. Both middle fingers way up high for him to see and keep walking. Who the fuck does he think he is?! I'm so fed up of him. It takes me hours to walk home. By the time I got there, I was exhausted and couldn't even make it to my bed. I crashed on the couch. Exhaustion taking over and shutting my body down.

***

It's been three weeks since I last saw Jasper at the supermarket, and I've been avoiding Liam at all costs. My life has been work and sleep. That's it. Sometimes I go to my old room at my parents' house and play the drums, letting out my frustration. Therapy's been... helpful, I guess. I tried calling Jasper. He never picks up. The guilt gnaws at me, a constant, dull ache. The Velvet Rope, my purgatory, is buzzing with its usual Friday night chaos. Marcus is already on my case.

"Focus, Ezra. You need to make drinks faster." he barks, his voice cutting through the music. I hand a woman her drink, the clinking glass a sharp counterpoint to the throbbing bass. I'm a mess, juggling guilt, anger, and the relentless pressure of keeping up with the demands of the bar.

"I am focused, Marc."

"No, you're not. You broke five glasses and spilled two drinks. I'm about to send you home." He complains. I roll my eyes and proceed to make the next person's drink of choice. I try to focus, to shut out the noise, to forget the way Jasper's eyes used to look at me .

"Why are you avoiding me?!" Liam shouts. I furrow my brows and scowl instantly at the sight of him.

"You can't just show up at my job causing a scene, Liam. Get out." I said, gripping the edge of the bar top tightly. I hate the way his presence always seems to highlight everything I've done wrong. Liam ignores me, pushing forward, insistent.

"No, I'm not leaving. Why are you avoiding me?"

"Ezra, go home. You're done today. Take pretty boy with you. He's bad for business." Marcus said, a scowl on his face. Fuck. I glare at Liam.

"Let's go." I said, dragging him outside by the arm.

"Oh, you're pissed now?! That's brilliant. Bring it on, Ezra. I have all fucking night." He said. His attitude is obnoxious and he aggravates the hell out of me.

"Yes, I'm fucking pissed! You want to talk so bad?! Fine! We'll fucking talk!"

"Oh, no. Not out here we're not. I'll meet you at your place." He yanked his arm out of my grasp and walk off to his car. I groan. I hop on my motorcycle and speed off. My anger does not care for the speed limit. I arrive at my apartment in no time. The first thing I do is take off my shirt and toss it on my bed. I walk into the bathroom and turn the sink on. Splashing cold water on my face. My reflection in the bathroom mirror shows a man barely recognizable.

"Ezra." I hear Liam shout. I dry my face and walk out my room.

"Sit the fuck down. Let's talk." I demand, my voice tight with barely contained fury. Liam smirks and sits down. His smirk is infuriating, a blatant disregard for the damage he's caused.

"I'm sorry I showed up at your job. I didn't know what else to do." He said. I scoff.

"You obviously can't take a hint. Let me make it perfectly clear for you. I. DON'T. WANT. YOU." I spit out, each word a carefully aimed dart. He gets up, his movement sharp and predatory, closing the distance between us.

"STOP LYING!" He shoves me, his hand connecting with my chest, sending me stumbling back. The physicality of it is a shock, but the rage that follows is a familiar, unwelcome companion.

"I'm not lying!" I shove him back, the force of my anger surprising even me.

"You do want me! Just admit it!" He shoves me back with more force.

"Oh my god! You're fucking crazy! I don't want you!"

"Fuck you!" He punches me in the face. I punch his face. He tackles me to the floor. I punch him again. He punches me back. I shove him off of me. He tackles me again. I flip us and lift my fist again but I don't swing. I laugh. I cover my face with my hands and scream all of my frustrations out. Maybe I'm the crazy one.

"You want me so bad, fine. Get up." I said, while getting off of him. I walk towards my bedroom. I'm breathing heavily. Liam enters shortly after. I grab his throat and slam him against the wall. He grunts at the impact, a pathetic sound. I tighten my grip.

"I hate you so fucking much. You reek of fucking desperation. I'm not going to be gentle and afterwards, I never want to see your stupid face again." I said, my voice was raw, devoid of any tenderness. I look into his wide hazel eyes. I drag him by the throat and push him down onto my bed with such a force his body bounced on the mattress.

He takes off his shirt and tosses it on the floor. I unbutton and unzip his jeans, pulling them off with his underwear. His hard dick sprang free. I feel nothing while looking at his naked body. It was just... a body. A vessel for my anger, my self loathing. I stripped myself bare, feeling no shame, only a dull ache. I grab a condom from my nightstand drawer and put it on. I spread his legs aggressively and position myself at his entrance. He grabbed my wrist, his voice a hesitant whisper,

"Ezra, maybe we should talk. I don't—" I cut him off, my voice cold, hard as granite.

"Do you want me to fuck you or not?"

"Yes." He whispers, letting go of my wrist.

"Then shut the fuck up." I push inside his hole all in one go. He hisses and grips onto my shoulders tightly. I didn't ease in. My thrusts were harsh, deliberate, fueled by the bitter ghost of Jasper's touch. I thrust hard and deep. I meant it when I said I wouldn't be gentle. He grunts with every snap of my hips. I close my eyes and think of Jasper. The way his body moves with mine. The faces he makes when I pleasure him. I think of his dark curly hair, his blue eyes, his long eyelashes, his plump lips moaning for me.

God, yes!! I love the sounds he makes for me. My thoughts are disrupted by Liam's moans. I open my eyes to find hazel ones looking back at me. His blue hair splayed on my pillow. I put my hand over his mouth to shut him up. I aggressively pump my cock into his ass. I close my eyes again. I think of Jasper's body. His broad shoulders, every muscle and how they flex, his huge dick and how great it feels when he fucks me. I can feel the build up of my release. I moan and think of the warmth of Jasper's lips on mine. How his hot load feels, when he finally cums inside of me.

"Jasper." I moan out as I climax, a sudden, violent release that felt more like a purge than pleasure. My seed filling up the condom. I open my eyes and pull out. Liam's eyes water but he looks pissed off, not sad. He sits up.

"You're an asshole!" He shouts, an angry tear rolling down his face. I toss the condom and put on some sweatpants.

"It was the only way I could do it. I told you, I don't want you. Now get out." I said, pointing at the door. He gets up and puts on his boxers then his jeans. He wipes away his tears. Before he walks out with his shirt in his hands, I grip his face with a bruising force.

"Remember that I never want to see your ugly ass face again." I said, as I watched his tears fall from his eyes. He flinched under my touch, a fleeting moment of vulnerability before the mask hardened again.

"The feeling is mutual. I hope you rot in hell, Ezra. I didn't deserve this." He walks out of my room and hopefully out of my life forever. I sink to the floor with my head in my hands. I don't even recognize myself anymore. I laugh until I cry hysterically, hyperventilating, a ragged, animalistic sound ripping through the silence of my apartment. I scream and shout, meaningless words tumbling out, fueled by a rage that feels both alien and terrifyingly familiar.

I tug on my hair, the sharp pain a welcome distraction from the gnawing emptiness inside. The destruction begins... things fly across the room, shattering against the walls. Then the sheets. Liam's blood, a dark stain against the pale fabric, is the final trigger. It's the physical evidence of our hate sex, the sordid culmination of my guilt and self loathing. I toss the sheets in the trash, the act feeling pathetically inadequate.

After a while, the storm inside me subsides. The adrenaline drains away, leaving me drained, utterly spent. I lie on my back, staring at the ceiling, the cracks in the plaster mimicking the fissures in my own soul. The numbness is a strange comfort, a blanketing silence after the deafening cacophony of self destruction. The apartment, a mess of broken glass and discarded clothing, reflects the wreckage within.

Liam is gone, but the ghost of his presence lingers, a chilling reminder of the irreparable damage I've inflicted on myself and everyone I've ever claimed to love. The weight of my actions settles, heavy and inescapable. I am left alone with the silence and the chilling certainty that there is no easy way out of this self made hell. The silence is too much to bare...I grab my phone and dial Jasper's number. It rings three times then a female's voice answers the phone.

"Hello?—Stop, Jasper! I'm on the phone!—Hello?" She giggles. I swallow the lump in my throat.

"Can I talk to Jasper, please?" My voice is low and I'm feeling vulnerable. She keeps giggling.

"That's my phone, Emmie. Now hand it over before I tickle you some more." I heard Jasper's voice say.

"Here you go, My Love. You can have it. Just stop the tickle torture." She giggles. I just stay on the line listening to them.

"Hello?" He says. His voice sounds cheerful.

"Hey." I manage to say.

"Ezra?"

"I need my best friend, Jas." I whisper. The words catch in my throat, heavy with unspoken apologies and a desperate plea for forgiveness.

"Where are you? I'll be there."

"On the floor of my apartment." I answer, pathetically. The admission hangs between us, heavy and shameful.

"Ok, let me tell my girlfriend that I'll be leaving. I'll be there in a few minutes." He said. *Girlfriend*. That cut deep. He hangs up. I don't move. I just wait for him on the floor.

CHAPTER 31

JASPER'S POV

"Hey, Em. I gotta go but I'll be back later." I said, while getting out of bed. I grab a shirt off the floor and put it on.

"Where are you going?" She pouted. I kiss her lips and smile.

"You're cute when you pout. I'm going to Ezra's place. He needs me."

"Is that something I should be worried about?" She asks. I shake my head.

"I do still love him but I'm not going to get back with him. That's over. I'm with you now, Emmie." I reassure her. She smiles and nods. I kiss her again then walk out the room with my keys and phone.

During the car ride, I think about how different things are now. Emilia is actually my girlfriend now. Like for real. No pretending. We were practically acting like a couple anyway. Minus the sex. She stayed at my place some days and I'd stay at hers the rest of the week. She'd cook and take care of me. I'd fix shit and helped her reach high places. We'd cuddle and fall asleep together. We'd joke and laugh. We were a couple. So, I made it official. Now I get to kiss her but that's as far as I've gone. It doesn't feel right to have sex with her when I'm in love with someone else. She knows that. I'm honest with her.

I knock, the sound swallowed by the silence of the building. Ezra's always been a creature of quiet solitude, but this... this feels different. The unlocked door confirms my apprehension. I enter his home and close the door behind me.

"Ezra!" I call out to him. I walk towards his bedroom. He's on the floor, a crumpled mess of black hair and misery. His brown eyes, usually so full of life, are red rimmed and swollen. I carry him to his bare mattress and lay him down. The warmth of his skin against mine ignites a familiar ache in my chest, a ghost of the feeling we once shared, a feeling Emilia will never understand. I sit on the edge. I wipe away his tears.

"You're starting to scare me, E. Say something."

He stares at me. Drinking in my face with his intense brown eyes. His hand cups my face. I ignore the warmth I feel deep within my chest at his touch.

"I can't believe you're here. It feels like a dream." He whispers, his voice thick with emotion.

"Well, you'll always be my best friend, Ezra. You were there for me when I was drunk and needed a friend." I manage, forcing a smile. He removes his hand away from my face.

"Do you still drink that heavily?" he asks, a ghost of a grin playing on his lips.

"No. Emilia would kill me if I came home drunk." I said. His smile vanishes, replaced by a frown at the mention of her name. The inevitable question hangs in the air.

"How did it happen? You and her."

"Ezra—" I begin, but he cuts me off.

"Just tell me."

"She was there for me. We got close. Things happened. Now she's my girlfriend."

Ezra scoots over, patting the space beside him. I lie down, our bodies close, our faces inches apart.

"I'm sorry." He whispers.

"Ezra, I forgave you. I don't need another apology." I say, trying to sound stronger than I feel.

"I fucked up. I ruined ever—" I cut him off.

"I don't want to talk about that, E." I said. His fingers trace my lips. My breath hitches, and I close my eyes, the memory of his touch too potent, too familiar. I want to kiss him, desperately, but Emilia's face flashes before me. I can't. I won't. I have to be faithful to her. Still, I can't help but caress his face. My thumb rubs circles on his cheek.

"Can you stay with me tonight?" he asks, his voice barely above a whisper. If I stayed, I would not be able to hold myself back. I know this because I'm still in love with him. Does he still love me? I don't dare ask him.

"I can't. I promised my girlfriend that I'd be back tonight." I say, pulling my hand away.

"Can you stay until I fall asleep, then?" he pleads, his red, puffy eyes looking up at me. I can't say no.

"Yeah. Close your eyes." I manage, my voice wavering slightly. He takes my hand, our fingers intertwining, a familiar comfort. He closes his eyes, and in the ensuing silence, I hear him whisper, "I still love you."

My heart stutters, a painful rhythm against the silence. I don't respond. Awhile later, he's at peace. Hopefully, dreaming about good things. I don't leave right away. I look at his gorgeous face and wonder where it all went wrong for us. The sadness becomes too much to bare and I have to leave. I kiss his forehead, my lips lingering there and let go of his hand. I turn off the lights. Close his door. There are too many memories here.

***

I enter my apartment, the key scratching softly in the lock. My hair falls into my eyes as I shrug off my jacket, the scent of Ezra still clinging faintly to the fabric. Guilt, a familiar companion these days, settles in my chest. Emilia is asleep, or so I thought.

"You're back. How did it go?" Her soft voice startles me. Her brunette hair spills across the pillow, framing her kind brown eyes.

"We talked for a while, and then he fell asleep." I lie, the words taste like ash in my mouth. I couldn't tell her about the intimate hand holding or caressing his face or even about the lingering around long after Ezra fell asleep.

"I kinda thought more than that would happen." she admits. I look up at the ceiling, avoiding her gaze.

"I wanted to kiss him, but I didn't. I couldn't do that to you." I confess, the confession a weight lifting, yet also adding to the burden. She turns my face towards her and kisses me, a soft, gentle press of lips. I kiss her back, giving into the familiar comfort of her touch. Her tongue explores my mouth, a tentative dance that quickly escalates. She wants more. I know that she wants more. But I pulled away. Kissing her is one thing. It's a distraction, a temporary solace. Sex is a whole other thing.

"I can't give you more than that, Emmie. It's wrong. I'm in love with someone else. I'd be using you. I don't want to use you. You deserve more than that."

"Do you know what the J on my skin stands for?" she asks, her voice barely a murmur.

"It stands for Joyful. I remember." The memory of going together to get tattoos fresh in my mind. Ezra's name on my flesh the perfect gift. I push away the memories.

"No, I lied... It stands for Jasper because I love you. I know you're in love with someone else but you won't start to love me, if you don't try. I need you to try for me. Please?" She said, her hand rests on my chest, her touch surprisingly firm. When did this happen? When did this quiet, optimistic girl with the sunshine smile fall in love with me? Her patience has been unwavering, and the least I can do is try.

"Ok, I'll try for you. I'd do anything for you." I said. She smiles, a genuine, radiant smile that melts away some of my guilt, and kisses me again. This time I don't stop her. As the kiss deepened, she straddled me, her hands tugging at my pants. It felt wrong, profoundly wrong, but I kept trying, trying for her, for the love she so freely offered. Realizing that I haven't hardened, She grabs hold of my member and begins to stroke it in her tiny hand. Emilia is patient. She takes her time until I've become erect. She moves her damp panties to the side and guides my cock to her slick entrance.

"Wait." I choked out. Emilia stopped, concern etched on her pretty face.

"Are you ok?" She asks, softly.

"I'm fine. I just need to breathe for a second. Just give me a moment." I mumbled, fighting back tears. It was pathetic. What is wrong with me? This was sex, for God's sake! I've done it plenty of times. I should be able to get through this. She's a great girl. I should feel lucky that she wants me. But I think of Ezra. How right it felt to become one with him. I'm so in love with him but I need to try to love Emilia. This is what she wants. I can give her this. She waits patiently for me to get my shit together. A grace I didn't deserve.

"Ready?" She asks. I took a deep breath, steeling myself, and nodded. In one swift motion, She slides me inside her. She's warm and wet. I grab onto her hips as she rides me. I close my eyes and try to enjoy myself. My thoughts immediately turned to Ezra.

"Don't think of him. Look at me." She says. I open my eyes and look into her brown eyes. The wrong pair of brown eyes. She smiles as she bounces on my dick. Her breasts bouncing with her, spilling out of her tank top. She's beautiful. She really is but she's not Ezra. Frustrated with myself, I flip us and begin to pound into her. She's moaning. I'm grunting. The bed is squeaking and banging against the wall.

"Yes! God, yes! Keep going!" She shouts. Her fingers digging into my back. I do as she requests and keep going. Harder, deeper, faster. The climax comes fast, brutal and messy, and I pull out, the release a hollow victory. I jerk off and cum on her belly. The act feels violating, even though she's the one who encouraged it. The image of Emilia, covered in my cum, solidifies the wrongness of it all. I feel dirty even though she's the one covered in cum. I get up, pulling my pants up around my knees, the fabric bunching awkwardly. The bathroom seems a million miles away. I don't want to see her face.

The guilt is a suffocating weight. Even though Ezra and I are over, I feel like I betrayed him, cheated on a ghost of a past relationship. The betrayal is a twisted knot in my gut. The water stings my eyes as I splash cold water on my face, trying to wash away the feeling of being dirty. I pull my pants up, the gesture feeling clumsy and awkward.

As I walk back into the room, she's asleep, her breath soft and even. As I look at her, I realize that I can't let this happen again. I don't feel right. I feel filthy. I need to end this. I don't want a girlfriend. I don't want to replace Ezra. They say the quickest way to forget about someone is to get under someone else but I did that and there's just no forgetting my first love. I crawl into bed and gently nudge Emilia awake.

"Emmie. Emmie, wake up. We need to talk." I said. She slowly opens her eyes and mumbles something I couldn't hear.

"Please, wake up. I can't sleep until I get this off my chest." I plead. She sits up and rubs her eyes.

"What is it?" Her sleepy voice said. I feel guilty but I need to do this.

"Emilia, you are really wonderful. You're patient and loving. You have been my rock. I really couldn't have coped without you. You are my most cherished friend and I really hope you don't hate me but I need to break up with you. It doesn't feel right. I tried. I really tried but I can't keep pretending to be in a happy relationship. I won't ever love you the way that you deserve to be loved." I said as gently as I could. She's wide awake now. I can't read her face. It's just blank. No reaction. No emotion. She's not even blinking. Did I break her or something?

"Emmie?" I said, waving my hand in front of her face.

"Hmm." She hums, as she finally blinks.

"Did you hear me?" I asked.

"Yes. I heard you." She replies.

"And?"

"Is this because of Ezra?" She asks, her fingers fidgeting. I take deep breath after that question.

"No. I'm not going back to him. I just can't be with anyone else either. It's me. It's definitely not you. I just don't need to be in a relationship right now. I'm sorry it took having sex with you to realize that."

"You will go back to him. I know it. It's only a matter of time. I'm not mad about it. It does suck that you're breaking up with me but I understand. I'm still going to be there for you." She smiles and holds my hand. I sigh, feeling relieved.

"Thank fuck. I thought you'd hate me. You really are amazing. Geez, can we go to sleep now? I hate talking about feelings and mushy shit." I said, returning the smile and completely ignoring the bits about Ezra. She giggles and nods.

CHAPTER 32

EZRA'S POV

The blaring sound of my alarm clock startles me awake. I groan and turn it off. My eyes flutter open, and the hazy remnants of sleep clear, replaced by the sharp, exhilarating jolt of remembering that Jasper was here. Last night. He was here. He actually came to see me. The overwhelming need to see him again, to feel the ghost of his touch, the memory of his smile, crashes over me. I want him. I need him. I get up, the floor cold beneath my bare feet, and head to the bathroom. Brushing my teeth, the idea—stupid, reckless, brilliant—forms. I'll get drunk and call him. That'll work. It has to. Could I have just, you know, invited him over like a normal person? Yes. Will I inevitably embarrass myself? Probably. Am I thinking straight? There's nothing straight about me, especially not when it comes to Jasper.

I finish my morning routine, a flimsy excuse for a shirt barely concealing my racing heart. Alcohol for breakfast. What could possibly go wrong? My tiny kitchen feels strangely vast, the silence amplifying my nervousness. I gather every drop of alcohol I own—a half empty bottle of wine, a lonely tequila sunrise, some questionable liquor I'd forgotten about—and arrange them on the counter like a morbid still life. Here goes nothing. The wine is half gone before I even register the act, the sweet burn already loosening my inhibitions. I can do this. I will finish it. One more desperate gulp, and the bottle is empty. The world starts to tilt, the edges blurring. My stomach lurches, a protest against the assault. I ignore it. Shakily, I grab my phone, my fingers fumbling as I dial Jasper's number. It rings four times before he answers.

"Hello?" His husky sleepy voice brings back so many memories.

"Sober friend needed." I slurred.

"What?" he mumbled.

"Sober…" hiccup. "Sober friend needed."

"Ezra, are you drunk? It's only eight in the morning." He said. I sat on my kitchen floor, the cheap linoleum cold against my skin.

"Yup. It is and I am."

"Where are you?" he asked, sounding more awake, the concern edging out the irritation.

"Home." I replied, the word heavy with unspoken things.

"I'll be right there. Don't move." He said in an exasperated tone. He hangs up. I drink some more, the cheap tequila burning a path down my throat. A few minutes later, there's a banging on my door. I staggered my way over and opened it, stumbling into his arms. He caught me effortlessly. It wasn't just the alcohol. I genuinely wanted a hug, a desperate need for his familiar warmth.

"Ezra, what the fuck?! This isn't like you." He said, dragging me back inside and shutting the door. He's upset, but the anger is laced with concern, a familiar note in his voice that always cuts through my self destructive tendencies. He's here and he's holding me, and that's all that matters right now.

"Your hugs are the best." I slurred, the words thick with alcohol and emotion. He lets me go and looks at my face, his eyebrows furrowed, a deep frown on his lips.

"What is this? Karma coming to get me. I'm getting drunk calls now."

"I'm not karma. I'm Ezra. Don't you recognize me, Baby?" I pouted, the words childish and pathetic even to my own ears. He shakes his head, amusement flickering in his blue eyes despite his obvious displeasure. He guides me to my room, then into the bathroom. He forces me into the shower and turns the water on.

"Fuck! That's cold! That's fucking cold!" I shriek, the shock momentarily clearing my head. My clothes stick to my body, my black hair plastered to my forehead.

"Time to sober up." He smirks. I glare at him, shivering from the cold, hating the way my clothes cling. I hate wet clothes. I take my shirt off, dropping it on the floor. Jasper blushes, a surprising flush spreading across his usually confident features.

"What are you doing?" *Isn't it obvious?* I thought.

"My clothes are wet." I said, pulling off my sweatpants. I'm not wearing any boxers. I can feel his heated gaze on me as I stand there, naked under the cold spray. He grabs a towel and holds it up, partially blocking his view. He looks up at the ceiling, muttering things under his breath. I chuckle, the sound surprisingly clear despite the lingering fog in my brain.

"Nothing you haven't seen before, Jas." I flirted, the words slurring slightly.

"Alright. Get out. Before you die of hypothermia." He said, strained. I get out of the shower and wrap myself in the towel, the chill air hitting me like a slap.

"It'd be your fault. Now I'm shivering cold and I'm still drunk." I said. I nearly lost my balance on the slippery floor.

"Nobody told you to drink this goddamn early. That's on you."

"I don't feel so good." I said before bending over the toilet and throwing up. This is not pretty. Definitely not my greatest moment. The taste of cheap alcohol and regret burned my throat. Jasper's hand, strong and reassuring, rubbed my back, sending shivers down my spine that had nothing to do with the cold. His touch was electric.

"What made you do this to yourself?" He asks, his tone laced with a sadness that mirrored my own self loathing.

"Desperation." I croaked, the word tasting bitter on my tongue. I get up with his help and brush my teeth again. He looks lost in thought. I wonder what is going on in that head of his. He led me to my bed, his hand finding its way to the small of my back, guiding me as if I were made of glass. He retrieved clothes from my dresser, his movements fluid an d efficient. He puts my shirt over my head and helps me put my arms through the sleeves. He then kneels on the floor and proceeds to put my legs through the proper holes in my boxers. I remove the towel as he drags my boxers up my legs. My thoughts, clouded by alcohol, swirled with a mixture of mortification and something undeniably, thrillingly sexual. He looks so good on his knees.

Unfortunately, these thoughts rushed blood straight to my dick and it began to rise right in his face before my boxers covered me up. Jasper bites his lip and looks up to my eyes.

"I'm sorry. My body has a mind of it's own." I bury face in my hands. He continues to pull up my boxers until I'm finally covered up. Not that it matters much since you can still see that my dick is still as hard as stone.

"Don't be embarrassed. It happens." He said, his voice low and reassuring. I remove my hands from my face. He smirks, a slow, knowing curve of his lips that sends a shiver down my spine. The familiar pull towards him threatened to overwhelm me. He grabs the sweatpants and helps me get dressed in them. The act felt intimate, charged with unspoken words and lingering feelings. He stands up to his full height and grabs my hand, his touch warm and grounding.

Dragging me to the kitchen, he initiates a silent, efficient clean up. Dumping the remaining alcohol down the sink, then tossing the bottles and cans into the trash. The rhythmic clatter of the bottles against the trash can somehow mirrored the frantic rhythm of my heart. He's incredibly efficient and methodical in his movements, and I find it strangely comforting. He scrambles eggs, toasts bread, and places the simple meal before me with a bottle of water.

"Eat." He demands. The word hangs in the air, laced with an authority that both excites and intimidates me. A dominant daddy, the thought flickers across my mind, a forbidden thrill weaving its way through the shame and self loathing. He lifts an eyebrow, catching the fleeting grin on my face.

"Thank you, Da—Jasper." I managed, my face heating up from what I almost called him. I eat, the blandness of the food oddly satisfying after the fiery onslaught of alcohol. He watches me, his gaze unwavering until the last bite is gone, the last drop of water consumed. If he keeps taking care of me like this, bossing me around, I might just cum in my pants.

"I have a question but I don't want you to be upset when I ask it." Jasper says, while putting the plate in the sink. His dark curls fall over his forehead, those captivating blue eyes filled with a hesitant concern that mirrors my own.

"I think I'm sober enough to answer your question." I said. He turns to face me, the light catching the worry etched onto his usually confident features.

"How long were you cheating on me with Liam?" He asks. The question catches me completely off guard. Any and all arousal still buzzing from earlier dies instantly, replaced by a cold dread.

"I wasn't cheating on you with Liam. He kissed me once when he was drunk. I told him it could never happen again. He said it was a drunk mistake. I believed him. Then he kissed me again and you saw that one happen. I did kiss him back the second time. I regret that. It was stupid. It was nothing compared to kissing you." I said, as truthfully as possible, the words tumbling out in a rush. Jasper runs a hand down his face and slowly nods his head.

"This sucks. This really sucks. I shouldn't have asked." He said. I grab his hand and intertwine our fingers, the familiar comfort a lifeline in this turbulent moment. He looks me in the eyes, his blue eyes searching mine. I continue, desperate to explain, to make him understand the messy, infuriating truth of Liam.

"I got caught up in the moment. It was a mistake. I had every intention to push him away but you had arrived before I got the chance. He's not in my life anymore. We fought and argued all the damn time. We hate each other." I said. He lifts an eyebrow and scowls.

"You sound like an old married couple." He said, a bitter jealousy dripping from his words.

"No, an old married couple bickers because they love each other. We threw fists at each other's faces. He stalked me and insisted that I show him how I felt about him. Even after I clearly told him that I didn't want him and he could never be you. He was annoying and persistent. He pushed me until I cracked and did some things I'm not proud of." I said. I run a hand down my face, the frustration palpable. I don't want to talk about Liam. His name leaves a bad taste in my mouth.

"What did you do?" He asked. A question I saw coming but still left my heart in my throat. What if Jasper doesn't want me after hearing the answer? I tried to swallow the lump in my throat. I didn't dare look at him in the face.

"We were arguing and it turned into a fist fight. There was a point where I was just going to bash his head in but I stopped myself. My fist froze in the air. All I could feel was the rage within me and...Well, I told him that if he wanted me so badly then fine. He followed me to my room. I grabbed him by the throat and slammed his body against the wall. I told him how much I hated him and I really did mean it. He looked like a scared child. I warned him I wouldn't be gentle then shoved him onto my bed. Should I keep going?" I looked at his face at the end. Jasper's hands and jaw were clenched tight but he nodded his head.

"I'm not proud of how I treated him. I'm sure he expected something more caring. That's not what he got. I didn't prep him or anything. I know I hurt him but he didn't complain because I told him to shut the fuck up. I was rough. I felt nothing looking at him. I had to think of you to enjoy any of it. It was frustrating. I wanted you there. I wanted to feel your skin. I said your name out loud. He didn't like that very much. He started to cry but I didn't care. I told him I never wanted to see his stupid face again and kicked him out." I finished explaining. Saying it out loud, I realize how bad it all sounds. It definitely doesn't paint a good picture of me. I'm worried that Jasper will think lowly of me. I don't usually get into fights. I don't treat other people like shit. I'm usually very calm. Liam pulled the ugliest parts of me out. I never want to be that guy again. The silence stretched, punctuated only by the faint hum of the refrigerator in my small apartment. I waited patiently for Jasper to say something. He just stood there, quietly. His eyebrows deeply furrowed and his lips in a tight line. I don't know what he's thinking. It scares me.

"I don't like Liam. I never will but I don't like who you're becoming more. That didn't sound like the Ezra that I know. The Ezra that I knew would never treat someone like that. He wouldn't drink himself stupid so early in the morning. He definitely wouldn't have been crying on the floor. What is going on with you? I don't even know you anymore, E." He said. His words hit harder than any punch ever could.

"I'm a man with nothing to lose, Jas. I lost everything the moment I lost you. I don't sleep right without you, eating seems pointless, I don't care about anything anymore. You took my heart with you. Now there's this gaping black hole in my chest. It's been six weeks, three days, eight hours and thirty two minutes and I don't know if I can even survive another second without you. The light has been snuffed out of my life. Do you get it? Do you understand? I know you have a girlfriend now. I'm happy that you're happy. I would never do anything to jeopardize that but I don't know how to live without you in my life." I said. The tears came, hot and unstoppable, a physical manifestation of the gaping black hole I described, a hole that had swallowed my joy and left me hollow.

"No, you don't get to do that. You don't get to make me feel bad for leaving you. You hurt me. You told me that you were just friends and made me feel like I was crazy. You ate his goddamn face and had your tongue down his throat. You gave him my kisses and touched him with the same hands that touched me. You told me that I was safe with you. You broke my heart and made me wish I was dead. How could you do that to me?! I loved you. I have never loved anyone. I was perfectly fine before you came into my life and turned everything upside down. I changed so much about myself just to be with you, Ezra. Did none of that even matter to you?" He choked out. His words were a mirror reflecting my own actions, each syllable a brutal reminder of my betrayal. He had been so vulnerable, so trusting, and I had shattered that trust with the carelessness of a drunk man. He was right. I had been a monster. I gulp down the guilt I feel, a dry pill choking me. My actions had not only destroyed me, but had irrevocably damaged the one person I ever truly loved. I had lost him, and deserved every bit of the agony that followed.

"Of course, it all mattered to me. I know what you sacrificed for me. I counted myself lucky that you loved me back. I never intended to hurt you. I made a mistake. One that I will never make again. Not ever. I swear on my life. I love you so fucking much, Jasper. I'll wait for you forever." I said, the alcohol had finally begun to recede, leaving behind the stark reality of my situation. Jasper shook his head, the tears streaming down his face unchecked.

"I have to leave. I can't breathe in here." He said, pacing back and forth.

"Don't run. Please, just stay. We can talk about something else. Anything else. Just don't go." I plead. He stops pacing and looks up at me.

"Why do you make it so difficult?! I can't stay angry with you and it's so fucking frustrating! I need to stay angry. I want to punch you in the face and kiss you at the same time. You are so frustrating! God, I can't breathe! This feeling in my chest is crushing me." He clutches his chest, breathing heavily, eyes squeezed shut. My heart ached for him. This man, my Jasper, was crumbling before me, his carefully constructed walls crumbling. I stood, my hands finding their place on his shoulders.

"Jasper, I need you to calm down. Take deep, slow breaths. Focus on my voice. Listen to what I'm saying. Deep, slow breaths."

He listened, his breathing slowing, his blue eyes opening, meeting mine, then falling to my lips. The air crackled with unspoken promises, with a history of stolen glances and forbidden touches. Simultaneously, we reach for each other, a silent understanding passing between us, a moment suspended in time. But we stopped, the space between our lips a chasm of unspoken realities. Instead, we both close our eyes and rest our foreheads together. I will wait forever for him. I will wait until he's not a taken man.

"Damn you. You know me too well." he whispered, eyes still closed, hands still gripping my neck.

"I know everything there is to know about you. I've been obsessed with you since day one." I confessed, my gaze fixed on his full lips, a bittersweet ache in my soul. Gently, I pulled his hands from my neck, breaking the spell. His eyes fluttered open. For a fleeting moment, time seemed to stand still. I wanted to freeze this moment forever, to memorize the nuances of his expression, the way the light caught the strands of his dark hair. God, he's breathtakingly perfect.

"I can't stay all day. I promised Emmie I would have lunch with her." He said. My heart plummeted. I slowly stepped away and sat down again. I don't want him to leave.

"I understand. I'll be fine. Thanks for coming over." I said, trying not to sound so deflated, the words a thin veil over the raw ache in my chest.

"I don't trust you. So, you'll just have to come with me."

"You're going to put your ex and your girlfriend in the same room? And you actually think that's a good idea?" I couldn't believe what I was hearing. The absurdity of the situation was almost comical, if it weren't so agonizing.

"She's not my—" He started to protest, but his phone rang, cutting him off. He pulls his phone out.

"Hello?...Hey, Em...I didn't forget...It's not lunch yet...brunch?...Fine but I'm bringing Ezra with me...Yup...No...No...I'll be there in a few minutes...ok, bye." The conversation was a blur of rushed apologies and explanations, punctuated by the casual mention of me. He slipped his phone back into his pocket, his expression unwavering.

"You're crazy. I can't sit in a room with her." I said, incredulously.

"You have no choice. You're coming and that's that." He said, the confidence in his voice both infuriating and strangely arousing. Well, fuck me. I guess I'm going to an awkward brunch with the girl who's fucking the love of my life. Just great. A bitter laugh escaped me as I got up, the familiar ache in my chest intensifying. Putting on my boots and leather jacket felt like a ritualistic preparation for war. Grabbing my phone, wallet, and keys, I felt a familiar wave of despair wash over me. I know I'm supposed to be sobering up but for this I might have to consume more alcohol.

"Alright, I'm ready to go." I said. Jasper drags me out by the hand. I'm too focused on the fact that he's holding my hand. It makes me grin, a stupid, lovesick grin that betrays my carefully constructed facade of nonchalance. The warmth of his hand, the familiar feel of his touch, it's a drug I'm hopelessly addicted to. We make it outside to his car and he lets go of my hand, the abrupt absence leaving a hollowness in my chest. I sit in the passenger seat, the leather cool against my hands. He sits behind the wheel and starts the car. He drives, glancing at me occasionally, those blue eyes holding a mischievous spark.

"Are you seriously pouting right now?" He chuckles.

"I'm not pouting." I scowl, trying to appear indifferent, but my heart feels like a trapped bird, fluttering against my ribs. He makes a sharp right turn, the car tilting slightly, and the smile on his face grows wider.

"You are definitely pouting. You're like a big baby. Aw, how cute." He cooed, like he was talking to an infant.

"Shut up. Focus on driving." I groaned, my brown eyes fixed stubbornly on the passing scenery. He chuckled, that deep, throaty sound that always sends a shiver down my spine. I didn't even notice that we had driven a good distance, my mind preoccupied with the strange mix of excitement and apprehension churning within me. A few minutes later, we arrived. It was a small house nestled in a nice neighborhood. Nothing special, just...a house. We get out of the car and walk up to the door. We didn't even have to knock, Emilia opened the door with a bright smile, brunette waves swaying behind her. She must have been sitting by the window or something. She instantly threw herself into Jasper's arms excitedly. He caught her with a big smile and squeezed her tightly.

"Hey, Emmie. I made it." He said. He then let her go and gestured towards me. "I brought Ezra. Be nice."

She smiled and extended her hand. I shook it.

"Welcome to my humble abode, Ezra." She said, cheerfully.

"Um, thanks." I replied. We all walked into the house and followed her into the kitchen. The air thickened with an unspoken tension, a silent acknowledgment of the complicated triangle we formed. I feel really uncomfortable. I don't want to be here.

"Alright, you guys can take a seat at the table. I'm almost done making brunch." Emilia chirped, oblivious to the silent war raging between us. She began plating some French toast.

"I'm going to the bathroom first. Don't start without me." Jasper said, before disappearing down the hall. I sat down, feeling awkward about being alone with her. Emilia's gaze bore into me.

"So, how does it feel to be the ex in this situation?" Her voice was laced with venom, a smirk twisting her lips. The question hung in the air, thick and suffocating. My own carefully crafted calmness shattered.

"How does it feel to be another fuck on his long list of girls?" I countered, my voice sharper than intended. The retort stung, I could see it in her flicker of surprise. But her defensiveness quickly hardened into triumph.

"Fact is you're the past, Ezra. You're the third wheel in this equation. You get to watch what you can't have." she declared, settling across from me. The memory of almost kissing Jasper moments before, the warmth of his nearness, fueled my response.

"Listen, I get why you're being catty. Jasper is fucking great. Anyone would be possessive over him, if they were to walk in your shoes. But tell me, does he kiss you hungrily? Does he fuck you passionately? Does he look at you like you're the only one in his world? No, he doesn't. Want to know why? It's because he gave ME his heart. I hold it in the palm of my hands. I effectively ruined him for all the rest. He's mine. So, enjoy the loveless kisses and the lackluster fucking because when he's done playing house with you, he'll be running back to me." I said, calmly. The color drained from Emilia's face, her bravado crumbled. Her carefully constructed facade shattered, tears welling in her eyes. Jasper's return went unnoticed. Emilia was already on her feet, fleeing the room, leaving behind a silence heavier than the unspoken tension before.

"Emmie, what's wrong?" he'd asked her, his voice gentle, the same voice he used to whisper sweet nothings in my ear before Emilia. The way his voice softens when he's around her makes my blood boil. The jealousy is a bitter poison, corrosive and all consuming. The sound of a door slamming closed echoes in the house.

"What did you say to her?!" He confronts me, those infuriating blue eyes blazing.

"I told you it was a bad idea to put us in a room together." I said.

"What happened?" he presses.

"She was rubbing my nose in your relationship. So, I put her in her place."

"Emilia is the sweetest, most caring person I know. She wouldn't do that." He said, in her defense. That irritates me.

"Ok, defend your precious girlfriend." I mutter, my voice laced with bitter sarcasm.

"Are you...jealous?" He asks. A chuckle escapes me, a hollow sound.

" Yes!" I hiss, "I'm a thousand percent jealous. And you know what, I'm not a liar. I'm telling you she's not innocent. She started it." I cross my arms.

"You've lied before." He remarks, his voice flat. The ghost of Liam, my one transgression, rose up to haunt me. His name felt like a physical blow, a raw nerve exposed.

"I didn't lie to you! Liam was just a friend! I never lied to you! I kept one thing from you but I never lied!" My voice cracked, the shout echoing the desperation in my heart. His sigh was heavy, laden with weariness as he runs his hand down his face.

"I have to go check on her." he said, leaving me alone in the kitchen, the silence amplifying the turmoil within. I watched him go, his silhouette swallowed by the hallway's dim light.

CHAPTER 33

JASPER'S POV

I was happy sleeping peacefully. Then Ezra calls me drunk and my day has been a roller coaster ever since. Don't even get me started on seeing him naked today. He's been making it difficult to stay away. I don't want him back. I love him. He is definitely attractive and makes me think sinful thoughts. I just can't be with him. I knock on Emilia's door.

"Emmie, open the door." She opens it, her usual sunny disposition absent. I enter her room, the air thick with unspoken tension.

"What happened?" I asked, needing to understand her perspective. She looks at me with sad eyes.

"Ezra was being an asshole towards me. So, I walked away." She said. I nod my head slowly but my gut tells me there's more to the story.

"What did you do to provoke him? Because it's obvious to me that you did provoke him. He's a very calm guy. I've never seen him just attack someone for no reason. So, cut the shit." I said. She was taken aback by my tone with her. I don't have any patience left. I need her to be straight with me.

"I asked him how does he feel being your ex." She said in a soft voice.

"Well, that's a stupid question. Considering you know exactly how it feels. Since you're my ex." I said, pointing at her.

"He didn't know that." She said, crossing her arms defensively.

"I'm trying to be friends with both of you. Don't complicate things by being petty, Em." I plead, sinking onto her bed, the exhaustion hitting me hard.

"Well, you can't be friends with both of us. It's me or him. Take your pick." she declares, her voice hard. I flinched as though I were hit by a physical blow to the stomach. She's making me choose? What the fuck? I can't choose. Ezra is my best friend. He knows everything about me. I love him. Emilia has been there for me. She helped me cope with my break up with Ezra. I care about her deeply. I can't choose between them.

"Emmie, you know I can't choose between you. I love him and I care about you. Don't make me choose." I said in a low voice.

"You heard me, Jasper. ME OR HIM?!" she repeats, her voice rising. She's not letting this go. I can almost hear my heart crack all over again. A single tear escapes my eye.

"Him." I whisper, the word barely audible. She stands there, stunned into silence. I walk out of the room. I find Ezra in the kitchen still.

"Let's go, E." I said, my voice cracking in the process. He immediately got up and cupped my face in his hands.

"Whoa. What's wrong? Why are you so upset?" His voice laced with concern. His rough hands were warm and comforting. I really wanted them to embrace me, to hold me and never let go.

"Get out of my house! I don't want to see that gay bastard all over you! Get out!" Emilia screamed. The venom in her voice was shocking. The Emilia I knew, the fiery but ultimately loving woman, was gone, replaced by a monster fueled by jealousy and possessiveness. Ezra clenched his jaw and if looks could kill, she would have been dead already. He wrapped his arms around me protectively and walked me out of her house. She just kept screaming, throwing plates in my direction. They shattered into pieces. Her aim was trash but her intentions were enough to hurt me. Ezra took my car keys, his touch a calming reassurance. He sat me in the passenger seat, then slid behind the wheel. The engine roared to life, a powerful counterpoint to the silence in the car.

"Crazy bitch." He muttered under his breath but I heard it. I couldn't come to her defense, she was acting like a lunatic. I'm still so shocked. Did I know her at all?

"I'm not going to rub salt in your wounds but I do expect an explanation." He said, his eyes on the road.

"Explanation?"

"Yeah, like why you came out of that room upset and your girlfriend suddenly went psycho on us." He glanced at me. I should probably tell him that Emilia's not my girlfriend. Just the thought made my stomach clench. Once I admit it, he'll probably pursue me with renewed vigor, and frankly, I'm not ready for Ezra to try and win me back.

"Firstly, I didn't know that Emilia had crazy in her. Secondly, I don't want to talk about what happened. All that you need to know is that I'm sorry I called you a liar." I said, watching the world blur past.

"You fought because of me? Jasper, I'm sorry. I should have kept my mouth shut. She was just irking my soul. I couldn't help myself. I should—" Ezra began, his voice laced with genuine remorse.

"Stop. Just stop. I don't want to talk about it anymore." I interrupted, the frustration bubbling over. Every relationship I try to build, crumbles. I am destined to be alone, it seems. Honestly, I just want to drink my problems away. I haven't touched a drop in months. Ezra's voice cut through my bleak thoughts.

"I know what will cheer you up." He smirked, that infuriatingly charming smirk that always managed to disarm me.

"Oh, noooo.. not one of your bright ideas. Just take me home, E. I'm serious. I'm not in the mood for your shit." I groaned. But did he listen? No, he did not. He dragged me to a trampoline park. He parked the car, a mischievous glint in his brown eyes, completely ignoring my glare.

"Ready?" He said, cheerfully.

"No, Ezra. This is not home. I specifically said to take me home." I grumbled. He chuckled.

"Come on, Grumpy. It'll be fun." He said, as he got out of the car. I sigh and reluctantly followed him. We walk inside the amusement center, sign a waiver, pay for an hour of jumping around and grab the socks they give us. We take off our shoes and put them in a locker, along with our phones. The special socks felt ridiculous over my own.

Ezra grabbed my hand, pulling me toward the trampolines. He launched himself onto the springy surface, a chaotic burst of energy. He looked completely out of place, a tattooed bad boy bouncing around like a kid in a candy store, but the sight of him, the genuine joy on his face, warmed something cold inside me. A smile slowly broke through my own gloom. He really was an idiot, in the best possible way. I ran and jumped in, the initial awkwardness melting away as I found my rhythm.

"I hate you!" I shout with a grin, surprising even myself. He flopped dramatically, grabbing his chest.

"Ugh. You wound me!" He shouts back. I laughed, the sound echoing around me, and jumped towards him, the anger and sadness fading with each bounce.

"Take my hand." I said. He didn't hesitate. He stood, his hand in mine, a smirk playing on his lips.

"Now what?"

"Now jump with me. As high as you can." I challenged, a newfound confidence blooming in my chest.

"Alright. One, two, three, JUMP!!" We jump, reaching higher and higher, the worries and anxieties seeming to melt away with each bounce. The air was filled with laughter, the kind that comes from the gut, from a place of pure, unadulterated joy. He was smiling. I was laughing, and for the first time in a long time, I wasn't thinking about the past. He was right. This was so much better than drinking my sorrow away. This cheered me up.

"I bet you can't do a back flip." I said. He let go of my hand and what do you know... the idiot can back flip.

"Your turn." He said. Damn it. I jump and flop on my back. He dissolved into laughter, collapsing beside me on the springy surface. We were both panting, our eyes locked.

"You're beautiful. It's not fair." He said, his voice softer than I'd ever heard it. My face burned. I look away.

"Shut up." I mumbled, my heart a frantic drum against my ribs.

"It's true. Your blue eyes are so pretty. Your lips are plump and kissable. Your face... just one look from you and you can have whoever you want." He said, a dreamy haze in his eyes. Meanwhile, I must resemble a tomato right now.

"Yeah. Well, you're not so bad looking yourself." I said.

"My eyes are a shitty brown." He chuckles. I frown at that statement.

"Your eyes are not a shitty brown. When you first open your eyes in the morning and the sun catches them, they're like pools of honey. Your eyes have an intensity to them. They are worth getting lost in them. And your lips are just as plump as mine. They are soft, warm and inviting." I said, truthfully. I can't even blame Liam for wanting to kiss Ezra's lips. I want to kiss Ezra right now. I can't allow myself to do that though. I stand up and walk off the trampoline. I glance over my shoulder. He's sitting up. He runs a hand through his hair and looks lost in thought. I leave him behind. I walk into the bathroom and throw cold water on my face. I look at my reflection in the mirror for a few seconds.

"Come on, Jasper. Snap out of it." I tell myself. I grab a paper towel and dry my face. I hear someone else enter the restroom. Soon after, I feel a hand turn me around. Ezra backs me up against the wall. His body pressed firmly against mine, hands on my waist. He leans in but I cover his mouth with my hand before he kisses me.

"We're just friends." I said, shakily. Ezra removes my hand and intertwines our fingers together.

"Friends don't stare in each other's eyes the way that we do." he murmured, that familiar smirk playing on his lips. The logic was undeniable.

"Whatever stopped you from kissing me earlier, use it now." I challenge, attempting to push him away. His grip tightens. He moves closer, his body pressing against mine, a familiar weight I both crave and dread. He rolled his lower half into mine roughly. I bit my lip to prevent myself from moaning.

"She's not a good enough reason anymore. She doesn't deserve you." He whispered into my ear.

"Oh, and you do?" I asked, enjoying his light kisses on my neck.

"I probably don't but I'm selfish and I want you all to myself. You're mine. You said so yourself." He said, then he sucked on my neck. Fuck. The memory of Liam, the reason for our separation, fades into the background as Ezra's touch consumes me, leaving behind only the intoxicating reality of his presence.

"Mmm." I moaned involuntarily. I shut my eyes and gave him more access to my neck. He kissed, suck and licked all the way down to my collarbone. I'm ridiculously hard right now. My mind is intoxicated with Ezra. We hear someone else enter the restroom and we quickly pulled apart. The man gave us a weird look. Ezra grabbed my hand and pulled me out of the restroom. A smug smirk on his face. We grab our personal belongings from the locker and leave. I unlock the car from a distance with a push of a button. Before I open the car door, I catch my reflection in the window. I gasp. I touch my neck.

"Ezra! What the fuck?!" I groan. He just grins, that infuriatingly charming grin that always makes my knees weak, even now, even after everything.

"You wouldn't let me kiss your lips. I had to taste something." He said, settling into the passenger seat. I sat in the driver's seat, the leather cool against my skin, a stark contrast to the burning heat blossoming on my neck.

"You left like a million hickies. How am I supposed to cover this up?!"

"But you look so beautiful with my mark." he pretended to pout, that little upward quirk of his lip a familiar, agonizingly sweet sight. I started the car, the engine rumbling beneath us like a restless beast mirroring the turmoil in my gut.

"I work at weddings. No bride wants her bartender to look like they've been attacked." I explained, my voice tight.

"If it makes you feel better, you can give me some hickies. Fair is fair." He offered, a little too happily. Unsurprisingly, I had the mental image of my lips and tongue devouring Ezra's skin while he moaned in my ear. I shake the thought away. That would quickly escalate to fucking and I can't allow that to happen. Shit, the tent in my pants is uncomfortable. I shook the thought away, clinging to the road, the focus of driving a shield against the relentless pull of him.

"Oh, that's NEVER happening again. You are back in the friend zone. Nothing more will happen between us." I clarified. Every word felt like acid on my tongue. How can you just be friends with someone you're in love with? How can you just be friends with someone who looks so delicious and sexy all of the damn time? I have to be careful or I'll be eating my words. I sneak a glance at him at the stop light.

"We've been just friends before. We can start over. You'll end up in my bed just like before and gradually we'll start right where we left off. I'm in no rush. You're mine. It's just a matter of time." He said, with a smirk. As if everything was truly that simple.

"Things have changed, Ezra. You aren't who I thought you were." The light turned green and I remove my foot off the break. He groaned.

"You're talking about Liam again. I really don't want to discuss that anymore. He's a mistake that I regret deeply. I don't want to relive it every time that I'm with you, Jas. I'm human. I'm not perfect. I apologized and I swore that would never happen again." He said, his eyes staring at me intensely. I park the car in front of his place. I turn to look at him.

"You were perfect to me, Ezra. You said the perfect things at the perfect time. You never lost your temper. Always spoke respectfully. Never once made me feel unloved. You were a tiny bit jealous but I never minded it because it was cute as hell. Then you kissed Liam and everything felt like a lie. So, now we can only be friends because I don't want to be the dumb ass that goes back to his cheating ex and looks stupid the whole time."

"Jas, I love you. I won't ever jeopardize what we have together again. All this time without you has been hell. I have completely lost my mind. Please, just give me a chance, Baby." *Ah, fuck.* He called me *Baby*. I need to stay strong. I can't just go back running into his arms.

"Ezra, Go home. It's been a long day." He grabs the back of my neck and pulls me forward. Our faces are so close. He looks at my lips then my eyes. He kisses my cheek then the other and then my forehead down to my nose until his lips hover over mine. It's so tempting to lean forward and close the gap. My throat is so dry. I put a hand on his firm chest and almost wish I didn't because I can feel the muscles just beneath the fabric of his shirt. I push him away, swallowing hard.

"Bye." He said, then left my car.

CHAPTER 34

JASPER'S POV

~One week later~

I haven't heard from Ezra in a week. I have called and texted like a million times and no answer. Who does he think he is, ignoring me like that?! He can't almost kiss me one moment and then disappear the next! I storm out of my car and go up to his apartment. I bang on the door with my fist. A shirtless, dark skinned man opens the door. His gaze is intense, trying to intimidate, but those dark eyes hold no real threat for someone like me. My father made sure of that. A million thoughts are racing in my head but one thought stands out among the rest, is Ezra's fucking this guy?

The thought made my stomach churn, a hot, angry acid rising in my throat.

"Who the fuck are you? Where's Ezra?" I blurted out. The man lifted an eyebrow, crossing his arms, leaning against the door frame.

"You must be the ex boyfriend. Jasper, right?" He said, his tone dripping with something akin to amusement.

"Yeah, that's me. Who the fuck are you?" I spat back, a scowl permanently etched onto my face. He chuckled, a low rumble in his chest.

"Go home, Jasper. Ezra doesn't need little boys like you." he sneered, a smirk playing on his lips. My blue eyes narrowed.

"Respectfully, the only little boy I see here is you. So, how about you go get Ezra out here like the good little boy you are." I retorted, a grin spreading across my face, mirroring his earlier arrogance. His amusement quickly melted into anger.

"Yo, don't get your ass beat. I ain't playing games with you. Get lost." he threatened, attempting to shut the door in my face. I stuck my foot in the way, my resolve hardening.

"I don't give a fuck who you are, I don't take threats lightly. You want to fight me?! Then bring it on, motherfucker but I will see Ezra. TODAY."

Who the fuck does this guy think he is?! He has no idea who he is threatening. The killer residing inside me is itching to get his hands on this man. I'm ready to fight my way inside. He hesitates, then opens the door fully, his face a mask of furious frustration. I remove my foot.

"You persistent little bitch. He's not here! He's out fucking the next available dude in a club! Now beat it!" he roared, slamming the door shut. Ezra is out fucking strangers? What the fuck? The shock is a physical blow, but the anger is quickly eclipsing everything else. Oh, I'm going to find him and when I do, I'm going to make him regret the day he thought he could play with fire. I'm going to burn you, Ezra Valenti. I'm going to drag you to hell with me. I storm out of the building and get in my car. I dial a number on my phone. One I thought I never had to use again. Frank. My father's...associate. A man who knows too much about me, about my past, about the brutal training I endured as a child. I hate relying on my shitty father's resources, but desperation is a potent cocktail. The call goes through.

"Hello, Mr.Rowan." God, I hate that voice, smooth as melted butter, yet dripping with something insidious.

"I need you to find someone for me, Frank." I demand, my voice low and tight. The usual charming Jasper facade is gone. Only raw need remains.

"Name."

"Ezra Valenti." Frank's voice, smooth as polished granite, cuts through my anger.

"Born in a middle class family. His mother is an elementary school teacher and his father is a marine soldier. Only child. Had two serious relationships. His criminal record is as clean as a whistle. This is an ordinary person. Why do you want to find him?"

"I don't need his background, Frank. I need his coordinates!" I snap. My fingers tighten around the steering wheel, knuckles white. Frank chuckles, a sound that grates on my nerves.

"That's too easy. Pin dropped at his home address. Oh but hold on, I can do better than that. Hacked his phone. Looks like you'll be crashing a party. Formal event. I'll send you the details." His smug, annoying voice is infuriating, yet I can't deny the effectiveness.

"Thanks. Oh, and Frank, you didn't hear from me."

"Understood, Mr.Rowan." The call ends, replaced by the buzz of a new message. Ezra's life, laid bare on my screen. But I don't need that. He's home. He wouldn't see me there. The new boyfriend lied. That stings. But he will see me tonight. He will see me at that formal event. I start my car, the engine roaring to life, mirroring the tempest brewing inside me. The formal event isn't just a chance to see him. It's a stage for a confrontation. This time, it won't be a whispered conversation in a dimly lit apartment. This time, it will be a declaration. Tonight, Ezra Valenti will hear me, and the truth will unravel, no matter the cost. The party awaits.

***

EZRA'S POV

"Jeremiah, who was at the door?" I asked, while towel drying my hair. My reflection in the mirror showed my black hair still damp, clinging to my forehead. Brown eyes, usually bright, felt dull. Jeremiah, tall and lanky, a black man with a booming laugh, looked up from his phone, a grin spreading across his face.

"No one important. Hey, did Mariana text you yet?"

"I must be going crazy. I thought I heard Jasper at the door. But um, no not yet. She's still pissed at me." I said, walking back into my room. Jeremiah doesn't follow me. He's one of those straight guys that thinks men shouldn't change in front of each other, some fragile masculinity thing. It doesn't bother me. He's a good guy, just... different.

"She's being such a girl! You didn't even fuck the guy!" He shouted from the living room. His voice, usually jovial, held a note of disbelief.

"Actually, I did fuck the guy. It wasn't great. I thought of Jasper the whole time." I admitted, pulling on boxers.

"When did that happen?! My best friend is finally a slut and you didn't tell me?" He roared with laughter. I snort.

"I'm not like you, Jeremiah. I don't see playing around with people as an accomplishment. I fucked up." I said, slipping into a black suit, leaving a few buttons undone to showcase the tattoos snaking across my neck and collarbone. I slick my hair back but a few strands fall on my forehead kinda sexily.

"You didn't fuck up. You're a man. You had needs." His words grated on me. That reductive view of men as primal beings lacking self control felt insulting.

"Do me a favor and shut the fuck up. Yeah?" I said, walking into the living room.

"Man, you look like death personified dressed in all black. Who's soul are you going to take, Grim Reaper?" He chuckled, his earlier bravado replaced with genuine concern.

"Maybe I should own a scythe." I laughed.

"No but seriously, you look scary."

"I'm a man with nothing to lose. Think about that. I'm heading out. Thanks for letting me use your car." I said. I didn't wait for a response. I left my apartment and got into Jeremiah's car.

***

The drive was smooth and easy. I arrived at the event in no time. I'm not usually the type to attend formal parties but I was offered the chance of a lifetime to start a career in business.. All I had to do was impress a few people at this ridiculously opulent shindig. If I can help run a business then I can own a business. Plus, it's another thing I can add to my résumé. The venue itself was breathtaking—chandeliers glittering like captured starlight, gold leaf shimmering on every surface. A waiter offered me champagne, which I almost declined, but then she appeared. A woman whose diamond necklace could probably fund a small country, who engaged me in endless small talk, her words a blur against the overwhelming opulence. I looked around at the many faces until one caught my eye but at the last second they turned away.

"Excuse me, I have to go." I mumbled to the diamond encrusted woman, escaping into the throng. I had to find him. I quickly walk through the crowd and try to get a glimpse of the man. I swear I just saw Jasper. But he was gone. Vanished. I spin around looking for him but nothing. I gulp down the the entire glass of champagne I had been babysitting up until this point. I must be losing my mind. I spotted the open bar and made my way over, scanning the room as I went. And there he was. I take a sharp breath and release it slowly. He's a vision in a crimson suit, black shirt paired with a black tie, looking like the prince of hell sitting in his throne. His posture was effortlessly masculine, leaning back in his chair, legs spread, hands resting on his thighs. His blue eyes, usually warm and playful, were now intense, burning into me, a smirk playing on his full lips—a smirk that only someone like Lucifer could pull off.

I don't know when I started walking towards him, but he rose to meet me. Hands in his pockets, he licked his lips seductively, his gaze never leaving mine until we were face to face. His hands were suddenly on the back of my neck, his lips crashing down on mine. It took a second to respond, but oh god, it felt so good. His tongue battled mine, and he won. I wanted him to have me. He pulled away, and I found myself instantly pursuing his lips again. He turned and began to walk away, and I followed, knowing he knew I was behind him.

He strode confidently down a dimly lit corridor, entering a room on the left. The instant I stepped inside the dark space, he pushed me against the wall, his lips finding mine again. This time, it was rougher, almost angry. The anger, the passion, the sudden reappearance...it was all a whirlwind of confusing, intoxicating emotions.

"Stop. Stop. Stop." I manage to say but he just kisses my neck instead.

"What are...Mmm... what are... you doing here?" I practically moan out. He palms my dick through my pants. Fuck.

"Is that what you're really focusing on right now?" He whispered in my ear before nibbling on my lobe.

"No." I breathe. He chuckles.

"I'm going to fuck you, Baby." His promise more of a threat than anything else. God-damn. That was hot. He quickly unbuckled my belt, undid the button and pulled down the zipper, dragging my pants down with my boxers. My dick throbbed and my hole clenched with anticipation. I wanted him so bad. I've waited so long to feel him again.

"I'm yours, Jas. I've always belonged to you." I confessed, the words a raw, vulnerable confession in the near darkness. I don't know when he undid his pants but I felt his cock rub against mine and I immediately grabbed both in my hands, stroking them together. We moaned at the same time. His hand grabbed a fistful of my hair and forced my head back. His tongue left a hot trail until I felt his teeth sink into my neck. The masochist within me purrs with satisfaction at the rough way Jasper is handling me.

"Turn around." He demanded. His command was unnecessary. My submission was absolute, unquestioning. He slapped my ass cheeks five times, each more painful than the last, before spreading them apart and licking my hole. I was a fucking goner. I mewled and ground my ass on his face, desperately. Seeking more pleasure. Jasper stiffened his tongue and fucked me with it. My cock was weeping. I needed relief. My cock felt as though it were made of steel from how hard it was. Jasper abruptly stood up and guided his cock to my eager wet hole.

I arched my back and bent forward a little, both my hands resting on the wall. He pushed inside slowly, teasingly, drawing out my frustration until it became agonizing. I wanted more. I groaned impatiently. He chuckled, his voice a low rumble in the dark.

"So greedy. Does my little slut want to be fucked that badly?" His voice a low murmur against my ear. The final plunge was exquisite. The fullness, the invasion, is utterly consuming. He gripped my hips and began thrusting in and out of me. Our skin slapping together.

"Fuck, yes! I missed this!" I moaned out. His sexy grunts and moans filled my ears and turned me on. My blood is running hotter in my veins. Everything about him arouses me.

"Yeah? You missed my thick cock?" I could hear the smirk in his voice.

"Yes. Fuck, yes. Fuck me harder."

Jasper picked up his speed and pounded into me harder. Hitting the bundle of nerves every single time. It was ecstasy. Pleasure vibrated through my veins. That familiar warmth and pressure built up until I couldn't hold my release any longer. I cried out from the high I was feeling. He didn't stop, he kept going chasing his own release. His fingers digging into my skin around my hips. Surely bruises will be left behind.

"Tell me what I fucking want to hear." His husky voice said. I knew exactly what he wanted me to say. My heart fluttered in my chest and the words spilled out of my mouth.

"I love you, Jasper! Fucking hell, I love you so much!"

With his chest against my back, his arms wrapped around me tightly and his face buried in the crook of my neck, he roared while hot semen coated my walls. Jasper didn't stop, he kept rutting into me, continuously releasing ropes of his cum. His moans muffled against my skin. I could feel his heart beating wildly. He held me like that for a few minutes, until he stopped moving his hips.

"I've missed you, Jas." I sigh, happily. He pulls out of me and I can hear him trying to redress himself in the dark. I search the wall until I find a light switch and turn on the lights. He's tucking his shirt back into his pants. I pull up my clothes and fix myself up. I notice he's avoiding looking at me. Once he has fixed his appearance, he finally looks at me with those beautiful sapphire orbs. His hand grips my jaw tightly and his lips kiss me hungrily, a possessive force that leaves my lips bruised and burning.

"You're such a good fuck." He said, without emotion. His voice cold. I suddenly feel cheap and small. He let's go of my face with a cruel smirk.

"This was just a good fuck to you?" My eyes water with the realization that I've been used and discarded. My heart splinters. My world slowly crumbling under my feet, the carefully constructed fantasy of reconciliation dissolving into dust.

"Don't text or call me." he says, the finality of it, a crushing blow. The happiness I felt seconds ago, melts away and in it's place a soul crushing sadness takes over. He tries to leave, but I desperately clutch onto his shoulders.

"Jasper, don't do this to me. Don't play with me like this." My voice cracks as I fight the urge to cry.

"Say hello to the boyfriend for me." He says, removing my hands and walking out. What the fuck is he talking about?! My mind struggles to process his words, the reality of the situation crashing in.

"Jasper! Wait!" I shout as I run after him.

"I love to hate you!" he throws over his shoulder before disappearing into the crowd, leaving me standing alone amidst the glittering spectacle, my heart in ruins. What the fuck did he just say? He hates me? The elegant venue, filled with laughter and music, becomes a suffocating cage, the brilliant lights mocking my despair. I'm left standing there, in the wake of his callous departure, the weight of his words crushing me.

"Mr. Valenti, we've been looking for you." An older gentleman approaches me.

"Sorry, I have to excuse myself." I say quickly and walk passed him. I pull out my phone from my pocket. I call Jasper. I exit the building and walk towards the car. He's not answering. I leave a voicemail instead.

"Jasper, call me back. There's clearly been a misunderstanding. Please, let's talk."

I call again. No answer. Another voicemail left.

"There is no one else. Do you hear me, Jas?! There's only you. Call me back."

I call a third time. No answer. Another pathetic voicemail was left.

"Jasper fucking Rowan, there will be hell to pay if you think you can just fuck me and walk out of my life."

I sit in the car and try to think rationally. Jasper is clearly angry and jumping to conclusions. I probably shouldn't have ignored him for a week. He thinks I have a boyfriend. What boyfriend? The only person I've been hanging out with is Jeremiah.

Then I remembered someone knocked my door earlier today and I thought it sounded like Jasper. I start the car, the engine groaning slightly as if mirroring my own internal struggle and head straight home.

***

I immediately shake Jeremiah awake.

"Wake up, man."

"What?" He groans, half asleep on my couch.

"Wake up! Who was knocking on my door earlier today?" He blinks a few times.

"Pretty boy. Can I go back to sleep now?"

"What the fuck, dude?! What did you tell him?! Because he seems to think you're my boyfriend!" The panic in my voice is palpable, even to me. At the tone, he sits up, looking confused.

"What? I didn't mention anything about a boyfriend. I just told him to get lost." He said, his voice laced with innocent nonchalance.

"Why the fuck would you do that?!" I yell, the frustration bubbling up threatening to boil over. He stands, hands up as if approaching a growling dog. Cautiously.

"Calm down, Ezra. I can explain myself. Just calm down." He said.

"Go ahead. I'm listening. I'll even sit down." I said, forcing myself to sit on my couch, hands clasped tightly in my lap. The anger felt hot, a simmering volcano threatening to erupt.

"Cool. So, dude came here knocking all pissed and puffing his chest out and shit, right. So, I figured you didn't need that kind of energy around and told him to get lost but dude wouldn't give up and was ready to fight. So, I told him some bullshit lie and slammed the door in his face. I was just trying to be a good friend and take care of him for you." He explained. Internally, I am furious, a raging fire in my chest, but my face remains stubbornly unreadable.

"What was the lie you told him?" I asked, monotonously, chillingly controlled. He seems a little panicked now, the casual facade crumbling.

"Does that really matter?" he stammered.

"Don't make me ask again." I ground out, my jaw clenched tight.

"Just remember that I was just trying to be a good friend and get rid of him for you...um, I told him you were out fucking someone else."

I let the weight of the situation sink in. I glide my hands down my face. Frustration seeping in, taking a hold of my body. I'm going to kill him. I might just commit murder tonight. FUCK! I take a deep breath, trying to regain control before I actually do something I regret. The absurdity of it all...Jeremiah had single handedly sabotaged my fragile hope of reconciliation with Jasper.

"Get out." I demanded, the words sharp and cold, laced with a pain far deeper than mere anger. The air crackled with the silent scream of a heart betrayed.

"Bro, really—" he started, but I cut him off with a roar.

"I SAID GET THE FUCK OUT!! TAKE YOUR SHIT AND GET THE FUCK OUT OF MY FACE!! GET OUT!!" He quickly grabbed his things and fled. I was so angry, I didn't know what to do with myself. Everything felt so irrevocably fucked up. A cold shower seemed the only logical course of action.

The icy water did little to soothe the burning rage within. As the frigid spray pounded my skin, Jasper's words echoed in my mind.

'You're such a good fuck.'

'I love to hate you.'

They weren't declarations of undying affection. They were barbed compliments, laced with a bitterness that reflected the toxicity of our relationship. Yet, despite everything, despite the cruel jabs and the hurtful words, I loved him. The love was a stubborn weed, refusing to be uprooted, even as its roots were being gnawed at by doubt and hurt. The exhaustion after the shower wasn't just physical. It was a bone deep weariness born of the emotional turmoil. I didn't even bother changing before collapsing onto my bed. My dreams were filled with fragmented memories of Jasper. His smile, the way his eyes crinkled at the corners when he laughed, the tattoo of my name on his body, a thousand tender moments of the man I love.

Chapter 35

Jasper's POV

"You're such a good fuck."

My words kept haunting me. I broke my own heart. I had no intentions of having sex with him, when I showed up to the event. I planned to give him a piece of my mind and probably make him jealous but when my eyes caught sight of him...Fuck. He looked so good. Sexy. I was turned on instantly. I had to take a seat and admire him from a distance. My anger almost dissipated. Almost. I quickly remembered the fact that he ghosted me and replaced me with a little bitch. Speaking of ghosts, Ezra was looking around like he'd seen one. I was practically electrified when his dark eyes found mine. I don't know what came over me. I was filled with a need to have him. Fuck my stupid heart for loving him.

I hated the effect he has on me. I forgot all about my anger the minute his lips touched mine. I called it *fucking* but you can't just fuck when your heart is involved. I made love to him. I let passion drive me and when it was all over, I just had to hold him. I couldn't let go yet.

My heart was beating too fast and I thought, *'Fuck. I love him.'* Then I caught myself slipping and I quickly harden my face and stiffened my posture. It angered me that he said he loved me and missed me when he clearly belongs to someone else. He spilled lies like water. The words just came to me. *'You're such a good fuck.'* How easily he believed me. That hurt. But I have no desire to become his side piece. I needed him to let me go. We were done. It was over. No more mind games. We couldn't even be friends. It's too difficult. *'I love to hate you.'* In a way, that was true. I love him soo much and I hate him for it because all it's done is cause me headaches, heartaches and fuck him for that.

I toss and turn in my bed but sleep does not find me. I try to justify my behavior so the guilt doesn't kill me. I mean he really is a good fuck. He's the best sex I've ever had. I could have just been talking dirty. I do love to talk dirty. Especially, to him. But he knows I wasn't attempting dirty talk, I was implying he's easy and that what we did was a one time thing. Guilt. Ugh. I hated it. I hated him. He deserved it! He was playing around with me! God, when will I finally fall asleep?! These thoughts are killing me. Fuck Ezra and his stupid beautifully handsome face.

I literally just laid in bed until the sun rose and watched as my once dark room lit up with morning light. I don't even know what time it is. I don't care. I keep my eyes closed and just lay there. I hear a knock at my front door. Ugh. It's probably my sister, Lily. I can't deal with her today. I ignore the knocking. Abruptly, the knocking stops and I thought it was over but soon after I hear the door slam shut. Fuck. I forgot to lock the door. She's probably snooping in all of my stuff now.

"Jasper, wake up." A very familiar *masculine* voice demands. That's definitely not my sister. My eyes shoot open.

"What the fuck are you doing in my apartment, Ezra?" I ask, my tone harsh as I prop myself up on my elbows. He's very obviously checking my naked upper body out as he stands at the foot of my bed.

"You thought you could just treat me like some slut and walk out of my life? Well, you thought wrong. Fuck you for making me feel like shit. But you were clearly fed some bullshit and I'm here to clear that up." He said. I didn't like his tone. I haven't slept shit and I'm not in the mood for an argument.

"Ezra, I don't have time to play games with you." I said.

"Shut up and listen. The guy at my place yesterday was not my boyfriend. He lied when he said I was out fucking and he's straight. Now you probably had the right to be angry that I ignored your texts and calls for a week but rejection stings and I needed space."

"Alright then—"

"Oh, I'm not finished. What you did was totally uncalled for and we could have avoided all of this nonsense with a simple conversation. I said what I had to say." He turned around and began to leave. Panic began to rise and I jumped out of the bed so fast that I stumbled a few steps but I managed to grab his arm and turn him around. Hugging his waist tightly with my face buried in his neck. I couldn't think of anything clever to say. I was never great with words. My actions always spoke louder. He didn't hug me back. I leaned back to look at his face. I would describe his facial expression as confused. I slowly walked him backwards against a wall. I grab the back of his neck and kiss him. Slowly and softly, at first but then it deepened and became heated. Like we're starved for each other. His hands explore my bare chest. I bend my knees slightly and lift him by his thighs. I grind my crotch against his. He moans, a low, guttural sound that sent a thrill through me. I smirked, enjoying the power, the knowledge of all his sweet spots, all the little tricks to get him exactly where I wanted him—under me, completely at my mercy. I kissed his neck, trailing my lips along his jawline.

"Jas...ahh" he moaned, his voice thick with pleasure.

"No talking." I said, continuing my assault on his skin.

"Mmm...marry me." He moaned again, the words unexpected, a jarring interruption to the physical symphony we'd orchestrated. I stopped, abruptly pulling away, setting him down. His touch, suddenly, burned.

"What the fuck did you just say to me?" I breathed out, my heart hammering against my ribs. The sudden shift in the atmosphere was palpable. He smiled, his eyes heavy with lust, and buried his fingers in my curly hair.

"Marry me, Jasper. I love you. I want you to be my husband." He said it dreamily.

"Why the fuck would I marry you, Ezra?" I asked, my voice tight.

"Because you...love...me?" He said, almost questioningly. I stood silent. His face changed, the color draining from his cheeks as if he'd suddenly glimpsed a horrifying truth.

"You don't love me?" he whispered, his hands falling to his sides. A single tear tracked a path down his cheek.

"For fuck's sake. Don't cry." I groaned, my voice rough with frustration and something else... something akin to panic.

"Fuck you, Jasper! You fuck with my emotions, reject me and then demand that I not cry!" he spat, his voice laced with righteous anger. The words hit harder than any slap.

"It's not my fucking fault you jumped to conclusions. I never said I didn't love you. Fuck. If anything I love you too much. God, I fucking hate it. I love you so much that I hate you. You make me so fucking crazy and every little damn thing you do affects me. Then you go and ask me to marry you?! Fuck." The word vomit just fell from my lips, a torrent of raw emotion. My heart was pounding against my chest, my hands slick with sweat.

He smashed his lips onto mine and I didn't hesitate to kiss him back. Our passion lead us to the bedroom and soon enough he was naked underneath me with my cock deep in his ass. I rocked my body in and out of him with vigor. Our lips locked, my head in the clouds. So many sensations running through me. So many emotions crashing like waves inside my chest. His sounds of pleasure like a song consistently playing in my ears.

He's mine. I want him. Nobody else can have him. He is MINE.

"Who do you belong to, Baby?" I grunt, the question a guttural whisper lost in the rhythm of our bodies.

"You, Jas." He breathed out, the words a sigh against my skin.

"Yess. Ahhh. Yes, you're mine. Mmm. You feel so good, Baby." I said in between moans, his tight grip around my cock a delicious agony. His moans are a counterpoint to my own, a symphony of lust building to a crescendo.

"Fuck." He groans, a sound that sends a jolt of pure, primal satisfaction through me. I pick up my pace, drilling into him harder, my hand simultaneously stroking his cock.

"Say it." I demand, the words harsher than intended, yet fueled by the desperate need to hear those three words, the drug that keeps me hooked.

"I love you! Fuck, I love you!" His sexy, deep voice cries out. He's close to coming. I can tell by the way his eyebrows furrowed, cheeks red, lips parted and those beautiful brown eyes glazed over, pupils dilated like he's high off of our sex. I stroke him faster, thrust harder, the rhythm of our bodies a frantic dance.

"It should have been me asking." I say, breathless, the words a confession hanging in the air between us. He cums hard into my hand, his warm seed leaking between my fingers and onto his abs. I can feel my own release rising as the pressure builds. I moan as I finally cum, filling him up with every last drop.

"Yes!" I cry out, collapsing on top of his body, my heart thundering in my chest.

"Yes." I whisper, answering his earlier question.

"Yes?" He whispers back. I pick up my head off his shoulder and look into his eyes.

"I'll marry you, E."

Ezra's shock is palpable, his eyes widening before a slow grin spreads across his face, his eyes sparkling with unshed tears. He blinks them away, then attacks me with kisses, frantic and joyful.

"Oh my god! I'm going to be married! This is like a dream! Am I dreaming?!" His excitement is infectious, bubbling over with unrestrained happiness. I pulled out and rolled onto my side.

"No, you're not dreaming. I'm really going to marry you. My stupid heart fell in love with you and now you're all that I want. There's no one else for me. You're my other half. Just know that I'm absolutely terrified right now and I may look calm but internally I'm screaming. My heart is beating wildly and I'm pretty sure I'm having a heart attack." I confessed while clutching my chest. Ezra smiled and grabbed the hand on my chest, intertwining our fingers together.

"Do you want a big wedding or are we eloping?" He asked, his voice a low rumble against my skin. There was no thinking about it. I don't want a big fancy wedding.

"Do I look like the type of man to have a big fucking wedding? I just want you and I, at the courthouse. And you better be in white." I said, the words tumbling out between breathless laughs.

"Why am I in white? I'm not a bride." He chuckled, while playing with my fingers.

"You're always in black. I want to see you in white. What better time than our wedding day, Princess?" I smirked.

"Fine. I'll be there like a virgin in white. Just for you." He said, blissfully. I trace his tattoos with my fingertips. Enjoying the feeling of his soft skin. I must be out of my fucking mind. We break up then literally skip so many steps and jump straight into marriage. Love makes people stupid. I'm living proof of that fact. I just don't care anymore. I love him and being apart fucking sucks. Breaking up was a dumb decision.

"What kind of ring does my virgin bride want?" I asked, playfully nudging him. He thought about it quietly, his brow furrowed in concentration. The contrast between his serious contemplation and the absurdity of our situation made me laugh.

"I think a plain silver band will do just fine."

"Let's get dressed and go buy one right now." I quickly got up and grabbed a wet wipe and cleaned us both up. The urgency to solidify this impulsive decision, to make it real, was overwhelming. Ezra puts on his clothes back on and I dig in my closet for something to wear. I settled on a long sleeved burgundy shirt and black jeans with black sneakers. I throw on a silver chain and put some products into my curly hair. Done. I grab a jacket, my phone, wallet and keys, a surge of exhilaration coursing through me.

Just as we were heading out towards the front door, there was a knock. I opened the door to find my twin sister frowning at me.

"What on earth possessed you to contact Frank?!" She yells at me, getting straight to the point. She walks into my apartment, a whirlwind of dark hair and frantic energy.

"Sure, come in. Not like I was about to leave or anything." I said sarcastically, as I leaned against the door frame.

"Jasper! Now he'll find you! And after he finds you, he'll find me! I don't want to be found!" she shrieked. The panic in her voice was palpable. I sighed, the weight of our shared history pressing down on me. Ezra looks confused. He stood patiently, his hands shoved deep in the pockets of his leather jacket.

"Who will find you?" He asks. Shit. I really hate talking about my father. Lily looks startled, like she didn't notice Ezra standing in the room when she barged in.

"Our dad." Lily whispered, her eyes starting to water.

"There's a lot you don't know about my family, E. Things I rather not talk about." I said, carefully choosing my words. He frowned, his brown eyes searching mine.

"Ok, then who's Frank?" He pressed.

"A very shady man that works for my father." I answered, knowing this would only pique his curiosity further.

"Why are you in contact with a shady man?" He furrowed his eyebrows, concern etched onto his features. I really didn't want to answer that question. How do you explain to your fiancé that you hacked his phone and stalked him without sounding like a complete psycho? They both looked at me expectantly.

"I wasn't invited to last night's event. I followed you there with a little help." I smiled awkwardly.

"Have you lost your goddamn mind?! You called Frank for something that stupid?!" My sister yelled at me. Ezra quickly connects the dots in his head.

"So, your father has connections with shady people and is hunting for you as we speak? Who the fuck is he?! Al Capone?! And we are definitely circling back to the fact that you were stalking me." Ezra said. My sister and I share a glance.

"Something like that. Let's just say, he's not a good man." I answer vaguely. The truth was far more complicated.

"Jassy, we need to run. We need to go." Lily pleads, fear dripping off every word.

The flashbacks of my father beating me, ran through my mind and anger slowly rises in me. I know that's why Lily is scared. She witnessed the beatings I took in her place.

"I'm not running anymore. What's the worst he can do? Shoot me?" My blue eyes hardened with a dangerous resolve.

"What the fuck?!" Ezra shouts with an incredulous look on his face. I unlock my phone and dial Frank's number. It rings five times before he answers.

"You just couldn't keep your trap shut, could you, you little bitch? Tell my father to meet me at the warehouse at midnight." I hung up without letting him speak. Lily gasps. Ezra doesn't look too happy either.

"You are not going to walk to your death. You're supposed to be marrying me, remember?!" Ezra shouts. I cup his face in my hands.

"I learned to shoot a gun when I was seven. I will be fine." I said.

"That's disturbing information but good to know. Only you don't own a gun, Jasper. I'm coming with you." He said, his voice laced with a mix of disbelief and something akin to fear.

"Actually, I do own a gun. A few guns. I also have cash put away." I confess, the admission feeling strangely liberating. The years of hiding this part of myself, the part forged in violence, are finally ending. I watch Ezra's perfectly sculpted features morph with surprise. He just blinks a few times, processing the information.

"What. The. Fuck." He whispers to himself. He starts to hyperventilate, his breath coming in ragged gasps.

"Hey, Baby. Stay with me. Don't panic. Everything is ok. Everything is fine. Look at me, Baby. I'm still me. I'm still Jasper." I try to comfort him, my voice soft, my touch gentle, a stark contrast to the brutality I've known. My sister is pacing the room, tears streaming down her face. Ezra looks at me, his eyes wide with a terror that's deeper than I've ever seen. I start to worry, a new kind of fear clutching at my heart. This isn't the calculated risk I anticipated, this is something else entirely. I kiss his cheek softly and hug him tightly. I whisper in his ear.

"I love you. Everything will be ok. I'll keep you safe. You won't ever have to even look at a gun. Nothing changes. I'm going to marry you and we'll grow old together. It'll be me and you against the world. I promise."

He pulls away from me, my arms falling to my sides. He looks at me briefly, a strange mixture of fear and something else—disgust maybe?—in his eyes, and then walks out of my apartment without a word. Fuck. I tug at my hair and decide to run after him. I throw open the door of my apartment—a space I'd carefully curated, a haven from the shadows of my past—and run after him. I catch him on the second flight, I grab hold of his waist and walk him backwards against the wall.

"Let go of me." He said angrily.

"No." I reply, the word a low growl, and I kiss his lips softly, a desperate attempt to bridge the chasm that's suddenly opened between us. He tries to push me away, but I don't budge. The blue of my eyes, my father's eyes, must be mirroring the cold fury in his.

"I don't even know who you are, Jasper! Let go of me!" He shouts, struggles, but I hold firm.

"You know the parts of me that nobody else knows, Baby. You know me the best. You didn't need to know about where I came from. It wasn't important."

"It wasn't important?! Are you fucking kidding me?! You're the son of a Mob Boss. You probably killed a man by the age of nine! You're a dangerous person with a lot of fucking secrets! I don't know you at all!" He argued. Dangerous person? That's when it hit me. The fear in his eyes, the way he flinched at my raised voice, the silent struggle fading into stunned stillness.

"Are you afraid of me?" I asked. He doesn't answer.

"Are you fucking afraid of me?!" I shout, the fear morphing into something darker, angrier. He flinches again, a small, heartbreaking movement that unravels me. My breath hitches. I let him go.

"N-no." he lies, the lie thin as cigarette smoke. I smile bitterly, a twist of self loathing tightening my chest. I shake my head in disbelief.

"I love you. I would never hurt you. I have never hit you. I would never put a bullet through your head. On the contrary, I would take a bullet for you. And to answer your unasked question, I have never killed a person willingly. And if you must know, my father would beat me to a pulp. He was a ruthless, heartless man who wanted to train me to be like him but I left and I took my sister with me. My mom was too loyal and stayed behind. The guns and the money are for protection. I've been on my own since seventeen. Is that what you want to know? That's the big secret, Ezra. But since I'm such a dangerous person, you can walk out of here and never have to worry about seeing me again." My face hardened and my jaw clenched tight, I began to climb back up the stairs.

"Jasper." He called my name, his voice laced with a vulnerability that mirrored the turmoil in my own soul. I stop but don't turn around. My heart, usually a steady, controlled rhythm, hammered against my ribs like a trapped bird.

"I just didn't expect any of this. You should have told me. It makes sense why you hate feelings and relationships. I'm sorry you grew up that way. I'm not afraid of you. I'm...I don't know what I am but I grew up with a mom who baked cookies in the suburbs. This shit is scary for me. But I'm mostly scared for you." He admitted. I turned, descending the few steps to stand before him again. Looking into his deep brown eyes, I made a decision. I wouldn't let him go. I would marry him, buy him a goddamn house in the suburbs, let him bake all the cookies he wanted. Fuck, I'd do anything for him.

"Are you still my fiancé?" I ask, knowing damn well that I wouldn't accept any other answer other than a yes. He bit his lip, eyes getting teary and looked into my eyes for brief moment. Fuck, he's going to say no and leave me.

I looked to the side and blinked the tears away.

"I'm going with you. I won't allow you to walk to your death and if you die, then I will follow you into the afterlife. Fuck. I'm in too fucking deep to give you up now." He said. My eyes snap back to his. Relief washed over me, potent and overwhelming. I pulled him into a tight embrace, burying my face in his hair.

"Oh, thank fuck. I really thought I'd have to kidnap you and tie you to my bed." I half joked. Ezra hugs me back and buries his face into the crook of my neck.

"That's not creepy at all." He said sarcastically. I laugh, the sound echoing in the stairwell.

"Come on. My sister must be having a total mental breakdown in my apartment." I said, as I tug him back up the stairs. As I approached, my door I realized I left it wide open in a rush to catch Ezra. Walking in, I found Lily sitting on the couch, a mug of coffee clutched in her trembling hands. Her face was stained with tears and smeared makeup. I crouched down, gently taking the mug and setting it on the table. I held her hands.

"Lily, you don't have to be afraid. I'll keep you safe. Haven't I always kept you safe? I'm going to end this once and for all. You won't have to hide anymore." I said softly. She looks down at our hands and nods her head.

"But what if you die?" She whispers.

"I've tried dying. Death just doesn't want me. So you're stuck with me for a long time, twinsie." I said, forcing a reassuring tone. She offered a small, unconvincing smile.

"Listen, stay here. I've got a few things to do but I will be back and we can order pizza or something." I told her, standing and kissing her forehead. I walked towards my man and kissed him softly on the lips.

"Stay with her. I'll be right back." Worry was etched on his face. I kissed him again, lingering a little longer than intended. The urgency of the situation, the weight of my family's history, it all pressed down on me. My father's training, years spent honing my lethal skills, had prepared me for this. It was time to finish what he'd started, to ensure Lily's safety, even if it meant putting myself in harm's way. I quickly walked out of my apartment. Slipping into my car, I started the engine, my mind already focused on the task ahead.

My first stop was a jewelry store. I bought Ezra a ring. My second stop was two hours away, a secluded spot in the woods. I retrieve my guns and cash in a travel bag I had buried in the dirt. I throw the bag in the backseat of my car. Half the day was already gone. My third stop was Ezra's apartment. Picking his lock was easy. I packed his clothes, cash, a gun, and left detailed instructions in case I didn't return. He needed to be safe. His bag joined Lily's in the backseat. Time to head home. I have a family to protect. This wasn't just about protecting Lily. It was about ending the cycle of violence that had plagued our family for generations. I knew what I had to do, and I knew the risks. The weight of the bag in the backseat was nothing compared to the weight of my resolve. Tonight, the nightmare ends. Tonight, I finish what my father started. But this time, it's for my family, not his twisted ideals. Tonight, we survive.

CHAPTER 36

---o---

JASPER'S POV

Finally, at nine at night, I made it back to my apartment. My sister is asleep on the couch. The TV playing some random show. Ezra was waiting up for me. He's sitting by the window. A cigarette in his hand, unlit. I drop his bag on the floor and walk over to him. I pluck it out of his hand and toss it towards the table. I know he's stressed. I sit on his lap, straddling his hips. I run my fingers through his black hair. I tug his head back, the moonlight lighting half his face. He looks blankly at me but his eyes tell me everything I need to know.

"Where did you go all day?" He questioned, monotonously.

"Shh. Just love me." I whisper. I lean down and kiss him with all that I've got. He kisses me back, his hands on my thighs. I don't want to waste time. I have wasted so much of it already. I wish I met him sooner. I wish I didn't waste my time dating Cindy, when all I really wanted was right there in front of me. I wish I didn't waste my time with Emilia, when we could have worked things out. I wish for more time but time is slowly running out. So, I kiss him and he kisses me. I get off of his lap without breaking the kiss and he follows me, rising from his chair.

We blindly make our way to my bedroom, lips still locked. We fall together on my bed. I pull away just to take his shirt off and I quickly place my lips on his skin. His neck, his shoulder, his chest, I kiss and bite it all. My tongue toys with his nipple and he makes the most beautiful sounds. I make my way down lower, licking his well defined abs. I unbutton his jeans and unzip them. Looking at him through my eyelashes, I grab hold of his cock and put his length in my mouth. It feels smooth and throbs as my tongue swirls around his flesh. I suck and watch him bite his lip, trying to stifle his moans. I take him in until he hits the back of my throat and he can't stifle his moans any longer. He lets his sounds of pleasure out.

A siren's song that only encourages me to keep going. Ezra's fingers dug into my scalp, holding me in place as he began to fuck my face hard and fast. I gagged, struggling to breathe, but I didn't stop him. A rush of heat flooded south, and I felt my own member hardening, even further than it already had. Sitting up, I took a lungful of air, the oxygen burning sweetly in my lungs, and began to shed my clothes. When I was naked, I moved to Ezra, his black hair falling across his forehead. I stripped his jeans completely, then hovered above him. I slipped my fingers into his mouth, his saliva coating them instantly, before lowering myself to his hole. The tight ring of muscles offered a thrilling resistance. I slid my fingers in and out, a slow, deliberate rhythm that mirrored the way I devoured his mouth with mine. Ezra reached up and took hold of my cock, his touch firm and unwavering. I pulled my fingers out and guided him onto me, feeling the deep press of his body. I thrust in and out, picking up the pace until I was viciously pounding his tight hole. The sound of skin slapping together mixed with our moans and grunts, filling the small space of my bedroom. He wrapped his legs around my waist, his hands gripping my shoulders, pulling me closer. The warmth of his body, his smooth skin against mine—I committed every detail to memory. I don't plan on dying but this may very well be my last time. I slow down at that thought. I needed to savor this, to fully embrace this act of love.

"Faster, Jas. Please." Ezra begged.

"Let me worship you. I promise I'll make you feel good. I don't want to rush this." I said, my face buried in the crook of his neck. I kept thrusting my cock slowly into his needy hole.

Ezra wasn't satisfied with my speed. He suddenly flipped me onto my back and began to ride me. His hard cock bobbing against his abs. The head glistens with precum.

"Fuck, Ezra!" I moaned. My hands grip his waist and attempt to slow him down but to no avail. My greedy lover kept bouncing like horny rabbit. He smirked down at me. He has me wrapped around his goddamn finger and he knows it.

"Ok, fine but remember you asked for it." I said, then I flipped us again. Ezra chuckles.

"Ok, Baby. Now what?" He said with an amused tone.

"Face down, ass up. Now." I demand.

"Yes, sir." He quickly gets into position. I knead his bottom and then spank his flesh. Ezra moans. I spank him again and again, until his cheek is red with my hand print.

"Please, Babe. Please." He groans. I smirk, knowing exactly what he wants from me but I want him to beg for it.

"What do you want, Baby?" I said in a low sultry voice.

"I want your cock." He breathed out. I grab my manhood and begin to thrust into my fist.

"How bad do you want it?"

"Stop teasing me, Jasper." He whined and picked his head up to look back at me. I quickly push his head into the mattress and thrust into him without warning. He groans in pleasure. I rock back and forth, drilling into his hole mercilessly. Unleashing the passion within me onto him. His hands grip the sheets as he mewls.

"Is this what my baby wanted?" I grunt, my abs flexing with each thrust of my hips. My hand is still holding his head down, pressing into the mattress. His hole squeezes my cock tight. YES!

Ezra's moans answer my question. Sounds of skin slapping together and the bed creaking fill the air. With a few more rough, sloppy thrusts, my seed fills him to the brim. It just keeps coming, more and more. Leaking out as I ride my high out.

"Don't you dare stop. I'm so close. Don't stop." He pleads. I keep pumping my cock into his hole. Hard and fast. Hitting the special bundle of nerves inside of him.

"Yes! Oh, Fuck! Yes! Right there. Jas, I'm gonna...ahhhhh!" He moans out, breathlessly. His cum spurting out onto the sheets. I grab his shaft and jerk him off. He spurts out some more with a cry of ecstasy. I rub my thumb on the tip, making his dick twitch. We both collapse, breathing heavily. I pull out and roll off of him. Settling on his side. I check the clock. It's eleven at night. I have to get going. My heart beating wildly in my chest for a different reason now. I kiss Ezra's shoulder up to his neck then find his lips. I don't want to leave him here but I have to. It's for his safety.

"E, I gotta go. If I don't come back when the sun rises, grab the bags I left at the front door and run with my sister. I left instructions inside the bag." I said, as I caressed his face. He quickly scowled.

"I'm not staying behind! Like hell you are going to leave me! We're going together! And what the fuck do you mean you left instructions and packed bags?! You plan to die tonight?!" He seethes. He quickly gets up and starts pacing around the room.

"Babe, you can't come. It's too dangerous for you. No, I don't plan to die but it's a possibility and I don't need you there risking your life as well." I explain as I walk into my bathroom to wash up with a wet rag. He stops pacing and follows me into the bathroom.

"You really just fucked me like some form of saying goodbye and expect me to be cool with it?! What the fuck, Jasper!" He shouts.

"I wasn't saying goodbye, E."

"No, you were just fucking me just in case you died and never returned to me, I'd have that as my last great memory of you. It's the same shit, Jasper. You're saying goodbye."

"I'm not going to die, Ezra! I'm going to fight like hell and come back to marry you! I wasn't just fucking you! I just wanted to show you how much I love you but you wanted it rough so I gave you what you wanted!" I shouted back. I exit the bathroom and grab my clothes.

Ezra gets dressed to. I watch him.

"I'm coming with you and that's final! Welcome to marriage, Hubby." He insisted. I groan in frustration and tug at my hair. He's leaving me no choice. I grab him from behind and push the pressure points on his neck until he's limp in my arms. I carry him bridal style and place him on my bed. He is going to be very angry with me when he wakes up and finds me gone but we can deal with that later when I come back. I glide my fingers through his hair and kiss his lips.

"I love you. I'll be back." I whisper. I get dressed, grab my phone and wallet then stuff two guns in the waistband of my pants. I tug my shirt down to hide them. I take one more look at the man who stole my heart then walk out. I get into my car, start the ignition and drive to the warehouse to meet my father. Knowing him, he'll be alone because he doesn't see me as a threat. That'll be his mistake.

***

An hour into my drive, my phone rings. I reach for it and check who is calling me. One glance at the name has me cussing. It's Ezra. Fuck. I decline his call. He keeps calling though. After ten phone calls, he sends me a text.

Ezra: You fucking asshole! I can't believe you did this to me! You best believe there will be hell to pay!

Yeah, he's definitely pissed off. That's going to be fun to argue about later. Sigh. I just want him safe. I arrive at the warehouse. A black jeep is already parked here. I take a deep breathe and exit my car. Let's get this over with. I enter the abandoned warehouse my family owns. The only light coming from a dim light bulb hanging above my father's head. After all this time, my father hasn't seemed to age a bit.

"My boy! Look at how much you've grown. Come give your father a hug." He said once he seen me enter.

"Skip the bullshit. I know you want me dead. I left your precious mafia. That counts as a betrayal and the punishment for that is death." I spat out, bitterly. He chuckles and pulls out his gun, holding it loosely at his side.

"Here I thought, I could have my son back. I see you rather die instead. Brave choice, my boy. Respectable."

"You don't want a son. You want a soldier. But you're right. I'd rather die than be a part of the family business, as you call it. I don't plan on dying though." I pulled a gun out from my waistband. He smiles.

"That's my boy! There's that fire you were trained to have! Tell me, boy, do you have a wife? Children?" He asked with a cynical smile. I gulped.

"No but I have a husband to get back to. So, can we get this over with?"

My father's face twisted with disgust. He raised his gun and I raised mine.

"All this time you've been a faggot! No son of mine will be a disgusting abomination! You disgust me! Your mother should have aborted you!" He spat venomously.

"Don't talk to him like that, you piece of shit!" I know that voice. My eyes widen and my head snaps around to see Ezra.

"Who the fuck are you?!" My father shouted angrily. Ezra smiles devilishly.

"Your son in law." He replied, proudly. Then Ezra looks at me and blows a kiss.

"Thought you could just leave and I wouldn't find you, Baby? Well, surprise." He directs to me. I'm too angry to say anything. I just shove him behind me and use my body as a shield.

"Ugh. Look at that disgusting filth. You really searched at the bottom of the barrel for this scum. I thought I could convince you to come back but now I see I don't have a son. I raised a bitch. A disgusting cocksucker. You're a disgrace to the family. I will end your miserable life!" My father spewed his hatred and suddenly gunshots were fired. Everything happened so fast. Ezra falls to the ground with a scream of agony escaping his lips. I don't think. I just react. I pull the trigger and I don't miss. A bullet through my father's head ends his miserable life and his body drops. I quickly turn to Ezra and fall to the floor beside him. I cradle his body to me and look for the bullet hole. His blood is soaking his shirt and I can't tell where he's been hit.

"Don't you dare die on me, Ezra!" I cry out. Tears falling from my eyes. I carry his body to my car and lay him in the backseat. We are out in the middle of nowhere but that doesn't deter me from racing down the road to find a hospital. I quickly search on my phone for any hospitals nearby. I pick the first one and drive there. Forgetting about the speed limit. I look in the rear view mirror every few seconds. Ezra is lifeless and bleeding profusely. No, he can't die. I refuse to let him die. Why didn't he listen to me and just stay home?! If he dies…I can't live without him… I just can't.

Finally, after what seems like forever, I arrive at the hospital. I don't even shut off the ignition. I just put it in my park, throw my door open and carry the love of my life into the hospital.

"HELP!! HELP, PLEASE!! HE'S BEEN SHOT!!" I scream as soon as I enter the building. Immediately, a medical team approaches me with a gurney and takes Ezra away. I run after them as they rush him away. They stop me as they enter a room and shut the doors.

I look down at my hands covered in dried blood. My clothes stained red. My eyes widen at the realization that I'm covered in my lover's blood. Shock takes over my body. Suddenly, I can't breathe. There isn't enough air in my lungs. The corners of my vision start to darken and the walls are closing in on me. Ezra was shot. I killed my father. Ezra's blood is on my hands. My father's blood is on my hands. What the fuck… WHAT THE ACTUAL FUCK!! I didn't even hesitate. One look at Ezra falling down and my fingers automatically pulled the trigger. I would have gladly taken that bullet in his place. It should have been me. It should have been me who got shot. Not the love of my life. No, he's innocent. He didn't deserve it. I rush through the halls and find a bathroom. I quickly scrub at my hands. Desperately trying to wash off the blood but it cakes under my fingernails and nothing I seem to do can erase the fact that I held Ezra's bleeding body in my arms. That memory is a stain in my mind that can't be wiped off. Exhaustion takes over my body. I fight my eyes to stay open but this is a fight I don't win.

CHAPTER 37

JASPER'S POV

Beep. Beep. Beep. The sound of a heart monitor is the first thing I notice. I try to open my eyes. It takes a few tries, but they finally squint open. Ugh, that bright light. Beep. Beep. Beep. What the fuck happened? I look around. Hospital. My brows furrow. Hospital? My eyes widen.

"Ezra!!" I shout, as I begin to sit up and yank out the IV in my arm. A female in baby blue scrubs rushes into the room.

"Whoa! Let's calm down! I can answer all of your questions!" she says, grabbing my arm as it leaks blood.

"Why am I here? Where's Ezra? I should be with Ezra!" She bandages my arm.

"You passed out from exhaustion. Whatever you put your body through was a lot. I don't know about your friend Ezra, but I can look it up." She answers calmly. I nod, my dark curly hair falling over my face, and wait for her to leave. My blue eyes dart around the sterile room, anxiety gnawing at me. When she's gone, I get up and look for Ezra myself. I find the front desk and ask for him. Relief washes over me when I find out he's out of surgery and recovering well. I hurry to his room. When I enter, he's awake, and my carefully constructed calm crumbles.

"What the fuck were you thinking?! You got yourself shot, E! You scared the living shit out of me!" I yell, my voice cracking with unshed tears. He jumps, startled by my sudden appearance.

"I swear to God or whoever the fuck is up in the cosmos that if you died, I would have followed you into the afterlife and found a way to kill you all over again!" I continue to rant, my hands clenched into fists. Slowly, a smirk begins to play on his lips, that infuriating, charming smirk that always melts my anger. The audacity of it!

"Are you done, Baby?" he says, the grin growing on his handsome face. I glare at him, my anger momentarily replaced by a wave of overwhelming relief and love. "Good. Now come kiss me. I just took a bullet for you." Needless to say, I walked the short distance from the door to the bed and kissed him with fervor. My hands cradling his face, emotion choking my throat. I pull away, breathless.

"Don't ever scare me like that again." I whisper, my voice thick with unshed tears. He pulls me closer, his brown eyes full of affection.

"It's just my shoulder. I'm fine." I roll my eyes at his nonchalance. Always so damn calm, my Ezra. But under the anger and fear, a deep, quiet happiness settles in my heart. We'd faced a bullet, and we'd faced it together. And somehow, that made everything right.

***

EZRA'S POV

~Four weeks later~

I look in the mirror, checking my reflection for any imperfections. I'm in a white suit, at the courthouse. It's finally happening. I'm about to marry the man I fell in love with at first sight at a coffee shop all those months ago. He chose me.

"Damn. You look good in white, Baby." Jasper's voice echoes in the restroom. I turn around, smirking. He licks his bottom lip and stares at me with fuck me eyes. Those blue ones that always feel like a call out to sea and drown me in them.

"Do you want to marry me or do you want to fuck me? We only have five minutes. Your choice."

Before Jasper could reply, Marcus walks in.

"Let's get this show on the road! Lily is getting antsy and she gets talkative when she's antsy."

I chuckle and Jas rolls his eyes. We all walk out to meet the judge. I felt like I was floating the whole walk to the room, that looked more like an office than a court room. I was in a dreamy head space. I barely heard the judge speak because I was lost in Jasper's eyes. His hands shook and his face was rosy pink but somehow he stood there confidently, all at once. Before I knew it, it was time to share our vows. Jasper went first. He cleared his throat and opened his mouth to speak.

"I'll start this by saying that, you know I'm not good with words but here goes it. Ezra, meeting you turned my life upside it's head. You showed me that I am worthy of love. That I am capable of things like forgiveness and compassion. You make me a better man. You're my best friend, E. I look forward to making a happy life together. I love you. Let's take this world by storm."

For someone who claims that he isn't good with words, he articulated what he wanted to say beautifully. I'm smiling so much and my eyes are a watery mess but I am too full of happiness to care. Lily was crying silently and Marcus was cheesing.

"That was perfect, Babe. I guess it's my turn now." I let out a nervous chuckle. "I love you, Jas. It's a simple truth that dances in my heart, but it's weight is profound. Meeting you at that coffee shop felt like an accidental moment, a delightful coincidence that sparked something beautiful. Yet, finding you again at my new job? That was fate, weaving our paths together with threads of destiny. Every day with you feels like an adventure waiting to unfold. The thought of being married to you fills me with joy and excitement. I can already envision the laughter and warmth we'll share in our little world. Together, we will create memories that shimmer like stars in the night sky. You are my partner, my confidant, and my greatest joy. With each passing moment, I am grateful for the love we've found—an extraordinary blend of chance and purpose. Here's to a lifetime of fun, laughter, and endless love. It's you and I, against the world, Baby."

After those heartfelt words that bared my soul to everyone in the room, the judge declared us married and I tongued the fuck out of my husband. No fucks given. Marcus hollered and whooped. Lillian, well, she cried and clapped to her hearts content like a proud sister. Jasper smiled against my mouth, breaking the kiss. My damn heart fluttered and danced. I managed to get the man. It took blood, sweat and tears but I would do it all over again. Minus some mistakes. With our fingers intertwined, we walk out of the courthouse. I look at my new husband. His curly dark hair, long eyelashes, plump lips, and that sexy black suit. Yeah, that's all mine.

"Hey, Jas. Want some coffee?"

He smiles, knowing that's where this all began.

"Yeah, coffee sounds awesome."

EPILOGUE

---◆◇◆---

JASPER'S POV

~The Honeymoon~

I can't fucking believe that a man like me is fucking married. If anyone asked me a year ago or even a few weeks ago, if I envisioned myself happily married in the future, I would have said no. But the fact is that I am. I'm so fucking happy that I'm terrified. Ezra is fucking perfection and I'm obsessed with him. The turquoise water laps gently against the shore, the sun warm on my skin. My dark curls are plastered to my forehead from the ocean swim, and I can feel Ezra's eyes on me as I sit here, sipping a ridiculously expensive cocktail. He's sprawled out on a sun lounger nearby, his heavily tattooed arms spread wide, his black hair against his tanned skin looking almost fierce. It's funny, this whirlwind romance culminating in a lavish honeymoon in some tropical paradise. It still doesn't feel real, but goddamn, the reality is delicious.

My blue eyes scan the beach, still marveling at the stunning view, but mostly focused on Ezra. His brown eyes, intense and warm, hold a depth I'm only just beginning to understand. Before him, my life was a string of fleeting connections, fueled by my own ego and a desperate need for validation. Ezra saw past all that, past the carefully constructed facade, and somehow, found something worthwhile within me. He challenged me, called me out on my bullshit, and loved me fiercely, flaws and all. That's the thing that's terrifying—the depth of his affection, a complete and utter acceptance that I don't deserve, yet somehow possess.

He knows about my past, about the years of training my father put me through, the brutal lessons in survival and killing. He doesn't flinch, doesn't judge. He just... accepts it. A part of me still expects the other shoe to drop, that this idyllic paradise will shatter and reveal a harsh reality. But looking at Ezra, at the peaceful curve of his lips, the way his chest rises and falls with each breath, I feel a strange calm settle over me. A calm I haven't felt since… well, ever.

Maybe this is it. Maybe this terrifying, beautiful, unexpected love is exactly what I needed, what I always secretly craved, buried beneath layers of cynicism and self preservation. The sun dips below the horizon, painting the sky in fiery hues of orange and pink. Ezra sits up, reaching for my hand. His touch sends a jolt of electricity through me. He smiles, a genuine, unguarded smile that melts away any lingering doubt.

"Beautiful, isn't it, Jas?" he murmurs, his voice low and husky. I nod, unable to speak, my heart overflowing with a love so profound, so unexpected, it leaves me speechless. Instead, I let my body do the talking. I straddle his lap and kiss that sinful mouth. My fingers rake through his thick hair as I tug his head back, my tongue tasting the sweat on his neck. Yes, this is love. This is happiness. I think to myself as Ezra moans. My father's "business" is no more. Everything he ever worked for has crumbled to the ground and then been set on fire, just for the hell of it. Ezra is mine. All mine. I bought him that house in the suburbs. We move in as soon as we get back. Nothing can beat this moment in time.

"Jas, fuck me. Right here. Right now." Ezra murmurs, his hands tugging my swimming trunks down. My manhood springs free, fully erect and dripping already.

"Aren't you afraid of someone catching us in the act? This is a public beach." I smirk, knowing no one will see us because I had the place closed for the day. It's just us.

"Please, Baby. Please. I need it." He begs, his fist tight around my cock. The desperation in his voice, the raw need in his eyes, is a potent aphrodisiac. Fuck. He knows what he's doing to me. He always does. His touch is masterful, his body a familiar haven.

"You are too good at this game, husband." I manage to say, as I thrust into his tight grip. Ezra smiles devilishly, his eyes hooded with lust and dick straining deliciously against his swimming trunks. I want to see it. I want to feel it against mine. I pull his manhood out and grip us both in my hand. His precum mixes with mine and I'm so fucking turned on by the sight that I could climax but I hold back. I want to be inside of him. I want his puckered hole to open wide by the girth of my cock.

"What are you thinking about, Baby?" Ezra moans out, knowing my thoughts are filthy, knowing by the look on my face. I don't need to tell him, I'll show him.

"Face down. Ass up, E." I say, my voice like gravel. He obeys instantly, his beautiful face resting on the sun lounger, his perfectly round ass presented to me. I spread his cheeks apart, spit on his hole and push the crown of my cock in. Both of us groan in pleasure. I push in further, sheathing myself completely, then hold still, giving him a moment to adjust to my size.

"Fuck me hard and deep, Jasper. Now." His wish is my command. I pull out to the tip and thrust in hard, the rhythm of our bodies a perfect symphony against the backdrop of the ocean's gentle roar. I fuck him good and long, pulling two orgasms from him; his cum splatters the lounger. I hold out long enough to build to my own peak. I've held out long enough. I piston my hips, loving the sound of our skin slapping together and the erotic view of his beautiful ass swallowing me whole. I cum with such a ferocity that my vision blurs. I see stars for a whole minute. Fuck, that was good. I withdraw, then quickly, before my cum can leak out, I fuck it back in with my tongue. Ezra is a moaning mess, exactly how I like him. With the same dirty mouth, I kiss him. I kiss him and don't care that my lungs scream for oxygen because I love him.

"I love you, Ezra. Thank you."

"What are you thanking me for?"

"For saving me from myself."

"I love you, Jas. I always will."

THE END

ABOUT THE AUTHOR

ANNIE SILVA IS A devoted mother of four and a loving partner, residing in the charming town of Bethlehem, Pennsylvania. As a high school graduate, Annie has embraced the role of a stay-at-home mom, where she manages the beautiful chaos of family life while nurturing her children's growth and development. Her daily experiences are filled with the joys and challenges that come with raising a bustling household.

Despite the vibrant life she leads, Annie is candid about her struggles with depression and other mental illnesses. She shares her journey with honesty and authenticity, demonstrating resilience in the face of adversity. Annie believes that opening up about her mental health challenges not only helps her but also provides comfort and understanding to others facing similar battles.

Annie is also an emerging author, finding solace and purpose in the written word. Through her writing, she connects with her readers, sharing insights that stem from both her personal experiences and her observations of the world around her. Her passion for storytelling reflects her love for reading, which has always been a significant part of her life. With a steaming cup of coffee in hand, she often finds herself lost in the pages of a good book, drawing inspiration from the stories that have shaped her.

In her free time, Annie enjoys the simple pleasures of life—whether it's sipping coffee on the porch while watching her children play or diving into a new novel that transports her to another world. Her love for reading not only provides an escape but also fuels her creativity as she weaves her own narratives.

Annie Silva is a testament to the power of perseverance and the importance of mental health awareness. Through her journey as a mother, a writer, and an advocate for mental health, she seeks to inspire others to embrace their own stories, no matter how challenging they may be. With every word she writes, Annie hopes to create a sense of community and connection, proving that no one is truly alone in their struggles. Her debut into the writing world is fueled by the belief that every person has a story worth telling, and sometimes the most powerful voices come from the kitchen table rather than the ivory tower. When asked about her inspiration, Annie simply says, "Life doesn't give us perfect stories. It gives us real ones. Those are the ones worth telling."

https://www.tiktok.com/@author_annie_silva

https://www.instagram.com/author_annie_silva

www.ingramcontent.com/pod-product-compliance
Lightning Source LLC
Chambersburg PA
CBHW060949030726
47503CB00003B/795